My left side hurt so badly it was hard to think for a moment, and I wondered if he'd broken any ribs. I held my side and spooled my earth magic. Green flames sparked on my skin as a five-foot-long whip-like stream of cold fire emerged from my right hand. I lashed the Porsche's front tire, and it split with a loud *bang* and the hiss of air escaping. I smiled grimly. No quick getaways for him.

PRAISE FOR THE WORKS OF LISA EDMONDS

"Edmonds's prose is energetic...Alice is both spunky and self-deprecating, with incredibly advanced magical powers...There is promise in Edmonds's melding of the supernatural and the everyday."

- Publishers Weekly

"What a cracking read...ages since I read a new fantasy story that's gripped me like this, that I so enjoyed. It's up there with my favourite reads and I hope Lisa is hard at work with the next book."

- Jeannie Zelos Book Reviews

"There is NOTHING better than finding a fantastic new paranormal series. *Lisa Edmonds* has started a series that grabbed and held my attention...HEART OF MALICE successfully shows me the new world as it's experienced. With a little info here…and a little info there, I wasn't bombarded all at once and I got to see it all live and in action."

- Stacey is Sassy

"Add everything together, great writing, great characters, interesting pasts, and great plotting, I can't wait to read more! Highly recommend!"

- Librarian, Penny Noble

"A powerful vampire wishes to have Alice's blood, but her freedom depends on no one finding out what she is through her blood. Too many people are now looking her way. A powerful fire mage, the paranormal agent, Charles the vampire. Deception, lies, magic, and one heck of a thriller."

- ARC Reviewer

LISA EDMONDS

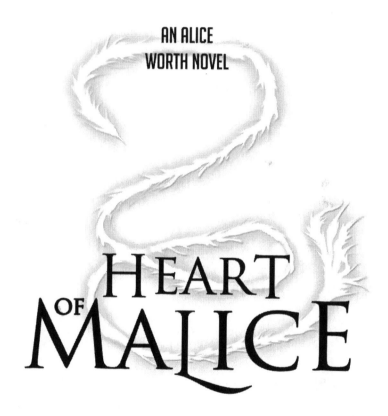

AN ALICE
WORTH NOVEL

HEART of MALICE

CITY OWL
PRESS

HEART OF MALICE
Alice Worth, Book 1

CITY OWL PRESS
www.cityowlpress.com

Cover Design by Olivia at MiblArt. All stock photos licensed appropriately.

Author Photo by Madison Hurley Photography.

Edited by Heather McCorkle.

For information on subsidiary rights, please contact the publisher at info@cityowlpress.com.

Print Edition ISBN: 978-1-944728-34-2

Digital Edition ISBN: 978-1-944728-35-9

Printed in the United States of America

To Bill, Mom, and Susan Michelle,

and everyone who stays up late to read just one more chapter.

CHAPTER 1

I was just finishing my second beer when someone leaned down to whisper in my ear. "Want to do something insane?"

As pickup lines went, it wasn't half bad.

I set my glass on the bar and looked up. He was dark-haired, gorgeous, and tall, dwarfing me by almost a foot—and at five-six plus heels, I wasn't exactly short. I took a moment to savor the close-up view of his impressively muscled chest and let my appreciation show in my voice when I answered, "Absolutely."

He drained the last of his bourbon and tossed a crisp hundred on the bar next to our empty glasses. "Then let's get out of here."

I let him help me slide down off my barstool. His eyes moved approvingly from my tall boots to my thighs and over my short dress to my cleavage, where they paused for a moment before meeting my gaze. "Scott," he said and held my jacket while I put it on.

I smiled up at him. "Alice."

"Nice to meet you, Alice." He offered his hand, and I took it. We plowed through the crowded bar toward the front door.

When we finally emerged on the sidewalk, I tucked my arm through Scott's and fell in step beside him. Despite the cold, he didn't need a coat; I felt his warmth even through my leather jacket. He smelled smoky and woodsy, like a forest fire.

"What's on the agenda?" I asked as we strolled along Ninth Street, past a dozen bars and late-night cafés.

"Have you ever flown the 101?"

I laughed. "I've *driven* the Pacific Coast Highway. I didn't know you could fly it."

He grinned at me. "In my car, we can."

"Let's do it." I squeezed his arm. "Where are you parked?"

"Up ahead a couple of blocks."

The March wind was bitterly cold on my bare legs. Though we walked quickly, within minutes, I was shivering.

"Come on—we're almost there." Scott squeezed me against his side with an enormous arm.

"How did you manage to get parking down here on a Saturday, anyway?" I asked, pouting a bit. "I'm all the way over on Fulton, in a pay lot."

"I know the guy who owns McGovern's Steakhouse," Scott replied. "He lets me park in his alley whenever I'm here."

"Well, that sure is convenient."

Scott flashed me a smile. We were in front of McGovern's, which was already closed for the night. At one a.m., there weren't many pedestrians around. It was cold enough that anyone who was out was in a hurry to get where they were going, and the most popular bars were back in the direction we'd come from. Where Scott was parked, there was nothing but long-closed restaurants and shops. I saw one other couple about a block behind us, wrapped in long coats, their heads down as they talked quietly, but no one else was in sight. The sharp staccato sound of my boot heels echoed as we walked.

Finally, we rounded the corner and started into the alley behind the steakhouse. It was a relief to be out of the wind. Ahead, by the light of a single streetlight, I saw a black Porsche 911 Turbo parked in front of a large sign that read AUTHORIZED VEHICLES ONLY.

"Nice car," I remarked as we approached it.

"Thanks," he said, and punched me.

I felt him tense up and managed to turn a fraction of a second before he swung, so his massive fist connected with my side instead of my stomach.

Pain exploded in my ribs. I gasped and hit Scott's chest with both hands. Magic flared, and he flew backward into the side of the restaurant, leaving a man-sized crater in the brick wall. He landed in a crouch with a snarl, his eyes blazing bright red.

My left side hurt so badly it was hard to think for a moment, and I wondered if he'd broken any ribs. I held my side and spooled my earth magic. Green flames sparked on my skin as a five-foot-long whip-like stream of cold fire emerged from my right hand. I lashed the Porsche's front tire, and it split with a loud *bang* and the hiss of air escaping. I smiled grimly. No quick getaways for him.

"Bitch," Scott growled. His voice was deeper and more gravelly now that he was no longer pretending to be human. "My car!"

"I guess you won't be flying the 101 anytime soon," I said. "And by the way, that's a terrible line."

The half demon glowered at me. Above us, the streetlight buzzed and flickered. "What do you want?" he demanded.

"You're coming with me. I've got a Court summons with your name on it."

His eyes glowed brighter with anger. "I don't answer to the *humans*," he snarled.

The corner of my mouth turned up. "No, the *other* Court."

Scott hissed. I tensed and shifted my weight, ready for him to attack.

Instead, the bastard ran.

I cursed and took off down the alley after him, feeling a burst of sharp pain in my side with every step. My boots and short dress might have worked well to catch his attention in the bar, but they were far from ideal for a foot chase. By the time I reached the end of the alley, Scott was already almost a full block ahead of me.

As we ran down the deserted sidewalk, headed farther from the relative safety of the bar district and possible witnesses, I set my jaw and blocked out the pain. Scott Grierson was not getting away from me tonight, not after all he had done.

Up ahead, Scott darted across the street. Between gasping breaths, I groaned. He was headed for Fields Park. If I lost sight of him in there, he was gone.

I put on an extra burst of speed, breaking into a full sprint. Half-demons were larger and stronger than humans, but it was heavy muscle mass. They might get off to a fast start, but they weren't built for running long distances. By the time Scott ran through the gates of the park, I'd cut the distance separating us in half.

The moon, a day from being full, hung bright in the clear sky, and I could see my quarry ahead of me, his steps crunching in the gravel path.

Scott heard me gaining on him and suddenly veered off the main path toward some trees. I cut across the grass, hoping to intercept him before he found cover. Behind me, I thought I heard running footsteps back near the gate but couldn't turn to look. If he had an accomplice, I'd deal with that when I had to; right now I couldn't chance him getting away.

When I got within twenty feet, I raised my hands. White magic sparked on my palms, and I unleashed a gust of air that sent the half-demon sprawling into the grass with a surprised grunt.

Scott rolled to his feet with a growl and turned to face me. His eyes glowed brightly in the darkness. "Who sent you?"

I stopped ten feet away, breathing hard. "I'm here because of Maggie."

"Who?" I couldn't see his expression clearly, but his tone sounded genuinely puzzled, and it infuriated me.

"Maggie Hill, the girl you picked up a month ago from the same bar we were just in."

Scott grinned. Unfortunately for them, a lot of women had found his smile to be charming. Of course, they hadn't seen it paired with his red eyes—at least, not until it was too late. "Was that her name? I had no idea."

My jaw clenched so hard that it hurt. "Did you know *any* of their names? Maggie? Alison? Katie?"

"Nope," Scott said with a shrug. "Honestly, I didn't care. I don't even know what *your* name is."

Suddenly, his arm moved.

A flash of metal glinted in the moonlight and I lashed out with my cold-fire whip. The bright green arc of lightning intercepted the blade in midair and sent it flying back in the direction it came from.

And buried it to the hilt in the half-demon's right eye.

It was over in a heartbeat. For a moment, Scott remained upright, his single red eye wide open in surprise. Then he fell backward and landed on the grass with a solid *thump*.

I approached him warily, my whip still crackling at my side. The half-demon was dying. His remaining eye stared up at me, glowing faintly. Dark blood ran from his right eye socket, where a four-inch knife handle protruded. His mouth moved, but nothing came out.

My fingers itched to pull the knife out and put it through his other eye. Instead, I crouched next to him as my whip coiled back into my hand and vanished. Disappointment left a bitter taste in my mouth. He didn't deserve a quick death; it should have been slow and painful. Maggie deserved that, at least.

"My name," I told him coldly, "is Alice."

Scott exhaled in a long, rattling wheeze. His eye dimmed, then went dark.

* * *

I sat on the grass next to the body while I caught my breath. Pain lanced through my side, and the chill of the night started to seep into me. Running had made me sweat, and now the wind felt icy on my damp skin.

My jaw ached from clenching my teeth, and my fingers dug into the ground in frustration. "Damn it, Alice," I chastised myself. When Scott threw the knife, I'd acted to defend myself, drawing on years of training that had become instinct. Unfortunately, as a result, he'd escaped justice, and now instead of presenting him to the Vampire Court as my prisoner, he would have to be tried *ex mortem*. I hoped the Hills could at least find some answers and closure from that.

Time to call the vamps to come get the body. I reached into my pocket for my phone.

I heard footsteps running from the tree line a half second before two flashlight beams blinded me. "SPEMA! Hands on your head!" The voice was loud and male, its tone unmistakable. My night had just gone from bad to infinitely worse.

Slowly, I pulled my hand out of my pocket, showed that it was empty, and clasped my hands on top of my head, half expecting to hear gunshots ring out and bracing for bullets that never came. Through the glare of the flashlights, I saw two dark figures in long coats, both pointing guns at me.

"My name is Alice Worth," I said calmly over the pounding of my heart. "I'm a licensed private investigator and a registered earth and air mage. My ID is in my wallet in the left pocket of my jacket."

"Do not move," the other agent, a woman, warned me.

I kept my hands on my head as the larger of the two shadows moved the beam of his flashlight to point at Scott Grierson's face. He swore and walked over to check the half-demon's pulse. "Dead. Goddammit, did you have to kill him?"

I blinked. I wasn't dumb enough to admit anything—even self-defense—in front of two federal agents, but the frustration and anger in his tone made me think these two hadn't just happened to be taking a late-night walk in the park.

I looked closer at them, and then it clicked. "You were following us, back on Ninth," I said slowly. "Why?"

No reply, not that I'd really expected one. These two federal agents were the "couple" I'd seen as we walked from the bar to Scott's car. I remembered hearing footsteps behind me on the path in the park. Had the agents seen and heard the entire thing? And who had they been following: Scott, or me?

The male agent held me at gunpoint while his partner walked around behind me. She was a few inches taller than me, built solidly, wearing a long coat over a dark suit. "On your feet, slowly," she ordered me. I heard metal clinking.

Carefully and a bit stiffly, I stood. She grabbed my left wrist and twisted my arm down behind my back. The movement made pain flare in my side. "You're under arrest," she said, closing a spell cuff on my wrist. She pulled my right arm down and cuffed it too.

The instant the first cuff closed on my wrist, my magic was suppressed, and I jerked in the agent's grip as the dampening spell settled on my skin like an itchy blanket. The discomfort made my stomach churn.

Once I was cuffed, the female agent recited the Miranda warning, and I acknowledged with a simple yes that I understood my rights.

She went through my pockets, starting with my wallet. "Alice Evelyn Worth," she told her partner. "Mage private investigator's license, SPERA registration, and current permits. Are you carrying any weapons or spells?"

"Air magic healing spell and spell cuffs in my right pocket," I said.

"No weapons."

When my arms started to ache, I laced my fingers together and tried not to pull on the cuffs. They drained your strength if you did, which was why I'd planned to use a pair on Scott. They worked well to restrain half-demons, vampires, and others with superhuman strength. Between the cuffs and a sleep spell, I should have been able to get Scott Grierson to the vamps without much trouble. I glared at the half-demon's body. I ought to have just dropped him the instant we got into the alley instead of waiting until we were completely out of sight from the street. The consequences of my hesitation grew more dire by the second.

The agent continued the search, dropping each item, including my cell phone, in the grass as she went through my jacket pockets. Then she frisked me very efficiently and thoroughly. When her hand slid over my ribs, I had to bite the inside of my cheek to keep from flinching.

The male agent, who had been crouching next to Scott's body, stood and came over. He was well over six feet tall and blond, wearing a long coat and dark suit like his partner. He picked up my wallet and read through its contents for himself.

"Alice Worth," he said quietly, as if to himself. Then he looked at me, his eyes hard. "Why were you with him?" he asked, hooking his thumb at the body.

I kept my mouth shut. If I had the right to remain silent, I was going to use it.

The male agent looked over my shoulder at his partner behind me. Whatever unspoken conversation they had, he didn't like it. His scowl deepened, and he stared at me. I fixed my gaze on his chin and stayed still, even though the discomfort of the spell cuffs and the pain in my side made me want to shuffle my feet.

Finally, he grunted, pulled out his own identification, and stuck it under my nose. "Special Agent Lake of the Supernatural and Paranormal Entity Management Agency," he said brusquely. "My partner is Special Agent Parker. We believe Mr. Grierson might have been involved in a series of disappearances in the area."

I said nothing.

A muscle moved in Lake's square jaw. "Since August of last year, we have six cases of young women going missing. A few days ago, we obtained camera footage from an ATM that showed the latest victim, Maggie Hill, on the night she disappeared, with a male suspect we believe to be Grierson. If you have any information tying him to these disappearances, or know anything about the whereabouts of these women, now is the time."

I thought about it. As with most supes and mages, my distrust of SPEMA agents ran deep. They had nearly limitless power and authority, and we had so few rights. I was acutely aware that Lake and Parker could haul me off and I would disappear into one of the Agency's supe prisons, never to be seen or heard from again. I'd killed Grierson in self-defense—by accident, really—but it would be difficult to prove that. As such, I wasn't particularly inclined to say anything.

The longer I stayed silent, the angrier Lake got. He stepped closer to loom over me. "I can take you down to our office, if you'd be more comfortable talking to me there," he said grimly. We both knew my comfort didn't figure into the equation, and the odds of me walking back out of the Agency office were slim at best. "I want some answers. I've got six families waiting for news, and so help me, if you know what happened and you're not telling me, I will find a way to get it out of you."

I stared at him, my face blank. He'd gone from intimidation to explicit threats in a blink. Neither was anything new to me. If he expected me to be rattled, he was destined to be disappointed. I'd spent the first twenty-four years of my life being threatened with—and suffering—far worse torments than he could even begin to imagine.

"Forget it," Parker said. "She isn't going to tell us anything. Let's go." She yanked on my cuffed wrists, and I barely suppressed a wince.

Lake held up his hand and met my gaze. The anger in his eyes faded, replaced with grim determination. He sighed. "We saw what happened," he told me.

From behind me, Parker made a disgusted noise. She let go of my arm and stepped back, as if to distance herself from Lake.

"We overheard you tell him that you were here because of Maggie, and we heard him confess to taking the girls," Lake said. "We saw him throw the knife. You didn't mean to kill him; you were protecting yourself. If I take those cuffs off you, will you tell me what you know?"

"For God's sake, Lake," Parker exploded. "You can't do that."

"I can and I will," Lake snapped. "You want to go back and tell them we don't know where their girls are?"

Parker stayed silent.

"Do you?" Lake demanded.

"No, but—"

"Take the cuffs off." Lake glowered at Parker. A full minute passed.

Apparently Lake won the staring contest, because suddenly I heard a jingle of keys. I braced myself, but when the cuffs came off, the surge of released magic caused me to stagger before Lake caught me by my left arm.

Before I could stop myself, I grimaced at the pain in my side as my weight pulled on my arm. "Are you injured?" Lake's eyes narrowed as he looked me over.

"No." I pulled away from him and forced myself to stand up straight. "Just stiff from the cuffs." If he thought I was hurt, he might try to force me to go to the hospital, and that was something I had to avoid.

Lake looked like he wasn't sure he believed me, but luckily for me, he was more interested in Grierson than any bumps or bruises—or cracked ribs—that I might have. "Tell me what you know."

I'd thought at first that Lake's change in attitude was simply a tactic to get me to talk, but he looked sincere. Grierson was dead, and as far as the agent knew, so were his chances of finding out where Maggie and the other girls were. My instincts were telling me that Lake cared far more about finding them than about throwing me in prison for accidentally killing a half-demon.

My only way out of this might be to tell him what I knew. I was about to take a very big—and very uncharacteristic—gamble with my freedom and my life. "Two weeks ago, I was hired by Maggie Hill's parents to look for their missing daughter. They were frustrated by the lack of progress the task force was making, and thought a private investigator might be more successful."

Behind me, Parker made a derisive sound. My eyes narrowed, and Lake gave her a quelling look. "How did you connect Maggie to Grierson?" he asked.

"I canvassed all of the bars Maggie's friends said she liked to visit and got nothing, just like the cops did. I started checking other bars close to her apartment and didn't have much luck until I got to the bar we were in tonight. The bartender there said Maggie had been in a couple of times, and he thought he remembered her with a flashy guy who liked to brag about his car. I got a physical description and a first name. I staked out the area for a couple of nights until I saw a guy matching the description parking his Porsche in the alley behind the steakhouse. I followed him home that night. This was about a week ago."

"That was before we got the surveillance footage." Parker's tone made it clear she wasn't happy I had identified their suspect before they did.

I continued. "Once I had Grierson's name and address, I did some digging into his background. It didn't take long to figure out that he was half-demon; I'd already guessed it from his size."

As I talked, Lake wrote in a little notebook. He paused at the last, his eyes narrowing at me. "Why didn't you pass his information on to the police or SPEMA?"

"At that point, it wasn't anything more than a possible lead. I needed something that would tie Grierson to Maggie, or to one of the other girls. I hoped I could find physical evidence I could give to the police."

"*Did* you find any evidence?"

"How familiar are you with magic trace, Agent Lake?"

Parker snorted.

Lake's mouth compressed into a grim line. "Parker, Mr. Grierson's vehicle and the alley behind McGovern's are a crime scene. I need you to head there and request a CSU."

"I can't leave you here alone with a suspect," Parker said. "It's against regulations."

"She's not a suspect; she's a witness. I'll call in for additional agents and a second CSU," Lake told her. "We'll be fine here in the meantime. Go secure the other scene."

Seething, Parker spun around and headed off in the direction of the park gate. Lake watched her go, then turned back to me. "I'll have to report this soon. She'll be sending more agents out here." In other words, get to the point.

I tucked my cold hands into my jacket pockets. "Maggie and the rest of the girls went missing the day before a full moon. I suspected the timing might indicate some sort of ritual magic. I went to Grierson's house to look around. When I got close enough, I could sense traces of what felt like a demon summoning. It was strong enough that I could sense it through the house wards, which meant if I was right, Grierson had summoned a very powerful demon."

It was hard to tell in the moonlight, but I thought Lake looked pale. "What did you do then?"

"The house wards were strong enough that if I tried to unweave or break them, he would know immediately. I asked an acquaintance to come with me and try scrying, to see if he could see anything that might have taken place in the house." I'd cashed in a big favor to get Michael to do it.

A pause. "What am I going to find in that house, Ms. Worth?"

"Not what you were hoping to find," I told him. "You'll need to unweave or break Grierson's house wards first. You'll find a basement with black wards. Make sure you bring a strong blood mage, and be aware that it will take some time to get through."

"What's in the basement?" Lake demanded.

"A very large summoning circle. Grierson was summoning his father from the demon realm and using the girls' blood to bring him over on the night of the full moon."

"When the boundary between the demon realm and ours is thinnest."

"Yes."

Another pause. "Did Grierson kill the girls to bring his father over?"

I hesitated.

"Tell me," the agent commanded, stepping back up into my personal space.

Despite our height difference, I didn't move away. "Grierson used their blood for the summoning circle. When the demon appeared, he ate them."

Lake staggered back like I'd hit him.

When Michael saw what happened to Maggie, he'd vomited,

packed up his scrying mirror, and told me never to call him again. He wouldn't even let me take him home; he called a cab and walked away without a backward glance.

"I'm not sure you'll find any physical evidence showing that the girls died in the basement," I said as Lake visibly reeled. "He probably used a burner spell to clean up the blood, but you may find something else that puts the victims in his house—hair, fingerprints, maybe bone fragments." Michael had told me enough before he walked off for me to know that Maggie hadn't died quickly. Demons liked to play with their food.

Lake stared at me. "Please tell me the Hills don't know how she died."

"No," I said, and he looked relieved. "I told them she was sacrificed as part of a summoning ritual, and it was over quickly."

"What were you going to do with Grierson?"

"At the request of Maggie's parents, I was going to turn him over to the vampires. The Hills believed, as did I, that the best chance for them—and the rest of the families—to get justice was in Vampire Court. They wanted him punished, and the vampires have the facilities to ensure he wouldn't have known an hour of peace for the rest of his long and miserable life. I didn't want Grierson dead; I wanted him to suffer."

If Lake was taken aback by that, he didn't show it. "If he did clean the basement with a burner spell, there might not be any physical evidence left. The Vampire Court could have been the only chance for a conviction. None of the magic-related evidence would have been admissible in human court." He seemed to be reasoning out loud to himself. I let him think.

Finally, Lake turned to me. "All of the victims had long, dark hair and were similar in height and body type. We speculated it was the work of a serial killer."

"I don't think you were wrong," I told him. "He selected his victims based on their appearance. It's possible that if you dig into his past, you'll find the woman he hated, who he felt he needed to kill over and over again. He needed blood for the summoning, but he didn't need to feed the girls to his father. He enjoyed watching them suffer."

After a moment, Lake said, "You went into that bar and used

yourself as bait, knowing you were his type. You risked your life to get justice for Maggie and the other girls." I could see grudging respect in his eyes.

I stayed quiet.

Lake turned back to Grierson's body, his face set. "You need to leave. The official report is going to say that we confronted Grierson in the alley and then chased him into the park, where he died resisting arrest. I don't need to tell you that saying anything to the contrary would be inadvisable."

"What about your partner?"

"Parker's report will match mine. I'll be visiting with the Hills privately. Other than sending them a bill for your services, I don't think there's any need for you to have further contact with them, do you?" His tone made it clear that it would be in my best interest to agree.

Ah, there it was: that trademark SPEMA arrogance. It was a good reminder that when it came down to it, even someone like Lake, who obviously cared a great deal about getting justice for Grierson's victims, had no trouble letting me know exactly who had the power in this scenario. I'd identified a serial killer, risked my life to capture him, and revealed what had happened in Grierson's basement, but it was Lake calling all the shots.

If he was worried that I wanted publicity, I could at least dispel that notion. "You can have the credit; I don't care about any of that. If everything had gone according to plan, no one outside the Vampire Court would have ever known I was involved, except the Hills."

"Good." Lake bent down and picked up my phone, healing spell, cuffs, and a few other items Parker had dropped on the ground, and handed them to me, along with my wallet. "Take your stuff and go."

I put my possessions back in my pockets and paused, looking at Grierson's body. It was just beginning to sink in that I had killed him. He was far from the first person to die by my hand, but at least I had no doubt he'd deserved his fate. So many others hadn't. I took a shaky breath.

Lake had his phone out. "What are you waiting for?"

I turned on my heel and headed for the main gate. Behind me, I heard Lake barking orders into his phone. I resisted the urge to hold my side as I walked, even though each step sent a bolt of pain through my ribs. The moon disappeared behind the clouds and I shivered.

Nausea surged, and I paused just outside the park gate, leaning against a lamppost while I swallowed hard. It was the closest I'd come in five years to getting caught. Part of me wanted to run, to put as much distance between myself and Lake as I could, but I forced myself to walk calmly and not attract attention.

My car was six blocks away, eight if I took a route that completely avoided Parker and the alley behind McGovern's, which seemed like a good idea. My feet and calves were starting to hurt, but I could make it. I'd go home, use a healing spell on my ribs, and crawl into bed.

In my mind, in an endless loop, I saw the glint of a blade and the bright green flash of my cold fire, and heard the sound of Grierson's knife going into his brain. I wrapped my arms around my middle and walked, my boot heels echoing like gunshots on the empty street.

CHAPTER 2

Two weeks later

"The worst part about being a ghost," the ghost confided, "is that you don't get to pick who you end up haunting. I know that seems counterintuitive, but there's a system. Of course, you can put in a request, but there are a ton of forms to fill out, which is a bitch if you're noncorporeal. By the time all the paperwork goes through, what usually ends up happening is you get someone from the priority list— the list of people who deserve to have a demented spirit running around ruining their lives. And that," he added happily, clicking his long, pointed fingernails together, "is how I ended up here with you."

"Fantastic." I sighed.

All three of the ghost's faces were hideous. One visage was alight with excitement, his red goat eyes with their slit pupils zipping around my office, taking in the economical furnishings. Another set of eyes, so black that they seemed more like holes than actual eyes, focused on my MPI license where it hung, slightly crooked, on the wall above my head. The third set, the multifaceted eyes of a spider set in an arachnid head, were fixed on my face. His black robes moved as though hordes of beetles crawled on his body beneath the silk. An unidentified purplish-black goo dripped from his fangs. I had to give him credit: he was thoroughly gruesome.

I blew out a breath. "Look, nothing personal, but I'm probably going to have you exorcised. I can't afford to have a ghost on the payroll; the supe insurance alone would *kill* me."

Three sets of angry eyes focused on my face. "Is that supposed to be a joke about me being dead? Because I find that to be in particularly poor taste."

"Honestly, I really don't care."

Two monstrous mouths fell open in shock. One was full of rows of very sharp, jagged teeth, while in the other, spider fangs clacked in consternation. The third face—the one with the black-nothingness eyes—had no mouth. He'd probably been expecting a much different reaction, based on the form he'd chosen to take. I might not be his first haunting, but I was going to be his last. I had no use for petty ghosts who got their kicks trying to make living humans miserable, even if I had earned my spot on the "priority list."

Some would say that threatening exorcisms or making puns about death to a ghost was cruel, but I'd never really gotten the hang of being nice.

While the ghost sputtered in indignation, I picked absently at the underside of my new desk. A particularly disgruntled client with surprisingly powerful telekinetic powers threw a fit in my office a little over a week ago, and I was still trying to get repairs completed and the furniture replaced. The remains of the old desk, along with pretty much everything else that had been in the office, were now in the dumpster out back. The large cabinet behind my desk, a heavily warded antique, was the only piece of furniture to withstand the dwarf's tantrum. The sole other survivor was my framed mage private investigator license, though it looked a bit worse for wear.

The ghost finally recovered his power of speech and gave me a truly grotesque arachnid smile. "I see you're an MPI, Alice Evelyn Worth," he said silkily. "Surely someone in your line of work has use for someone with particular…talents?"

I scoffed. "How long were you in the Null since your last haunting? Ghosts aren't a new thing anymore. If I need to get results, I'd have better luck summoning a demon, or hiring one of those crazy half-vamps, a dhampir. At least people are scared of them. You. Are. Not. Scary."

The ghost's red goat eyes flared in anger. I met his gaze without fear. He wasn't the first nightmare-form ghost to show up in my life, and I'd dispatched all the others as quickly as they'd arrived. There wasn't anything he could do or say that would make me want to keep him around.

Of course, just as I thought that, he proved me wrong.

The ghost raised his clawed hand. Bright blue-and-green flames danced along his fingertips.

Drawing on my air magic, I threw up a protective circle around me and my chair just as my desk—and everything on it and in it—went up in cold bluish-green flames. In seconds, there was nothing left but ash.

It was my turn to be momentarily speechless. "Well, that's different," I said finally.

* * *

Turns out, the ghost had a very particular set of skills—skills that had apparently put him at odds with someone who decided he didn't need to be walking around alive anymore.

Now rather intrigued, I poured myself a cup of coffee from the coffeepot that had, thankfully, been sitting on the little table behind me and not on the second desk I watched get destroyed in the past week. I used my desk generally to make my office look more professional, and to create a psychological barrier between myself and my clients. I'd been forced several times to use a desk as a shield, and twice as weapon. The new desk hadn't been around long enough to be used as any of those things.

The ghost looked disappointed that I wasn't all that upset about the loss of my desk and its contents, but I'd long ago ceased to worry about the destruction of office furniture. When you're a PI specializing in the paranormal and supernatural, it didn't pay to get attached to office décor. Not all my clients left satisfied, and the nature of my business often brought angry supes of various species to my door— which, though heavily warded, has had to be replaced six times in three years. I wasn't very popular with the building's management.

The ghost watched me sip my coffee. I couldn't help but notice he was smirking. The spider mouth might also be sneering, but it was hard to tell. Well, I still planned to have him exorcised, so that ought to wipe those smiles right off. He'd thrown me a pretty epic curveball with the speed and precision of his cold fire, though, and I was curious about his past. If nothing else, I'd be adding to my knowledge of ghost abilities, and that was worth fifteen minutes of talking with this dead jerk.

"Tell me about yourself," I said. With no desk to put it on, I held my coffee cup and made unflinching eye contact with my uninvited guest.

The ghost's goat eyes sparkled with something like humor. Strangely enough, most ghosts found their situation funny, even when their deaths were violent and unexpected. I had yet to figure out why this would be the case. My working theory was that being in the Null for any length of time made them all a little unhinged.

"My name is…Malcolm," the ghost said slowly, as if recalling his own name took a moment. "I was a mage."

I snorted and gestured toward the pile of ash that had once been a perfectly respectable secondhand desk. "No shit."

He made a raspy, wheezing noise that I realized was laughter. While his goat head was speaking to me, the other two sets of eyes went back to looking around my office. The three pairs of eyes looking in different directions were starting to make me feel queasy.

"What kind of mage?" I asked.

"Earth," he said, confirming my suspicions. The cold fire was unique to earth mages. Then he surprised me again. "And water."

My eyebrows raised, despite my intention to stay only mildly interested. "Earth *and* water? That's very unusual."

I carefully opened my shields enough to get a better sense of the ghost's magic. I recognized the cool blue of his water magic and the peaceful green of earth magic. His aura sizzled along my senses. I realized he was definitely a high-level mage, and well trained; his control of his cold fire was precise.

"Unusual enough for me to end up on a good payroll," Malcolm was saying as my senses turned outward again. "It was a good living, for a while." He stopped talking, and the goat's eyes wandered over to look out the window. Since it looked out on the dirty bricks of the building next door, I figured he wasn't lost in the view.

"Let me guess," I said. All three sets of eyes suddenly focused on my face. "Everything was great at first. Then they started asking you to do things you didn't like, then things you didn't want to do, then things you'd swore you'd never do, and then things that made you not be able to sleep at night or look at yourself in the mirror. And then...." I stopped. I noticed that my hands had clenched and forced them to relax.

"And then, I died."

I nodded. These days, it was a common story.

"I worked for Darius Bell." For a moment, the ghost sounded almost proud, but then his shoulders slumped. I was sure at one point he'd been honored to be a part of Bell's cabal, one of the most powerful, wealthy, and well-connected on the West Coast. Hard on the heels of that flash of pride would be the recollection that his boss had him killed—and that for all his hard work and loyalty, he was rewarded with what had probably been a very unpleasant exit from this plane of existence.

The ghost—who I was grudgingly starting to think of as Malcolm, despite every effort not to, damn it—settled in to tell his story. Apparently tired of the effort it took to maintain all three nightmarish countenances, he suddenly re-formed with a single human face and head, with spiky, blond hair and bright blue eyes. His robes turned into a button-up shirt and jeans. His claws retracted into his sleeves, then pushed back out as normal, even delicate-looking human hands.

Transformation complete, he peered at me through the wire frames of quite unnecessary glasses—after all, who'd ever heard of a nearsighted ghost? The affectation was almost quirky, and completely unexpected after the gruesomeness of his nightmare form. I had no idea whether this was how Malcolm appeared when he was alive, but now he looked like a cute librarian.

The total package, I had to admit, was not unpleasant—you know, for a dead guy.

"I went to work for Darius right out of college," Malcolm said. "Well, I say that, but it's not really true. I left college to work for him. Two semesters to go before I had my chemistry degree and probably a decent career as a research chemist, and I let a recruiter hand me a signing bonus and the next thing I knew, I was signing a ten-year contract and moving across the country."

I whistled. A ten-year contract *and* a signing bonus? Malcolm must have had some serious talent. I looked at my noncorporeal guest with new respect.

I felt a familiar hollowness when I thought of the years I spent as a mage for my grandfather's cabal: the sleepless nights, the misery, the blood—both literal and metaphorical—on my hands. Even now, I could see the telltale signs of blood magic in my aura that even the strongest spellwork couldn't hide completely. If it weren't for my spelled tattoos, my bloody history would be visible for any ghost or sensitive to see.

I wrapped my hands around my mug and refocused my attention on Malcolm's face. Behind those superfluous glasses, Malcolm's eyes looked...concerned? Troubled? I raised my eyebrows, waiting for him to continue his story, and hoping he couldn't see anything in my aura but the light smudges of someone who'd only dabbled in blood magic once or twice.

Malcolm went on. "At first, they gave me the best assignments: bringing rain to crops that needed it, enriching the ground for farmers, shoring up land for housing developments, nothing bad or even questionable. I felt good about the work I did. I spent the first year wondering where all those horror stories about the cabals came from. I finally decided the stories were made up by anti-magic activists and people who weren't good enough to work for the cabals. I really believed it was all lies. God, I was so stupid." He hung his head.

I stayed silent. In a weird way, I envied Malcolm's lost innocence; as the granddaughter of Moses Merrum Murphy, I'd never had the luxury of *not* knowing the truth about the cabals. My earliest memories of magic involved the suffering of others, and always—*always*—the pursuit of profit and power, the two things Moses Murphy and Darius Bell and pretty much every other cabal leader, or Davo, lived for.

While there were certainly plenty of smaller cabals out there that had no interest in criminal activities and whose members used their magic to help rather than harm, all of the very powerful ones were organized crime syndicates. These cabals, like any other criminal organization, ran on brutal efficiency, demanded unwavering loyalty, and cared about two things: money and power. There were a dozen major cabals in the US and a host of smaller ones, each run by a powerful Davo and his or her lieutenants. Like the Mafia, cabals made money through various criminal enterprises. Mages bound to cabals did whatever was required to make these ventures profitable.

Malcolm was speaking again. "So, after about a year of getting the cushy, easy jobs, they started me on the ones I didn't really like very much: causing droughts and floods, destabilizing the ground under particular building projects, disrupting shipping routes. Then they came to me with the rough stuff: landslides, washouts, attacks on construction sites and building projects owned by other cabals. People were hurt. People died. I tried to refuse, but that contract...." He rubbed his wrists with recollected pain, and my own wrists throbbed in sympathy.

I remembered all too well the agony of trying to break a contract once I had been forced to accept it, the crippling white-hot lashes of pain that scoured my body whenever I tried to refuse to carry out an assignment. Even now, just *hearing* the word *contract* still brought on nausea at unexpected moments.

"It got worse and worse," Malcolm continued. "By that time, I realized the stories about the cabals were true—and they weren't even close to the worst things they were responsible for. But something tells me," he said, regarding me much too closely for my own comfort, "that you know that just as well as I do."

"What I know or don't know is none of your business, ghost," I snapped, setting my forgotten mug down on the side table so hard that lukewarm coffee sloshed over the side. I stood.

Malcolm's eyes went suddenly wide with fear. The familiar power of my magic surged and swirled around me. Unlike Malcolm's brightly colored earth and water magic, mine was black and red and purple, dark and malevolent and dangerous. Without me having to consciously call for it, the energy spooled around my fists, waiting to be unleashed.

"Blood magic," he whispered. If it was possible for a ghost to turn pale, Malcolm was doing it.

And now he knew how I got on that priority list.

* * *

The midmorning sunshine poured in through my office windows, glittering on dust particles in the air. The light was diffused as it passed through my guest and made strange, indistinct shadows on the floor. We stood unmoving, Malcolm frozen in place with fear, and me struggling to get control of my anger.

It took nearly a full minute, but I pulled the magic back inside myself, and the residual energy faded. When my arms finally stopped prickling, I breathed deeply, sat back down in my chair, and looked across the pile of ash at Malcolm.

Despite his initial fear, he looked calmer now that I no longer seemed like an immediate threat. It occurred to me then that his death could have been at the hands of a blood mage, and that my loss of control might have triggered some very unpleasant memories.

Malcolm eyed me with obvious unease. "I'm sorry I upset you."

"It's fine." I started cleaning up the spilled coffee with a handful of Kleenex. Malcolm waited silently.

Finally, I dropped the gloppy, wet tissues into the trash can and turned back to him. "So, they were giving you assignments you didn't want...," I prompted.

Malcolm nodded. "I had no choice but to do what they told me. I belonged to the cabal for ten years, but I didn't make it that long, obviously. By my fourth year, I was fighting them every step of the way. I'd developed a tolerance for the pain, and it was taking them longer and longer to get me to comply. Sometimes I'd be unconscious for days and they'd end up having to use a different mage who wasn't as strong. I told them I wanted different work or I wanted out of my contract. This went on for another year."

I was surprised Malcolm resisted his contract so openly for that long and survived as long as he did. It was a testimony to how talented he was that a) he'd been strong enough to resist the power of the contract, and b) that the cabal had been unwilling to kill him for resisting. To the end, I doubted Bell really wanted to kill Malcolm. A strong mage with both earth and water magic was a rare gem, one that any Davo would be very reluctant to part with.

"So what finally got you killed?" I asked.

Despite the bluntness of my question, he laughed a little. "Well, that's pretty direct," he said. "I guess they finally got tired of my shit, figured out that I wasn't going to stop fighting. They handed me over to a blood mage. Three days later, I was dead."

I was right, then: he'd been killed by a blood mage. A normal person probably would have felt guilty for unleashing blood magic in front of a ghost who had died that way, but thanks to my grandfather, I had never really been any kind of a normal person. The best I could come up with was some empathy. Those three days had probably felt like three hundred years. I was willing to bet Malcolm had welcomed death in the end; after even an hour with a blood mage, many would. I knew that from personal experience.

Suddenly, realization hit me. "Wait…how are you here?" I asked in confusion. "How did you end up bound to *me*, instead of Bell's cabal?"

Malcolm shook his head. "I don't know. I was under contract when I died, so I should be back at the cabal." He shuddered. Bound ghosts were often simply "stored" in spell crystals and foci, where their energy could be used in spellwork and continuously drained like magical self-charging batteries. It was a horrible fate for any mage. "Unless Darius freed me, but why would he do that?"

"I have no idea. I can't imagine he would let a mage as powerful and skilled as you be unbound."

"But what other explanation is there?" Malcolm asked. "It's got to be punishment of some sort, but I can't think of a scenario where being a bound ghost isn't worse than coming back as a haunt. Sorry about that, by the way," he added.

I shrugged. "Not your fault."

"Maybe he expected me *not* to come back as a ghost, and instead end up in the Underworld. Considering the things I did, I can't imagine that would be very pleasant for me."

I sat back and thought.

Why would Darius Bell do something as unheard of as let a mage's ghost be unbound? Malcolm's theory of punishment was possible, I supposed; death wasn't necessarily the end of suffering. Ghosts, unless exorcised, remained incorporeally on earth, tied to a person or place, tormented by their inability to connect with their loved ones or find peace and rest. If exorcised, they went to the Underworld, but, as Malcolm said, there was no guarantee he'd find any peace or rest there. I didn't know the extent of the things he did while working for the cabal, but I could guess. There were a lot of theories, few of them cheerful, about what happens to those in the afterlife who caused suffering in this one, even if they were coerced into doing so.

So had Bell freed Malcolm so he would be unbound? If so, why? Had he wanted to ensure Malcolm ended up in the Underworld? He could just as easily have destroyed Malcolm's essence completely, wiping him out of existence, but it would mean Malcolm would no longer be suffering. So if punishment was the goal, I could see some kind of logic in sentencing Malcolm to a noncorporeal afterlife.

But somehow it didn't seem right. To say cabal mages never got their contracts nullified and their ghosts unbound would be an understatement. What was less frequent than never? Was there a word for that? Never*er*? Never*est*? That was how often it happened. So this had to be an extraordinary circumstance.

I raised my eyes to look at Malcolm, who clearly shared my unease. "You don't think it's punishment."

"I don't, not in the way you're thinking. It's something else. There's a plan for you. It may involve more suffering—in fact, it almost certainly does—but it's not as simple as just condemning you to being a ghost and haunting someone like me." I fell silent.

Malcolm's face went blank, but I could feel his disquiet as if it was my own. For some reason I couldn't quite articulate, there was something very disturbing about Malcolm's story, beyond the obvious parts about the things he was forced to do while under contract, or his terrible death at the hands of a blood mage. I couldn't shake the feeling there was something going on in Bell's cabal, and that Malcolm being bound to me was a clue to it, which meant I wasn't going to be exorcising Malcolm now or anytime soon, not until I had some answers.

I stood, and Malcolm floated back a few inches. "Well," I said with a sigh, "welcome to Looking Glass Investigations. You're the newest member of the team."

CHAPTER 3

Article 1, Section 34.1 of the Supernatural and Paranormal Entity Registration Act stated that I had seventy-two hours to register my new ghost with SPEMA. That, I believed quite sincerely, was going to be a problem. If Bell had indeed given Malcolm his freedom so that the mage would return to earth as a ghost, then he would be watching the Agency's registration system for his name to pop up, and then the entire cabal would be on my doorstep. I had a bad feeling nothing would keep them from taking both of us. It would likely mean either my death, my undeath, or my return to the cabal I'd escaped five years ago. Obviously, I wasn't going to be making that call to the Agency.

"How long have you been dead?" I asked Malcolm, hands on my hips, as I thought about what to do with the pile of ash that had been my desk and its contents.

"Um, I don't know." I glanced at him with raised eyebrows. "Things have been a little crazy," he said defensively. "I wasn't really thinking clearly when I died, and it's not like I had a watch or a calendar. What's the date?"

I told him. He stared at me, clearly stunned. "Two…no, almost three years? I've been gone that long?"

"Apparently." I turned away to give him some space to process that revelation. I went to the storage closet and emerged with a broom, dustpan, and bucket. I'd long ago given up on having carpet in my office and resorted to bare, stained concrete. What it lacked in aesthetics it made up for in convenience when it came to cleaning up the inevitable messes my visitors tended to leave behind. There were other benefits as well; my second sight revealed the shimmer of the circle I'd inlaid into the floor around my chair. The ash had settled around it in a semicircle, the only visible hint of the circle's existence.

"Let me—" Malcolm started to reach for the broom, then stopped with a grimace. "I'm sorry about the mess," he said instead.

"Don't worry about it." I swept ash into the dustpan and then dumped it into the bucket. There really wasn't as much ash as you might think there would be; magical fires didn't tend to leave as much behind as mundane ones. Even entire houses and all their contents could be consumed and leave less ash than would fill the bucket I was using. Memory flooded through me, despite my best efforts to keep those images locked away. My fingers tightened on the broom handle, and for a moment, it was hard to breathe.

"Are you all right?" Malcolm floated a little closer.

"I'm fine," I said shortly, focusing on sweeping. You could never get it all, though, really, I thought absently. I'd have to clean it with more than just a broom or mop to remove the traces of Malcolm's magic. I didn't need anyone knowing I'd had a high-level earth and water mage in my office, much less a dead one.

Once the ash was swept up, I put the dustpan and broom into the bucket and left it sitting in the middle of the floor where the desk had been. "I need to get rid of this," I told Malcolm. "If we're going to keep you off the radar as long as possible, there can't be any of your magic trace left behind, so try not to incinerate anything else. If you do, just use basic earth magic. That's easy enough to disperse."

"Do you think it's possible to hide me from Darius and his people?"

I made a face. "Honestly, I'm not sure how long we can keep you under wraps. I'm not about to register you with the Agency, but that doesn't guarantee your—our—secret is safe."

It occurred to me that the consequences of breaking one of SPERA's most strictly enforced laws would probably mean I'd never see daylight again if we were caught, and if the rumors were true, I'd probably be begging for death before it was all over. I saw a flash of a blood-splattered room and heard an echo of my own screams. Ice seemed to form in my veins, and suddenly my vision tunneled and again it was hard to get a breath.

"…Sit down! Sit down!" Malcolm was saying, as if from a long way away. I found my chair and sat, bending over to put my head between my knees. I focused on breathing deeply and slowly. The ghost hovered a few feet away.

Finally, I raised my head to look at Malcolm. I don't know what my face looked like, but he flitted back a few feet in that way ghosts could move when they got really spooked—so to speak. I smiled mirthlessly at my pun, and something in my expression made him flit again.

"This could be a death sentence for me," I said quietly. "And there are rumors that there are punishments for ghosts as well, not just exorcism. I've heard there are traps that capture the ghost, and…." I paused. "Blood mages designed the traps to torment the ghosts. I don't know the details, but we can assume it would be better for us both if we stay far away from SPEMA."

Malcolm looked anguished.

"If it comes down to it, I'll try to have you exorcised before they can catch you. If that's not possible, I can discorporate you."

His eyes widened as he realized what I meant. My own special set of blood-mage skills included the permanent dispersal of a ghost's noncorporeal form. It wasn't something I did very often, and I'd only ever discorporated wraiths and poltergeists. They were so far gone by that point, they didn't know what was happening to them, but Malcolm would be self-aware enough to know.

I spoke quietly but purposefully. "It would mean a one-way trip to the Underworld, but some might say that would be preferable to ending up in one of those traps. I need to know ahead of time if that's what you want, because we may not have time to think or talk if the Agency or a cabal catches us. I'll have a few seconds at most, just long enough to—"

"Do it," Malcolm broke in. "If it comes to that, send me on. I don't know what will happen to me down there, but I know I don't want to spend eternity in a trap, or back at the cabal being used as a focus." He stopped as realization dawned. "But if you spend those last few seconds taking care of *me*, you won't be able to do anything to defend yourself. They'll take you."

didn't tell him that I had one final option standing between me and the tortures of the Agency or a cabal. Inside my left leg, a so-called "divine wind" spell was carved into my femur. Only the most sensitive and focused X-ray would be able to spot it, and it couldn't be sensed before I invoked it. It was basically my nuclear option, and one I would never use unless I had no hope of escape. I knew it was a better alternative than the suffering I would have to look forward to at the hands of either the Agency or a cabal. And if my grandfather ever caught me…well, nuking myself would be the only choice. At least I would take a lot of them with me when I went, in true kamikaze style.

I resisted the urge to glance down at my leg and shrugged with a nonchalance I certainly didn't feel. "Odds are, if they catch on to us, they'll send a small army. I'm strong, but not strong enough to take on the kind of combined firepower they'd send. The best I can do is try to keep you from being caught. At some point, we need to figure out why Bell gave you your soul back."

I had no earthly idea how we were going to do that, but what the hell; it was a Wednesday, and I always came up with lofty goals on Wednesdays.

* * *

My phone beeped a reminder that I had a downtown lunch appointment with a potential client at noon. I turned to my new ghost companion. "We've got to head out. Can you leave the office and hang out unseen in the hallway for a moment? I need to clean up in here."

Malcolm nodded and vanished. I waited until I could sense that he had gone past my wards before pulling some of the energy to me that had spindled earlier. I focused on the little tickle in my senses that represented the remaining traces of Malcolm's earth and water magic. "*Obliterate.*"

The metaphysical blast that radiated out from me would have staggered a less powerful mage, but long years of practice and training kept me steady as the wave swept through my office, taking apart Malcolm's handiwork and dispersing it. The atoms weren't gone, of course; magic still obeyed physical laws. In less than a heartbeat, no trace of ash remained, in the bucket, on any surface, or in the air. In a few minutes, even the trace of his energy would disperse.

The air felt heavy and smelled like ozone, as it always did when I used magic in an enclosed space. I peeked into the bucket for a visual confirmation of what my senses already told me: the ash was capital-G *Gone*.

I stuck the cleaning supplies back in the closet, grabbed my messenger bag, and locked up the office. I could feel Malcolm's presence nearby, like a gentle, distinctly blue-green pressure in my mind, but he stayed invisible as we traveled down the elevator to the parking garage below the office building. Neither of us said a word until we were in my car and on our way out of the garage.

Finally, I gave voice to what had been going through my head. "I have a spell that should mask your energy. To other mages, you should feel like a nonmagical spirit. If you don't attract attention to yourself, it should hold up fine, but I don't have time to do the spellwork right now. To find something that will withstand scrutiny, I'm going to have to do some work. Depending on what this case is, I might be able to look into that tonight. You're going to have to stay invisible until we can work something up."

"How do we keep other mages or ghosts from sensing me in the meantime?" Malcolm's voice was quiet, either because he wasn't manifesting physically, or from apprehension, or both.

"I have a thought," I said slowly. "But you may not like it."

* * *

When I walked into Janie's Downtown Café forty-five minutes later, I walked in alone. I told the hostess my name and said I was meeting someone.

She glanced down at her notepad, then pointed. "Redhead in the third booth from the back. She's been here fifteen minutes already." There was clear disapproval in her tone.

I glanced up at the clock and frowned. I wasn't late; it was only just noon. I'd intended to be here ten minutes ago, but construction caused me to have problems finding a place to park. Plus there had been the matter of dealing with Malcolm....

I resisted the urge to touch my right earring and headed for the booth she'd indicated. "Natalie Newton?"

A petite young woman in an emerald-green shirt and khakis looked up, startled. "Yes? Are you Alice?"

"That's me." I sat down across from my client and studied her. Her hair was a remarkably bright red. A smattering of freckles made her look younger than she was. I guessed her at about twenty-five. She was very thin. Her hands played with her teacup while she fidgeted under my gaze. I sensed no magical ability in her.

"How can I help you?" I asked. "Your message indicated that you're worried about some missing items."

Natalie dropped her eyes to the table and sighed, rubbing her forehead. "Yes, that's right." Her voice was as thin as the rest of her. "My grandmother passed away about three months ago." She paused.

I'm not very good at social cues, but even I could figure that one out. I murmured, "I'm sorry," and she nodded graciously.

"Thank you. It was a car accident; a drunk driver swerved over the center line and hit her. My grandmother raised me after my parents died when I was ten, and I'm an only child, so...it was hard." Her eyes filled with tears.

I waited. No one had come by to ask if I wanted something to drink, so while Natalie was sniffling and wiping her eyes, I waved at a server and mimicked drinking a cup of coffee. She gave me a quick smile and headed for a coffeepot.

Finally, Natalie cleared her throat. "My grandmother left me everything. I have three aunts and an uncle and some cousins, but they hadn't really spent much time around Grandma for years, so...." She shrugged. "I was surprised, since I thought I'd be dividing things with the rest of the family, but her will was pretty clear. I own the house and everything in it, as well as her money." She didn't sound happy about it. Inherited money was often bittersweet, but I got the impression there was more to Natalie's unhappiness than just her grandmother's death.

"How is the rest of the family taking the news about the will?" I asked as the waitress brought my coffee.

Natalie made a face. "Some of them aren't taking it well at all. My aunt Elise hired an attorney to argue that my grandmother wasn't of sound mind when she made the will, which is such a terrible thing to say about her own mother." Her eyes filled with tears again. "I don't think anything will come of it, since there are plenty of folks who will testify that she was thinking very clearly. In the meantime, my grandmother's lawyer got me a restraining order to keep them out of the house, but it's not Elise's lawsuit I'm worried about."

She took a long drink of hot tea and looked at the cup like she wished it held something a lot stronger. "I think one of my aunts or uncles has stolen things from my house. And…." She swallowed hard, coughed a little, and looked away. When she met my eyes again, there was real fear in her gaze. "I think I'm being poisoned."

I sat back and looked at her more closely. Her hands trembled with more than just emotion, her eyes looked dull and listless, and I saw that instead of healthy pink, the skin under her fingernails was white and bloodless, as if her circulation was poor. Clearly something was wrong, but it could be as much anxiety and grief over her grandmother as anything else. "What makes you think you're being poisoned?"

She gestured at her body. "I've lost almost twenty pounds in the last few months, and it's not because I don't eat. Or *try* to eat, at least. I'm always nauseous, and often I can't seem to keep anything down. I've been to four doctors, and they all run tests and then tell me it's a stomach bug and it will pass. I know what they're thinking: I'm depressed about my grandmother, I'm worried about my aunt's lawsuit, I'm making myself sick. But I swear to you that's not what's happening."

Natalie leaned forward and reached out, as if she wanted to grab my hand. I picked up the coffee mug and took a drink. Generally speaking, I don't like to be touched.

If Natalie felt slighted, she didn't let on. Instead, she took a drink from her own cup, her hands shaking. Finally, she said, "I don't care if you don't believe me either, but I just want someone to take me seriously, and no one else will listen to what I'm saying. That's how I ended up calling you; the last private investigator I called told me that I might be better off talking to a PI who specializes in unusual cases, and I got your number from the Internet. I'm willing to pay you to find out what's going on. I need to know if I'm really being poisoned, and by whom. And why, although I can guess," she added bitterly. "I loved my grandmother, and I love our home, and the things we shared. My aunt and the rest of them don't care about Grandma at all. All they want is the money, and all they see when they look at the house and what's in it is what they could sell it for."

"You said some things were missing," I said. "What's missing? Valuables?"

"Not really, not in the way most people would think. It's books that are missing." She looked at me like she expected me to scoff at her. I got the feeling others had.

Some people wouldn't be concerned about missing books, but I was intrigued. There were all kinds of books: books that educated, books you read at the beach or on planes, books that sold bad advice...and books that could level whole cities. I wasn't psychic, but I had an inkling that the missing books weren't celebrity memoirs. Suddenly Natalie's grandmother and her house were a lot more interesting.

Finally, a harried-looking server came by to see about food orders. Natalie made a little face and ordered a salad with chicken, dressing on the side. I ordered my usual: a grilled cheese and bowl of tomato soup.

After the server left to put in our orders, I turned my attention back to Natalie. "I'd like to come take a look at the house, especially the place where the missing books were kept, and we can talk more about the rest."

Natalie's eyes got big. "You believe me?" she asked hopefully, and I could see in her expression that my belief meant a lot more to her than I thought it would.

I imagined myself in her place, going from doctor to doctor, being told not to worry, that it was just a stomach bug that would pass; week after week, month after month of no one listening. It must have felt very hopeless and lonely and frustrating. Still, I tried to be as honest with potential clients as I could be. "I'm not sure of anything yet."

Her face fell.

I held up my hand. "I am certainly willing to believe your intuition may be right," I added. "I think we have...special senses sometimes, and that we don't listen to our instincts as much as we should. So if you think there is something going on here, I'll help you find out for sure."

As fast as she'd withdrawn, Natalie's face lit up with pure happiness. "Thank you." Her eyes filled with tears again. She cleared her throat as our server brought the food and we focused on our lunch.

I attacked my sandwich and soup like a starving werewolf, but Natalie, despite her flash of joy, only picked at her salad. She watched me eat with undisguised envy. It probably didn't say anything good about me that even her obvious misery didn't affect my appetite. I'd only had a piece of toast for breakfast, and doing the kind of magic required to clean up after Malcolm, plus capturing and hiding his energy in the earring dangling from my right ear, had drained me somewhat.

Thinking about my ghost, I felt the urge to fiddle with my earring, and once again I forced myself not to draw any attention to it. I'd used my crystal earrings to smuggle magical energy, spells, and even a fragment of a poltergeist once. (That was a long story that involved the destruction of several cars, a storage building, and a small section of a local cemetery.) This was the first time I'd hidden a ghost in one of them. I'd spent many hours crafting the earrings by hand to be both pretty and functional. Unless someone physically touched my right earring, there would be no way to know a powerful ghost resided in it.

I used the last bites of sandwich to mop up what was left of my soup. Natalie had eaten about a fourth of her salad and given up, sipping her water while I ate. When I finished, I pushed away the soup bowl and reached for the check.

Natalie snatched it up. "Let me. It's the least I can do for you listening to me."

"Thank you." As Natalie handed her credit card to the server, I asked, "Are you available to go back to your house right now and have me look around?"

"Absolutely." A little life came back into her pale face as she signed the receipt. We stood, I slung my bag over my shoulder, and we turned to leave.

At that moment, the front door of the café opened and three SPEMA agents walked in.

For mundane humans, their presence was supposed to be reassuring, or so I have been told. For this reason, most agents displayed their credentials and wore Agency jackets or vests everywhere they went. Their visibility was designed to give people a sense of security in a dark and scary world full of monsters and magic and things that went bump in the night.

For supes and mages, however, agents were far from comforting; on their word, someone could be hauled away in spell cuffs, or even put down on the spot if deemed a danger to citizens' property or their safety. It didn't take much to be labeled a threat and killed. It was most common with supes like shifters, vamps, half-demons, and dhampirs, but it happened to mages too.

I evaluated the newcomers in a split second with the practiced eye of someone who had spent her entire life avoiding contact with agents whenever possible. Their body language was natural and relaxed. While the blond man in front spoke to the hostess and held up four fingers, the other two scanned the room, not as if they were looking for anyone in particular, but just keeping an eye on their surroundings. My conclusion: it was simply lunchtime for them as well.

Time to make a casual exit via the side door. I turned to Natalie. "Where are you parked?"

"Two streets over, on Powell."

Drat; that was in the direction of the front door. "Well, I'm in the garage. Walk with me? I'll take you to your car."

"Sounds good!" Natalie followed me as I wove between the tables toward the garage entrance.

Just as we made it through the lunchtime crowd and approached the side door, it jingled open.

Special Agent Lake stood inside the door, three feet in front of me, his hand on the door handle and eyes locked on my face.

CHAPTER 4

As Moses Murphy's granddaughter, I never had the luxury of anonymity—not from the public, the Agency, or anyone else. Even as a child, I was famous, and feared. My face was known, even if the extent of my skills was a closely guarded secret. Moses kept me on a short leash, cultivating my mystique by leaking information now and then, teasing outsiders with hints and rumors about what his granddaughter was capable of doing.

I remained in the public eye until my escape. I moved across the country, established a new identity, earned my MPI license, and redefined myself in a world that hated and distrusted my kind. I had to leave behind the name and the face that were so well known to so many. Alice Worth bore little to no resemblance to the deceased granddaughter of Moses Murphy, physically or otherwise.

In my new life, I kept my head down and avoided all publicity and contact with SPEMA. Anonymity was key to my survival. Being instantly recognized by a SPEMA agent was not in the plan.

Lake's stare became impersonal. Apparently, we were going to pretend not to know each other, which was fine with me.

"Sorry, wasn't looking where I was going," I said politely.

"Not a problem." Lake studied us for a moment, then stepped aside to hold the door open for us to walk past him into the alley. Behind me, I heard the door close.

The tension faded from my shoulders with every step away from the diner. "I think I'm parked on the fourth level," I told Natalie, heading to the garage elevator. "I'll drop you at your car and follow you back to your house."

"Thanks!" Natalie hummed quietly to herself as we took the elevator up.

I ferried Natalie to her car in my blue Toyota, a nondescript three-year-old sedan that worked well for surveillance. To my surprise, she drove a bright red Mustang convertible, which was definitely not the type of vehicle I thought she would be driving. I followed her out of the downtown area and toward the west side of the city.

As I drove, I thought about Special Agent Lake. Two days after Grierson's death in Fields Park, SPEMA announced the half-demon the media had dubbed the "Full Moon Stalker" died trying to elude capture. The public reacted with predictable horror at the news that Grierson had sacrificed the six known victims as part of demon-summoning rituals. Lake and Parker appeared on a handful of national news channels for bringing Grierson's reign of terror to an end. I watched one of their interviews on CNN. Lake looked uncomfortable in the spotlight, but Parker seemed more than happy to take the credit for catching Grierson.

I never did send an invoice to the Hills. I don't know what Lake said to them, but they mailed me a sizable check anyway. I made a donation to a women's shelter in Maggie's name and sent flowers to her memorial service.

After a fifteen-minute drive, Natalie turned into the driveway of a tidy single-story house, and I parked at the curb.

There was a Lexus SUV parked in the driveway when we arrived. The back window featured several stickers representing extremist anti-magic organizations and anti-supe hate groups. Fantastic.

Natalie parked next to the SUV and flew out of her car to confront a middle-aged bleach-blonde in a lime-green designer track suit. The woman stood on the front porch holding a high-end digital camera. I watched for a moment to gauge their interaction.

When Natalie started yelling, I decided it was time to find out what was going on. I grabbed my bag and exited my car.

"You have no right to be here," Natalie shouted as I strode across the yard. "The court has ordered you to stay off my property. Get out of my house!"

"I am not *in your house*," the woman said, in a snotty tone I would have thought was impossible for someone who was not sixteen years old. "I am on the porch of *my mother's house*, and by the time my lawyers and I are done, you won't be living in it."

This must be Aunt Elise. "Excuse me," I said loudly.

The woman turned on me. "Who the hell are you?"

"An order of protection prohibits you, your vehicles, and your agents from stepping foot on or in property owned by Ms. Newton. At this moment, you are in violation of the law and I am dialing the police." I held up my phone and began hitting buttons.

"Who is this?" the woman demanded of Natalie.

"I am Ms. Newton's representative." I advanced on Natalie's unwelcome guest with an expression that caused her to step back before I got within ten feet of the porch. "I have one more number to push before I hit Call, so you have approximately five seconds to get out of here before you'll be needing bail money."

Elise glared daggers at me. "This is my mother's house," she hissed, but she headed toward her SUV.

"What's on the camera?" I asked.

Elise clutched it to her chest. "None of your business," she spat. Then she saw my crystal jewelry and her face switched from fury to terror and back to fury as she put two and two together and rounded on her niece. "Who is this *freak* you're bringing into my mother's house?" she screeched. "I won't allow it!"

I hit Call on my phone and waved it. Elise's face turned tomato red as she sputtered expletives. I stared at her impassively. I'd looked full demons in the face and been flayed alive by a blood mage, so the wrath of a soccer mom didn't faze me in the least.

I acted like someone had answered the phone while it rang in my empty office. "Yes, this is MPI number 230492-394." I rattled off my license number. "I would like to report a violation of a protection order—"

"*Bitch!*" Elise screamed and hurled a small potted plant at me before running to her SUV. I flicked out a finger and used a tiny stream of air magic to soften the plant's landing so that it came to rest unharmed in the grass three feet to my right. Elise jumped into her SUV, slammed the door, and backed out of the driveway, narrowly missing my car. She flipped me off and shouted a few more curses out her open window before peeling out, tires squealing.

I sighed and joined Natalie on the porch. She sat on the front step, sobbing.

I stuck my phone in my bag, returned the plant to where it belonged, and leaned against the porch railing while my client cried herself out. It took a while.

Finally, Natalie wound down. Sniffling, she got up and unlocked the front door. I paused outside the threshold, getting a sense of the place.

Someone who had lived here was *definitely* magical. Judging by the faded magic I could sense, I was betting it was the recently deceased grandmother. Odd that Natalie had no such talents; they usually ran in families. There were wards on the house, but they had faded without upkeep from their creator.

I touched the doorframe gently, running my fingers along its smooth wooden surface. I closed my eyes and listened to the house.

It sang. It was beautiful. There had been a lot of love within these walls.

"What are you doing?" Natalie's voice was curious.

Slowly, I opened my eyes and looked at the young woman as she stood, still shaken, in the entryway to the home her grandmother had left to her. Strangely—since such sentimentality was very unlike me—I felt compelled to do what I could to find the secrets of this house and protect both it and Natalie from those who would wish them harm. This house had told me it was worth saving—that they were *both* worth saving.

"Listening to the house. May I come in?" I asked.

She looked surprised. "Do you have to have permission, like a vampire?"

"No," I replied, smiling despite myself. "It's just polite to ask. And also, incidentally, it's not true about vampires either."

She paled.

* * *

Looking around Natalie's living room, I wondered if she had changed much of anything after her grandmother's death.

The deceased had been very fond of cats, it would seem; in addition to four actual cats living there, the décor was cat-themed. There were cat sculptures, cat paintings, cat knickknacks, cat-shaped rugs, cat refrigerator magnets, photographs of cats in cat-shaped picture frames, and even a wall-mounted grandfather clock with different breeds of cats as the hours. Normally this level of obsession would have irritated me, but for some reason, it didn't. It was like a peek into a world of a sweet, cat-loving, old granny I'd certainly never known.

The grandmother's room had been kept more or less the same since her passing; Natalie confessed a reluctance to clean it out and use it as her own. I made a noncommittal sound. Due to my unique upbringing, I lacked not only social etiquette but also most of the sentimentality that seemed to make life difficult for those who were more sensitive. The master bedroom was much larger and had its own bathroom. From my perspective, it would be a better room for Natalie to live in.

The master suite also connected directly to the library, the room I was most excited to see. Natalie opened the door and walked inside. I started to follow her in—

—and was promptly knocked on my ass with a hard *zap* of magic that singed my shirt, sucked the air out of my lungs, and left me seeing honest-to-God stars.

Startled, Natalie yelped as I fell. Since she was nonmagical, she could not have seen or felt the bolt that hit me; it would have just looked like I ran into an invisible wall and went down.

Dazed, I propped myself up on my hands and wheezed.

The library door pulsed with wards that had been dormant probably since the grandmother's death. They'd flared to life with my attempt to unknowingly trespass, and now I could feel them sizzling on my skin.

The power of the wards was enormous. That probably meant the library had been where the grandmother practiced her craft and kept important books. It would be warded with the strongest whammies she could cook up—spells that would not have faded as easily as those around the house. The wards seemed designed to permit passage to specific individuals, since Natalie was able to come and go freely.

I was furious with myself for not being more cautious. Even though I hadn't sensed any magic inside the house, I should have used a spell to detect hidden wards. In fact, I was lucky I hadn't blundered into deadly black wards. Mistakes like that can cost a mage her life.

Natalie was speaking to me. "Are you all right? What happened? Did you faint?"

"I'm fine, I'm fine," I said crossly, embarrassed by my carelessness. I swatted her hands away and hauled myself to my feet, shaking my head to clear the cobwebs. Damn it, my shirt was ruined. There was a scorched two-inch hole just to the left of my breastbone. Double damn. Through the hole, I saw an angry red burn over my heart. *Triple* damn. If I'd walked into those wards right after the grandmother's death, right now I'd be hanging out in the afterlife with her.

I suddenly had way more respect for Natalie's grandmother, and a hell of lot of questions. First, I had to see if I could untangle these wards so I could get into the library.

"Um, Alice? Ms. Worth?"

I'd almost forgotten about Natalie, who looked at the hole in my shirt in confusion.

Well, even *I* knew this would be an awkward and possibly very upsetting conversation. In a situation like this, there was only one thing to do.

"Do you have any coffee?"

* * *

Much to my dismay, Natalie was a tea drinker and did not have so much as a single coffee bean in the house.

Some time later, after we'd consumed an entire pot of tea and I'd eaten several homemade oatmeal-raisin cookies, Natalie sat in stunned silence in the living room, a cat in her lap and two others on the back of the couch next to her.

I sat in an armchair across from my client, holding a bag of frozen peas to the burn on my chest and waiting for her to process what I'd told her. It was a lot to think about, I supposed, wiping cookie crumbs off my ruined shirt.

Finally, Natalie stirred and rubbed her forehead. "So…my grandmother was a mage."

"Yes," I said, somewhat impatiently. "She had very strong skills with air magic, and possibly fire. I need to take a closer look at the wards on the library to know for sure."

Natalie frowned. "I thought mages only had one kind of magic."

"Most do," I told her. "Magic of any kind is rare; they say less than a half a percent of humans have it. Of those, almost all have only one of the four types of natural magic—earth, water, air, or fire—but some have two kinds. I have both earth and air. Some mages have what's called blood magic."

"That's death magic, right?" Natalie said.

I hesitated. "It's highly volatile dark magic, and it's illegal, but it's not necessarily 'death magic.' It has other uses."

Natalie was quiet for a bit. "This is a lot to take in. It's not that I don't believe you…."

"I understand," I said, even though I didn't. Magic just *was* for me; it wasn't a thing to be believed or not. "If she never showed any of her abilities to you, and kept them so well hidden that her family didn't know, she did it for a reason, possibly to avoid the kind of reaction we saw today from your aunt."

"Oh my God, my aunt." Natalie's eyes widened. "Her *own mother* was a mage, and she hates supes and mages so much."

I shrugged. "People are ignorant. They're afraid of what they don't understand. There's a lot of anti-supe propaganda out there that people like your aunt believe. Maybe if she'd known about your grandmother, she'd think differently, but who knows. Prejudice and bigotry aren't logical."

"Aunt Elise *cannot* know about this," Natalie said vehemently. "If she did, she'd burn this house to the ground."

I thought about Elise's hateful eyes and didn't disagree. "Well, she won't hear about it from me, but if she came here with someone who was sensitive, they could tell the house has wards. That wouldn't prove your grandmother was a mage," I added at Natalie's sudden look of panic. "Lots of non-mages have protective wards on their houses; it's more effective than hiring an alarm company. If someone encountered the wards on the library, though, they'd know for sure someone who lived here was a mage. They might think it was your grandmother, or they might suspect it was you."

Natalie looked terrified, but she needed to know the truth. Hiding it from her could only do more harm than good.

"Here's my thought. I need to examine the wards on the library closely to understand them. If I can take them down, I will, then replace them with my own. That should divert suspicions. I can also put wards on the house to help prevent any more trespassers from getting in, including your aunt."

Natalie looked hopeful. "Really? That's great!" She paused. "Will it hurt her?"

I considered the possibilities. There were aversion spells, or even stronger options, if you wanted to take a more aggressive approach to home defense. My mind conjured up an image of Aunt Elise going up in a bright green fireball, and my mouth twitched. "Not too much," I said finally. "At least, not unless she gets overly enthusiastic about getting in the house. In that case, she might get a nasty surprise."

Natalie grinned. "Good."

* * *

Two hours later, I sat down on the grandmother's bed and wiped sweat off my forehead. While the house wards were easy to take down and replace with my own, the wards protecting the library were another thing altogether. The spellwork was exquisitely complex.

I discovered her grandmother had set the wards so Natalie could come and go safely through them. The intensity of their defense was based on the strength of the mage trying to cross them, which confirmed my initial evaluation that those wards would have killed me if I'd walked into them when they were at full power. Anyone without magical ability would feel an aversion to the library, which probably meant the rest of the family would simply avoid going in without giving it much thought. Whatever was in that library was both magical and worth killing for, but not something the grandmother feared Natalie would find.

Of course, all this begged the question of how someone would have gotten in there to steal the books Natalie said were missing, but I'd cross that ward when I came to it.

I had to admit unraveling the wards by myself would take at least a day. Conveniently, I'd recently made the acquaintance of a ghost who also happened to be a very strong mage. I was willing to bet he was at least decent with spellwork.

I took a piece of chalk from my pocket and drew a circle around myself on the floor, then removed my right earring and held it in the palm of my right hand. Against my skin the earring buzzed as if it held a very slight electrical charge. "*Release.*"

"*Holy shit!*" Malcolm yelled.

I jumped. Malcolm, still in his cute librarian ghost form, stood in my circle, looking shocked. I broke the circle with the toe of my boot, and he flitted back away from me, half disappearing into the grandmother's neatly made bed.

"Holy shit!" he shouted again.

"Hey, buddy," I said. "How are you doing?"

Malcolm flew around the room, a ghostly whirlwind. "That…freaking…*sucked*," he declared as he zipped around. Trying to keep track of him made my eyes cross. "It was so dark. It felt like forever, or a second, or both. I don't know!" He came to a stop in front of me. "*Please* don't put me back in there," he begged. "It was awful. There has got to be another way."

"I'll try to think of an alternative. But hey, in the meantime, you wanna help me with something?"

Malcolm paused to take a closer look at the hole in my shirt. "What happened to you? That looks nasty."

"It could have been a *lot* worse." I gestured over my shoulder at the doorway to the library.

That brought an end to his snit. "Whoa," he said in awe, gliding over to take a look at the wards. As a ghost, they would be evident to him, like neon signs. "This is grade-A work. Kind of faded," he muttered to himself. "They must have been *intense*." He sounded impressed.

"Hey, Alice? Who are you talking to?" Natalie appeared in the doorway to the bedroom, steaming mug of tea in hand, looking around the room as if she thought someone was hiding.

Well, hell, in for a penny…. I walked over to where Malcolm was reading the wards and grabbed his arm. I funneled energy into him, and

Malcolm went from invisible to partially opaque. "Natalie, this is my ghost, Malcolm. Malcolm, meet Natalie Newton, my client."

Natalie stared at Malcolm. After a moment's hesitation, Malcolm waved.

Natalie walked over and sat on her grandmother's bed. "Wow," she said weakly. "This has been a *day*."

* * *

I let go of Malcolm's arm and he went invisible again, but Natalie sat on the bed and watched me have a one-sided conversation with thin air.

After about ten minutes of careful scrutiny, the ghost pronounced that together he and I could dismantle the wards in a couple of hours.

"I need to rest for a bit," I said. "That zap earlier really got me, and that was on top of all the other magic I've used."

"Take all the time you need." Malcolm's eyes were on Natalie. "So, what's her story?"

"We can talk about that later," I said, frowning at him. Natalie, who could only hear my side of the conversation, looked puzzled. "He's asking about you."

"Oh, he hasn't been here all along?" Natalie asked.

"Well, he was, but not in a form where he could listen."

"Damn right I wasn't," Malcolm griped.

I glared. "Well, that's gratitude."

He looked abashed. "Sorry. I know you're doing your best for me, but...."

"I know it was rough," I said. "If there is any other way to hide you, I'll try to think of options."

"Why does he have to hide?" Natalie asked.

I debated how much to tell her and decided on a portion of the truth. "He's in hiding from someone who wants him for a reason we don't understand. So if anybody ever asks you about Malcolm, you never saw him."

"Saw who?" Natalie quipped.

"Exactly."

Malcolm grinned. "I like her. She's cool."

"Settle down, Ghost of Don Juan." I lowered myself to the floor and folded my legs with practiced ease. I placed my hands on my knees and began to breathe deeply and evenly, closing off outside distractions as I sought the calm, centered core of myself that would help me focus on the serious business of unraveling someone else's wards.

For whatever reason, that calm center was difficult to find. I supposed it had something to do with the surprise arrival of a mage's ghost, a narrow escape from SPEMA agents, and a new client with a loud-mouthed bigot of an aunt and a mysterious magical grandmother with near-deadly wards.

It took several minutes, but I was finally able to relax. I meditated until I felt sure I was prepared to do the dangerous work ahead of us, and then I opened my eyes.

Natalie was curled up on her grandmother's bed. At first I thought she was asleep, but her eyes were open and she seemed to be looking through the open door into the library. I might have been imagining it, but I thought she seemed to have a bit more color in her face and sparkle in her eyes than earlier in the day.

Malcolm was still examining the wards, his fingers moving as he formulated a strategy for unraveling them.

"What was your grandmother's name?" I asked, my voice breaking the silence of the room.

Natalie jumped. "Morrison. Betty Morrison."

The name didn't ring any bells. I got up and stretched. Natalie rose as well. "You should probably go into the other part of the house, just in case."

She looked disappointed. "I was hoping to watch you work. Will it really be dangerous?"

I considered. "Probably not for you, since the wards were tuned to let you in and out, but everything we're going to be doing will be invisible to you since you aren't a mage. If you want to stay in the room with us, I'd be more comfortable if you would at least sit over there to the side, away from the wards."

"Okay." Natalie moved to the far side of the room and sat.

Malcolm hovered next to me. When I slipped into my second sight, I saw the complex runes connected by threads that pulsed like power lines. The wards formed a perimeter around the library at floor level, with additional reinforcement around the doorway. The wards were orange and white, the signature colors of fire and air magic.

Faint black threads were the last remaining evidence of how deadly the wards had once been. It wasn't hard to imagine that anyone running into them when they were at full strength might have been reduced to a smoking ruin. Betty Morrison had been playing hardball. I rubbed my chest.

"How do you want to do this?" Malcolm asked.

I contemplated the wards and the threads connecting them. "Could you break it?"

He tilted his head, considering. "Maybe, but honestly, I'm not comfortable doing that. It looks like there is a *lot* of energy still stored up in there. There's no telling what it will do if we break the ward, since the person who set it isn't here anymore to control the flare. We might level the house, or take out the entire neighborhood. If we cast a circle strong enough to contain the surge of energy, we'd have to tap a ley line to hold it, and that would attract a lot of attention we definitely don't need."

I sighed. "That was my assessment too. An unweaving would probably work best. That's gonna take a while." I rolled my neck and shoulders to loosen myself up. "Give me a minute to get focused, then find me."

I closed my eyes and opened the tiniest chink in my shields. The wards buzzed on the edge of my senses like a hive of bees. Slowly, I reached out with my magic to feel the threads of Betty's wards.

The fabric of the wards pulsed in a tapestry of runes and power. I observed the threads, feeling my way through them to understand the patterns. I sifted through the wards like fingers moving through the finest beach sand. The wards were works of art, and I regretted having to destroy them.

As my shields lowered, I could sense Malcolm's magic. It was lovely, colorful and light, with none of the darkness mine held. His magic was like a symphony playing Beethoven. By comparison, mine sounded like a bunch of xylophones falling down the stairs. With a jolt, I realized I was actually jealous of a ghost.

As quickly as the feeling flared, I squashed it. Now was *not* the time. Even faded by time and lack of maintenance, Betty's wards could be dangerous, even deadly if we lost control over them during the unweaving. I had to stay focused. Everything else would have to wait.

Slowly, painstakingly, I slowed the sifting of the sand until I could feel individual grains. Vaguely, I was aware of Malcolm following my lead. I focused my senses on a single mote of power. Using my own magic, I slipped inside it and pulled gently, and it fell apart with a tiny pulse of energy and a sound like a distant chime. Somewhere near and yet in another universe, I heard and felt another chime as Malcolm took apart a different thread. It tugged on my awareness, like someone gently pulling at a single hair and then letting go.

Two grains of sand gone from the beach. I focused on my task while somewhere on the edge of my awareness, Malcolm did the same. The wards began to fall.

CHAPTER 5

Hours later, I hugged the toilet in the master bathroom and heaved miserably. My stomach felt like it was full of razors, and I tasted blood. I was aware Malcolm was hovering nearby while Natalie stood outside the bathroom door, but I didn't care much about either of those things.

The moment the last thread of Betty's wards disintegrated, agony and nausea ripped through me, sending me fleeing on rubbery legs toward the nearest bathroom, half-blind with pain. I barely had time to slam the door closed and fall on my knees in front of the toilet before I threw up everything I'd eaten today, and then it felt like I threw up everything I'd eaten in the last week. The spasms that racked my body were so violent, I was surprised my shoes didn't come up too.

"Alice, what should I do?" Malcolm's hands felt ice-cold on my shoulders.

Blinded by pain and sickness, I flailed at him. "Get away!" Another spasm tore at me. This time, I threw up mostly blood. Dimly, I thought, *Shit…that* cannot *be good.*

Through the haze, the rational part of my mind figured out that I had triggered a curse hidden within the wards designed to punish anyone who tried to disassemble the library's protections. Curses and spells concealed within other spells, commonly known as landmines, were one of the most dangerous hazards mages faced when interacting with unknown spellwork, since they were virtually undetectable until tripped.

This landmine didn't seem to have affected Malcolm; it was possible it simply did not include noncorporeal beings as targets. I couldn't really think about it very much right now. The pain was endless.

I heard Natalie through the door, asking if she should call for an ambulance.

"No," I rasped. "No," I said again, louder, so she could hear me. I convulsed and vomited blood so violently that it splattered across the toilet and floor. I spat several times and wiped my mouth with the back of my hand. "No ambulance. I will...be...okay," I managed to say. I hoped she heard me.

A minute passed, and though I dry-heaved and spat up more blood, the worst of the vomiting seemed to have passed. The pain was lessening by degrees. I flushed the toilet again and lay down on the cold tile of the bathroom, shivering with shock. My vision had gone gray, and vertigo made the bathroom spin around me.

The bathroom door swung open. "Oh my God," Natalie said, horrified. After a moment, I heard soft noises and water running, and then a cool, wet washcloth began cleaning my face.

I had no strength or will to move, so I let her clean me up a little while sensation crept back into my limbs. I didn't realize I'd closed my eyes until water trickled over one eyelid. I opened my eyes and was somewhat surprised I could see again.

Natalie appeared, a bloody washcloth in her hand, her eyes wild with fear. "Can you hear me?"

I took a ragged breath and whispered, "Yes."

"What happened?" Natalie wiped my face gently with a different, cleaner washcloth. "I don't know what to do to help you."

"You...don't have to do...anything," I said, my voice gaining some strength. "I will be okay."

She looked incredulous. "There is blood *everywhere*." I thought she might be on the verge of losing it completely.

I tried to move but stopped when it felt like broken glass ripped through my stomach. I moaned and curled up in a ball. "Don't call anyone," I whispered. "I just...need to rest." Then I let go and passed out.

* * *

The next time I opened my eyes, the pain in my stomach had faded to a dull ache. For a moment, I was disoriented and confused, my mind a jumble of fractured memories and pain. I remembered lying on the cold tile in the bathroom, but what was under me felt warm and soft.

When the fog cleared a bit, I realized I was on the floor in Betty's bedroom, wrapped in a thick cocoon of heavy blankets and quilts. I turned my head and saw Natalie sitting on a pillow next to me, her back against the bed. She was focused on her phone, tapping on the screen and frowning.

I felt a jolt of fear. "Who are you calling?"

She jumped and dropped her phone with a clatter. "Nobody!" she said, sounding defensive, scared, and angry all at once. "I was reading what to do for someone in shock that didn't involve calling 9-1-1." She stared at me pointedly.

I closed my eyes. "Okay." I cleared my throat gently. It was still raw and painful from vomiting. The gross taste in my mouth defied description. "Okay," I repeated, opening my eyes again to look at her. "I just…can't go to a hospital." They'd run tests, call SPEMA—or, if I was really unlucky, my grandfather—and I'd disappear.

Natalie picked up her phone and put it on the bed behind her. I noticed she was even paler than before. My condition must have really frightened her. "I'm glad you're awake," she said. "I didn't know how long you'd be out. You were shivering so badly, I got every blanket in the house and wrapped you up in them." She gestured at my blanket nest.

"Thank you." I felt weak but clearheaded, which was good. I'd half expected to wake up dead. "I'm sorry about the mess in your bathroom. When I can get up and around, I'll clean it up." The way my arms and legs felt, it might be a little while before I was mobile, though.

"Don't worry about it. It's clean."

I sighed. "Oh. I am so—"

"I didn't do it," Natalie interrupted me. "The ghost did."

Welp, I was completely awake now. "Malcolm?"

She nodded.

I looked around the room and saw my ghost hovering near the door to the library—a doorway no longer blocked by wards. He looked like he'd expended a lot of energy. "Did you use magic to clean the bathroom?"

Malcolm shrugged. "I had to. I didn't know when you were going to wake up, and all that blood...." He shook his head.

"Thank you." My blood could never be left behind. It could be used against me and was one of the few things that could connect my current life as Alice Worth to my real identity. Despite my order to not call an ambulance, Natalie might have done just that if my condition hadn't improved, and Malcolm had done his best to protect me.

The windows were dark, and it occurred to me that I had no sense of how much time had passed. "What time is it?"

"About eleven o'clock," Natalie told me. "You've been unconscious for almost three hours."

Whoa. So the unweaving of the wards had taken something like four hours, then I'd been knocked out by what I was now sure were the remains of a landmine, no doubt put in place by Betty and designed to bring an abrupt and agonizing end to the life of anyone brave or foolish enough to try and dismantle her wards. My admiration of Betty's skill rose another couple of notches, along with some other less pleasant emotions arising from the fact I'd been hurt twice in one day since coming into contact with the dead woman's magic.

I started to wonder if all the cutesy cat crap in the house was camouflage. Who was Natalie's grandmother? Why would she put black wards around her library, then double down by hiding a death curse within them? And what the hell was in that library?

I tested my arms and legs and found that strength was creeping back into them. I started peeling back layers of quilts and realized I was in my bra and underwear. "Where are my clothes?"

"Soaking in cold water," Natalie said. "They were really bloody. I'll get you something to wear."

"How did I get into the bedroom?"

"I rolled you onto a blanket, then slid you across the floor into the bedroom. I wish I could have put you in bed, but I couldn't pick you up."

"Thank you for what you did," I told her sincerely. I realized

Natalie was sweating and looking a little unfocused. "Are you okay?"

"I don't know. I don't feel very good." She shivered hard.

"Alice—" Malcolm began, his voice urgent.

Natalie gasped and white magic flared around her hands for a split second before it vanished. She sagged back against the bed, her eyes wide with panic.

"She's a mage!" I shouted at Malcolm as I kicked frantically to get myself loose from the blankets that were tangled around my legs. "Malcolm, knock her out and drain her! *Right now!*"

Malcolm got to Natalie just as she shrieked and an orange fireball erupted from her hands. I dove to one side to avoid it and heat rolled over me.

Natalie's cry cut off abruptly. When I looked back, she was on the floor, unconscious, and Malcolm's hands were on her shoulders, draining her magic as fast as he could pull it. He began to glow.

I finally freed myself from the blankets and staggered to my feet, dizzy and achy. I was cold but didn't have time to worry about trying to find clothes. "Do we need a circle?"

"I don't think so," Malcolm said tersely. "I'm almost done."

"Did you hit her with a sleep spell?"

"Yes." Malcolm drifted back from Natalie's body. He was so bright from the surge of energy, I had to squint a bit. "She's drained for now, but we need to bind her magic. A blood magic spell would be stronger than my earth or water magic."

"I'm low on magical energy right now, but I think I have enough to bind her." I knelt beside Natalie and used a hidden edge in my ring to open my right index finger, then pulled down the back of her shirt to expose her right shoulder blade. I drew a rune on her back in my blood and used most of my remaining energy to bind her magic. My blood hummed with power, then the mark faded.

I used the bed to push myself to my feet, and Malcolm and I looked down at Natalie as she slept.

"It looks like Granny Betty isn't the only person in the family with a secret," I said.

"Do you think she knows anything about her magic?"

I shook my head. "I don't believe she knows. I'm thinking Betty found a way to hide Natalie's magical ability from everyone, including

Natalie."

"Why would Betty not want Natalie to know about her own powers?"

I shrugged. "Could be lots of reasons. Betty hid her abilities well, probably to stay off the Agency's registry. Maybe Betty was worried Natalie would screw up and out the whole family so she cast a suppression spell—more likely a shitload of layered spells—to bury Natalie's abilities so deep that even Natalie doesn't know she has them. Then Betty died without releasing the spell or telling Natalie the truth."

I had a new emotion to add to my complicated feelings toward Betty: disgust. What did she think would happen if Natalie's magic escaped the binding spells?

Malcolm moved over next to me. "Those would have to be some powerful spells. I mean, *seriously* powerful. And why are some of those powers breaking out now?"

"It might have something to do with the fact Betty's wards are fading and we just finished unweaving the wards on the library. There was a lot of power in those wards." I pressed my hands to my aching stomach. "Maybe some of that power was anchoring the binding spells on Natalie. We disrupted them, and now the cat's out of the bag." I glanced around at all the cat décor. "So to speak."

Betty's magic had been impressive, and she'd been an expert at wielding it, as the library wards and the pain in my chest and stomach could attest. How much power did Natalie have?

"We've stumbled into a mess here." Malcolm gave voice to the thoughts in my head. "What are we going to do?"

I sighed and rubbed the bridge of my nose. "We have a couple of choices." I was startled to notice how easily I'd started using the pronoun *we*. "Worst-case scenario, unweaving the wards started a process and Natalie's powers will manifest in full, like a dam breaking."

"That could be bad."

I snorted. "Yeah. If she's got as much power as Betty did, and it flares, she could level the house, or worse. She'll have no control, no discipline, no training. SPEMA will put her down. The only question is how much destruction she'll cause before they nuke her, and how much collateral damage there will be when they do."

Malcolm looked stricken.

"Best case," I continued, "her powers manifest slowly enough that someone can train her." Who the hell that person might be, I had no idea. I didn't even know anyone who could—or *would*—take on an adult whose magical abilities had been suppressed her entire life. I'd have to find someone powerful and trustworthy enough to control Natalie's magic until she could. I sighed. I'd have more luck finding a unicorn, and no one had seen one of those on this side of the fae realm in more than a hundred years.

"Well, we know she has both fire and air magic, but how much she has, I don't know. It was a small flare, but for all we know, she's as strong as her grandmother."

I realized Malcolm was very studiously avoiding looking at me in my underwear. I glanced down at myself. "I need clothes. I'm going to find something to wear and get my go-bag out of my car so I can clean up."

"While you're doing that, I'll start working on the library wards. You don't look like you have much magical energy left."

"I don't. The binding spell took about everything I had." As Malcolm moved over to the library door, I went in search of clothes. A few minutes later, wearing one of Natalie's T-shirts and a pair of her yoga pants, I hurried barefoot out to my car, got the black duffel bag out of the backseat, and returned to the house.

I used the toiletries in my go-bag to shower, and then put on jeans and a comfy T-shirt that advertised a great local supe band with a half-demon lead singer named Cam who'd shared my bed for a sizzling-hot six weeks. After I was clean and dressed and had brushed my teeth, I felt almost human again.

When I returned to the bedroom, Malcolm was putting wards on the library. He was focused on his work, so I sat cross-legged on the bed and gently rubbed my sore abdomen as I watched him. His fingers were quick and deft, forming runes and symbols, stringing them together, and then layering the strands. He was using earth magic only, and I couldn't see or sense anything that might lead anyone to believe they were placed by anyone other than a strong earth mage. It was exquisite workmanship.

By the time he finished with the wards, it was almost three a.m. I had gone from sitting up to lying down on the bed. When Malcolm finally turned around, his energy looked somewhat depleted, but he looked like he had enough left for me to pull from. I might not be powerless for much longer if he could be talked into sharing with me.

I'm not usually one for compliments, but I had to give him credit. "The wards are incredible. Some of the best I've ever seen."

Malcolm smiled. "Perimeter wards are one of my specialties."

I sat up slowly to avoid strain on my sore stomach. "Looks like mostly aversion spells, but the defenses are going to hit mages pretty strong."

He glanced back at the wards. "Yeah, I figured we want to keep anyone out who has magical ability, until we know what's in there." He paused. "Do you want me to set it so that Natalie can pass?"

I thought about it, then shook my head. "We better not, until we know how much magic she has. We don't know what Betty left in the library."

Now I had a decision to make, and I found I wanted Malcolm's opinion on it. "Should we put the stronger spells in?"

He looked at me. "Like the ones that almost killed you?"

"Yeah." We were silent for a moment. "There's something in there that Betty was willing to kill to protect. Until we know what it is—or was—I'm wondering if we need to up the threat level on the wards."

Malcolm went quiet and frowned while he gave that some serious thought. "If I funnel enough energy into these wards, and we maintain them, they'll incapacitate up to a half dozen mages trying to get in at once. If you want black wards and landmines, that's not something I can do—not something I *will* do. I did enough for Darius. I'm done with death."

I rubbed my face. I could do them, if I had enough energy. I didn't even need my blood magic; my air magic was strong enough that I could replicate both the black wards that had burned me and the landmine I'd tripped during the unraveling. I was running on fumes, however. Time to test our partnership. "If you let me siphon energy from you, I can set the wards."

Malcolm and I stared at each other. I had no idea what he was thinking about me or my request. It had been a rough day for both of us. He'd been threatened with exorcism and stuck in an earring. I took two big hits from deadly wards and now I was as low on magic as I could ever remember being.

I let him think.

Finally, Malcolm made a decision. "If you take enough energy from me to do what you need to do, I'll be very weak for a while. You'll have to hide me and protect me until I get my strength back." He looked at my earring with a grimace.

I took a deep breath and slid off the bed. "I will try to figure out a better way to hide you. I can't promise it will be much of an improvement, but maybe there's another option. For now, we've got to get these wards up, and then I'm going to go out."

"Go out?" He glanced at the clock. "By the time you do all that, it will be four o'clock in the morning."

"I know. It's cutting it close, but as long as I get there by five, he'll still be there."

"Who will be where?"

"I've gotta go see a vampire."

"A vampire? What vampire?"

"His name is Charles Vaughan. He's a member of the Vampire Court."

Malcolm flitted back in surprise. "You know a member of the Vampire Court?"

"I've worked for them for a couple of years. Charles is a friend. More importantly, he's a broker."

"A broker? Of what?"

"Treasures and secrets, mostly." I smiled. "Charles likes to say that he buys and sells only things that are priceless. Also, he knows people who know people. If we're going to find a master mage to teach Natalie how to control her magic, I'll need his help."

"Okay," Malcolm said finally. "I guess we better do this, huh?"

I took Malcolm's arm, closed my eyes, and reached out with my senses until I felt the hum of his magic. I began to draw it into myself, slowly at first, then faster as our connection opened wider.

Malcolm's magic tasted sweet and pure, like rain. I felt parched, like I'd been stranded in the desert for days without water, and had to fight not to siphon every drop. When I felt him getting weak, I closed the connection between us and released his arm.

Energy rose and crashed within me like an ocean wave breaking on a beach. I kept my eyes closed and allowed it to settle into me, soaking into my bones. Even when it was at rest in my skin, I felt buoyant, lighter on my feet.

I opened my eyes. Malcolm hovered in front of me, almost invisible. He opened his mouth, tried to speak, then shook his head. I hadn't left him with enough energy to communicate.

I reached out my hand and he took it.

I'm sorry. I took too much, I thought at him.

His eyes widened in surprise at hearing my voice in his head. He focused on me and thought back, *It's okay. I should probably…rest.*

With my other hand, I reached up and touched my earring. *"Contain."* The spell flared, and Malcolm vanished. The earring buzzed; the ghost was in residence.

The room felt emptier without Malcolm's presence. I shook my head. *Don't be ridiculous*, I thought. *Stay focused.*

Upgrading the library wards didn't take long; I knew the spellwork well enough to do it in my sleep. I upped the aversion spells for nonmagical intruders and then set black wards for magical trespassers.

I frowned at the door to the library. I really wanted to know what was in there, but I wasn't about to go into Betty's library low on magic. The woman had put black wards around it and woven a death curse into them. Who knew what was waiting in there?

For now, I needed to put Natalie in bed and get to Hawthorne's before Charles went to sleep for the day. My client was such a tiny thing, but I was still weak and sore. As a result, it was embarrassingly difficult and painful to hoist her up onto the bed and get her under the covers. I took her shoes off and tucked her in.

I replaced Malcolm's sleep spell with a compulsion that would wear off in about six hours. Natalie murmured and snuggled deeper under the covers. Because of the spells, she'd wake a little confused, and probably with no memory of her magic breaking free. That was good, because I really didn't need her to panic when she woke up.

I found a pad and pen on the nightstand and jotted a quick note: *You fell asleep while we were working, so I put you in bed. We're still working on making the library safe, so don't try to go in there yet. I'll give you a call in the afternoon. Alice.*

I propped the note up on the nightstand where she'd see it, made sure I had all my belongings, and locked the door on my way out. After I checked to make sure the house wards were up, I headed to my car and took off for Hawthorne's.

CHAPTER 6

Hawthorne's was one of the few bars I really enjoyed frequenting. Named for a famous literary friend of its owner, it sat in the trendy neighborhood known as The Heights, in the middle of a block of very expensive retail lofts all owned by Charles Vaughan. Its patrons tended to be late twenties and older, professional types more likely to be discussing stock portfolios over expensive bourbon than sports over beers.

Since Hawthorne's was open until dawn, it was popular with both human night owls and nocturnal supes. Despite the diverse clientele, things generally stayed peaceful. There were two main reasons for that: Adri and Bryan, two of Charles's enforcers who often worked as security to keep an eye on the crowd downstairs while their employer conducted business in his offices above.

When I walked up, Adri stood at the door checking IDs. As always, the tall woman wore all black—black turtleneck, black pants, black boots—with her shoulder-length, brown hair in a ponytail. With her height, her striking features, and a body toned by mixed martial arts and free climbing, it was impossible not to feel intimidated next to her, even if you didn't know she could pick a grown man up and toss him across the room.

"Alice." She greeted me with a half hug.

I squeezed her back with real affection. "How are you, Adri?"

"It's a slow night. It's good to see you, *chica*. You here for fun or business?"

I sighed. "Business, unfortunately. Is Charles in?"

"He is. Go talk to Bryan."

"You're a doll," I told her.

She snorted and waved me in.

The inside of Hawthorne's, like its owner, radiated subtle elegance: all dark wood, low lights, and brass fixtures. Patrons took up only about half of the tables and booths, talking in low murmurs over the sound of clinking glasses and Eddie Money on the jukebox.

Pete, the manager and my favorite bartender, was pouring out shots in a long row on the bar. He grinned as I came up. "How you doing, Alice?"

"Doing okay, Pete. How have you been?"

"Not too bad." He finished pouring the last shot with a flourish and slid the bottle back onto the shelf behind him. "What can I get you?" A waitress put the shots on her tray and headed off to distribute them.

I started to ask for a beer, then shrugged mentally. All things considered, I thought I deserved a real drink. "Scotch. The good stuff."

Pete reached up to the top shelf as I slid onto a barstool. He poured me two fingers of whisky and pushed the glass over.

I took an appreciative sip. "Is Bryan around?"

A hand the size of a catcher's mitt landed on my shoulder. I somehow managed not to drop my drink and screech as Bryan's laugh rolled through the bar. "Damn it, Bryan, don't do that!" I scolded him, giving his massive bicep a punch that hurt my hand but only made him laugh harder. I scowled and nursed my drink.

"Mr. Vaughan is meeting with a client," Bryan said when he finished laughing at my expense. His voice sounded like boulders rolling down a mountainside. "If you can wait, I'll let him know you're here and take you up when he's available."

"Not a problem." I jerked my chin toward the back of the bar. "I'll be over there whenever he's ready."

My favorite booth was in the corner, where I could sit with my back to the wall and watch the bar. There wasn't much light in the back, and the lamp that hung over the table hadn't worked in ages, which was why it tended to be a popular booth for couples, or solitary souls trying not to be noticed. I sipped my Scotch and retreated into the shadows, staring off into the distance while my mind wandered.

My solitude lasted for all of about five minutes before a deep voice interrupted my thoughts. "Can I join you?"

I looked up.

The tall, dark-haired newcomer wore jeans and a button-up shirt and held a bottle of craft beer. Ruggedly handsome and muscular with about two days' worth of stubble, he had the casual confidence of a man used to hearing yes to that question. As delectable as he looked, what I liked most was the way the corners of his eyes crinkled when he smiled, as if he smiled a lot.

Despite the flutter in my stomach, I took a drink of my whisky and gave him a level stare just this side of unfriendly.

Apparently undaunted, he propped an elbow on the back of the seat across from me and raised his eyebrows.

I should say no. Then again, it had been a long day, and he wasn't the worst-looking man in the bar. "Why not."

He grinned and dropped into the seat opposite mine. "I'm Sean."

I hesitated. "Alice."

"Hi, Alice." Sean set his beer down on the table and stuck out his hand.

I stared at him and thought about how the last time a man tried to pick me up in a bar, he ended up dead with a knife in his eye.

Sean waited.

I reached out and shook his hand briefly. His skin was very warm.

"What are you drinking?" he asked.

I saluted him with my glass. "Dalwhinnie."

He looked surprised, but pleasantly so. "Rough day?"

"You could say that."

"I know what you mean." Sean leaned back in the booth, stretching out. His right leg brushed against mine. "Sorry," he said. He didn't look all that sorry. I was pretty sure he'd done it on purpose. Maybe it was the Scotch talking, but I didn't really mind. "I had to work overtime, didn't get off till three. Then I didn't feel like staying home, so I decided to go out for a drink."

"Where do you work?"

"I own a private security firm." I liked that he didn't say it as if I was supposed to be impressed. "One of my employees called in sick for the second time this week and I had to cover his shift. I think he's got a new girlfriend." He laughed and I smiled. "So, tell me about yourself, Alice. What do you do?"

I took a drink to give myself a moment to think. Normally I claimed to be an administrative assistant if anyone asked, since most people started peppering me with annoying questions if I told them I was a mage private investigator. If he was private security, though, he probably wouldn't be all that awed with my job, or ask me how many vamps I'd staked—three—or if I'd ever seen a full demon—yes, right before I sent him back where he came from. "I'm an MPI."

"Wow, I never would have guessed."

I gave him a flat look. "Why? Because I'm female?"

"Not at all." Sean smiled good-naturedly. "I actually know several female mage PIs. We have a couple on retainer as consultants, but all the ones I know are ex-law enforcement, and you don't strike me as a LEO."

I took that as a compliment.

He finished off his beer. "So what's keeping you up tonight? Working late on a case?"

"I was," I said. "Client meeting ran late. I decided to stop by to see…a friend."

"Oh?" Sean looked around the bar. "Is she…or he…joining you here?" He was plainly wondering if I was meeting a date.

"Sort of." I glanced around for Bryan but didn't see him. I supposed that meant Charles was still in his meeting and wasn't ready for me. "I guess he'll be around at some point." I shrugged. Part of me was impatient, wanting to talk to Charles about finding a master mage to help with Natalie, but I found myself enjoying Sean's company.

I raised my glass and drained the rest of my Scotch. I caught Pete's eye and pointed at Sean's beer, holding up two fingers. He gave me a thumbs up, grabbed two bottles from the cooler, uncapped them, and headed our way.

As Pete put the beers down in front of us, Sean spoke up. "Thanks. You can put her drinks on my tab."

"Oh no," I said. "That's not necessary."

"Please, let me—"

Pete looked back and forth between us, his eyebrows raised.

"No, thank you," I said. "I've got it." I didn't want any misunderstandings between us. Men who buy drinks for women in bars near closing time get certain expectations. Sometime soon I'd be leaving him sitting at the table whenever Bryan came back to get me, and that would be that.

"Okay, okay." Sean held up his hands in surrender. "Just thought I'd offer."

"I appreciate it."

Pete took Sean's empty bottle and my glass away and returned to the bar. I asked Sean what brands of craft beer he liked, and we talked microbrews for a while. As I was telling him about a popular local beer I enjoyed, I noticed him studying me intently, his brow furrowed.

I broke off in midthought. "What?" I asked.

"Alice, are you hurt?"

I frowned. "Why do you ask?"

"You've been flinching, and you're holding your stomach like you're in pain."

I realized my arm was wrapped around my sore abdomen and I hadn't even noticed I was doing it. I moved my left hand on top of the table and straightened. "I'm fine."

"What happened?"

I lifted one shoulder in a careful half shrug. "I ran into some black wards at my client's home earlier in the evening and tripped a landmine hidden in the spellwork."

I watched several emotions—surprise, anger, then alarm—cross Sean's face as he processed what I told him. "Black wards *and* a landmine? Aren't those both deadly?"

I shook my head. "Not always. These were just very…intense. I survived."

"Do you need to go to a hospital?" Sean looked me over, I think for visible injuries.

"Seriously, I'm fine," I insisted. "No permanent damage. I was lucky. I know better than to just walk into a room without checking."

"I'm a security consultant," Sean reminded me. "Can I do anything to help? Was the person who set the wards arrested?"

I shook my head. "Really, I can't talk about it. Client

confidentiality."

Sean looked unconvinced, but he sat back, apparently willing to let it go, at least for now.

Despite how self-conscious it made me, I appreciated both his concern and that he took my word that I was all right. Since my parents' murder when I was eight, I hadn't had anyone to fuss over me when I was hurting. Even now, five years after my escape from my grandfather, I didn't spend much time around what few friends I had, and wasn't used to others worrying about me. The only people I counted as friends were Adri, Bryan, Pete, and maybe Charles, if a vampire could be said to be anyone's friend. The longest dating relationship I'd had was with Cam, the singer, and that was pretty much just sex. My fear of being found out kept me from getting close to people.

Looking across the booth at Sean, I suddenly felt lonely. I'd long ago accepted my isolation as a condition of being in hiding. It wasn't like me to feel maudlin about it, but to my horror, my eyes burned with angry tears. I hoped the bar was too dark for him to see them.

I took a drink and stared absently in the general direction of the front door. I caught sight of Adri turning away a pair of teenage boys. They watched with wide eyes as she tore their fake IDs in half twice and handed them the pieces. The offenders slunk away, dejected, and Adri smirked, leaning against the doorway. She caught my eye and winked.

"Alice?"

I blinked.

Sean was leaning toward me again. I got the impression he'd been talking, and I hadn't heard a word he'd said. "I'm sorry, I spaced out for a minute. What did you say?"

"I was asking what was wrong."

I forced a little laugh and glanced at my phone. If I was going to see Charles, it would have to be soon; dawn was an hour away. "Like I said, it's been a long day. I'm not sure my friend is going to have time to see me tonight, and I'm starting to get tired. I'm just not the best company right now."

Sean reached out. I started to pull back, then forced myself to be still as his hand covered mine.

I'm so tired of being afraid. The vehemence of my own thought startled me.

"You okay?"

"Yes. I'm all right." I curled my fingers around his and his grip tightened.

The part of my brain that was always on guard, always worried about giving myself away, wanted to yank my hand back, but the warmth of his skin felt good. It occurred to me that the stress of the day—Malcolm's troubling story, a run-in with Special Agent Lake, two close calls with Betty's wards, and Natalie's magic manifesting unexpectedly—had left me feeling out of sorts. On another night, I'd probably have told Sean to go away. I might never have told him what I did for a living, or let him hold my hand. Knowing that on an intellectual level didn't change how good his touch felt, however, or how much I appreciated having a good-looking man show interest in me.

Sean brushed my palm with his fingertips. "Is your friend not coming?"

"I'm not sure. He said he'd be along, but...." I shrugged. "It's getting really late."

"Or early, depending on how you look at it," Sean joked. "The sun will be up soon."

"I know." I finished my beer and toyed with the bottle.

We studied each other. "What are your plans if your friend doesn't show?" Sean asked finally.

"No plans per se. Probably just home to bed."

The subtext hung in the air between us like a chandelier.

"I'd like to take you home," Sean said.

My brows shot up. So much for subtext.

Sean chuckled at my expression. "You seem like the sort of woman who doesn't play games. You've probably already decided if you're interested in me or not. Now that I've gotten to know you a bit, I thought I'd take the direct approach and see what happened."

I nailed him with a look. "What do you think you know about me?"

Sean leaned forward, meeting my gaze—and my challenge—head-on. "You're a private detective. You work hard, you're loyal to your clients, and you aren't afraid of the risks that come with the job or going in where others fear to tread. You're tough, and other people's respect is important to you. You don't like to be the center of attention, but you want the person you're with to listen when you talk. You're on constant alert. I bet if I asked you to close your eyes and describe every person in here, you could do it. And you enjoy good Scotch, good beer, and good music."

I tilted my head. "Leaving the other items aside for the moment, how do you know what kind of music I like?"

"I've been watching your reactions to the songs that played while we've been sitting here. You liked Guns N' Roses, scoffed at Starship, and lost your train of thought twice while listening to 'Purple Rain.' That tells me a lot about you right there."

"It *is* a great song," I mused.

"Alice."

We both looked up. *Way* up.

Bryan stood at the booth, looking at our hands with raised eyebrows. Suddenly self-conscious, I pulled back from Sean and put my hands in my lap. "Yes?"

"Mr. Vaughan sends his regrets. Unfortunately, he won't have time to see you tonight. Unless it's an emergency?"

I thought about that. Charles and I had known each other for almost five years, but you had to be very careful around vampires. The situation with Natalie probably didn't qualify as the kind of emergency that would justify pulling him out of his meeting, and if he got angry with me, he might not help me.

I sighed and shook my head. "Not an emergency, Bryan, but if you could get me in to see him tomorrow night, I would appreciate it. I have a situation where I need his advice."

"I'll put you on the schedule and text you a time," Bryan said. "Do you need a lift home?"

I wasn't drunk, but the Scotch and the beer on an empty stomach had given me a buzz and I knew I wasn't okay to drive. I frowned.

Sean spoke up. "I was just about to offer Alice a ride home."

Bryan focused on Sean. "Oh?" He managed to pack a lot of suspicion and distrust into that one word.

Sean returned his gaze, totally unfazed, then both men looked at me. I had a decision to make.

Bryan could get someone to take me home. Probably Pete, or either he or Adri if I hung out while they closed.

Or I could call a cab.

Or I could do something completely irresponsible and ask a security consultant with beautiful eyes to give me a ride home.

What the hell. "If you could take me home, I'd really appreciate it," I told Sean. He grinned.

Bryan didn't look happy about my choice. "Call up here when you get home. We'll drop your car off in a few hours."

"You are such a sweetie. I'll go settle up with Pete." I slid out of the booth and walked to the bar.

"You headed out?" Pete asked me as he ran my credit card.

"Yep." I filled out the receipt, left a generous tip, and handed him my key. "That's for my car. Bryan said he'd drop it off in a bit."

Pete stuck the key in his pocket, then printed off Sean's tab. Sean handed him a twenty and a ten and told him to keep the change.

"Thanks, buddy." Pete dropped the tip into the jar before turning to grab a bottle from the beer cooler.

"After you." Sean gestured grandly at the front door. We said good night to Adri as we passed.

Sean's car was a silver Mercedes, and he'd managed to get a parking spot right near the door. I sank back into the leather seat and buckled in. Sean put my address into the car's navigation system, and we were off.

We chatted about music as the car glided smoothly and quietly through the nearly deserted city streets toward my neighborhood on the east side. I leaned my head back and closed my eyes as Sean talked. Despite my interest in what he was saying, I found myself drifting.

I jolted awake when I felt Sean's hand on my arm. "We're here," he said softly.

I looked out the windshield and rubbed my eyes. We were parked in my driveway. It was a twenty-five-minute drive from Hawthorne's to my house, and apparently I'd been asleep for most of it. The car's engine was off. I got the feeling we might have been here for a couple of minutes before he'd woken me up.

I stretched and something popped in my back. "Sorry I fell asleep," I murmured, fumbling around for the door handle.

"It's okay." I heard the smile in his voice. "Your snore is adorable."

I gasped and turned back to face him. "I do *not* snore!"

We stared at each other in the faint blue light from the dashboard. In the east, I could see streaks of orange and red on the horizon. Dawn was breaking. Desire stirred the air like a fan.

I'm not sure who made the first move, but we suddenly closed the distance between us. Sean's kiss was hungry, and his stubble scoured the skin around my mouth. I ran my fingers through his thick hair and held on as the kiss deepened. When our tongues met, it felt like a shock ran through my body. He pressed me back against the seat, his hands coming up to touch my face. The warmth in my belly from the Scotch moved lower and I made a little sound.

When we came up for air, Sean held my chin. His eyes looked very bright in the early dawn light. "Do you want to go in?"

I took a moment to consider. That guarded part of my brain was still voting that I end the evening here and now, but my hormones were redlining and my desire was drowning out the anxiety. Besides, I had a lot of built-up tension and stress from the day that I wouldn't mind working out of my system. "Let's go inside."

Sean kissed the tip of my nose. We got out of the car and I led him up the sidewalk to the porch.

As I unlocked the door, I ran my fingertips along the doorframe to lower the house wards. I opened the door and stepped inside with Sean behind me. I shut the door and raised the wards again. They would let us out, but anyone trying to get in would get a nasty surprise.

I switched on the light in the foyer and Sean looked around. I'd bought the house, a beautiful but neglected Victorian, for far less than it was worth when I first arrived in the city. The previous owner had passed away, and his children lived out of state and didn't want to deal with fixing it up before they sold it. The neighborhood wasn't fancy, but it was quiet. After extensive renovations, the house was beautiful, if simply furnished.

I turned to put my bag on the small table by the door. Sean wrapped his arms around me and trailed kisses up my neck from my shoulder to my jaw. As I leaned back against him, he burrowed his face into my hair and inhaled deeply. I shivered and turned around to take his hand. "Upstairs."

Sean let me lead the way. When we got to the landing, he followed me down the short hall to my bedroom.

We stood in the middle of the room, looking at each other in the light from the streetlight. He really was a fine-looking man.

Suddenly, Sean twitched, as if he'd just thought of something. "Call the bar."

"What?"

"You were supposed to call the bar to let them know you got home safely," he reminded me.

Oh. Right. I dug my phone out of my pocket, pulled up my contacts list, and scrolled down to the *H*'s.

The phone rang four times, then: "Yes." A familiar rumble.

"Hey, Bryan, I'm home."

"He dropped you off?"

I looked at Sean. "Yep," I lied.

"Are your house wards up?"

"Yep."

"You going to bed?"

"Yep." That's me, the witty conversationalist.

A pause. "Good. We'll drop your car off in about an hour. I'll text you about seeing Charles tonight."

"Thanks. Good night."

"Good night, Alice."

I ended the call, put the phone on my nightstand, and looked at Sean.

"Why did you tell him I dropped you off?" he asked, his voice mild. I couldn't tell what he was thinking.

I shrugged. "None of his business either way." I leaned down and unzipped my right boot, then slid my foot out. I did the same with the left, then pushed them aside.

Sean watched me silently. There was something fierce in his eyes, and I liked the intensity of his gaze. He waited for me to make a move, to let him know what I wanted.

So I did.

I grabbed a handful of his shirt and pulled him to me. Sean crushed my body to his and lifted me. I wrapped my legs around his hips and clung to him, kissing him hungrily. He took a couple of steps forward and we dropped onto the bed. My hands fumbled at the buttons on his shirt while he slid his hands up over the skin of my stomach. He helped me get my T-shirt off over my head, and then I went back to unbuttoning his shirt. My fingers were clumsy from urgency.

Evidently, I was taking too long. He made an impatient noise and pulled his shirt and undershirt off, revealing a muscular chest that looked like it belonged on the cover of one of those cheap romance novels. I stared at him in wonder.

He paused, looking down at me. "What's wrong?"

"Not a thing." I gently raked my fingernails across the flesh of his hard stomach, leaving scratches I couldn't see in the dim light. He made a growly noise and kissed me hard while he lifted my torso and unhooked my bra. It went flying and suddenly his mouth moved from my lips to my right breast. My back arched and I moaned as he licked my nipple, then gently sucked, watching me as he teased me with his tongue.

I wanted his skin on mine, but his jeans were out of my reach and I made a complaining sound.

Sean chuckled and rose, unbuttoning my jeans. I wiggled as he pulled them off, leaving me in my underwear. He stood above me, shirtless, jeans riding low on his hips, looking me over like a starving man in front of a five-course meal.

I stretched my arms above my head and looked at him through half-closed eyes, running my bare foot up his leg. "Are you waiting for a formal invitation?"

In a flash, he was back on top of me, pinning my hands to the bed while his mouth teased first my right breast, then my left. His hands slid down to my hips as I trembled. It had been months since I'd been touched.

I felt a tug on my Wonder Woman underwear and looked down. Sean was sliding them off slowly, his eyes on mine, looking for permission. In answer, I raised myself up a little and he grinned, and then the underwear was gone too. When his gaze moved down and settled between my thighs, I blushed.

Sean moved up my body to kiss me. "You are so fucking beautiful," he said roughly.

I started to make a snarky comment about him not having to pile on the compliments since I'd already invited him to my bed, but then he did something with his fingers that made me forget what I was going to say. Sean's mouth trailed down my throat, and his tongue moved slowly down my abdomen to my navel, where he gently tugged on my belly-button piercing with his teeth. When I moaned, he slid down the bed, bent his head, and licked me.

I cried out, arching my back. The resulting pain in my stomach was no match for the pleasure. I clutched his head with my hands, my fingers in his hair, as he raised my hips and caressed me with his tongue.

Soon, I was shuddering under his touch. I felt like if he wasn't inside me soon, I'd lose my mind. I tried to pull him up, but he refused to budge. The pleasure was too intense, and I was reduced to begging. "Please. *Please.*"

I felt him move away and heard the sound of his shoes falling on the floor, then a zipper and the rustling of clothes. When I opened my eyes, he was naked, and I swear my heart skipped a beat at the sight of him.

"Condom," I said breathlessly, reaching for him. There was no chance of me getting pregnant, but it was always best to be safe.

He produced a small square packet as if by magic, rolled the condom onto himself, and returned to the bed. Despite his attentions, it had been a while and he was a tight fit. He groaned and I screamed again, my nails digging into his shoulders. Starbursts filled my vision as I wrapped my legs around him. I cried out, but it sounded like someone else. I'd never felt anything so good in my entire life.

A wonderful pressure began to build low in my abdomen. I opened my eyes and looked at him. He was sweaty and gorgeous in the morning light, his eyes on my face, watching me closely as I moved beneath him.

Suddenly, in the midst of the passion, a bolt of fear made my stomach clench. The nagging worry I'd managed to drown out earlier was back at the worst possible time. I was afraid of being found, of being caught, of losing control and being vulnerable. I went from delirious with desire to guarded and tense. I was suddenly unable to lose myself in the moment, and the climax that had begun to build faded. I closed my eyes in despair and my grip on Sean's biceps loosened.

His movement slowed. "Alice?"

I opened my eyes.

Sean bent down to press his lips to my ear. "Let go," he told me, moving his hips in some magical way that made me cry out. "Let go. I've got you." He kissed my ear, then bit it.

I looked into his eyes. Maybe he saw my fear; he seemed to be able to read me pretty well. "I've got you," he said again, this time with more force in his voice. He cupped my face with his hand and held my gaze. "Let go. Come for me, beautiful girl." He shifted position a bit, catching my knees with his forearms. My gasps turned into one long cry.

As the rush of pleasure swept over me, I let go of my fear, my anger, and the worry I would be found, and did something I had never done before: I threw off the tight control I kept over my magic, and as Sean began to shudder, my magic poured out of me and rushed around us in a hurricane of green-and-white energy. I thought I heard things crashing in the background as he groaned, but I didn't care. I lost myself in the storm.

Sean collapsed onto his forearms to keep from putting all his weight on me. My magic drew back inside me and settled into my core. Through the haze, I could feel that my energy level was nearly back to normal. Good sex can build magical energy quickly, and that was *very* good sex.

I was still breathing hard, my heart racing. Sean looked down at me, his eyes dark with passion, and nuzzled my neck. "Holy shit," he breathed into my ear. "I don't know what just happened, but that was incredible."

I couldn't have spoken if my life depended on it, but I definitely agreed with his assessment.

We lay there for a few minutes to catch our breath, then Sean slowly disengaged and got up while I stayed where I was. He disappeared into the bathroom. I heard the toilet flush and the sound of water running in the sink.

He returned to the bedroom, still naked, and pulled the covers back. He scooped me up and I squawked. He laughed and settled me into the bed, then climbed in beside me and pulled the covers over us.

He drew me close to snuggle with my head on his chest.

My exhaustion had been replaced with contentment. I lay in bed and listened to Sean's heartbeat.

"What are you smiling about?" he asked, pressing a kiss to the top of my head.

"Your heart is going a million miles an hour." I tilted my head up to look at him. "And it's hot under the covers. You're like a furnace."

He grinned and flipped the comforter back so we were just covered by the sheet.

"Ahhhh, that's much better," I murmured with a sigh.

My brain slowly came back online. I saw my bedroom and sat bolt upright in shock.

Unleashed, my magic had swept through the room like a tornado. Clothes were everywhere. Everything that had been on top of my dresser or hanging on the wall was on the floor. My lamp and hamper were turned over. The files from my nightstand were scattered across the room.

Sean sat up next to me. "I take it this isn't something that happens around here very often?" he teased.

"Um, no. This would be a first for me."

Sean looked smug then. *Men.* I rolled my eyes.

We settled back into the bed, and he wrapped his arms around me. It was officially morning; I heard cars going by outside as my neighbors headed off to work. Daylight streamed through the window. I stretched, but from the bed I couldn't reach the curtains. Sean reached up and pulled them closed and the room fell into near-darkness.

"Do you want me to stay?" Sean asked.

I couldn't see his face, but he didn't really sound like he wanted to leave. I was hardly a dewy-eyed romantic who demanded her lovers stick around afterward, but it might be nice to go to sleep with someone warm in my bed. My stomach still ached, and I was rattled from the run-in with the landmine.

"If you don't have any place you need to be, you're welcome to stay," I told him.

"I don't have to be anywhere." Now that we had recovered somewhat and cooled off a bit, I was starting to feel chilly. Without being asked, he pulled the comforter back up over us. "One of the benefits of owning the company is that I have flexible hours most days. I don't have to be in the office today until a meeting at three." He rubbed his stubbly chin on the top of my head, and the bristles scratching my scalp felt good. "We can sleep in if you want."

"I do want." I yawned and rolled over onto my other side. Sean spooned up behind me, fitting his body against my curves. I let him wrap his arm around me and pull me close.

As good as the sex was, and as much as I appreciated that he seemed to really care that it was as satisfying for me as it was for him, Sean was a one-night stand. A damn fine one, though, and with any luck, after we'd slept, he'd have at least one more chance to show off his skills before I sent him on his way.

Just before sleep pulled me under, I remembered my earrings. I took them out, stretched over the edge of the bed, and tossed them lightly onto the nightstand before settling back into the warmth of Sean's arms. I felt his breath on the back of my neck.

As I was drifting off, Sean whispered, "Sweet dreams, Alice."

Good night. I wasn't sure if I thought it or said it. Between one heartbeat and the next, I was sound asleep.

CHAPTER 7

When I wake up, I will be a different person.

In a city a thousand miles from where I grew up and two thousand miles from where I am headed, I stand in front of a mirror looking at my face for the last time.

In a few minutes, a plastic surgeon will begin the long and painful process of turning me into Alice Worth, an unremarkable earth and air mage who is about to move to the West Coast to start a new life. My face will be completely different. This me, the one in the mirror, will be gone forever. I am trying to figure out how I feel. I should be scared, I suppose. Maybe relieved or angry. Instead, I just feel numb.

After the night I left the cabal compound, it took me nearly a week to get here and another week before I found a plastic surgeon who could be trusted to do the work I needed. The surgeon is a mage whose family was killed by a cabal. He knows who I am and he wants to help.

There is a picture taped to the mirror of the real Alice Worth. I run my fingertips over my face, feeling my forehead, my eyes, my nose, my lips, my chin, and try to imagine looking into the glass and seeing that other woman looking back at me. Somehow, I already feel like this isn't my face anymore, like it's been on too long already. I'm impatient to have it be gone so I can start recovering. It will be at least another week before I am able to resume my run across the country to my final destination.

Although I have heard nothing to make me think I am being pursued, and the news is filled with images of my grandfather openly grieving over my death, I can't help but feel like danger is nipping at my heels. I want to be moving on, but this stop is necessary. I can go no farther wearing this face.

There is a quiet knock on the door. It's the surgeon, asking if I am ready. I've been ready for this moment for as long as I can remember.

As I lie back on the table, the surgeon asks again if I am sure I want to do this. With no hesitation, I tell him yes. I look at the world as Moses Murphy's granddaughter one last time, and then an ocean of soft darkness sweeps me away.

* * *

I woke to the unfamiliar sensation of a very large, very warm body pressed up against my backside and an arm curled around my middle. Sean was nuzzling my neck. He'd opened the curtains a bit to let some afternoon sunlight into the room. I blinked fuzzily at the clock on the nightstand to see it was a little after one. I'd had about six hours of sleep and felt pretty good. I yawned and started to stretch.

Agony flared in my stomach, and I gasped and curled into a ball. Either my sore abdominal muscles had tightened up and they were simply cramping, or it was actual injuries from the landmine I'd triggered. The pain made me breathe in short, panting breaths.

"Alice, what's wrong?" Sean was wide awake in an instant. "You're hurt."

I gritted my teeth and managed not to whimper.

He looked at my stomach, but there was nothing to see. The injury, whatever it was, was on the inside. I focused on breathing through the pain, and it started to recede.

"The wards…from yesterday," I finally managed to say. "It's just a muscle cramp. I'm okay."

Sean made a snarly noise. "You keep saying you're fine and you're okay, but it's pretty clear you're not." He sounded angry. "I can smell blood. You may be bleeding internally."

I froze and looked at him—like, really, really looked at him.

In the daylight, I could see a faint gold sheen over his eyes that reflected the light in a way no human eye did. Add that to his muscular physique, body temperature, tendency to rub his face against me, and ability to smell an internal injury, and….

"Werewolf?" I guessed.

Sean went perfectly still. We stared at each other.

A number of emotions were visible on his face: worry, anger, and…fear? What was he afraid of, that I'd turn on him? I supposed it was a legitimate concern for a werewolf these days, when we were all afraid of each other and the Agency.

I sighed and gingerly rubbed my abdomen where the pain had faded to soreness, like I'd done too many sit-ups. I wasn't worried that Sean was a werewolf. If it were nearer the full moon, I might have been concerned, but as it was, I doubted he'd be going furry on me. Since a bite from a werewolf in wolf form was the only way to contract the virus, I was more bothered by the pain in my stomach and the possibility of internal injuries.

Sean cleared his throat. "Should I leave?"

Carefully, so I didn't strain my stomach muscles, I turned so I could face him. His arms were still around me, but he looked grim.

I took his face in my hands and kissed him.

At first, he didn't respond; I think I surprised him. Then he kissed me back with a hunger that took my breath away. When we separated, he met my gaze with dark eyes that shone gold. How I'd missed the signs last night, I had no idea. I must have been too preoccupied with the events of the day.

Sean touched my face. "So you're not angry?"

I shook my head. "I don't care that you're a werewolf. Sure, I'd have preferred it if you'd told me last night, but it wouldn't have changed anything. It's not like I can catch it from having sex with you."

That made him relax a little, but he looked concerned as he placed his hand carefully on my stomach. "What kind of wards did you walk into yesterday? What magic could hurt you like this?"

I debated what I could tell him without breaching client confidentiality. "The wards were set by a woman who died a couple of months ago. When I walked into them, they did this." I pointed to the burn on my chest. It was still red, and it hurt the way burns did: a steady, hot, stinging sensation that hadn't faded much since last night.

Sean paled. "That's right over your heart."

"Yep. The wards were designed to kill. I was lucky they had faded." He stared at me.

I kept talking. "I needed to take down the wards for my client. The unweaving went fine, but apparently there was a landmine, and it got me." He didn't say anything. "I threw up a lot, and some of it was blood. That's probably what you're smelling. Honestly, I don't think

I'm actually still bleeding internally—"

Sean lost it.

I squeaked as he wrapped his arms around me and pulled me against his body with a growl. He was careful not to hold me too tightly, though his arms felt like steel. "I want to kill the person who hurt you."

"You can't; she's dead already," I said into his chest. "I don't need a protector, Sean. I'm not looking for someone to take care of me, or fight my battles for me."

"I know, but I'm an alpha. My instinct is to protect..." He hesitated. "People who are injured."

"Females and the weak," I corrected him. "I know. I'm familiar enough with werewolves to understand that, but I'm not part of your pack, or yours to protect. I'm just your one-night stand."

Sean pulled back. "Is that what this is?" He looked startled, as if that hadn't been anything close to what he expected me to say. I wondered if he was used to women who got emotionally attached to one-night stands. He wouldn't have to worry about that with me; emotional attachments weren't really my thing.

I patted his chest affectionately. "Sean, we both had a good time, but I don't have any illusions about how this goes."

Sean's expression went flat. "How do you think 'this' goes?"

I ran my hands over his chest, scratching him lightly with my nails, and he made that growly sound I liked. "We lie here for a while longer, since neither of us has to be anywhere immediately, then we have sex again because you're that damn good at it, and then we part company with good feelings and good memories."

Sean leaned close to me. Before I realized what he was doing, he inhaled deeply. I recoiled, taken aback by his suddenly very werewolf behavior. "What I'm smelling isn't old injuries from yesterday. I'm pretty sure you *are* still bleeding internally. You need medical attention, Alice."

I put my hands on my aching stomach and knew he was right. "I have healing spells," I told him with a sigh. "Give me a minute." I started to slide off the bed.

"Do you need help?"

I shook my head and stood, heading for my bathroom. "This won't take long. There's another bathroom down the hall if you need to use it." I went in and closed the door.

After I used the toilet, I dug around in a drawer and took out my first aid kit, a small wooden box with runes carved on all sides. The runes were spells that hid the energy stored within. I traced three runes on the lid, then opened it. Inside the box were crystals containing healing spells of various strengths, color-coded from light green—minor injury—to dark purple—possibly fatal wound. I took out a green crystal, held it gently against the burn on my chest, braced myself, and said, "*Helios.*"

Magic flared and I sucked in a breath as the spell went to work on the burn. It felt like a hundred tiny needles were stabbing me. The sensation lasted for about thirty seconds before fading. When I took my hand away, the burn was gone, leaving a faint scar. I set the crystal aside to be respelled when I had time.

Whatever the landmine had done to my insides, it was going to take a stronger spell to fix it. I rooted around in the box and came up with a mid-range blue crystal. This one was going to hurt. Mindful of Sean in the next room, I turned on the shower to help mask any sounds and grabbed a hand towel. I sat down on the bath mat next to the tub, pressed the crystal against my stomach, and invoked the spell.

I stuffed the towel into my mouth to muffle my cries. Now the needles were inside me, and it felt like they were ripping through my insides as the spell went to work on the damage. This much pain from the healing spell meant there really were significant internal injuries. I'd always thought healing spells should feel good, not hurt, but no one had ever been successful at creating one that wasn't painful. I bit down on the towel and tried to be quiet.

Minutes crawled by. When the pins-and-needles sensation finally faded, I dropped the empty spell crystal on the rug and pushed myself to my feet using the side of the tub. My stomach felt tender in the way that recently healed injuries do. I put the box away in the drawer, washed my face and rinsed my mouth, and turned off the shower.

When I opened the bathroom door, Sean was sitting on the edge of the bed, looking very tense. He'd probably heard enough to know that the healing spells had hurt. He stood and looked me over. "Are you all right?"

"I am now. All healed." I wrapped my arms around his neck and kissed him warmly. He relaxed against me and kissed me back.

We returned to the bed, and Sean pulled me into his arms. My fingers traced over his shoulders, feeling the definition of his muscles. His hands moved up my back, caressing.

"Where did you get these scars?" he asked.

I stiffened. The scars on my back were from another lifetime. My phoenix tattoo covered most of the damage, but the lines were still visible if you looked closely. Healing spells and even plastic surgery could only do so much. The only thing that might heal them completely would be slicing the scars off and pouring vampire blood over the wounds, but I had no desire to undergo that particularly extreme measure.

"I used to know some bad people," I said.

He stilled. "How bad?"

"Very bad." I moved my head so my lips were against his neck. The smell of him eased the tension in my shoulders. I wondered absently if alphas gave off calming pheromones.

"I saw the scars while you were asleep." Sean's fingers traced the lines. "I assume healing spells were used…after?"

"Yes. A lot of them, for a long time." My voice was level.

He took a deep, involuntary breath. "And these scars remain?"

Intensive healing spells could heal most severe injuries with minimal or no scarring. Right now, he was imagining how bad the wounds had been for the spells to have been unable to heal me completely. I didn't have to imagine anything; I'd been conscious for all of it. I knew my back looked butchered when the blood mage had finished with me. For it to look as good as it did now was nothing short of miraculous.

I was suddenly cold. I wanted heat and to be distracted from the memories, and I knew one sure way to get both.

I drew his hand up to my mouth so I could lightly bite his fingers, and he made a snarly wolf sound that sparked an instant reaction. I was suddenly very aware of my breasts brushing against his chest. I reached down and stroked him gently.

Sean groaned and shifted on the bed. "Alice—"

I nipped his bottom lip and his eyes turned gold. I pushed him onto his back and moved to my hands and knees so I could lick slowly across his chest. He reached for me, but I moved away and bent over him, teasing him with my mouth and tongue and making him writhe. I found I liked having an alpha werewolf at my mercy.

He moved so quickly, all I saw was a blur. One second I was leaning forward to draw him into my mouth again, and the next I was on my back and he was on top of me, his hand between my thighs, and I was crying out. Blissful minutes later, I was gasping and screaming and trying to pull away from him, but he held me tight until I stopped shuddering.

When I opened my eyes, Sean looked at me with an expression of such fierce passion that I went still. "Condoms?"

"Nightstand. Bottom drawer," I panted.

The drawer opened, the box tore, a packet crinkled, and then Sean was back. "Up," he commanded, raising me and turning me over onto my stomach.

I resisted, self-conscious about my scars in the daylight, but then he was kissing my back and suddenly I didn't care anymore. He pulled me onto my hands and knees, his hands on my hips, and then he pushed into me from behind. I arched my back with a cry.

He moved carefully and gently. It was wonderful, but I wanted and needed something else. "Harder," I gasped. "Faster."

He bent over to run his lips across my back and I shuddered. "Are you sure?" His voice was deep and growly and it made me crazy. "Your stomach…."

"I'm healed," I told him breathlessly. "Please, Sean. Please don't go slow."

His fingers dug into my hips hard enough to leave bruises and suddenly the brakes were off. I grabbed the bedding as hard as I could as he growled—a deep, rumbling werewolf growl—that almost sent me over the edge. I forgot about everything else as the pleasure rose toward a crescendo. I called his name over and over and begged him to go even faster.

This time, I had none of the second thoughts that held me back last night. He reached around to stroke me and I came with a wail. A heartbeat later, he snarled and emptied himself inside me. We fell over onto the bed, gasping for breath.

"Oh my God," Sean rasped.

"Mmm-hmmm."

I lay on the bed while he went to the bathroom to clean up. He had, I thought appreciatively, a thoroughly magnificent butt.

When Sean came back, he climbed onto the bed and wrapped his arms around me. "I'm glad I went to Hawthorne's last night," he said, biting my earlobe gently.

I laughed. "Me too. And I'm glad Charles was too busy to see me. This turned into a really fantastic night—well, a really fantastic day."

"What brought you in to see the vampire?"

"A matter related to one of my cases." I shrugged lazily and glanced at the clock. "It's almost two. Don't you have to be at work at three?"

He groaned. "Are you kicking me out of bed?"

"We have to get up at some point. You've got to get to work, and I'm supposed to be getting a text about seeing Charles tonight. And I've got a client to see." And a ghost to check on, though I didn't mention that.

"You did get a couple of messages."

"What? Why didn't you wake me up?" I scooted away from him to grab my phone off the nightstand.

"I thought you needed your sleep."

I sat cross-legged on the bed and checked my messages. There were two. The first one was from Bryan, who'd texted me around eight a.m. *Meeting with Mr. V at midnight. Car is out front, key in the mailbox. Sean Maclin's car is in your driveway.*

Shit. I'd told them Sean had dropped me off. Now Bryan knew that not only had I lied, but that Sean had stayed with me. My face burned.

"What is it?" Sean watched me, frowning.

"Nothing." Damn it, I didn't answer to Bryan for anything, least of all my sex life. It was none of his business if Sean stayed with me. I supposed I shouldn't have lied, but Bryan had pushed me about whether or not Sean had dropped me off and maybe I resented him acting like it was any of his business. I wasn't really clear on my motives for lying. In any case, I would have to face Bryan tonight at Hawthorne's in order to see Charles. Fantastic.

Also, Sean's last name was Maclin. Good to know. Bryan must

have had someone run the tags of the vehicle when they saw it in the driveway. Maybe he was concerned about my safety, but whatever his reason, it felt like an egregious invasion of my privacy.

I scowled and fired back a terse text: *Ok will meet C at midnight.*

"Alice?"

I looked up from my phone. "Bryan texted me a meeting time for Charles when he came by. He was wondering why your car was parked in my driveway. And your last name is Maclin."

Sean sat up. "And you told him I dropped you off."

"Yes."

"Is this going to cause problems?"

"Why should it? I don't owe anyone an explanation for who I sleep with."

Again Sean looked surprised. Then he grinned.

"What?" I asked.

"I don't think I've ever met anyone quite like you before, Alice."

"You're probably right."

He laughed. I smiled briefly.

The second text was from Natalie. *Hi! Saw your note. Sorry I fell asleep. Call when you get a chance.* She signed the message with a smiley face.

I blew out a relieved breath. It looked like she didn't remember anything about manifesting any magic.

Sean moved over to me on his hands and knees and kissed me so hard that I dropped my phone. "What was that?" I asked breathlessly.

"I have to go to work, but at the risk of being cliché, I'd really like to see you again."

"In what way?" If he was interested in working out a bang-buddy arrangement, I would be willing to consider it.

"How about tonight, after your meeting with Vaughan? I'll be off work. We can have some drinks and talk about beer and music or whatever else is on your mind."

I stared at him. "You're talking about an actual date."

Sean's mouth quirked. "Yes, an *actual date*. What we do after that—if anything—is up to you."

"I'm not really looking for a relationship," I told him.

"Me neither, but I think we both had a good time. I'd like to get to know you better. How about one date, and then you decide where we go from there."

The sex had been very satisfying, and it was a tempting offer, but there was something in Sean's eyes that made me wary. I'd invited him into my bed thinking we were on the same page about this being a one-night deal. Maybe we'd started out that way, but it looked like he might be on a different page now, possibly a whole other chapter, and I wasn't even sure my book had that chapter in it.

Still, I could try to let him down easy. "Let me think about it."

He gave me a wolfish smile. "Did I not pass the audition?"

I was quiet for a few moments. "I thought we were clear about the plan for how this would go."

"Plans can change."

"Not mine." Mine was simple: stay cautious, stay under the radar, stay alive.

Sean leaned forward. "Give me a chance to change your mind."

"I said I would think about it."

He got up and started pulling on his clothes. I shamelessly watched the reverse striptease and couldn't help but feel a little sad when he was dressed.

As he sat on the bed putting on his shoes, he turned to me. "Well, you know my last name, but I don't know yours."

I hesitated but saw no reason not to tell him. He had my address; he could find out easily for himself. "Worth."

"Alice Worth." He finished tying his shoes. "Can I have your number, Alice?"

I tilted my head and considered. "Why don't you give me yours? If you need to get me a message, you can call Hawthorne's, and they'll see that I get it."

"You don't give an inch." Strangely, he was grinning.

"Nope."

Sean gave me his number and I put it in my phone under Wolf. He saw the nickname and laughed.

He rose, then bent down to give me a sizzling kiss. When he drew back, his eyes were gold. It occurred to me to wonder if the wolf in him enjoyed the idea of a chase. Too bad for him that I had no intention of playing along.

He moved his lips to my ear. "Give me a call," he said softly.

"Maybe."

He went to the door of my room, then turned back. We looked at each other.

"Have a good day at work, Alice," he said finally.

"You too, Sean."

He hesitated, as if he wanted to say something else, and then he was gone.

CHAPTER 8

I showered and washed my hair. When I got out, I wrapped myself in a bathrobe and spent several minutes straightening the mess left behind by this morning's magical hurricane. I stacked my files, put my dirty clothes back in the hamper, returned the scattered items to my nightstand and dresser, and hung the pictures back on the wall.

After I got dressed and dried and braided my hair, I ate a sandwich while setting out a replacement change of clothes for my go-bag.

With my preparations finished, I called my client.

"Hello!" Natalie's greeting was warm and cheerful. I felt a pang of guilt that she had no memory of what had happened last night. "How are you feeling? I've been so worried about you."

"Doing fine," I told her. "I'm ready to come take a look at that library."

"I'm glad you're okay. I haven't tried to go in there."

"I'm sorry about that, but until we know what's going on, I think we'd better err on the side of caution."

"Good thinking. I can't believe I was living in this house for so long with those wards." I could hear the fear and anger in Natalie's voice. I could understand the feeling; even knowing the wards had been keyed not to harm her, anyone not used to being around magic would have good reason to be afraid of spells designed to kill without warning or mercy. Hell, I'd been using magic since I was four and blood magic since I was twelve, and it was enough to rattle me.

"Well, it made for an interesting afternoon. What time should I come over?"

"Whenever you want. I'm here all day."

"I'm about ready to head out. I can be there in about an hour."

"Awesome." A pause. "Is Malcolm coming?"

"Yes. He's going to help me with the wards. See you in a few."

We said good-bye and disconnected. I put on my jewelry: rings, charm bracelet—with assorted spells—and a monogram necklace with a pendant shaped like the letter *A*.

Time to let my new sidekick out. I picked up my crystal earrings from the tray on the nightstand. I could feel Malcolm's energy buzzing in my palm. Yesterday, unsure of how much energy would be discharged, I'd used a circle to contain Malcolm when I released him, but it hadn't been necessary. Today, I simply held the earring and said, *"Release."*

With a yell, Malcolm popped into existence three feet in front of me. The wave of magic staggered me back a half step. Unlike yesterday, when he'd been disoriented and near frantic, today he just looked surprised. He also looked far more substantial than he did before. Hmm. I suddenly wondered if he'd gotten a boost at the same time I did when I was having sex with Sean. I'd been wearing the earrings and it seemed logical. I flushed.

"Hey, Alice." Malcolm moved back and forth slowly. "I feel...different, more solid and much stronger. Did you try another spell?"

"Sorta." He categorically did *not* need to know where the energy boost had come from. "Was it less rough on you this time?"

"Yes." He looked relieved. "It feels like it's only been a few minutes this time. The time before...." He shuddered. "It felt like forever, and like a split second too, if that makes any sense. It really messed with my head."

I tried to wrap my brain around that and couldn't. "I'll have to take your word for it. I'm glad it wasn't as bad this time. I'll look into a different spell as soon as I get a chance."

"So how long was I in there?"

"It's tomorrow afternoon. After I put you in the earring, I went to meet the vamp, but he was busy. I'll be seeing him tonight. Then I, uh, got some sleep, called Natalie to let her know we're on our way over, and here you are."

"Cool." Malcolm moved around the room. "So this is your house?"

"Yes." I gave him a quick tour of the upstairs, then grabbed the stack of clothes that were going in my go-bag and headed downstairs, Malcolm floating behind me. I showed him around the main floor— living room, kitchen, laundry room/downstairs bathroom, storage room—and then pointed at the basement door. "That's my library and my spellwork area. We'll be spending a lot of time down there."

"Right on." Malcolm stared at the door and whistled low. "Whoa."

I realized he was seeing the wards. I'd poured a lot of time, energy, and blood into those wards. They were the strongest and most intricate I'd ever made. Even the best mages wouldn't be able to get in. There were layers of deadly landmines strung throughout the spells. Trying to break the wards directly would mean death for the mage or mages who tried. Nuking the wards with focused energy would level the house and kill everyone in it. My basement was as secure as I could make it.

Malcolm looked at me with a combination of fear and respect. "Holy shit. I thought Betty's wards were intense. How long did it take you to do this?"

"The foundation spells took three days and eight pints of blood. The rest of the basic spells took about a week. I've been adding on to it and pouring energy into it since I moved in almost five years ago."

"It's incredible," Malcolm said reverently. "All that energy, and yet I couldn't even sense it from upstairs." He drifted forward, his fingers moving as if he was envisioning the process I'd used to layer the spells. "I've never seen anything like it. I *see* the energy, but I can't *feel* it. I can't even begin to understand the spells you're using to mask the trace. Unbelievable."

"Well, I couldn't very well let anyone sense the energy. It would be a beacon so bright, they'd see it from space. You're not even seeing the strongest and most deadly wards."

"What?" Malcolm's eyes widened.

"There are secondary spells hidden in landmines. Even if a team of mages came in here and tried to unweave the spells, they'd hit the landmines and release the cascades." Cascades were spells that triggered a series of other, more powerful spells, like an avalanche.

There were even more surprises hidden in the cascades: divine wind spells designed to travel back to the heart of whichever cabal attempted to break my wards and cause maximum destruction. If my library went—even if I went with it—I'd be going out with a very big bang.

Malcolm was silent for a long time. "With skills and power like this, you would be the most powerful mage in just about any cabal in the country," he said finally. He drifted back toward me and stopped close enough that I felt his energy buzzing. "There is no way any cabal would let you go. I know you used to belong to one; you knew what I was talking about when I was telling you about my past. At first I thought you'd completed your contract and negotiated a release, but there's no way." His eyes searched my face. "You feel like a mid-level mage, but you aren't, are you?"

I said nothing.

Malcolm's brows drew together and his anger prickled on my skin. "Alice—"

"No," I said in a cold, flat tone.

He closed his mouth.

"I belonged to a cabal. Now I don't. The rest of what happened isn't a story I can share with you, not right now, maybe not ever. You know better than most people what the cabals are capable of. Now you know at least some of what *I'm* capable of." I gestured at the wards protecting my basement. "Perhaps you can fill in some of the blanks for yourself, or at least hazard a guess."

I took a step toward him, despite the sizzle of his energy on my skin. It hurt, but I was no stranger to pain. I'd felt little else since I was four years old. "You're one of the best mages I've ever met. I think we can have a good long-term partnership. I want to know what's in Betty's library and what books were stolen from her. I want to know how strong Natalie's magic is and find her a mentor if she wants one. Big picture, I want to know what Darius Bell is up to and how you ended up bound to me. But from here on, you have to understand that my past is off-limits. No questions, no poking around. It's not personal, but I will protect myself. If those wards tell you anything, it's that I am not someone you'd want to cross."

Malcolm's mouth opened and closed several times. I stepped back.

Finally, he regained his power of speech. "Well, at least we cleared *that* up." He sighed—purely an affectation, as ghosts didn't breathe. "I get it. No questions."

"Good. We need to head over to Natalie's house." I put on my leather jacket and turned to gather my things.

"Wait, I do have one question."

I paused, my arms full. "Yes?"

"The blood in the foundation spells—all eight pints of it—it isn't yours."

I turned and gave him the kind of smile that made people twitch. "I never said it was."

Malcolm flitted back so fast, he passed through the couch and the coffee table and ended up over near the fireplace. "Okay then." He sounded strangled. "I'm glad we could have this talk."

"Come on, Malcolm." I opened the front door. "Let's go see a woman about some missing books."

* * *

The drive over to Natalie's house was more or less silent. When I parked in her driveway, I could feel the wards. They felt as strong as they had when I'd left. At some point, Natalie would be able to maintain them, but that would be a while yet, and that was assuming I could find someone to teach her.

I had to find Natalie a mentor, but I also had to be very careful. If she had strong magic like her grandmother, she'd be worth good money to a cabal. A mage without scruples would sell her out in a heartbeat. At the same time, I was hiding from the cabals. I couldn't very well go around making inquiries, but Charles could. As a broker and a member of the Vampire Court, he was powerful and connected. I was betting he would know someone who could train Natalie and wouldn't sell her out.

Was there any reason to doubt Charles? I thought back over all my dealings with him. He was ruthless, certainly; all vampires were. The older they were, the less human they became. Charles wasn't all that old by vamp standards; he'd fought in the Revolutionary War as an adolescent, which meant he'd been turned sometime around 1800. As a member of the Vampire Court and a successful businessman, he excelled in reading people, making alliances, and staying ahead of the competition. Could I trust him with Natalie's life? I'd been so certain last night, but now, in the cold light of day and looking at the home Betty had shared with her granddaughter, I started to wonder.

The X factor was how much power Natalie had. If she had a lot, it would make her a powerful bargaining chip, and for a vamp, that might be too irresistible of a prize if he needed something to establish an alliance with a cabal. Of course, if her power was mid-level or lower, she wouldn't be worth selling out.

"Are we going in?" Malcolm's voice made me jump. I realized we'd been sitting in front of Natalie's house for almost ten minutes while I thought through the problem.

"In a minute. I need your opinion." I laid it out for him. "Thoughts?"

"I definitely agree that we need to know how strong she is," Malcolm said. "If she's powerful, you're right—telling the vamp about her might not be a good idea. If she's mid-level or below, we're probably safe talking to him."

I nodded. It was great having a partner to talk things through with, especially when he agreed with my plan.

"I vote we tell Natalie the truth and let her decide," he added. "I think she needs to know what's going on and make an informed decision. I'm not sure we have the right to determine how much she gets to know about herself."

"You're right. If it were me, and I found out someone had been keeping this kind of information from me, I'd be furious. I'm worried about how she'll take the news, but she deserves to know."

"I think the best thing to do is tell her what we know, give her the options, and see what she wants to do. Hell, she may want us to bind her power completely. There are a lot of people who don't want any part of magic. There are a lot of days when I'd give anything not to have it. I suffered a lot because of my 'gift.'" He sounded bitter.

"Do you really wish you had been born without magic?"

A long pause. Then the ghost in my car said, "Honestly? Yes."

I sat back in my seat and tried to imagine my life without magic. No cabal, no blood magic. No Agency to fear. My parents would still be alive. I thought about all the pain I had endured since the day when I was four and my magic manifested and my grandfather saw in me the potential to be the strongest mage in the family's history.

I rubbed my face. It didn't matter if I didn't want the magic or not; I had it. I couldn't change anything about my past. The dead would stay dead. As an MPI, I tried to help people, as if I could do enough good to somehow make up for what I'd done for the cabal. It wasn't enough, but it was all I could do.

"Let's go talk to Natalie," I said finally.

* * *

Once we were inside, Malcolm went visible again. Because he'd drawn energy from Natalie the night before, she could hear him now. What surprised me was that she could sort of see him too, probably thanks to the power boost.

Natalie sat on the couch, I took the chair, and Malcolm floated three feet to my left. She was looking right at him. "I can see the outline of someone," she said in wonder. "Like when you stare at a geometric pattern and then a blank wall, and your eyes still see the pattern."

I pulled a folder out of my bag. "Before we get started, we should write up a contract and talk about payment. I should have done it yesterday, but things got unexpectedly…busy."

Natalie's hand flew to her mouth. "I am so sorry! I forgot completely about that. Let's do it now."

We spent about twenty minutes going over the contract. She argued when I told her I wasn't invoking the "extraordinary circumstances with personal injury" clause after what happened last night. I insisted that my burn and ruined shirt were my fault, but I let her talk me into adding a bonus for the landmine mishap. We agreed on a retainer and a daily rate plus expenses, and she wrote me a check and signed the papers.

With the legalities out of the way, it was time for The Talk. "Natalie, before I start working on the library, there's something we need to discuss. What's the last thing you remember from last night?"

She thought about it. "You'd been hurt by the wards," she said slowly. "I wrapped you in blankets and Malcolm was going to put new wards on the library. And then I…fell asleep?" She frowned. "That doesn't seem right. How did I fall asleep in the middle of all that?"

"You didn't." She blinked at me in confusion. "Some pretty strange stuff happened last night. I'm going to tell you everything, but you might find it a little upsetting."

"Just tell me!" Natalie demanded.

I told her about her fire and air magic suddenly manifesting, how Betty had suppressed her magic, and how I'd bound it again before tucking her into bed.

By the time I finished, Natalie was pacing around the living room, her arms wrapped around her middle. She looked mad and scared. I wasn't sure what would help her, so I waited.

Finally, she turned to face me. "What am I supposed to do?" she demanded. "Yesterday I found out my grandmother was a powerful mage who left killer wards behind when she died. I saw you hurt twice from what she did. Now you tell me I have magic too, but that my grandmother put spells on me so I wouldn't know I had it."

Malcolm and I waited quietly while she struggled to process what I'd told her. Finally, she dropped back onto the couch and sighed. "Okay, I can deal with this. Tell me what we need to do."

Briefly, I outlined the problem. "I'm pretty sure we can keep your magic bound. If you want no part of this life, I'm about ninety percent certain I can keep your magic from manifesting. I think the reason it flared last night is that Betty's spells weren't maintained after she passed away. They might have been tied to the library wards; I'm not sure."

I suddenly had a revelation. "You know how you told me you thought you were being poisoned because you've been sick and losing weight? I'm wondering if your magic trying to escape the binding spells might be causing you to be ill."

She looked shocked. "You really think so?"

"It's a possibility. Have you felt better today?"

She thought about it. "Well, yes, I guess I have. I ate a big sandwich for lunch, and normally I'm not that hungry. I thought it was because I got a good night's sleep." Suddenly she seemed more energized. "Well, *that's* a relief! One less thing to worry about. I guess nobody is really trying to kill me after all!"

"I'm not sure I'm right; it's just a theory for now," I said before she could get too excited. "The binding spell I put on you is tied to our wards, which are at full strength, so your situation should be stabilized for a while."

"Will the spell always be tied to the wards?" Natalie bit her lip.

"No. There's another way. A better way."

"How?"

"A tattoo." I pushed up my right sleeve and pulled down the back of my shirt to show her some of my own tattoos, including a dragon coiled around my upper arm and the phoenix on my back. "A tattoo can hold a spell pretty much indefinitely. It wouldn't have to be very big—maybe two inches square. Your own aura will power the spell."

"Would it have to be a particular design?"

I shook my head. "There would be runes, but a good mage tattoo artist can make them practically invisible within most any design. You could get pretty much whatever you want and put it wherever you want. I can take you to the mage who did my tattoos."

"You said ninety percent." Natalie seized on something I said earlier. "Why not a hundred percent?"

"Unfortunately, every spell has counterspells, and I can't anticipate every possibility. Most government buildings are protected by wards that disrupt spells, even ones anchored by tattoos. If you crossed one, the binding might fail. If you ever touched a null—"

"What's a null?"

"A null is a mage who can drain someone else's energy by touching them. They're not common, but they're out there. If you bumped into one on the street, you'd lose some or all of your magic and the suppression spell would fail. If you didn't get to me or someone soon to redo the spells, your magic would be uncontrolled as it regenerated."

Natalie closed her eyes.

"If you're looking for guarantees, I can't give them to you," I said. "That's life, pretty much. You'll be as safe—and nonmagical—as anyone can make you, if you decide that's what you want."

"And if I don't want it bound?" Natalie opened her eyes and stared at me. She might be tiny, but she was feisty.

"You'll need training. First, I need to know for sure what kind of magic you have, and how strong you are. Once I know that, I can find someone to take you on as an apprentice. You'll learn how to control your magic and use it. You don't have to become a practicing mage.

Your life won't have to change much. Once you learn control, it will be just like any other ability, like being able to paint or sing." Well, that was oversimplifying things, but the gist was true.

"How do we find out how strong my magic is?"

"Two choices. I can put you back in a sleep spell and Malcolm and I will find out, rebind you, and wake you up to tell you. Second option: you stay awake and find out at the same time we do."

"Which do you recommend?"

"It's up to you. One thing you might want to think about is that you have no memory of having magic, of how it feels. I can imagine it might be frightening for you if you're awake when we release the binding spells, which is why I suggested you be asleep. You might prefer to make the decision without the memory of being afraid."

Natalie was quiet. "How long can I think about this?"

"As long as you need," Malcolm said. "Your magic is bound. I know Alice would prefer that we at least find out today what kind of magic you have and how strong you are, but really it's up to you. If you want to do that today, and then decide later whether or not to bind the magic permanently, that's okay. For whatever it's worth, if it were me, I'd at least want to know that about myself before I made any long-term decisions."

Natalie took a deep breath. "Okay, let me think about this."

I stood up. "In the meantime, Malcolm and I are going to take a look at the library."

"I'm going to make some tea. You want some?"

"Sure."

Malcolm and I headed back to the master bedroom, and Natalie went to the kitchen.

We looked at the wards we'd put on the library the night before. I could see the beautiful green lines of Malcolm's spellwork and the darker colors of my own magic.

"What are you thinking?" Malcolm asked.

"I'm thinking we need strong containment wards. Whatever's in there, we don't want it getting out."

"I can do that. Can you take down your wards?"

I reached out and brushed my fingertips over the doorframe and my wards fell. Malcolm's fingers moved quickly, and in a few minutes, the library perimeter hummed with a strong containment spell. Nothing short of the magical equivalent of a nuke was getting out.

"Whew," Malcolm said. "I feel like I have so much more power today. Whatever spell you used, I like it."

Yeah, I like it too. I didn't say a thing.

I took a deep breath and opened the door to Betty's library.

CHAPTER 9

Yesterday, when I tried to walk inside, Betty's wards swatted me like a fly. Today, I felt only the prickle of the containment spell as I stepped across the threshold and flipped on the light.

The windowless library was as large as Betty's bedroom. Three of the walls were floor-to-ceiling bookcases. A heavy antique desk with matching file cabinet and a love seat took up the fourth wall.

The floor was hardwood, like the master bedroom, but a large rug lay in the center of the room. I felt a distinctive itchiness and a sudden urge to back away and walk around it. I gritted my teeth, lifted a corner of the rug, and flipped it back, revealing an inscribed circle. Even though Betty had been gone for months, it still hummed with stored energy. My fingers went numb from touching the spelled rug.

Natalie appeared in the doorway, a mug in her hands.

"Don't try to come inside," I told her.

"I never knew that was there." She stared at the circle. "I never even thought to look under the rug."

"There's an aversion spell on the rug." I rubbed my tingly fingers on my jeans. "She didn't want you to look."

Natalie sighed. "Here's your tea."

I came to the door and took it. "Thank you. Where were the missing books?"

She peered into the room and pointed, staying clear of the doorway. "Bottom shelf, second bookcase on the right. You see how the books all have gaps between them? It looks like someone took some books and then spread the rest of them out so there wasn't a big hole. I know that shelf was stuffed full."

"When did you notice the gap?"

She frowned and thought. "I'd say about two weeks ago, but I can't say for certain when they might have disappeared. All these books and papers were my grandmother's. Most of my books are on my e-reader or in the bookcase in my room. I've really never looked at any of these books. There's no reason to."

The sudden flat quality of her voice made me look at her in surprise, then stare suspiciously at the bookcases. I immediately got a strong feeling that I didn't need to look at any of the books.

I scowled. "Aversion spells on the bookcases too. Malcolm, would you be so kind?"

"No problem." After checking for hidden spells, Malcolm went to work unweaving the aversion spells in the library, starting with the rug, and then moving on to the bookcases.

"Start with the shelf where the books are missing." He dutifully went to the bookcase Natalie indicated.

I turned back to my client and sipped my tea. "With those spells in place, I'm surprised you even noticed the books were missing."

She pursed her lips and thought. "I was sitting in the love seat reading. I remember I just saw it out of the corner of my eye and thought it looked wrong. All those shelves were always crammed full. I used to tease my grandmother about it because she always bought more and never seemed to give any away." She smiled at the memory.

"That's probably why it worked. The aversion spells kept you from looking at the books directly or too closely until the last few days, but out of the corner of your eye, your subconscious saw what the spells kept your conscious mind from seeing. Without her here to maintain the spells, they probably lost some of their power. There's really no telling when the books might have been taken. It could have been any time in the last three months."

"How did someone get past the wards?" She asked the question that had been bugging the hell out of me. "And the aversion spells on the bookcase?"

Malcolm piped up. "I think I can answer that. Something I noticed last night but forgot to mention in all the excitement, but here it is again." He motioned me over to the bookcase, then held out his hand.

I closed my fingers around his. I felt a moment of disorientation, and then he was showing me what he was seeing in his mind. Betty's aversion spells had exclusions: herself, obviously, and one other. At first, it looked like Betty's own magical signature, but I realized it was slightly different. This person's fire magic was stronger than Betty's, his or her air magic weaker. The magic was so similar, though, I knew it had to be a close relative: a parent, sibling, or child. I closed my eyes and reached for that strand of magic, committing it to memory so that if I encountered it again, I would recognize it.

When I was done, I let go of Malcolm's hand and staggered, suddenly out of his head and back into mine. "Go ahead and unweave the aversion spells." Malcolm got to work, and I rejoined Natalie at the door. "Are Betty's parents still alive?"

"No, they died a long time ago."

"Does she have any brothers or sisters?"

"One brother and one sister, my great-aunt Helen and my great-uncle Robert. They're both in their late seventies."

"What about your aunts and uncles?"

Natalie narrowed her eyes. "What's this about?"

"Someone else in your family is a mage with the same skills as your grandmother. As far as I can tell, the spells haven't been disturbed since your grandmother passed away, so whoever is the mage is probably the same person who took the books. So tell me about your aunts and uncles."

She rubbed her forehead. "Well, there's Elise, of course, who you met yesterday, but there's no way *she's* a mage. All I ever heard about from her was how evil mages are, about how all supes should be put in camps or killed on sight. She joined a bunch of those anti-supe hate groups years ago."

"Still, I'd better check her out. She could be hiding behind all that hot air." I doubted it, though. Elise's hate seemed pretty sincere.

Natalie shrugged. "Her name is Elise Browning. I've got her address."

"Who else?"

"My mom had two other sisters and a half brother: Deborah

Mackey, Kathy Adams, and Peter Eppright. He was my grandmother's son from her first marriage. They all live in the city."

"I'll get their addresses from you and start checking them out. Any guesses as to which of them it might be?"

Natalie shook her head. "Honestly, no. If you'd asked me that yesterday, I'd have said none of them could possibly be mages, but it's becoming increasingly apparent that I don't know nearly as much about my family as I thought. What will we do when we figure out who stole the books?"

"Well, we'll find out what they took, and why. They're *your* books, so we'll try to get them back. At some point, you need to decide what to do with Betty's books." I gestured at the library. "You could keep them, or put them in storage, or sell them to collectors. If we find Betty's spellbooks, you might want to save those in case you want to hand those down." Spellbooks were usually family heirlooms. Even if Natalie didn't want her magic, someone else in the family might want those books. I coveted them myself.

I went to the bookcase where the missing books had been kept and knelt in front of the bottom shelf. I closed my eyes and reached out tentatively, focusing on what my senses might be able to tell me about the books that were still here, and the ones that weren't.

As I lowered my shields and stretched out my senses, I gasped as a punch of residual power and a wave of orange, gray, and black magic rolled over me. Dimly, I heard Malcolm asking if I was all right, but I couldn't answer. I had to focus on not being swept away. I could feel my knees on the hardwood floor in the library, and that physical sensation kept me grounded. If I could ride it out, I'd be able to extricate myself.

It took a lot of effort to think, but I was able to make some sense of what was happening. I was caught up in the echo of something incredibly powerful that had been in the library at one time but wasn't here anymore. The magic trace, as formidable as it was, felt diminished. If this was the amount of energy it had left behind, I shuddered to think what the actual object might feel like.

Slowly, the power receded, like a tide going out, and I started to surface. I became aware of my body, especially the pain in my knees from kneeling on the floor. My neck had a cramp from my head hanging down for so long.

The low, indistinct sounds I'd been hearing were becoming recognizable as voices. Now that the power wasn't rushing through me anymore, I raised my shields slowly, and my hearing and vision cleared.

"Alice, can you hear me?" Malcolm's voice came from somewhere near my left shoulder. He sounded worried but calm.

"I can hear you," I mumbled. I took a deep breath and raised my head.

Malcolm hovered nearby, but not close enough to have gotten caught up in the same surge of energy that had snagged me.

"What did you see?" I asked him.

"There was a massive power surge from the area of the bottom shelf. It was like nothing I've ever seen before. I thought I saw fire magic, but most of the trace was black and gray. I don't even know what that is."

"Yeah, me neither." I looked at the books on the bottom shelf. I saw Bradshaw's *History of Fire Magic*, *Air Magic and Storm Cycles* by Ann Lewis, and a bunch of other unremarkable texts. I ran my fingers carefully over each of the books. It felt like they had soaked up some of the power that had swept over me, but none of them were the source of it.

I stacked the books on the floor and hunkered down to look at the shelf itself, running my fingertips along the bottom edge of the bookcase. About six inches from the left side of the shelf, it felt like I ran my fingers over a razor.

"Ow!" I jerked back, looking at my hand. I expected to see blood, but there was nothing. What the hell?

"Malcolm, can you see anything right here?" I pointed.

Malcolm bent down next to me. "It looks like a blood ward lock. Hang on." His fingers danced in the air. "It's been opened, but the spell is still in place. Just a second." I felt a puff of magic. "Okay, it's gone."

I reached back in and felt around carefully. This time, instead of a sharp pain, I felt a raised edge. I lifted up and a lid opened, revealing a compartment hidden in the bottom of the bookcase. The lid was covered with runes that looked like an intricate containment spell, designed to shield whatever was in the compartment from being sensed when the lid was closed.

"Well, whatever was in here, it's gone now." I sat back on my heels. "It looks like they took something out of this compartment and a couple of books, then rearranged the shelf to hide the fact that anything had been taken. Since it doesn't look like any of the spells have been broken, whoever took the stuff was the person who these wards were designed to allow in."

Natalie pulled the wooden chair over from the other side of the bedroom and settled in to watch us work. "So, one of my aunts or my uncle."

"It looks like it." I pushed myself onto my hands and knees, then staggered to my feet. "Ugh. Jeez." I shook my head to clear it. "Whatever was in that compartment, it's a hell of a thing. I hope whoever took it can contain it."

"What could they want with it?" Natalie asked.

I shrugged. "Hard to tell until we know what it is. Your grandmother had it well hidden, but somehow this mystery mage knew about it and came and took it, we can assume after Betty died. Whatever it is, it's extremely powerful. I'd feel a lot better if I knew what it is, and what they intend to do with it."

"Me too," Malcolm said. "How do you want to go about looking for it?"

"Well, we've got a definite list of suspects." I glanced at Natalie. "How are you doing with all of this?"

"Honestly, a lot better than I thought I would be," my client said. "I think the big shock was finding out about my grandmother. The rest of this is just…." She shrugged. "My grandmother was a mage, I've got some weird magic situation going on, and someone in my family broke into my house and stole some mysterious *thing* out of my grandmother's library. Oh, and my grandmother's magic could have killed you." She made a *pfffft* sound. "I guess I'm all out of surprise at this point."

"Speaking of, any thoughts on what you want to do about your magic?" Malcolm asked.

"Whenever you're ready, I'm ready to find out what kind of magic I have. At least then I'll have enough information to be able to make a decision about my future."

I looked at Natalie. Yesterday, she'd been pale and fragile-looking; today, there was color in her cheeks, and though she was still painfully thin, there was an aura of vitality that hadn't been there before. I hoped I was right about her deteriorating health being tied to the weakening spell that bound her magic.

I gave her a smile. "I'm really glad to hear it. You want to do it now?"

She finished off her tea. "Sure, no time like the present, right?"

"You want to use the circle in here?" Malcolm asked.

I glanced at the floor. "No. Too many residual spells in here, and I don't trust anyone else's circles but mine. And yours," I amended. "Let's go into the bedroom again."

We stepped out of the library. I looked at Malcolm. "What do you think? I draw the circles, you power them?" He was still super-powered; might as well take advantage of it.

"Sounds like a plan," Malcolm said.

I pulled out my chalk and got to work, drawing a nested set of three circles. I was reasonably certain we'd be fine with just one, but I was cautious enough to have two backups in case things got out of hand. I'd had just about enough of surprises in this house.

"Let's do this," I said.

Natalie, who'd been sitting on the bed while I worked, stood. "Stand in the center of the circle," I told her. She moved into place and fidgeted.

I gestured at the circles I'd drawn. "The first thing I'm going to do is close this circle. When I do, you'll feel a tingle, like a small electric charge, but it's harmless. Then I'll charge the circle so it's strong enough to contain your magic. You'll feel the tingle get stronger. Malcolm is going to be out there to close and charge the other circles if we need to."

Natalie looked at Malcolm. He grinned and waved. "He's waving at you," I said.

She let out a nervous laugh. "Then what?"

"Once this circle is ready, I'll remove your grandmother's binding spells from you, leaving just my own. When her spells break, you'll feel a...pop, I guess is the best word for it. Nothing will happen because my spells will still be there. Then I'll start letting your magic out."

"What will that feel like?"

I thought about that. "For me, it feels like I'm exhaling. It feels wonderful. It will feel weird to you since you've never done it before, but if I do a good job with my spells, it will be gradual, like breathing out."

"Will I be able to hurt you?" Her eyes were wide.

"No," I said, though there was a chance. Uncontrolled magic was never safe for anyone, but I needed Natalie calm and feeling as secure as possible so she didn't panic. Panic would be bad. "I'll be protected within my circle, and with my own spell. Nothing you can do can hurt me."

Malcolm frowned at me. I gave my head a tiny shake to tell him not scare her.

I continued with my explanation. "Once your magic is freed at least partway, I'll be able to tell how strong you are. Then I'll bind your magic again until you make a decision about what to do, and we'll break the circle. Are you with me?"

Natalie took a couple of deep breaths, then nodded. "Okay. I'm ready. Let's do it."

"Okay. Here we go." I activated the protection spell on my bracelet, then closed the center circle around Natalie. She gasped.

"How does it feel?" I asked her.

She was quiet for a moment. "It feels so weird, like an electric charge, but really faint. It doesn't hurt at all." She looked immensely relieved.

"I did tell you it wouldn't. Now I'm going to charge the circle." I closed my eyes and reached out so I could feel the circle. In deference to Natalie, I transferred the energy slowly.

She sucked in a breath but stayed quiet as the power built. When I was happy with its energy level, I stopped the transfer and opened my eyes to check on my client.

Natalie's red hair floated in the air from the charge in the circle. "That feels amazing," she breathed. "It's like standing on a power line. Oh, I can see why people do this," she blurted out.

I laughed. "Malcolm, you ready?"

"Yep." Malcolm was in the third circle, ready to close it at a moment's notice if Natalie's magic broke out of hers.

"Natalie?"

"Let's do it." Her eyes were huge but she held her ground.

"Stand still. Here we go." I closed my eyes and reached out toward Natalie with my mind. Slowly, I lowered my shields and focused my senses toward my client. I could clearly see my binding spell as well as her grandmother's layered spells. They were degrading quickly. Some of the strands were sickly gray-green. Suddenly, my theory about the binding spells being the cause of Natalie's mystery illness was almost a certainty.

I began plucking at the strands of Betty's binding spells. They were weak and began falling apart faster than I could unweave them. In a few seconds, my gentle pulling tore clean through them like someone had taken a knife and cut them away. Natalie yelped in surprise.

"Are you all right?" Malcolm asked.

"Y-yes," she said. "Was that my grandmother's spells?"

"Yes." I opened my eyes. "Now I'm going to start removing mine. You're going to feel the magic coming out of you. Try to stay calm, and remember that you can't be hurt by your own magic, and you can't hurt me. Deep breaths."

I began unweaving my binding spells. After the first few strands fell away, I started to feel the magic rising in a breath of warmth with strands of cool white.

"Fire magic," I said quietly, knowing Malcolm would hear me. "And air as well."

"As we thought." Malcolm was equally quiet.

Natalie made little fearful sounds.

"You're doing fine. Everything's good. Stay relaxed." The magic I could sense dammed up behind my spell didn't feel like an overwhelming amount of power. I found myself hoping that would be the case. Natalie would probably be happier as a low-level mage.

I felt a rush of heat and air, and Natalie gasped.

I opened my eyes. Magical fire and air swirled around Natalie in the center circle. It was mild, but her eyes were wide with terror. "You're fine. It won't hurt you."

Natalie wasn't hearing me. Panic shone in her eyes. She was losing it.

"Natalie, don't—"

Several things happened pretty much simultaneously. Malcolm sensed trouble and closed the third circle. Natalie stumbled and hit her circle, which discharged energy and somehow broke instantly, releasing her fire and air magic into the larger second circle where I stood. Even protected by my spell, I felt the heat as the firestorm raged around us.

Startled by the power surge, Natalie shrieked and flailed blindly, striking me in the stomach. I saw a flash of telltale bright yellow just before I collapsed in a heap, my magic snuffed out like a candle.

In a split second of clarity, I realized Natalie was a null, and a strong one. I'd had no way of knowing that until now, and it was going to cost me big-time.

With no magic to sustain it, my protection spell failed. In the next heartbeat, Natalie's binding spell broke, and the full force of her fire and air magic tore free and roared through the circle—

—where, without a drop of magic in me, I was completely unprotected, and in the middle of an inferno.

CHAPTER 10

I screamed and pulled my leather jacket up and over the top of my head, trying to shield my head and face. *"Malcolm!"*

Fire scorched my skin and heat seared my nose and throat, the agony so intense that I almost passed out immediately. I clung to consciousness, desperately trying to think of anything I could do to save myself before I burned to death, but with no magic, I was defenseless.

I sensed an enormous impact of magic that felt like I'd been hit by an invisible bus. Natalie's screaming cut off abruptly, and the fiery maelstrom was suddenly gone. I couldn't see anything. I didn't know if the fire had blinded me or I was just in shock.

From the darkness, I heard Malcolm shouting my name. Something ice-cold hit my right shoulder and fresh agony surged. I tried to scream, but nothing came out. Malcolm's voice rose, and the cold feeling spread through my body, a wave of liquid ice followed by red-hot needles and then numbness. Whatever part of my brain was still functioning recognized an earth-magic healing spell. A second spell hit my left shoulder and I cried out, a pathetic, broken sound.

After that, all I could do was writhe on the floor while Malcolm's spells hit me one after another, trying to save my life. The numbness and pins-and-needles sensations rolled through my body in turns. When I had a moment of peace, I wondered what had happened to Natalie, but then another wave of pain hit and I couldn't care anymore.

Finally, mercifully, I blacked out.

* * *

I floated in darkness for what felt like a very long time, surfacing for brief moments just long enough to overhear indistinct sounds and feel intense pain.

Eventually, somehow, I was able to stay conscious for a few minutes. Above me, Malcolm floated, almost transparent. "Alice?" His voice was faint. "You've got to get help. I'm too drained to do any more healing spells. I don't know if you're going to make it if we don't get someone over here."

It took a few moments for me to process what he was saying. I realized I was sprawled on the bedroom floor. From where I lay, I could see my phone in my bag next to the library door. It wasn't very far, but I had no idea if I could make it. Every part of me that hadn't been somewhat protected by my jacket radiated agony, and all the skin I could see was red and splotchy. My brain refused to believe what I was seeing, or that I had nearly burned to death.

Slowly, I rolled onto my stomach and began pulling myself across the floor. Every movement brought searing pain. I lost consciousness several times.

Finally, I got to my bag. With swollen fingers, I managed to pull my phone out and drop it on the floor. I held down the button until the screen turned on, then I dragged my fingertip across the screen to unlock the phone. It took three tries.

When I got to the main screen, I used a numb finger to tap the Contacts button. I wanted to find the number for Hawthorne's, but my eyesight was fading. At the last moment, I saw Wolf, the most recent contact I had created, and in desperation tried to touch the green icon next to it.

My head hit the floor next to my phone. From beyond the growing darkness, I heard someone asking if anyone was there.

"Help," I whispered.

I thought I heard a voice say "Alice?" but it might have been wishful thinking. I fell into oblivion.

* * *

An eternity later, I surfaced again, roused by a surge of magic that ripped through my brain like talons.

I heard shouting and heavy footsteps, and then a male voice, growly and familiar. "Jesus. Alice?" Somehow, the werewolf had found me.

Gently, slowly, Sean rolled me over onto my back. I tried to open my eyes but couldn't. I sensed him leaning close as his fingertips pressed into my wrist, searching for a pulse. I moaned.

"Thank God." Strong arms scooped me up off the floor and I cried out in pain. "I'm taking you to a hospital."

"No." I kicked weakly. "No hospital. Malcolm...."

"Who is Malcolm?" Sean jerked, and I heard a vicious-sounding snarl. "Who's here?"

"Ghost," I whispered. "Help Malcolm...."

"Help him how?" Sean demanded.

Malcolm spoke. "Help me save her."

Sean jumped at the disembodied voice. "Where are you?"

"I'm right next to you," the ghost snapped. "I need to pull energy from you."

"Do it! Help her!" Sean ordered.

I summoned up enough strength to talk. "No hospital, Malcolm."

"I won't let him take you," Malcolm promised. Sean growled.

Malcolm said something else, but I was fading again and couldn't hear him. I felt an impact on my shoulder and another wave of cold rushed through me, followed by the white-hot needles of another healing spell, and then darkness again.

* * *

I had to be alive. You couldn't hurt this much and be dead.

I opened my eyes. Pain. I closed them again. That hurt too. Breathing also hurt. My throat was agonizingly dry.

I sensed movement behind me, and it felt like someone was sanding the skin off my back. I whimpered.

The motion stopped immediately. "Allie?"

I was momentarily confused by the nickname, but I recognized Sean's voice. I opened my eyes and blinked groggily, trying to figure out where I was.

After a moment, I realized I was in Betty's bed, under a mountain of blankets. A bleary glance revealed a familiar arm wrapped around my waist from behind, and that I was wearing a blue nightgown. The soft cotton was probably the best clothing for me to be wearing under the circumstances, but it still felt like the harshest sandpaper. Instead of the severe burns I'd seen before, my skin looked pink and felt sensitive and tight, like I had an all-over sunburn.

I'd been burned with uncontrolled fire and air magic, and I was really damn lucky to be alive and still have skin on my bones. I tried to sense my own magic, but there was nothing there. *Oh, right. Natalie freaking nulled me.* I was *not* getting paid enough for this shit. It might be time to invoke that personal injury clause in our contract. I felt dizzy and closed my eyes.

"Alice?" It was Malcolm.

"Let her sleep," Sean growled from behind me.

Malcolm's voice was patient and nonthreatening. He must have dealt with angry werewolves before. "She's been unconscious for five hours. I need to know what to do to help her."

I forced my eyes open. Malcolm floated in front of me. "Hey," I rasped.

The ghost touched my shoulder. I felt a light tingle of magic, and then he withdrew. "How do you feel?"

I took a deep breath. "Hurts," I said, my voice scratchy. I coughed.

"I know." Malcolm sounded grim. "Natalie nulled you, and your binding spell failed."

"I remember fire." I coughed again. "Water?"

Sean got out of the bed and disappeared in the direction of the kitchen.

"What happened?" I asked my ghost sidekick.

Malcolm looked relieved when Sean was gone. I was sure dealing with an alpha werewolf in protective mode had been difficult. "When Natalie nulled your spells and her magic escaped, I broke your circle, knocked her out, and drained her magic to make healing spells as fast as I could. You went into shock, I kept pulling magic and energy out of Natalie for healing spells until she was drained and so was I. You woke up and managed to call Sean."

I closed my eyes.

Footsteps approached. "Allie, here's some water."

I didn't want water. I was hurting and deeply shaken by how close I'd come to death. Hot tears slid from my eyes, burning like acid on my face.

Gentle fingertips tried to wipe away the tears, but even Sean's light touch was too much. Ignoring the agony of the nightgown scraping my tender skin, I rolled over and turned my back to them, burrowing under the blankets and shaking with pain and shock.

Sean swore. Footsteps moved around the bed. "Allie, you have to drink some water."

"Leave me alone." I meant to sound mean and threatening, but it came out choked and teary. Damn it, couldn't I just be left alone?

Apparently not. I felt the blankets lifted and then Sean got into bed next to me. "Drink the water, Alice." This time it was an order. Alphas don't make requests; they give commands, and they expect to be obeyed.

Well, *I* don't take orders, not anymore. I opened my eyes and glared. Sean was giving me the full-on alpha stare, gold eyes and all, and it made me furious. "Don't order…me around," I told him flatly. Anger gave me strength, and the tears dried up.

Sean's face softened, and his eyes went back to normal. "I'm sorry. I know you're hurting. Please, will you drink some water?" He held out a plastic cup with a straw sticking out of it.

Reluctantly, I leaned forward and drank. The tap water was room temperature, but it tasted like heaven. "Easy, don't make yourself sick," Sean murmured.

As slowly as I could, I drank every drop, then lay back down. Sean set the cup on the floor and gathered me carefully in his arms. I felt acutely uncomfortable. Cuddling together earlier in private was one thing, but now we were in Betty Morrison's bed in Natalie's house, and Malcolm was in here watching us.

"How did you find me?" I asked hoarsely.

Sean stiffened at my tone, though he didn't move away. "I was at work when I got your call. By the time I realized it was you needing help, you'd lost consciousness again. I called a buddy of mine to track your phone. When I got here, your car was out front, but there was no answer at the door. I came in and found you burned to holy hell in here on the floor. After Malcolm got you stabilized, I found something for you to wear and put you in bed so he could keep healing you for as long as we could."

My brain was having trouble catching up. "You came in through the house wards?"

"Yeah, he got a good zap." Malcolm floated into view. "He was bleeding from the nose and ears for a while."

For the first time, I saw blood splattered on the shoulders and front of Sean's green polo shirt just above the lettering that read *Maclin Security*. There were streaks of dried blood below his ears. Getting through the wards had cost him.

"Thank you." My voice was a dry whisper. "I'm sorry I got you mixed up in this."

"Don't be," Sean told me. "I'm glad you're alive. When I saw you, I thought you were dead. I wanted to take you to a hospital, but I guess you can't go to one." His eyes searched my face, looking for an explanation.

"No hospital," I insisted.

Malcolm spoke. "Alice, I gotta be honest with you…if Sean hadn't gotten here when he did, I'm not sure I would have been able to save you. As it was, we used so many healing spells back-to-back that your blood pressure was through the roof. We were worried you'd stroke out if I did any more. If you hadn't stopped seizing, I don't know what else we could have done."

"I told you—" I started to say.

"I know," Malcolm interrupted me. "I know, no hospital, no doctors, but damn it, you were *dying*."

I closed my eyes and dropped my head onto the pillow. "Where's Natalie?"

"She's asleep in her room," Malcolm said. "I used some of Sean's energy to replace the binding spell on her and he put her in bed. She'll probably be asleep until the morning."

"What time is it?"

"Almost midnight," Sean told me.

I jerked. "Charles!"

"Don't worry about that," Sean said. "I'll call and tell them you can't make it."

"I can do it. Can you get me my phone? I think it's over by the library door."

"Okay." Sean slid out of bed again.

I turned to Malcolm. "What's your assessment of Natalie's magic?"

"Mid-level fire, low-to-mid-level air," Malcolm replied. That had been my analysis too, before the proverbial shit hit the fan. "The nulling thing is rare, though. I've known mages who could null, but not as fast as she does. It takes time to drain someone, usually. She can null instantly, and break circles with a touch."

"Tell me about it," I griped.

Sean handed over my phone. I tried to sit up but didn't have the strength. I gave up and fumbled around with the phone, finally getting it unlocked and finding the number for the bar.

Three rings and then Pete answered. "Hawthorne's." I heard voices, laughter, and glasses clinking in the background. It sounded like a busy night.

"Hey, Pete, it's Alice."

"Hey, girl. You still coming in to see us this evening?" Only on VST—Vampire Standard Time—would midnight be considered "evening."

"I don't think I can make it in. I had a little…accident."

A pause, and then the background noise disappeared as Pete stepped into a back room. "Alice, are you okay? You sound like you're in bad shape."

"I'm okay."

Sean growled.

"I *will be* okay," I amended, though I had no idea why I was appeasing Sean. "But I'm not going anywhere tonight. Please extend my apologies to Charles. I'd like to reschedule for tomorrow night, if I can."

"Should I ask Adri to come over and help you?"

I hesitated, debating how to answer. Finally, I said, "I'm not alone. Someone is here."

Another pause. "Who's with you? The werewolf?"

Beside me, Sean went very still.

"Yes. What the hell, Pete? Are you keeping tabs on me now?"

"I'm not keeping tabs on you. We were concerned when you told

Bryan you'd been dropped off, but Maclin's car was still in your driveway when we came by with your car. Bryan checked the house, but when everything was quiet, we assumed you'd invited him in."

Sean's face was like granite. The thought Bryan had been snooping around in my yard this morning while Sean and I were inside asleep was enough to make me see red.

"Whether or not I invited him in is none of Bryan's business, or yours," I told Pete through gritted teeth. "Stay out of my personal life."

"Okay, Alice," Pete said quietly. "I'll tell Bryan you won't be in tonight, and he'll let you know when Mr. Vaughan will be available."

"Thank you."

"Good night."

I dropped the phone on the bed and closed my eyes. Whatever energy I'd had was suddenly gone. I felt completely drained, in more ways than one. I could barely move, but things needed to be done, and then I was going home. I wanted out of this house.

I opened my eyes, then pushed myself up until I was sitting. My arms shook and my tender skin hurt, but I blocked it out.

"Out of the bed," I told Sean.

He blinked at me.

"Scoot. Off." I made a shooing motion.

Looking confused, Sean got up. His expression switched from bewildered to angry a second later when I started inching toward the edge of the bed. "Stay there. Tell me what you want, and I'll get it."

I waved him back. "I need to get up. I can't just lie here."

Sean and Malcolm started to argue. If I'd had any magic, I'd have zapped them both. "Stop," I said, holding up a shaking hand. "Just stop, both of you." I swung my legs over the side of the bed, closed my eyes, and waited for the room to stop spinning.

"Allie, for God's sake," Sean said, exasperated.

I opened my eyes and glared at him. "I want to go home. Are the circles still on the floor?"

"Yes," Malcolm said.

"I need to clean those up. Somebody get me a wet towel." I started to get off the bed.

"Stay on the bed," Sean said, then added, "Please," when I glowered at him. "I'll clean up your circles." He stalked off to the bathroom.

"How much energy do you have left?" I asked Malcolm.

"Not much, but I'll give you what I can, and maybe that will get you on your feet and home."

"What kind of shape is Natalie in?" I asked as Sean came back with a wet towel. He began wiping the floor on the other side of the bed, his jaw clenched and anger rolling off him in waves. It occurred to me that he was probably feeling helpless, and that was not an emotion alphas dealt with very well.

"She's fine," Malcolm said. "She's been out since I knocked her out."

"Shit," I breathed. "She's going to be a mess. I'll have to leave her a note again and hope she's calm enough in the morning that I can talk to her. She'll probably think she killed me." I watched Sean cleaning the floor and despised how powerless I was.

I looked at Malcolm. He read my expression and floated over to me. "Do it."

When I touched his arm, I thought, *Thank you for saving my life. I owe you.*

Malcolm smiled at me. *Don't worry about it. I owe you more than I can ever repay for hiding me from Darius.* His face grew serious. *You have some of my magic signature now, since I used so many healing spells on you. You'll have to be careful so that no one senses it.*

All right. I closed my eyes and felt for Malcolm's magic. It was very weak. I slowly pulled energy from him into myself. There wasn't much for me to take; just enough to put him in my earring and maybe raise and lower my house wards.

When I opened my eyes, I could only see his outline; otherwise, he was completely transparent. I touched my earring, protected from the fire by its own spells, and in a heartbeat, he was contained. I could barely feel the earring buzz. I took a deep breath and stood.

I staggered, and in a flash Sean was there to hold me up. "I'm okay," I said in a voice that shook. "Give me a minute."

Sean touched my cheek gently, and even that was painful. "You're *not* okay. I can see how badly you're hurt. There's nothing wrong with letting others help you."

I looked around for the pad and pen I'd used the night before.

Shrugging out of Sean's grip, I walked slowly to the nightstand, using the bed to hold myself up, then scrawled another note with trembling hands: *Good morning. Don't worry and don't panic—I'm fine. Give me a call when you're up. Alice.*

I looked down and sighed. I didn't have the energy to change clothes, and it would probably hurt like hell anyway. Screw it; I'd go home in the nightgown.

"Can you grab my bag and my phone?" I asked Sean. He picked them up. Barefoot, I shuffled to the bedroom door, and Sean turned the light off. We moved down the hall at a snail's pace. When we got to Natalie's room, I could hear her snoring lightly. Sean put the note on her nightstand.

I was dead on my feet, but I kept moving like I was on autopilot. We went out the front door and Sean locked it behind us. The wards still felt at full power. I looked at Sean and shook my head. Going through them must have really hurt.

From the front steps, I looked at my car sitting in Natalie's driveway. It felt like a lifetime ago when I'd parked here this afternoon and sat talking to Malcolm. Sean's Mercedes was parked at the curb. The cool air felt good on my hot skin.

"Allie?"

"Yeah?" I realized I was swaying on my feet.

"I'll drive you home in your car. If that's all right," he added.

I appreciated that he was sort of asking. "Okay."

"Okay?" He looked surprised I wasn't arguing.

Things began to get very fuzzy, and I suddenly felt cold all over. "I think you'd better—" I started to say, and then the sidewalk rushed up toward my face and everything went dark.

CHAPTER 11

I rocked back and forth on a boat as someone gently wiped my forehead with a cold, wet cloth.

"Mmmrrrph?"

"Hey, baby. Wake up." Sean sounded really worried. But what were we doing on a boat?

I forced my eyes open and blinked a couple of times to bring my surroundings into focus. As it turned out, we were *not* on a boat. We were on the front porch swing at my house, and I was curled up in Sean's lap while he swayed us back and forth slowly with his feet. He had a bottle of cold water and was using his shirt to cool my face.

I blinked slowly, and time seemed to jump forward several minutes by the time I opened my eyes again.

Sean put the wet shirt on the swing. "Can you hear me?"

"Yes." My voice sounded like dry leaves on a sidewalk.

He kissed my forehead, visibly relieved. "Do you think you can lower the wards?"

I thought about it. I was awfully comfy, but I didn't know how long we'd been sitting out here, and Sean probably wasn't comfortable. "I think so," I murmured. "Help me up."

Instead, Sean stood up effortlessly with me in his arms and brought me over to the front door. I tried to reach out, but my arm just flopped uselessly. I frowned at my hand and tried again, but I had no strength. He stepped right up next to the door, and the energy from the wards ran over our skin like an electric current. I was able to touch the house. A little nudge, and the wards fell.

In a flash, Sean had the door unlocked and we were inside, and he kicked the door shut. I was so depleted, the ambient energy of the house wards felt like an invisible, prickly blanket.

"Can you put the wards back up?" he asked me.

"Yes." I reached out to touch the doorframe and focused with extreme difficulty. I got them back up, but it took everything I had. I went limp in Sean's arms, my head falling back while my vision went dark. I made a little noise and started to fade out again.

"No, no, no," he chanted to himself, shifting me so my head flopped onto his chest instead of hanging limply back over his arm. "Come on, Allie, stay with me now. Shit, I shouldn't have even asked about the damn wards."

He rushed through the foyer, up the stairs, and into my room before I could really process what was going on.

He got me under the covers and stripped down to his boxers. The bed dipped as he climbed in next to me and pulled me against his hot, bare skin.

I shivered uncontrollably. "C-cold," I told him, my teeth chattering.

"I know, baby." His mouth was pressed into my hair. "Hold on to me."

Okay, I could live with the nickname Allie, but that was twice now. "Don't c-call me 'b-baby,'" I mumbled, thumping his chest with my fist.

Sean snorted softly. He probably thought it was funny that I was burned to a crisp and bitching at him for calling me "baby." I'd have been mad if I wasn't so wretchedly cold. I buried my face into the side of his neck, and the smell of him was comforting.

We lay like that for a long time, me shivering and him holding me to share his heat. I was so cold that even his werewolf body temperature wasn't warm enough to drive away the chill.

I drifted in and out while he talked to me. I couldn't understand a word he said, but his tone was quiet and soothing. At some point, I cried for a while, though I wasn't exactly sure why. Eventually, I slept.

* * *

About an hour before dawn, I woke feeling marginally better, though my skin still felt tight, and I couldn't close my swollen hands into fists or move without serious pain.

Sean dozed, curled around me protectively. He looked exhausted. I reflected on how he'd come looking for me and forced his way through the house wards to get to my side, then let Malcolm use his energy for healing spells. He'd driven me home, sat on the porch until I woke up to let us in, carried me upstairs, and held me for hours while I shivered and cried and slept.

As I looked at him, I felt something strange and unfamiliar stirring in a part of me I thought was dead. I tried to remind myself that alpha werewolves were not boyfriend material, and I was not girlfriend material. I was a haunted house, and not the fun kind you visited on Halloween for cheap thrills. The scars on my back were nothing compared to the ones on the inside.

I realized with a start that Sean's eyes were open and he was watching me. "Did I wake you up?" he asked.

"No." I hesitated. I should tell him to go.

"What's wrong?" Sean brushed my chin with his fingertips.

He was so warm. "I don't want you to go." The words just tumbled out of my mouth before I could stop them.

He kissed me so gently that I barely felt it. "I don't want to go either, so that's fine. Just rest." He tried to hold my hand, but pain made me hiss and he quickly let go. "I'm sorry. Is there anything I can do to help you? Can Malcolm—"

I shook my head. "Malcolm's drained to nothing. Can you get my healing spells for me? There's a wooden box in my second drawer in the bathroom. Don't open it; just bring it to me."

"Okay." Sean carefully unwound himself from around me and slid out of bed. He went to the bathroom and returned with my first aid kit. He knelt next to me on the bed and looked at the box. "It's beautiful. What are these carvings?"

"Runes to keep anyone from sensing the spells inside." I took the box from him and traced three runes on its lid before opening it.

Sean watched as I used my swollen fingers to paw through the spells, then awkwardly lifted out a purple crystal. I closed the box and set it aside. I knew I needed a strong healing spell, and this was the second-strongest in the box. I also knew it was going to hurt, and that was going to make a certain werewolf very unhappy.

I tried to sound as clinical as possible. "This is a powerful healing spell. I'm pretty sure it will be enough to heal the burns and the rest of the damage, but it's going to be painful. I don't know if you've ever seen one used, so I just wanted you to know what to expect so you're not surprised. Don't touch me until the spell is done."

A muscle moved in Sean's jaw. "Will it be worse than the ones Malcolm used earlier?"

I considered. "Probably. Those were earth magic. Blood magic is more intense. Maybe you should go downstairs while I do this."

Sean's gaze turned steely. "If you can stand it, so can I."

"Okay. Give me some space, then, and get the trash can for me in case I need it."

Reluctantly, Sean moved to the edge of the bed and scooted the wastebasket closer.

I pulled up one side of the nightgown and grabbed one of my pillows. Before I had too much time to tense up, I held the crystal to my abdomen and invoked the spell. "*Helios.*"

Magic hit me like a freight train. I put the pillow over my face to muffle my hoarse screams as what felt like liquid ice and burning acid rolled through my body. Instinct made me want to throw the source of the pain across the room, and it took every ounce of my willpower not to. I squashed the pillow to my face as hard as I could and panted out breaths between shrieks as the crystal pulsed, discharging its healing energy into my body in waves. My skin tingled as the magic went to work. I hadn't used a strong healing spell in a while, and it hurt every bit as badly as I remembered.

Finally, an eternity later, the pulses began to slow, signaling that the spell was completing its work. As the waves began to ease and numbness set in, I took the pillow off my face. Through the fog of pain and healing magic, I heard a low, reverberating sound.

It took me a full ten seconds to realize it came from Sean.

He was pacing back and forth next to the bed and growling, his hands clenched into fists, his eyes bright gold. At that moment, he looked much closer to wolf than man. I felt a little stab of fear, though I knew it was the instinct to protect, not harm, that was calling his wolf close to his skin.

When he saw me looking at him, he stopped pacing and came to the side of the bed, leaning on it with both hands. "Is it done?"

I felt a whisper of magic from the crystal, then stillness as the last of its healing power gave out. I dropped the empty crystal on the bed. "Now it's done." My voice cracked.

Sean was shaking with the effort of holding himself back. "Did it work?"

I moved carefully, testing my limbs. I couldn't see my skin well in the darkness, but the pain and tightness of the burns were gone. I was achy and nauseous, but it didn't feel like I was going to throw up, thankfully. "I think it worked."

In a flash, Sean was on the bed and pulling me into his arms. "That was just about the worst fucking thing I've ever had to stand by and watch," he growled into my hair, squeezing me so tightly that my bones creaked. "You don't know how hard it was not to take that thing away from you."

"You know you can't interfere with a spell when it's working." His chest muffled my voice. "It's over. Now I'm all better."

He made a strangled sound. "A few hours ago, you were close enough to Death to look him in the eye. Then you went through a healing spell that looked like it hurt as much as a werewolf's first shift, and now you're 'all better.' How can you be so calm about this?"

I couldn't tell him how many times I'd looked Death in the eye, or how many strong healing spells I'd had to withstand over the years. I might not have had much use for them after I escaped my grandfather's cabal, but during the twenty years I was under its control, I'd teetered on the edge of the abyss many times, only to be yanked back unwillingly into the land of the living. Alice Worth hadn't had nearly as many run-ins with Death, but Moses Murphy's granddaughter was no stranger to the coldness of his scythe.

"I've used healing spells before," I told him.

He stilled, probably remembering the scars on my back. "I guess you have."

I moved the first aid box to the floor next to the bed and put the empty crystal on the nightstand. I got up, stretched carefully, then went to my dresser for pajamas. I grabbed a pair and changed into them in the bathroom.

When I came back out, Sean raised the covers in a silent invitation. I climbed in next to him, and he wrapped himself around me, as much for his own comfort as mine, I thought. In moments, I fell into a deep, dreamless sleep.

* * *

I woke midmorning to my phone blaring. I groaned, untangling myself from Sean to roll over and grab it from the nightstand. I rubbed my eyes, looked at the screen, and tried to sound alert when I answered. "Morning, Natalie."

I heard her sobbing. "Alice, I'm so sorry. Are you okay?"

"I'm fine. I got a little singed, but I'm okay."

Beside me, Sean growled. I elbowed him in the ribs and he grunted. Natalie sniffled. "Are you sure?"

"Yes." I stifled a grimace as I shifted to a more comfortable position on the bed and my sore muscles protested. Sean watched me like a hawk for signs of distress. "How do *you* feel?"

She made a sound like a half laugh, half sob. "Like I've got the worst hangover I've had since college. I could barely get out of bed."

"You'll probably feel a little weak for a day or two. We bound your magic again, so you're safe. I do have some good news on that front. You have fire and air magic, like your grandmother, but your power is low-to-mid-range, which is easier to learn to control. Also, it keeps you off the cabals' radar." I paused.

"What else?" Natalie prodded.

"You have an additional ability that's unusual. Do you remember what I told you about nulls?"

"Mages who can drain other people's magic?"

"Yes. You're a null."

"What's unusual about that? You said there are lots of them."

"It's unusual because you can do it so quickly. A lot of mages can drain someone else's energy, but it takes a while. Your ability is lightning fast, and you do it instinctually. You drained me just by touching me." She gasped. "It's fine—I'm recovering well enough, but it's one more thing that you'll need to learn to control. *If* you decide to learn, that is."

She went quiet. Sean rubbed my back and it felt really good.

"Don't make a decision right now when you're upset. We've got time. Your binding spell will hold for as long as you need to decide what to do. You can do something for me, though."

She took a deep breath. "What can I do?"

"If it's okay with you, I'll swing by your house with Malcolm. We'll double-check to make sure there aren't any more spells in the library, and then I'd like you to look through your grandmother's papers and books to see if she has anything that might indicate what was in that hidden compartment. In the meantime, I'm going to track down your aunts and uncle and try to figure out which one of them has been in your house. I'll need whatever information you have on them, like addresses, phone numbers, work info, photos, et cetera."

"I can do that," she said. Her voice sounded stronger. Giving her a project to work on helped her cope. "I'll have it for you when you get here."

"Great. I'll head over in about an hour." We disconnected and I flopped back in the bed.

Sean lay on his side and propped his head on his hand. "Sounds like a busy day."

"It'll be nice to do some actual *investigating* today. I don't want to tempt fate, but I sincerely hope I'm done with the near-death experiences for a while."

"Knock on wood," Sean said and rapped my skull lightly with his knuckles.

"Ha-ha."

We lay in my bed for a while, me on my back staring at the ceiling, Sean on his side facing me. It was a comfortable silence.

"What are you thinking about?" he asked finally.

I thought about different ways to answer that question, then settled on simply "You."

"What about me?"

"Well, for one thing, you got your wish."

"What wish?"

I gave him a wry smile. "To see me again."

He shook his head. "This was about as far from what I was hoping for as it can get." He paused. "Having said that…do I get a date?"

"You don't give up, do you?"

"No." The wolfish smile was back. "How about tonight?"

I sat up and leaned back against my headboard, putting some distance between us. "Do you think I owe you a date?"

"I don't think you owe me anything," Sean stated. "But I was hoping you might think it was at least worth considering."

"I told you yesterday I would think about it."

He gave me a look. "You and I both know you'd already decided."

He had me there. I didn't insult him by denying it.

"I get that you're cautious," he said. "I'm sure I would be too, if I'd been through whatever you've been through. I'd like to know what I need to do or say for you to give me a chance."

Sean could have reminded me of everything he'd done for me since I called him for help yesterday, but he didn't. He looked sincere when he told me I didn't owe him anything for saving my life. He was persistent, but I understood the value of single-mindedness; my own stubbornness had kept me alive more times than I cared to count. He was an alpha, but other than a brief moment last night when he'd tried to order me to drink water, he hadn't tried to control me. All those things were certainly in his favor, along with the great sex, the sense of humor, and our shared love of music and craft beer.

Unfortunately, on the other side of the equation was my life, and that was a pretty big consideration. It was a lot to risk for a slim chance at happiness.

Sean watched me for clues as to where my deliberations were headed. I thought I had a pretty good poker face, but he was probably even better than me at reading microexpressions. He sat up, looking resigned.

The sunlight coming through the window revealed dried blood on his neck and ears. The man had suffered and bled to save me. No one had done anything like that for me in a very long time, and that had to be worth something.

I took a deep breath. "You asked what you could do to prove yourself."

Sean tilted his head. "Yes."

"How long have you been in the security business?"

"Almost twenty years."

I blinked. He didn't look more than thirty-five, but shifters aged more slowly than humans. He must be in his early forties, then. "Permits and licenses current?"

"All of them."

"Willing to sign a nondisclosure and confidentiality agreement?"

His mouth twitched. "Is this a job interview?"

"Of a sort."

"Then, yes."

I was quiet. Sean waited.

Finally, I said, "Here's my offer. I have a full day ahead of me, as you heard. Come with me."

"In what capacity?"

"Colleague."

He grinned. "Colleague, huh?"

"That's the offer. I've got to do some work at my client's home, then track down four people who might have taken something from her house, something that might be dangerous."

He turned serious. "How dangerous?"

"I'm not sure yet. It's a magical item of some sort, possibly an object of power, or a focus. I'm still looking into that." I sighed. "Of course, this is all assuming you can take a day off from work. Is that even an option?"

"Already taken care of. I told my business partner last night that I wouldn't be in. He's got everything covered. I thought you might need me today."

I stiffened. "'Need' you?"

Sean's eyes darkened. "Yes, *need* me. When I texted Ron last night, I was holding you on your front porch and you were unconscious. You'd been burned, gone into shock, and were unresponsive for five hours. I thought you might be dying in my arms. You'd made it very clear I couldn't take you to the hospital—for reasons I haven't even asked about, I might add—so I sat there helpless, listening to you breathe and waiting to see if you would live or die."

I shifted uncomfortably. "Sean—"

"Alice, let me say this, please."

I waited.

"I took the day off in case you still hadn't woken up, or you needed someone to take care of you, even though you hate relying on anyone's help and get really unreasonably angry about it. Fortunately, thanks to Malcolm and me and the healing spells, you're well enough to drag yourself out of bed and carry on with this investigation, and I'm free to be a part of your day, as a *colleague*. And despite your tendency to think the worst of me and my intentions, I'd rather be with you than anywhere else right now."

I was shocked by the vehemence in Sean's words. I felt torn between my resentment and guilt for not thinking more about what he'd gone through.

I didn't do well with guilt; it made me angry. I spent so long under the cabal's control, the two emotions went hand in hand for me: shame over the things I did, combined with fury at my grandfather and his lieutenants for forcing me to make people suffer. On some level, I knew Sean didn't deserve my anger, but I felt guilty, and that made me mad. I didn't need any more guilt. I carried so much already, sometimes it crushed me flat.

On top of that, I was rattled by his statement that he'd rather be with me than anywhere else. This one-night stand was evolving into something that scared me.

My isolation began when I was eight years old and my grandfather murdered my parents—not that I had many friends before that, but after they died, I had no one. Twenty-one lonely years later, maybe I didn't have to be alone anymore. Everything Sean had done for me made me think that maybe I could allow him to try to earn my trust.

"I'm sorry," I said finally. "If you still want to come with me, you can." I didn't want it to sound like I was reluctantly granting him a boon, but I think that's how it came out.

Sean didn't look happy. "You don't sound very enthusiastic about it."

"I'm used to being on my own," I admitted. "And you're right: I don't like relying on other people, or needing help. I'm unreasonable about it, and I'm liable to try to take your head off at any time for no good reason. Sometimes I'm rude, and I'm no good at being friendly because I've never had many friends. They were just one more thing that could be used against me by the people who wanted to control me."

Sean's eyes softened, and he reached out to comfort me. I moved away, which clearly frustrated him. "I'm not looking for sympathy; I'm just stating facts. I'm trying to figure out if I can trust you, and maybe letting you come with me today will help me answer that question. Knowing all that, if you want to go with me and find out the hard way how difficult I am to be around, then let's do it."

Sean and I looked at each other. I had no idea what he was thinking. I half expected him to get up and leave.

Instead, he stretched and grinned at me. "So who gets the shower first?"

CHAPTER 12

I got the shower first while Sean went down to my car for his go-bag. I dropped the wards to let him go in and out without getting fried—again—and shut myself in the bathroom.

I took off my pajamas, stood in front of the mirror, and looked myself over. My skin looked normal, with no sign of burns. My head and face had thankfully been protected by my jacket, but my hair was a horror show; it had come out the braid I'd put it in yesterday and was sticking out wildly in all directions. Gah. If Sean hadn't run screaming at the sight of that mess, maybe he was tougher than I already gave him credit for.

I climbed into the shower with a wide-tooth comb and spent ten minutes just trying to unsnarl the colony of rats' nests that was my hair. It was painful and required a lot of swearing and conditioner. Finally clean and detangled, I wrapped my hair in a towel and myself in a bathrobe, brushed my teeth, and stuck my first aid kit back in the bathroom drawer before returning to the bedroom.

I found Sean lying on the bed in his boxers, chest bare and fingers laced behind his head. I took a moment to appreciate the mouthwatering view. From the gleam in his eyes, he was well-aware of the effect he was having on me.

"Is there any hot water left?" he asked, raising an eyebrow.

"Yes," I grumped. "Get in there before I change my mind and leave you behind."

"Yes, ma'am." He sprang out of bed and picked me up around the waist, kissing me so thoroughly, my toes curled. Then he put me down and went into the bathroom with his bag.

After the door closed and the shower came on, I checked my phone. There was a text message from Bryan that Charles would be busy tonight, but I could meet with him tomorrow night at ten. I texted him back that I'd be there.

I was already dressed by the time Sean stepped out of the bathroom wearing a black polo shirt and khakis. "Any idea where my jacket and boots are?" I asked.

Sean turned grim. "Your clothes were nothing but rags. Even the jacket and boots were pretty much destroyed."

I closed my eyes and sighed. "Those were my favorite boots. Son of a bitch." I went into my closet for my backup pair, then sat on the bed to put them on.

Sean started shaving in the bathroom. I realized he was the first man to do so, and that made me pause. I wasn't sure why it seemed so significant to me. Maybe because I'd never encouraged a man to stick around before? Hard to say. I found I liked watching him shave as I got ready and wondered what that meant.

I finished zipping up my boots, then put on my charm bracelet, rings, and monogram necklace. I picked up Malcolm's earring for the first time since last night and it buzzed in my hand. He at least had regenerated much of his magic; I, on the other hand, had been nulled so completely that I had almost none, and I hated how vulnerable it made me feel. I thought about having sex with Sean, simply to restore my magic. I watched him washing the rest of the shaving cream off his face and decided even I couldn't be that cold-blooded.

I left Malcolm where he was for now and put the earrings on. Sean was finished in the bathroom, so I traded places with him and put on my makeup and french-braided my damp hair while he packed up his dirty clothes and toiletries. In a few minutes, we were both ready. I stuck my phone in my bag and we headed out.

By the time we got in the car, we'd agreed to stop at Moe's, a fast-food place I liked that was between my house and Natalie's. I adjusted the driver's seat, which had been pushed all the way back to accommodate Sean's height, and we were off. If Sean's instincts were rebelling against being in the passenger seat, he didn't let on. It was a point in his favor.

I turned on the radio as background noise. "So, tell me about yourself," I invited as I drove.

"What would you like to know?"

"How old are you?"

"Forty-two." Which was about what I'd figured.

"Where were you born?"

"Here—well, on a farm not too far from here. My brother and his family live there now, with my parents." Sean seemed entirely comfortable answering questions. I tried to feel as comfortable asking them. As someone who was intensely private about her life, it was hard to feel at ease asking someone else to reveal personal details.

I really wanted to know if he'd been born a werewolf or been bitten, but that wasn't something you asked. He'd tell me himself if he wanted to. I asked about his security company instead.

"My friend Ron Dormer and I worked together for a different security company for about five years," Sean told me. "Then we decided to start our own business. It took a couple of years to build up a decent client base, but now we've got about thirty full-time employees, plus about two dozen part-timers. Our office is downtown, on Decatur near the park."

I pictured the area. "I know where that is. What kind of work do you do?"

"The personal security division does short-term bodyguard or security work. Our installation division sets up surveillance and security systems."

"And your friend who tracks cell phones?"

"Cyro's not an on-the-books employee. He's more of a consultant who works on a cash-only basis."

"With that kind of illegal equipment, I guess he would."

"He does more than track phones. I provided security for a woman last year who was going through a particularly nasty divorce. Her husband was abusive and threatening to take their kids out of the country. Cyro did some digging into the husband's financials, and it turned out he was laundering money for a cabal. Cyro sent the info to the Feds, and problem solved. Guy's doing twenty in federal prison, and the kids are safe with their mom."

"Good for him. Sounds like Cyro is a good man to know, and not someone you'd want to cross."

"That's for sure. He likes to see justice done, and he has the technology and expertise to make it happen."

"Interesting."

Sean glanced at me. "What are you thinking?"

"Not a thing."

His eyes narrowed. "Your tone sounded like you were thinking about something or someone in particular where some justice is needed."

"Nope."

Sean snorted. I ignored him and turned into the drive-thru at Moe's. I ordered a breakfast sandwich and coffee. He opted for three double bacon cheeseburgers, two large orders of home fries, and a large soda. I wondered if he planned to eat it all or if he'd ordered extra thinking I might need it. We focused on eating rather than conversation as I drove to Natalie's house.

By the time I pulled into her driveway, we'd finished all our food. I resisted the urge to steal from Sean's fries; his werewolf metabolism needed the calories after giving up so much of his energy healing me. He looked like he could have eaten more.

I knocked on the front door, and Natalie answered it. She looked pale—not surprising, after what happened yesterday—but her expression lightened when she saw me standing on the porch, as if she hadn't believed I was all right until she saw me with her own eyes. "I'm so glad to see you." She stepped back to let us inside. "I really thought I'd killed you."

"I'm okay." Sean looked like he wanted to say something, but I gave him a look and he changed his mind. "It was close, but we were fine."

Natalie looked at Sean. "Hi, I'm Natalie," she said, sticking out her hand. He shook it.

Oops. I'd forgotten they'd never actually met. "Natalie, this is Sean, my colleague. Sean, Natalie Newton, my client. Sean was over here last night to help with the…cleanup."

"Oh." Natalie's cheeks turned pink. "Well, I'm so sorry about yesterday. It was entirely my fault. Alice is very kind to not blame me for everything that's happened in this house. Thank you for helping."

"Not a problem," Sean said, though something in his eyes made me think he wasn't happy with Natalie's role in yesterday's events.

To distract him, I got down to business. "Do you have the info on your aunts and uncle?"

Natalie led the way into the kitchen and handed me a piece of paper that had been waiting on the counter. On it were the names, addresses, phone numbers, and work information for our suspects. I scanned the list.

"Did I forget anything?" Natalie asked.

"Nope, this looks good. Thank you. We'll start checking them out today. In the meantime, I think Malcolm and I will take a look in the library again." I stuck the sheet in my bag.

"Would you like some tea?" Natalie asked us.

"I would," I said.

"Sure," Sean added.

I headed down the hall, Sean trailing along behind me.

When we got to Betty's bedroom, I flipped on the light and gasped. The floor was badly charred, but there was an irregular unburned shape in the middle of the scorched area. I went cold when I realized that must have been where my body had lain. I'd been too out of it to notice the damage last night. The blood drained from my face.

"Allie?" Sean touched my arm lightly. "Are you all right?"

The sight of the burned floor paralyzed me. It was easier to pretend I hadn't been so badly injured when I didn't have to see the evidence of what happened.

Suddenly, the lingering smell of fire magic and burned wood and the scorched outline of a body catapulted me back in time to another house, where two similar body-shaped burns, one larger, one smaller, were plainly visible, as was the fact they'd been holding on to each other and died where they'd fallen. A terrified eight-year-old girl stood over the ash on the floor, shaking and crying, next to an old man with cruel eyes.

"The floor will have to be replaced." My voice sounded strange, distant, like someone else was talking.

Sean's hand wrapped around my arm. "Hey."

I pulled away. When I looked at him, I knew my eyes showed the darkness in my head. "What are you remembering?" he asked me softly.

"Nightmares." I didn't want to talk about it. I turned away from him and touched Malcolm's earring. "*Release*."

Malcolm appeared a few feet in front of me. This time, he didn't yell, and I didn't stumble backward from the force of his aura. We must be getting better at this.

He looked at me, clearly relieved. "Alice, I am so glad to see you up and around."

"I'm glad to *be* up and around." My voice still sounded a little off. "We need to check the library for any more spells before we let Natalie back in there."

Malcolm's eyes flicked to Sean and back. "You have a new partner?"

"I'm her *colleague*," Sean said, humor evident in his tone.

"It's temporary," I said. Sean shot me an irritated look that I ignored. "Let's check out the library."

Walking around the burned section of the floor, I opened the library door and flipped on the light switch. With a flick of my fingers, I dropped our perimeter wards. "Can you raise the containment wards again?" I asked Malcolm. Sean stayed outside the library, watching us through the open door.

Malcolm raised them. "What are we looking for?"

"I've asked Natalie to search through Betty's books and papers to see if there's anything that might indicate what was taken from that compartment. I want to make sure there aren't any spells or booby traps in here that she might trigger while she's looking, so we need to be thorough. Betty was tricky."

"Got it. You want to do that side, and I'll check over here?" Malcolm gestured to the wall to our left. I went to the right.

I started at the top of the bookcase. I raised my hand above my head, closed my eyes, and lowered my shields. I passed my hand slowly along the books, reaching out with my senses. I felt extremely low levels of air and fire magic, probably echoes left from the last time Betty had handled the books. When I cleared the top shelf, I moved to the next one, and the next. Across the room, Malcolm was doing the same.

We moved slowly and carefully. I cleared the first bookcase and moved to the second one. About halfway through the third shelf, I felt a spark of strong magic on a particular book. I carefully pulled it from the shelf. It was a very old book, stuck in among a bunch of newer texts on magical theory. Its cover and spine were blank, but inside a spidery handwriting covered the lined pages. A journal, perhaps? I set it aside and continued.

We made our rounds of the library, and then I checked the desk and file cabinet and found nothing while Malcolm double-checked the floor. The library appeared to be clean of spells.

At some point, Natalie had come with tea for Sean. When I finished with the desk, he was drinking from a large mug and sitting in the hard-backed chair in Betty's bedroom.

I swayed on my feet, shaky from having my shields down and senses wide open for so long. Sean watched me as I wiped my forehead with the back of my hand and took the journal to the love seat.

On the first page, Betty had written her full name: *Elizabeth Ann Finchley Eppright Morrison*. Below that was an incantation. I had no idea what it would trigger and obviously did not read it aloud.

I flipped through the pages. It looked like this was part of Betty's spell book, but all of the spells it contained were for her air magic. It looked like she kept her fire and blood magic spells recorded separately. I hadn't seen any other spell books. None of the other books in the library carried as much residual energy as this one, and even it was fairly light. I wondered if that meant that Betty had been focusing on her fire and blood magic before she died. Were the other spell books what had been taken from the compartment? Or were they the books that were missing from the bottom shelf, and the item from the compartment something else entirely?

I told Malcolm what I'd found, and my theories about the rest of Betty's spells. We looked back through all the books, but nothing we saw looked or felt like another spell book.

"I bet someone took them," Malcolm said, echoing my thoughts, when we'd come up empty from our second search of the library. "They were probably on that bottom shelf."

"Still no idea what was in that compartment." I collapsed back onto the loveseat to catch my breath. "We need a name for it so we don't have to keep saying 'whatever was in that compartment.'"

"We could call it the MacGuffin," Malcolm suggested.

"The what?"

"You know, the MacGuffin. That's what Hitchcock called the mystery objects in his movies that the characters were always after, like the microfilm James Mason was smuggling in *North by Northwest*."

I stared at him. "Okay. Fine. It's the MacGuffin."

"Excellent." Malcolm was pleased. Sean regarded us with his eyebrows raised, clearly amused.

Natalie appeared, holding a mug of tea. "Is it safe to come in?"

"Yes," I said.

Tentatively, Natalie stepped over the threshold and frowned. "I felt something."

"A containment ward, in case we triggered a spell in here, but everything seems neutralized," Malcolm told her.

"Oh. Good." Natalie handed me the tea and I took it gratefully. The hot liquid helped settle my stomach. "So I should look through the desk and the file cabinet?"

"Yes. It looks like there are a lot of papers in both." I held up the book I'd found. "We found one of your grandmother's spell books, but the other ones are missing. They might have been taken from the bottom shelf. We're not sure, but we need to try and find out what the MacGuffin is."

"The what?"

I made a face at Malcolm. "You explain it." I heaved myself up off the love seat and left the library, moving into the master bedroom to stand next to Sean while Malcolm explained the esoteric reference to Natalie. She was either fascinated by Malcolm's film history knowledge or doing a good job of feigning interest.

I didn't want to stay in Betty's bedroom with the burns on the floor. "Whoever was in here, we don't want them to be able to get back in this room. Malcolm, can you set up wards on the library that allow us and Natalie in and out and no one else?"

"Sure."

I turned on my heel and left the master bedroom with Sean in my wake.

When I got to the living room, I pulled the paper Natalie had given me out of my bag and looked at it. I was relieved my hands were steady. The flashback to my parents' murder had unnerved me. I needed to focus on looking for the person who had gotten into Natalie's house and taken the books and the MacGuffin from the library. There was no time for the horrors of the past to be sneaking up on me.

Sean stepped up next to me. "What's the plan?"

"I need to get within touching distance of these people in order to sense who has magic. I should be able to recognize their magical signature based on the wards that were set in the library if I can get skin contact with them for a few seconds."

Sean read the list over my shoulder. I started to bristle, then reminded myself to relax. He was a professional colleague with valuable advice.

"Well, this guy is an insurance agent." He pointed at Peter's name and info. "They meet with people all day long. Kathy is a real estate agent. Aren't we in the market for a new house?" He grinned at me, and I smiled.

Maybe this "colleague" thing wasn't so bad after all.

Elise and Deborah would be a little trickier. They were both housewives, and Elise had already met me. I might need a disguise for that one. I could either try to catch them at home or follow them and try to bump into them while they were running errands.

"Who do we want first?" Sean asked.

I considered. "Well, the insurance agent should be easy enough to get in to see. How about we call up for an appointment?" I pulled out my phone and called his office.

Once I got past the automated phone system, a cheerful secretary came on the line. "Eppright Insurance. This is Mandy."

"Hello. My name is Audrey," I told her, using one of my aliases. "My fiancé and I recently moved to the city, and we're looking for a local insurance agent for our home and cars. We wondered if Mr. Eppright might be available to meet with us?"

"Of course!" I heard computer keys clicking in the background. "When are you available?"

"We're free this afternoon, unless that's too soon."

"I have a two o'clock available."

I checked my watch. It was almost one. Plenty of time. "We can make it."

I gave her my fake name—Audrey Talbot—and a posh address in one of the city's newer gated communities. When she asked, I told her my fiancé's name was Sean and managed to say it without coughing. Much.

"We'll see you soon!" the receptionist chirped. We disconnected.

Sean grinned again. "Promoted from temporary colleague to fiancé in less than a day," he teased. "I must be doing something right."

"You definitely do *something* right. Keep up the good work, and I might be able to talk the boss into offering you a better position. With benefits."

A gold sheen rolled over Sean's eyes. "Tell the boss I am committed to the quality of my work, and I look forward to proving it in any *position* she wants me in."

A wave of heat settled low in my belly. I made a little sound and shuffled my feet.

Sean growled low in his throat and nuzzled the back of my neck. "You smell like sex," he whispered, lips against my skin.

I shivered and stepped away from him. Sean had that distinctly male self-satisfied look that made me simultaneously want to punch him and pull him down to the floor.

Fortunately, Natalie came walking into the room to save me from my hormones. "Malcolm's finishing up the wards. There's a lot of stuff in the desk and cabinet. What should I be looking for?"

I cleared my throat and avoided Sean's fiery gaze. "Hard to say. We don't know what was in the compartment, but your grandmother's fire and blood magic spell books seems to be missing too. So anything that refers to fire or blood magic, an object of power, or really, anything that just seems weird to you."

"This all seems pretty weird to me." She thought about it for a moment, then added, "But way less weird than it would have seemed two days ago."

I laughed at that. "I bet."

Natalie smiled. "You want some more tea?"

"We're going to be heading out to go see your uncle. What do you think of him?"

"We're not very close." Natalie leaned against the doorway. "As I said, he was my grandmother's only child from her first marriage, and I don't think he ever felt entirely comfortable around my mom or my aunts because he was nine or ten when his dad died and my grandmother remarried and his stepsisters were all so much younger. I always got the impression that he felt like a fifth wheel. My mom used to tell me that after he moved out to go to college, he didn't really come around that often."

A quick online search revealed that Eppright had no social media presence, but he'd been in the newspaper a year ago. I studied the picture. Peter Eppright appeared to be in his late fifties. He was posing with two other local businessmen, all wearing tuxedos and toasting champagne glasses.

I used my phone to pull up the location of Eppright's office, which was partway across town. It would probably take us close to a half hour to get there. "We'd better leave soon." I headed back toward the library.

When I got to Betty's bedroom, Malcolm was standing inside the library, finishing the wards. I marveled at their beauty as he wove the spells together to form a perimeter around the entire room. No rookie mistakes with Malcolm. Inexperienced and poorly trained mages often warded around doorways and windows, since those were obvious points of ingress, but walls, floors, and ceilings could be broken through, which is why *good* wards run around the perimeter of the room, top and bottom, blocking all four walls, floor, and ceiling.

I recognized my own magic signature in the wards, along with Malcolm's and Natalie's, which granted us free passage. It looked like they were set to incapacitate any trespassers. I thought about upping the ante but wondered if there was much point. Betty had tried to protect the library's contents with wards so deadly, they'd nearly taken me out months after her death, but it hadn't been enough; the MacGuffin and the books were gone, taken by one of the two people Betty thought she could trust. Malcolm's wards would knock out anyone who tried to get into the library. At this point, doing more seemed like closing the proverbial barn door long after the horses were gone.

Malcolm finished his work. "What do you think?" he asked, gesturing with both hands at the room.

"Looks damn good." I stepped over the threshold. "I had a thought. Can you add to the containment spell and make this a 'safe' room for Natalie?"

Malcolm frowned. "What are you thinking?"

"Here's what I want. If Natalie's magic breaks free of her binding spells, I'm wondering if we can set a containment spell so she could come in here. The spell would confine her magic and keep her from either destroying the house or attracting unwanted attention, and then drain her magic into the wards."

Malcolm was thinking. "So long as she doesn't touch the wards and accidentally null them, it will work. I can do it. It's going to take some time, though."

"Sean and I are going to check out Peter Eppright and see if he's our mage. Why don't I leave you here to work on the spells and we'll be back?"

Malcolm looked surprised and then nervous. I realized we hadn't parted company since he'd popped into my office two days ago. "You can sense me wherever I am, right?" I asked.

He nodded slowly. "You're like a beacon, but then again, I've never been very far from you."

"I know, but distance shouldn't matter. I speak from experience on this one. We could be in different states and you'd still be able to find me without too much trouble."

Malcolm looked a little less anxious. "Okay. No problem. We have to get used to this sometime." He sounded like he was talking to himself more than me. "Go on and go. I'll work on these wards while you're gone."

"Okay. Back soon."

I stepped out of the library and led Sean back down the hall to the living room, where Natalie sat on the couch with a cat in her lap. I told her Malcolm was staying to work on the library wards.

"Should I go back there and keep him company?"

I shook my head. "He's going to be focused for a while. He might come back in here when he's done, though. Hopefully he doesn't scare you too badly when he does."

Natalie laughed. "I'll have to remember he's here so I don't do anything embarrassing."

I grabbed my bag and headed out with Sean. I went to my trunk, opened it, and dug around in the large duffel I keep back there as an emergency disguise kit. I swapped out my crystal jewelry for a nice pair of gold hoop earrings. From inside a zippered pouch, I pulled out a sparkly ring and slipped it onto my left hand.

Sean looked at the ring. "You keep a spare engagement ring in your trunk?"

"It's just cubic zirconia. I had to investigate a bridal shop a few months ago." I closed the trunk and we got in my car.

I followed the GPS instructions across the city to Eppright Insurance and parked in front of the next building over.

"We keep the story simple," I said as we walked toward his office. "Just got engaged a month ago and moved to the city from Los Angeles. I'll do the emergency phone call ruse if he gets too pushy."

"Sounds like a plan." Sean opened the door and we stepped inside Eppright Insurance.

Chapter 13

A young brunette receptionist with a name tag identifying her as Mandy sat behind a large L-shaped desk right beside the door. A man and a woman in business casual chatted near the door of an open office. No one else waited in the lobby, but I could hear voices down the hall.

"Hi, can I help you?" Mandy asked.

"I'm Audrey Talbot," I said. "We have a two o'clock appointment?"

"Of course!" Mandy grabbed a clipboard and some forms and handed them to me with a smile. "Have a seat in the lobby and fill these out so Mr. Eppright has a better idea of your needs, and he'll call you in a few minutes."

I took the clipboard and went to sit in the small lobby. Sean got two cups of water from the cooler and came to sit next to me as I tapped the pen and looked over the questionnaire.

"Seems pretty standard," Sean said, glancing at the paperwork.

I started filling out our fake contact information, then moved on to the more detailed questions. As I was reaching the end of the questionnaire, a man's deep voice said, "Sean? Audrey?"

We looked up. Peter Eppright wore a button-up shirt, slacks, and designer shoes. He glanced at me, then focused his attention on Sean, beaming and holding out his hand. At another time, being dismissed might have annoyed me, but in this scenario, having Eppright's attention on Sean would work in my favor. While he was busy schmoozing with my fake fiancé, I would be taking the measure of his magic.

He shook Sean's hand first, then turned to me, almost as an afterthought.

I lowered my shields, smiled brightly, and reached out. His handshake was strong. A frisson of familiar magic trickled over my hand: air and fire, but only a trace. I drew on it gently. Eppright's smile faltered, as if he'd sensed something, but when I withdrew and raised my shields, it was back up to full strength. The entire exchange took about three seconds.

"Please follow me," Eppright said, gesturing at the hallway. Sean and I fell in step behind him as he led us past cubicles and offices to the end of the hall and a large corner office. "Have a seat." We settled into the guest chairs while he sat behind his desk.

I wanted to parse what I'd sensed about Peter Eppright's magic, but first I had a part to play. "Thanks so much for seeing us today," I said to Natalie's uncle, handing over our clipboard. "We didn't get quite all the way through."

"No problem, no problem," Eppright said, waving it away as unimportant. "It's just to give me an idea of what we might able to do for you." He looked over the questionnaire, and I took the opportunity to think about what I'd felt.

There was no doubt he was Betty's son. His magic felt very similar to hers, but was it the *same* magical signature from the library wards and the spell on the secret compartment? Perhaps, but he had so little magical energy, it was practically nonexistent. The signature in the wards felt strong. Still, I wasn't ready to dismiss Eppright as a suspect quite yet.

Eppright finished reading through the questionnaire. He must have liked what he saw, because he leaned forward in his chair. "I can see you are building a wonderful life together," he said, looking at my ring and then back at Sean. "And you need to protect everything you've both worked so hard for. I'm sure I can set you up with the best policies so you can sleep well at night knowing you're safe."

"We're just getting moved in," Sean lied with a smile so charming that even Eppright seemed to fall under its spell. "We don't have a whole lot of time here today because we have to be at another appointment by three o'clock, but we wanted to meet you and see if this was the right agency to handle our insurance needs."

Eppright's eyes widened. We'd dangled a tantalizing prize in front of him to get us in the door, and he had no intention of letting us walk out without signing on the dotted line.

Sure enough, Eppright quickly reached into his desk and started pulling out forms. "Well, we can certainly start by discussing home coverage and make a follow-up appointment for a complete review."

Sean leaned back comfortably and propped one ankle on his knee, fingers laced over his flat stomach. Eppright sucked in his gut and I hid my smile behind my water cup.

"I'm sure you understand this is not the kind of decision a man in my position is going to make in a half hour," Sean said to Eppright, still with that easygoing smile. "Our assets are extensive. We met with Rick Marshall yesterday."

I didn't know who that was, but Eppright's face went grim at the name.

"I have to be honest with you, though; I wasn't all that impressed with him," Sean added. The insurance agent relaxed. "My friends in town speak highly of you, Peter, and I'd like to think I'm a good judge of character."

"What business are you in, Sean?" Eppright asked.

"Risk management," Sean replied without missing a beat. "So, as you might imagine, I'm a cautious man. After all, there's nothing more important than protecting what's mine." He gave my hand an affectionate pat. He noticed my eyes narrow minutely, and the corners of his mouth twitched. "Tell me about your services," Sean urged.

Eppright launched into a lengthy recitation of the various types of products offered by his company. My eyes glazed over almost immediately, but Sean looked engrossed, asking questions and making notes on his fancy phone. While Eppright was intently focused on selling Sean on his company, I eased my shields open and focused on Natalie's uncle.

His air and fire magic were nearly identical to the magical signature in the library wards at Natalie's house, but something about it felt off. It *wasn't* exactly the same, I decided. It was a subtle difference, like having more versus less cinnamon in a recipe. Whoever the unknown mage was, it was someone closely related to Eppright, but it wasn't him.

I raised my shields. I didn't realize I sighed in relief until I noticed Eppright and Sean were looking at me. Sean's eyebrows were raised.

"Sorry," I murmured, rubbing my forehead. "I've suddenly got the *worst* headache."

"Oh, babe," Sean said, and the way he said it made me feel warm all the way down to my toes. "I'm sorry," he said to Eppright. "She's not feeling well. Can we continue this conversation another day? I need to take care of my fiancée."

Eppright looked disappointed but forced a smile. "Of course. I hope you feel better soon."

"Thank you," I said.

We got up to leave, but Eppright turned to his computer, clicking quickly. "I have a few appointments open tomorrow and Monday," he told Sean. "What time would be convenient for you to come back?"

Sean glanced at me. I tried to telegraph to him with my eyes that Eppright was not our guy. He gave me a nearly imperceptible nod. "We are booked solid until next week," he told Eppright. "But we have next Thursday afternoon open."

Eppright clicked keys. "Thursday at one, then?"

"Absolutely." Sean pretended to note the appointment in his phone.

"I hope I can count on you not to make any final decisions until we get a chance to really talk," Eppright said with an amiable smile and reached out for a handshake.

Sean shook his hand and I followed suit. The mage who'd been in Natalie's house had been strong. With my shields up, I felt no magic from Eppright at all. We could cross him off our list of suspects.

Eppright led us back down the hall to the lobby. I feigned my headache until we were out the front door.

Once we were inside the car, Sean said, "No joy?"

I explained what I'd felt from Eppright. "So it's going to be someone close to him, but it's not him," Sean said.

"Pretty much." I turned the key in the ignition.

"Well, we couldn't expect it to be the first person on the list," Sean said with far too much cheer. "That would have been too easy. At least I only had to sit through about ten minutes of sales pitch before you got us out of there."

I winced. "Sorry about that."

He grinned. "It's okay. I'll let you make it up to me at some point." His eyes glinted and my cheeks got hot. "It drives me crazy when you blush," he said and leaned over to kiss me. I lost track of time for a bit.

When we came up for air, I was out of breath. "You're pretty good at this undercover stuff," I told him. "Who was that guy you baited him with?"

"Huh? Oh, Rick Marshall." Sean shrugged. "He owns one of the big insurance agencies in town. We talked to them about insurance back when Ron and I started our company. So who do we want next?"

I pulled out Natalie's list. "How about Kathy the real estate agent? Fancy a look at a nice three-bedroom, two-bath in a good school district?" I typed Kathy's name into Google.

"Met you two days ago, and now we're engaged and house-hunting. My mama warned me about women like you," Sean teased.

I snorted. "Please. Your mama didn't know there *were* women like me out there, or she'd have never let you out of the...." My voice drifted off and I stared at my phone.

"What?" Sean asked.

I held up my phone so he could see it, and he whistled. "We're gonna need a change of clothes," he said. "And we need to switch cars."

* * *

The type of homes Kathy Adams sold were not the kind I would ever be in the market for. All of the houses listed on her website were valued at two million dollars and up.

Sean and I looked over the listings and chose a lovely mansion in a gated community—three stories, six bedrooms, five and a half bathrooms, listed for almost three million dollars. Lower-end, by Kathy's standards, but it looked like it had been listed for a while, and that probably meant she'd jump at the chance to get it sold.

I called Kathy's office and got put through to her assistant. I introduced myself as Audrey Keller and told her my fiancé and I were very interested in the house but we'd need to see it soon, preferably today. The assistant perked right up, and in a moment I was speaking to Kathy herself.

"I am so glad to hear you're interested in the Cherry Tree Lane property," Kathy told me. "My afternoon is pretty packed—"

"I know this is late notice, but my fiancé and I are taking the jet back to LA tonight—"

"—but I've just had a cancellation at four thirty," she said quickly. "Will that work for you?"

I checked the time. It would be tight, but we could make it. "Yes. Shall we meet you at the house?"

"Absolutely! I will see you then!"

Kathy hung up. I threw the car into reverse. "Are we closer to your house or mine?"

"Yours," Sean said. "Let's roll."

I broke every speed limit on the way to my house. When we arrived, I whipped into my driveway, parked, and dashed to the front door. I got the wards down and the door open in record time, then sprinted up the stairs. I went to my closet, grabbed my Armani suit and my Louboutin heels and handbag, and went to the bathroom. I stripped, refreshed my makeup, put on red lipstick, dabbed on some perfume, and changed my hairstyle from a french braid to a french twist. I swapped out my jewelry for real diamond earrings, then put on the suit and stepped into the heels.

I glanced in the mirror. The suit was dark blue pinstripe, and I wore it with a scoop-neck off-white silk top. Not bad for a ten-minute change. I blotted my lipstick and headed out.

Sean was waiting by the front door. When I appeared on the stairs, he looked positively gobsmacked. I grinned and headed down the steps, one hand on the railing for balance in the four-inch heels.

When I got to the bottom, I struck a pose. "Do I clean up good?"

"You look beautiful." I liked the way he looked at me when he said it.

I headed for the door, keys in hand. "Should we pick up your car next, or head to your place?"

"Let's get the car. It's on the way to my house. You want to ride with me to my place, or drive separately?"

"I'll ride with you." I locked up, raised the wards, and we were off to Natalie's.

At Natalie's house, we moved our stuff to Sean's car and took off. As he drove, I transferred my wallet and a few key items from the messenger bag to the handbag. It appeared Sean lived near Hawthorne's in The Heights.

By the time Sean parked in his driveway, my handbag was full and the messenger bag was on the floor in the backseat. As we got out, I studied the house.

It was two stories and all brick, with a three-car garage and a fenced backyard. There was a large black truck in the garage, and the third spot held a pair of jet skis on a trailer. I pictured him bare-chested riding a jet ski and nearly tripped over my own feet.

Inside, the house had a definite bachelor-pad feel. I smiled at the framed vintage concert posters on the walls.

"Do you want something to drink?" Sean asked.

"No, I'm good."

"I'll go change, then. Feel free to look around." Sean disappeared, leaving me in the kitchen.

I looked over his posters and music memorabilia while I waited. When I moved to the living room, I found a gigantic television and a state-of-the-art home theater system. I surprised myself by imagining us sitting on the couch watching a movie or playing video games.

The family pictures in the living room featured an older couple who were probably Sean's parents, and several other families I took to be Sean's siblings and their kids. On the mantelpiece I found a family photo. It looked like it had been taken in a park on a sunny day. Sean was standing with his parents while his siblings and their families flanked them. Everyone was smiling.

I wondered what it would be like to come from a big, happy family. I'd never had any brothers or sisters; my mother had told me once, not long before she died, that she'd always wanted at least three children but feared losing them to her father as she had lost me. I looked at the picture of Sean's family and felt a little stab of jealousy.

I heard footsteps behind me, turned, and stared.

Nothing could have prepared me for the sight of Sean in a silver-blue suit. I didn't know much about men's suits, but it looked expensive and perfectly tailored. My brain literally went blank.

Sean stood in the middle of the living room, one hand in his pocket, and grinned at me. Damn that man for knowing exactly how good he looked.

Finally, I cleared my throat and got my legs moving to walk over to him. "Well, you look *okay*." I brushed some imaginary lint off his lapel.

Sean caught my hand and raised my fingers to his lips. "You've got to stop looking at me like that." He pulled me toward the door to the garage. "Let's go, before I say to hell with this real estate agent and ruin our fancy clothes."

We got back in the Mercedes. Sean put the Cherry Tree Lane address into the car's GPS and we took off. I noticed him glancing at my legs as he drove and smiled to myself.

As we headed toward the east side, Sean seemed to be thinking hard about something. Finally, he asked, "How long have you been in the city?"

"About five years."

"Have you been a private investigator since you got here?"

"I worked for another MPI for a year and a half before I got my license. I've been self-employed ever since."

"What kind of work do you usually do?"

"A little of everything: magic tracing, spellwork and wards, summonings and banishments, tracking of magical objects. I also do mundane work like missing persons, skip traces, insurance fraud, background checks, and cheating spouse/divorce stuff. That's my least favorite type of case, but sometimes it's just about paying the bills."

"You work with anybody?"

"Just Malcolm. Other than that, nobody." I shrugged. "I like working for myself. It keeps things simple."

"I can see that." A long pause. Then: "I'm trying to figure out what I can ask about, and what I can't."

"Anything about the last couple of years here in the city, you can ask, and I'll probably answer. Nothing from before."

"Okay." Sean navigated through some heavy traffic before we got on the highway to head east out of the city. "This one might be off-limits, but can I assume the reason you can't go to a hospital is connected to whatever happened before you arrived in the city?"

I shifted uncomfortably in my seat. I'd asked questions of Sean on the way to Natalie's house and he'd answered them, but I couldn't reciprocate. He could never know anything about my life before I'd arrived in the city, and there were some things I would not—could not—discuss. It wasn't fair, but that was how it had to be. My life depended on it.

I decided on part of the truth. "There are some anomalies in my magic that I need to keep secret. I can't leave my blood anywhere, and I can't go to a hospital. I need to stay clear of SPEMA and anyone from a cabal, and there's not much more I can say about it." I paused, then added softly, "I'm sorry."

"It's okay." Sean squeezed my knee and his touch relaxed me. "I understand. I won't push you. If I ask something you don't want to answer, just tell me."

"Thank you."

We made the rest of the drive in silence. We turned onto Cherry Tree Lane at four twenty-five and found the house with no trouble. Sean parked in the driveway behind a white Land Rover. "Are you ready for this?" he asked.

"Definitely." We got out of the car and headed up the walk to the front door.

The door opened before we even got to the porch. "Welcome!" Kathy Adams called out to us. Her practiced eye looked us over, saw the shiny new Mercedes, and decided we looked the part. Her smile was even more radiant than Eppright's had been, and that was saying something. She ushered us inside and closed the door.

I could see the family resemblance to Natalie, though Kathy's perfectly coiffed auburn hair framed a narrow, almost hawk-like face, and her green eyes glinted with cool calculation. A hint of crow's-feet put her in her midforties. Her eager smile grew wider as she reached out to shake Sean's hand.

I dropped my shields and focused my senses as she turned that big, fake smile to me, hand outstretched. The instant our hands touched, I felt a tiny flare of very low-level air magic and no fire magic at all.

A sudden wave of dizziness made me stagger and almost fall. With my magic and energy still depleted, focusing my senses so intently was taking its toll.

Sean caught me by the arm. "Audrey! Are you all right?" It took me a moment to realize he was calling me by my alias.

I got my shields in place. Everything was a little out of focus and my head pounded, but I gave Kathy my best smile and stepped away from Sean. "I tripped. Such a klutz."

Kathy frowned and looked down at the spanish tile in the foyer, obviously trying to figure out what I could have possibly tripped on.

"New shoes," I told her, sticking my right foot out to show off my Louboutins, which she dutifully admired. "We're Sean and Audrey. What a cute little house!" I said, moving past her and looking around.

Kathy blinked at my "cute little house" comment but was immediately back on her game. "It may be small," she said agreeably, "but the space is amazingly well-designed. It's an open plan, so it feels like it's twice as big." And she was off, leading us farther into the house, going on about natural light and vaulted ceilings and other realtor-type talk.

Sean hung back. "You okay?"

"I'm good," I told him. "Just feeling a little run-down." He squeezed my hand and we hurried to catch up with Kathy.

As the realtor walked us around the house, I let Sean take the lead as he'd done with Eppright, engaging her in conversation and asking questions while I focused on sensing her magic.

Like Eppright, Kathy was not an exact match to the magical signature in the library wards. Hers was similar, but not as close of a match as her half brother's. We were in the right ballpark but still not the right person.

Once I realized Kathy wasn't our suspect, it was time to bring an end to our tour. My knees were getting wobbly.

As we walked into the master suite, which was as big as the entire top floor of my house and overlooked the pool and guest house, Kathy beamed. "Well? What do you think?" she asked us, gesturing at the enormous bedroom.

"It's lovely." I gave her a sad smile.

Kathy's smile faded. "What's wrong?" she asked anxiously.

"It's just too small for us," I said, shaking my head and wishing I could sit down. "I really thought, with the open floor plan, it would feel bigger, but...."

Sean put his arm around my waist to hold me up. At first, I resisted; it felt possessive, and I didn't want him to think I was relying on him, but I was cold and light-headed. I reluctantly leaned against him and he squeezed me gently.

"We did see some other larger homes on your website. I actually liked the one on Pinehurst quite a bit better than this one," Sean told her.

Kathy perked up again and led us back to the front door. "Oh, yes! That house is *lovely*." And listed for a million more than this one was. "Would you like to see it? I can arrange a walk-through for tomorrow."

"We'll be in Los Angeles for a couple of days." Sean pulled me tighter against his side as I swayed. "If you're available when we get back, we would definitely like to see it."

Sean took Kathy's card. She encouraged us to call her when we returned to the city. We promised we would, shook her hand again, and made our escape.

Sean helped me into the passenger side of his car. I leaned my head back and closed my eyes.

Sean got in, and I felt him throw his suit jacket into the backseat. "Are you all right?"

It was a moment before I could respond. "Yes." My voice sounded wispy.

Sean sighed. "Why do I bother to ask?" He touched my hand. "You're cold again."

I took a deep breath. "I'm just tired." He put the car in gear, pulled through the circular driveway, and accelerated away down Cherry Tree Lane. "It took a lot of energy to check the library this morning, and I've been running on fumes ever since. I just need to rest for a bit."

"It seems like you were asking too much of yourself to do all this today." Sean cleared his throat. "Not that I would have told you that, of course."

I snorted.

Sean drove in silence. Once we were on the highway, he asked, "Where are we headed?"

I thought about that, then sighed. "We need to check in with Malcolm and Natalie. I wish I felt up to tracking down Deborah and/or Elise today, but I don't."

"So swing by Natalie's house and pick up the ghost, then what?"

"After that, I need to go home. I'm just too worn out to think about doing anything else today." The rhythm of the tires on the road made me sleepy, and I let myself drift.

"What about tomorrow?" Sean asked suddenly.

"What about it?" I murmured, half dozing.

"I could take another personal day."

I opened my eyes and looked at him as he drove. It was rush hour, but we were driving back toward the city and the traffic wouldn't be bad until we got into town. The outbound lanes were bumper-to-bumper with folks headed home at the end of the day. "I appreciate it, but I'll be fine, and I'm sure you need to get back to work. I did enjoy having you along today. It's been fun, and that's not something I get to say very often during an investigation."

Despite my earlier misgivings, I *had* liked working with Sean. We'd fallen into an easy, comfortable partnership. He was a natural at undercover work, and I had no doubt having him with me today had made it easier to get access to both Peter Eppright and Kathy Adams. The thought of tracking down Elise and Deborah on my own tomorrow suddenly seemed unappealing.

Sean was talking. I turned my attention back to him. "I've got a lot of PT built up. Hell, now that I think about it, I haven't taken a vacation in over a year. Today was the most fun I've had in a long time. I'd much rather do undercover work with you than coordinate bodyguards for a client, or supervise the installation of a camera system at a law office, which is what I had on the schedule for tomorrow. Someone else can do that shit. I want to put on a disguise and help you find a secret mage and a MacGuffin."

I had to laugh, despite the turmoil in my head. "I'm still not clear on what a MacGuffin is exactly, but it seemed to make Malcolm's day to let him call it that, so I guess we're sticking with it. Seems like the least I can do after...after yesterday." And just like that, the mood went from light to serious.

Sean squeezed my knee. "Why don't we pick up Malcolm and go from there? We don't have to decide anything right this minute."

I sighed, leaned my head back, and closed my eyes again. "Okay."

For five years, I'd feared if I let myself depend on someone else in any way, I would lose the edge that kept me alive long enough to escape the cabal. After spending the past few days with Malcolm and Sean, however, I was starting to think that maybe having colleagues— or whatever Sean and I might be to each other—could be a strength rather than a weakness.

Or maybe I was just tired of being so afraid all the time. The problem was, after a lifetime of fearing everything and everyone around me, I wasn't sure I knew any other way to be.

CHAPTER 14

I sent Natalie a text that we were on our way, and Sean drove us to my client's house while I dozed in the passenger seat. When we arrived, I was able to get out of the car and walk up to her door on my own power.

Before we could knock, Natalie opened the door. "Come on in. Malcolm's in the living room. Would you guys like anything to eat or drink?"

"No, thank you," I said as we stepped inside. "Sorry it took longer than I thought to get here."

"It's okay, no problem." Natalie waved her hand and took us to the living room.

Malcolm looked up from where he was studying a chess board with a game in progress. He looked at me closely and frowned. "Hey, you guys look nice. What did you find out?"

"Neither of the people we talked to are who we're looking for, but the mage is definitely in the family. Both Peter and Kathy's magic felt very similar. It must be either Deborah or Elise. Did you get those spells set up in the library?"

"Yep. You want to see?"

"Definitely."

We all went back toward Betty's bedroom. This time I was more prepared for the sight and smell of the burned floor and was able to ignore it to focus on the library wards.

"Wow. Beautiful work," I breathed, looking at the spellwork. I could see the spells that would contain Natalie's magic, as well as the spells that would drain it into the perimeter wards. "Well done, Malcolm."

"Thanks. It took a little while, but I'm pretty happy with the result."

"Did you tell her what the spells do, and that she needs to avoid touching the walls so she doesn't null the wards?" I sidled away from the group to sit on the edge of the bed.

"Yes, he did," Natalie said. "And I really appreciate that you've done this for me. Knowing I have a 'safe room' to go to if I lose control of my magic makes me feel so much better."

Malcolm and Sean were watching me. "Alice, you look exhausted," the ghost stated.

"I'm fine," I said, at the same moment Sean said, "She's barely able to walk."

I glared at Sean. "*She's* right here, and perfectly capable of speaking for herself."

Malcolm looked unhappy. He floated over to me. "You should have asked me to share some energy with you before you left," he told me, holding out his arm. "Here."

"No."

Malcolm blinked at me. "What?"

"I'm not going to keep draining you every time I'm depleted," I told him flatly. "You're not a battery, Malcolm."

"That's not—"

I didn't want to have this argument in front of Sean and Natalie. "Malcolm, we can talk about this later. I appreciate the offer, but no."

Natalie's expression was dark. "You're still hurt from yesterday." She bit her lip. "I'm dangerous."

"No." I started to get up.

She held up her hands to stop me. "Yes. I'm dangerous, because I don't know how to control my magic. I wish my grandmother was here to explain why she did this to me, but I guess it doesn't matter now. I've decided I want training."

"Are you sure?" I asked.

"Yes. I've been talking to Malcolm, and he told me about the things you can use fire and air magic to do. Plus, I was so scared when my magic got loose yesterday. I need to be able to control it so I'm not afraid of that happening again. I'm done being afraid."

"Okay. It may take a little while, but I'll start looking for a teacher." I turned to Malcolm. "Did you test the containment spell?"

"Not yet."

Sean growled quietly. "We're not waiting around for that. You're going home."

I stiffened. "I'll go when I want to go. The containment spell—"

"Does not need to be tested tonight," Malcolm interrupted. "You can bring me back here tomorrow and we'll do it then. Nat's fine in the meantime. Sean's right; you need to rest. You look like roadkill."

I crossed my arms. "You realize you are scoring no points with me with comments like that."

"Totally rude, Mal." Natalie frowned in the ghost's general direction.

"Sorry," Malcolm said to me. "But seriously, you do."

I pushed myself to my feet. "Fine. I'll come by in the morning to drop off Malcolm so he can test the containment spell, if that's okay. When he's done with that, you can start looking through your grandmother's files while I check on Deborah and Elise."

"Thank you, Alice." Suddenly, Natalie launched herself forward to give me a hug. "You've been so awesome."

I patted her awkwardly on the back and extricated myself from her embrace. "No problem. I'll be back in the morning." I glanced at Malcolm.

He groaned. "Earring time, huh?"

"It's the safest thing to do for now."

"Okay," he said, sighing. "See you soon, Nat."

"See you, Mal," she said with a smile.

I touched my earring and invoked the spell. "*Contain.*" Malcolm vanished, and my earring buzzed.

"Does that hurt him?" Natalie asked.

"Not at all," I assured her. "It's kind of like being asleep."

"Okay. Well, I guess I'll hear from you in the morning." Natalie escorted us to the front door.

"I'll text you," I promised, and she closed the door behind us.

As soon as the door clicked shut, I took a step and stumbled.

Sean swung me up into his arms before I could argue. "That's it; we're going home *now*."

"Only because I say we are," I countered, but my retort didn't quite match the shakiness of my voice.

Sean sighed and carried me down the sidewalk to where we were parked at the curb. "Your car or mine?"

When I didn't immediately answer, he brought me over to his Mercedes and sat me on the hood.

I rested my weight carefully on the car and looked up at him. "You can't stay the night with me."

Sean gave me a long-suffering look. "Once again, you're assuming I have ulterior motives. I'm only thinking about getting you home and making sure you have what you need when you get there."

"All I'm going to need is my bed. I'll be asleep the minute my head touches the pillow. I need to recharge."

He hesitated. "I read somewhere that there's another, faster way to regenerate magical energy." He tilted my chin up and looked into my eyes. "Is it true?"

"It's true," I admitted.

Sean ran his thumb lightly over my lower lip. "Then why are you sending me home when I could be helping you?"

I opened my mouth to say something sarcastic about his motivations for offering me some sexual healing, but the seriousness in his eyes made me reconsider my response. "Because Malcolm is not a battery and neither are you," I said instead.

"You regenerated your magic with me the first time we were together."

"Yes, I did. That was part of the plan, when I invited you home with me."

He seemed neither surprised nor upset by my admission. "And now?"

"Now the plan's changed."

He absorbed that. "Speaking of plans, what did you decide about tomorrow?"

I tilted my head back, bracing myself with my hands on the hood of the car. Above the trees, the three-quarter moon shone against a darkening sky. Sean's wolf would be feeling restless, no doubt. I wondered where he and his pack went on the full moon, and what he looked like in wolf form. I was suddenly full of questions about him, and it was a strange feeling.

"I'll be ready at eight o'clock," I said finally.

Sean grinned. "Eight o'clock it is. Come on, Sleeping Beauty. Let's get you home." He held out his hand and I took it.

* * *

When Sean knocked on my door at precisely eight a.m. the next morning, he'd opted for a green button-up shirt that brought out the gold flecks in his dark brown eyes, and khakis that fit very, very well. I looked him over appreciatively before my eyes zeroed in on the enormous cup of coffee and bag of donuts in his hands.

"Now you're just buttering me up," I said after I'd inhaled a warm donut and drunk half the coffee in three large gulps. "And rather shamelessly, I might add."

He grinned. "Is it working?"

"Well, it doesn't hurt."

Sean snorted as he backed down my driveway. I snarfed another donut. "Hungry?" he teased.

I hadn't eaten anything since our late breakfast the day before. When I got home, I'd gone straight to bed and slept for eleven hours. "Famished. This coffee is fantastic."

"It's from a little coffee shop near my house," Sean said. "We heading to Natalie's?"

"Yep. We're going to drop Malcolm off, then go track down Natalie's other two aunts." I licked some frosting off my fingers.

"How'd you sleep?"

"Like a log."

"And your magic? Back to normal?"

"Getting there." It would take several days for my magic to regenerate completely on its own, but he didn't need to know that. "You were able to take the day off again without any problems?"

"No problems, though my partner Ron thinks I've been replaced by a pod person, since the 'real' Sean hasn't taken two workdays off in a row in a very long time."

"What's a 'pod person'?"

Sean stopped at a red light. "You're kidding. *Invasion of the Body Snatchers?*"

"Haven't seen it." I chomped into another donut.

Sean widened his eyes in mock horror, then stepped on the gas when the light turned green. "That's a classic. I can see we'll have to have a movie night very soon."

His casual remark caused me to pause with the donut halfway to my mouth. *Movie night.* I'd never had a movie night. For Sean, it was as unremarkable as buying coffee; for me, it would be a completely new experience, one of many I might be facing in the near future. My stomach knotted, and I dropped the half-eaten donut back into the bag.

Sean slowed down to make a turn and glanced at me. "What's wrong?"

"Nothing." How could I possibly explain why the idea of having a movie night caused me anxiety? There wouldn't be any easy way to justify how I'd managed to get to the age of twenty-nine without ever going to someone's house to watch a movie. It was another reminder of how difficult it would be to have any kind of relationship when I had to keep so much of myself hidden.

"Not having second thoughts already, are you?" Sean's voice sounded like he was teasing, but his shoulders looked tense.

"No." I realized my voice sounded like it was made up of second thoughts. I cleared my throat. "No," I repeated, more firmly. I'd made a decision, and I was going ahead with it.

"Okay." Sean took my hand.

I tried to pull away. "Don't—I'm all sticky from the donuts."

He grinned and squeezed tighter. "I don't care."

* * *

We dropped Malcolm off at Natalie's, then Sean and I headed to Deborah Mackey's house. As he drove, I reached into the small duffel bag at my feet and pulled out a baseball cap and a pair of large sunglasses.

Sean glanced at the cap. His mouth turned down.

"I know," I said. "But it's part of the ruse."

Sean's grip tightened on the steering wheel until his knuckles turned white. He didn't say anything. We drove in silence for a while.

Deborah lived on a typical west-side residential street. Sean pulled to the curb diagonally across from her house. According to Natalie's information sheet, Deborah and her husband Lawrence were childless. Their house was quiet. There was a new BMW parked out front.

"What's the plan?" Sean asked.

I dug out a clipboard. "Petition ruse. I'm a volunteer going door-to-door meeting people and collecting signatures."

"Signatures for what?"

"In this case, Prop 87."

Sean growled. "Well, that explains the hat."

I took his hand and squeezed it. If it passed, the proposed law would require vamps, shifters, and other supes to notify the neighborhood when they moved in, and would allow cities to designate certain areas, like around schools and churches, as supe-free zones. It was blatantly racist and horribly unfair. I was suddenly struck by the thought that if Prop 87 became law, Sean would have to reveal his werewolf identity to his neighbors, potentially making him a target of anti-supe hate groups like the one whose hat I was wearing.

"I'm sorry," I told him. "Maybe this isn't the best idea."

"No, it's fine. There are a limited number of ways to meet strangers and shake their hands. It's a good plan." Tension prickled on my skin as his anger disrupted his natural shields, and his emotions bled over to me.

I gave him a minute to deal with his fury while I took out a blank petition sheet and fastened it to the clipboard. I filled in the top with the information about the proposition, the date, and—after a quick Internet search—the state representative for this district.

"It's what they do to *sex offenders*, Allie," Sean snarled.

"I know." I swallowed hard around the lump in my throat. I'd signed a petition opposing Prop 87 and gone to rallies against it. Even though mages weren't included among those who were directly affected by the proposition, there was a good chance they'd be added to the list at some point. Today, shifters, half-demons, and vamps; tomorrow, mages like me.

"We can't go directly to their house; it's in the middle of the block," I said quietly. "We need to start at the corner."

Without a word, Sean eased back onto the street and reparked at the end of the block. I pulled out a small bag of pins and picked out a couple representing other anti-supe groups. I put them on my bag. I didn't ask Sean to put any on, and he didn't offer.

"You can stay in the car," I told him as we got out of the car.

"We're in this together." Sean shut the door hard enough to make me jump.

I slung my bag across my chest and adjusted my jacket. Clipboard in hand, I marched resolutely up to the first house on the block with Sean next to me. I rang the doorbell, plastered a perky smile on my face, and became Audrey Talbot, anti-supe crusader.

Ten minutes later, I was brimming with hidden rage, but I had my first two signatures from the couple who owned that house. They both had very strong opinions on supes, and they absolutely did not want any in their neighborhood. The husband confided they were members of Humans First, a radical "Human rights" organization that advocated creating walled-off reservations for supes and keeping them away from humans.

Sean made a few comments but let me do most of the talking. His jaw was clenched so tightly that I worried it would break.

We walked back to the sidewalk and stood silently, looking at each other. Sean reached out and I took his hand, recognizing his need for warmth and physical contact. The tautness in his shoulders made mine ache.

I drew him to me and kissed him. His body felt like caged violence. "Go back to the car," I told him, my voice ragged. "It's not going to get any better."

Those beautiful brown eyes turned stony. It wasn't in his nature to back away from anything, no matter what it might cost him emotionally. "Let's just do this," he said.

We went to the next house and had much the same experience, except I cut the couple off after a few minutes, telling them we wanted to get to as many houses as we could today. The elderly woman in the third house declined to sign and gave us an earful about the evils of prejudice and racism. I turned and left with tears burning in my eyes.

There was no answer when we knocked at the next house. I steeled myself and headed up the sidewalk toward the Mackeys' home.

Just as we were halfway to their front door, it opened and Peter Eppright, Deborah's half brother, walked out. Behind him in the doorway stood a slim middle-aged woman I recognized from Natalie's photo as Deborah. Neither looked very happy.

Beside me, I heard Sean mutter, "Shit." My sentiments exactly.

Nothing to do but soldier on. I summoned up a big, cheery smile and marched up to the porch. "Peter!"

Eppright looked at me, then at Sean, and recognition dawned. "Sean and...Audrey?" he asked in surprise.

Sean stepped forward to shake Eppright's hand and gave him a manly clap on the shoulder that almost made the older man stagger. "Peter, how are you?"

Deborah looked back and forth between us. "Sean and Audrey came to see me yesterday about some insurance," Eppright said to his half sister.

"What a small world!" I chirped. "Do you live here?"

"It's my sister's house," Eppright told us. "I was just leaving."

"I hope we haven't caught you at a bad time," Sean said.

Deborah stepped out onto the porch. "What do you want?"

I launched into a shortened version of my spiel about Prop 87, pointing to my various pins and waving the clipboard for emphasis. Eppright paused to listen.

"So, I was hoping to get your signature on this petition showing your support for protecting our neighborhoods," I concluded, shoving the clipboard at Deborah.

"Sure," she said hesitantly and took it and the pen from me.

As she was filling in her name and information, I opened my senses and focused on her, trying to sense if she had any magic. Almost none, I determined almost immediately. Like Kathy, she had only a trace of air magic and no fire magic at all. I'd know better after I shook her hand, but I was ready to cross Deborah off the suspect list.

She finished filling in her information and handed the clipboard back. I stuck out my hand. "Thank you so much for helping us today."

After a hesitation, she reached out and shook. A slight tickle of magic, barely enough to register. Definitely part of Betty's family—the magical signature was familiar—but not the person whose signature was in the library's wards.

I gave her a bright smile. "Have a wonderful day."

"You too."

Eppright walked with us down the sidewalk. "Are we still on for that meeting next week?"

"Absolutely." Sean shook Eppright's hand again. "We'll be there."

Eppright climbed into his BMW as we walked over to the next house. Deborah stayed on her porch. I gave them both a cheerful wave and rang the doorbell. Eppright backed out of Deborah's driveway and headed down the street.

The front door opened, and it was a young mother holding a baby on her hip.

"Hi! I'm Audrey with the Human Defense League...."

Out of the corner of my eye, I watched Deborah go inside her house. We went through the motions with the mom, who was joined at the door by two more small children. I could see she was totally frazzled and didn't push her for a signature. I wouldn't have even knocked on her door if we weren't being watched.

When the baby started wailing, Sean and I made our escape and headed back to the car.

When we were inside, I took off the offending baseball cap and pins and stuffed them out of sight into the duffel bag. "That was not ideal."

Sean's laugh was so loud and sudden that it startled me. "Definitely *not* ideal, but I think he bought it."

"I didn't see any indication he suspected us of anything, but we'll have to use a different ruse for Elise."

Sean pulled away from the curb. I put Elise Browning's home address into his car's navigation system and settled back into my seat.

"I take it Deborah's not our mage?" he asked.

"Nope." I told him what I'd sensed.

"That leaves Elise, then."

I grimaced. "Yeah, but I'm having a hard time believing she's a strong mage."

"She's the only sibling left," Sean pointed out. "It *has* to be her, right?"

"I guess," I said doubtfully.

"So what's the plan for Elise, then, if not the petition ruse?"

"Good question. Let's drive by her house and get an idea of what we have to work with."

As Sean drove, I got to work on my disguise. I used bobby pins to secure my hair tightly to my head, then put on a blonde wig. I used my fingers to comb through the wig hair and used the mirror on my sun visor to make sure it looked natural and my own hair wasn't visible. I put on a different pair of sunglasses, a sparkly pair that looked more like something the blonde would wear, and took off my jacket.

"I like you better as a brunette," Sean said, watching the transformation out of the corner of his eye.

"Good."

He laughed.

Elise lived on the northeast side of the city in a fancier area than her sister. I saw the SUV I'd seen at Natalie's house parked in the open garage of a large three-story home, along with a Mercedes and a Land Rover. A sticker on the Land Rover indicated that their children attended a very expensive prep school. Natalie had said that Elise's husband, Ray, owned a construction company. Business must be good for them to afford such a large home, private-school tuition, and three vehicles on a single salary.

Sean drove down the street slowly as I tried to see if there was any obvious way to gain entry to Elise's home. Nothing jumped out at me, and this wasn't the kind of street where we could park and watch the house waiting for her to leave. Nice neighborhoods like this meant people noticed strange cars and unfamiliar people lurking around.

"Lost dog," Sean said suddenly.

"Huh?"

"Lost dog," he repeated. "Our dog got away from us when we were walking it. We're going door-to-door asking if anyone has seen it."

I grinned. "That could actually work." We continued down the street, turned the corner, and parked. I went online and browsed pictures of yellow Labs. I saved several to my phone and decided to call the dog Mal. Sean laughed.

I put on a different ball cap over my blonde hair—this one representing the city's basketball team—and we headed out on foot. By the time we were getting close to Elise's house, I had real tears in my eyes over the plight of our poor lost dog. Sean seemed to be enjoying playing the role of worried dog owner.

We were in the yard next door to Elise's house, showing them the dog pictures, when Natalie's aunt came outside with two little dogs of her own on leashes.

"Elise!" Her neighbor, a pretty young woman named Tracee— "with two *E*'s!"— hollered and waved her over. We were in business.

Elise came over, looking irritated. "Hey, Tracee. What's going on over here?"

Her dogs bounced and barked their heads off at Sean. He stared at them, and I saw a glint of gold in his eyes. The dogs went silent and hunkered to the ground. I coughed to hide my smile.

"These poor folks' dog got away from them," Tracee said. "Show her the pictures."

I sniffled and obediently held up my phone. "His name is Mal. He broke the leash and ran in this direction. I'm so desperate to find him before he gets hit by a car. Have you seen him?" I stuck the phone under her nose.

Meanwhile, I focused my senses on Elise. I was shocked at what I felt.

Nothing. No magic at all.

"I haven't seen your dog." Elise seemed completely unmoved by my sniffling.

"Your dogs are so sweet." I reached down to pet one of them.

Elise grabbed my hand. "Don't—they might bite you."

Even with her touching me, I felt nothing. Elise was not the mage who had been in the library—not even close.

Which left me with exactly *zero* suspects. What the hell?

CHAPTER 15

I backed away from Elise and her dogs. I didn't have to fake looking tragic; my last lead had gone nowhere. "Well, if anybody sees our dog, please call us. My number is on his tag."

Tracee assured me she'd call. Elise didn't say anything; she was too busy trying to keep her little dogs from biting Tracee.

I headed back to the car, Sean beside me. "So?" he asked as we walked.

"It's not her."

Sean frowned. "How is that possible? You said it has to be one of them."

I rubbed my forehead. "It wasn't Peter, Kathy, Deborah, or Elise. All of them have weak or no magical ability. I would have *sworn* it was one of Betty's children. When I touched Peter, Kathy, and Deborah, I can sense that their magic is almost identical to the signature in the wards. It *has* to be one of them, but it isn't!" We got into Sean's car. I pulled off my hat and wig and tossed them into the duffel bag on the floor. "I don't understand this at all."

"Could the mage be one of Natalie's cousins?" Sean started the car.

I shook my head. "The magic was almost identical to Betty's. I'd have bet any amount of money the mage was one of her children. I'm trying to figure out what I'm doing wrong here. It makes no sense. Maybe Natalie found something in Betty's papers." I pulled my phone out and called my client.

"Hey, Alice," she said with far too much cheer, considering how my morning was going.

"Are the wards finished and tested?" I asked. "Have you had a chance to start looking through Betty's files?"

"Malcolm is working on the library wards, so I haven't gone in there yet. We still need to test the containment spell. How are you doing?"

"I struck out," I confessed. "I've contacted your uncle and all of your aunts, and none of them are the mage who was in your library."

A pause. "I thought you said it had to be one of them."

"I thought it did."

Natalie hummed a bit. "What about my grandmother's sister and brother?"

"It's possible," I mused. "You said they live nearby?"

"Yes. Should I text you their addresses?"

"That would be great. We can check them out this afternoon."

"Give me a few minutes to find the information—it's probably in my grandmother's address book."

"Thanks, Natalie."

"No problem!"

We disconnected. I picked up my empty coffee cup and looked at it wistfully.

Sean chuckled and pulled away from the curb. "Where are we going?" I asked.

"I saw a coffee shop a couple of blocks from here. Might as well take a little break while we wait."

It was almost fifteen minutes before Natalie texted me the addresses of her great-aunt Helen and great-uncle Robert. In the meantime, since it was nearing lunchtime, I bought us some much-needed caffeine and sandwiches at the coffee shop. Sean tried to pay, arguing that since he was buying three sandwiches that it should be his treat, but I was insistent. It seemed only fair, since he'd bought breakfast and he'd been doing most of the driving. I added a cherry turnover to the order when I saw Sean eyeballing it in the dessert case.

We settled in to eat at a table on the coffee shop's patio. Sean seemed to have recovered from the unpleasantness of the petition ruse. In between bites, he brought up *Invasion of the Body Snatchers* again and launched into a rather interesting explanation of how many of the science fiction films of the fifties, sixties, and seventies were thinly veiled references to the fear of communism. I ate my lunch and listened to him talk.

Sean Maclin, alpha werewolf and security consultant, was kind of nerdy. I liked it.

When Natalie's text finally came in, along with her apology for the delay, we looked up the addresses. Robert Finchley lived in an assisted-living facility in Springtown, a suburb about an hour's drive away. Helen Matson lived another hour farther away from the city, in a town called Hope.

"Who do you want first?" Sean finished his coffee and the last bite of sandwich number three. I was just finishing my half sandwich and still had most of my fruit salad to go. I was a little in awe of his appetite.

"Might as well start with Robert in Springtown."

Sean took the opportunity to respond to some work e-mails while I finished my food. We threw away our trash and got back in the car. Sean put Finchley's address in his GPS and headed out.

"Do you want me to do some of the driving?" I asked. "I feel bad that you've been chauffeuring me all over the city for the past day."

"I don't mind it. I drive for clients all the time." He paused. "And it's hard for me to ride shotgun."

"I understand." An alpha needed to be in control, and the past few days hadn't been easy on him in that regard. As much as it rankled me to be in the passenger seat, I could live with it for the rest of today. After that, we'd see. I didn't much care for riding shotgun either.

Sean talked more about movies during the drive to Springtown. He was already making plans for several double-feature movie nights.

When Sean finally turned into Pine Ridge Resort Village forty-five minutes later, my jaw dropped. I saw what looked like a nine-hole golf course, tennis courts, multiple pools, a network of shady sidewalks connecting brick townhouses, and dozens of very spry-looking seniors out and about on the grounds as we parked in front of the building marked Office.

"The old guy's not doing too badly here," Sean said as we got out.

"No freaking kidding." We entered the office and approached the reception desk.

"Can I help you?" a young red-haired nurse asked us.

"We'd like to see Robert Finchley," I said.

"Can I see your identification?"

Sean and I both gave her our driver's licenses. The nurse recorded our information, then handed them back, along with two guest badges on lanyards. We put them on.

The nurse checked the computer. "Unit 5B. Go out this door, then turn right. It will be the third building on your left."

We thanked her and headed back outside. "I don't think my parents would go for a place like this," Sean said as we walked. "But if it ends up that one or both of them need to move to a retirement community, this isn't so bad."

I wondered if he was fishing for information about my parents, but his tone seemed casual. "It's pretty far from your standard nursing home, that's for sure," I said.

We traded cheery hellos with several residents on our way to Finchley's townhouse. We found 5B easily, and I rang the doorbell. To my surprise, the door opened almost immediately.

The white-haired gentleman who answered held a cane in one hand, but he looked remarkably energetic for a man of nearly eighty. "The front office called ahead to say I had some visitors." His voice was strong, and his eyes were bright. "I'm Robert. What can I do for you?"

I smiled and held out my hand. "My name is Alice Worth. I'm a private investigator. This is Sean Maclin, my colleague."

It was Finchley's turn to be surprised. "Well, my goodness." He reached out to take my hand and eyed me with interest. "How exciting."

I lowered my shields as our hands touched and felt a flare of air magic. Mid-level, I thought—not weak like Betty's children. Interesting. I felt no fire magic, however, and was quickly sure Robert was not the mystery mage. He *was* a mage, though, and that made me wonder what he might know about the family's magic.

"Why don't you come in?" Finchley said, stepping aside.

Sean and I entered the spotless house. "Can I get you some iced tea?" Finchley asked.

We declined. The elderly man led us to a small sunroom off the living room, and we settled into a wicker love seat while Finchley lowered himself into an armchair. "How can I help you, Miss Worth?"

"I was hired by your grand-niece, Natalie Newton, to look for some books that have gone missing from your sister Betty's personal library."

Finchley's bushy eyebrows drew together. "I see," he said heavily. "Of course, you won't mind if I call my niece to verify that you are who you say you are?"

"Please do. I have her number handy, if you need it."

"I appreciate that." Finchley reached for a cordless telephone, and I read Natalie's number off for him as he punched in the numbers. We waited as the phone rang.

When Natalie answered, our host said, "Natalie, good afternoon. This is your Uncle Robert." Finchley looked at me. "I have some surprise visitors today. I wonder if you could tell me who they are?"

Finchley listened. "And these people...they know about your grandmother's *library*?" Finchley asked, his voice hardening. If the family had taken such pains to keep their magic secret, I could well imagine he would not be happy about the information getting out.

I couldn't hear Natalie's response, but it was lengthy. Her tone sounded urgent and apologetic.

Whatever Natalie said, it seemed to mollify Finchley. He exchanged a few pleasantries with her, then hung up.

"My niece seems to think you're trustworthy." The older man nailed me with a hard look. "I have to say I'm less than thrilled you know about our family's private business."

"My contract with Natalie includes a confidentiality agreement. Beyond that, I'm a mage myself," I told him frankly. "I have no love for SPEMA, and I violate SPERA regulations more than I follow them. I assure you, no one will ever hear about your family's secret from me."

Finchley looked at Sean. "And you, Mr. Maclin?"

Sean didn't hesitate. "I'm a shifter." I was surprised he volunteered that information, but Finchley didn't even blink. "Like Alice, I have no use for the Agency, and I've signed a confidentiality agreement."

Our forthrightness softened Finchley's expression, and the tension left his shoulders. "I appreciate your honesty," he said gruffly, leaning back in his chair and reaching for a glass of iced tea on the table beside him. "It hasn't been easy, obviously, to keep our family out of SPEMA's records."

"Is that why Betty bound Natalie's magic?" I asked.

Finchley started. "She never told me about that. That poor girl. I suppose Betty's binding spells failed?"

"They did, but luckily, I was there when it happened."

The old man sighed. "I wish I could say I was surprised my sister would do something like that, but I suppose I'm not. Betty was always cautious. We've all had to be careful, of course, but she was always so worried we'd be found out. I don't understand why she didn't want Natalie to know she had magic, though. No one in our family has ever been bound once they were old enough to learn control."

"We certainly haven't come across any explanations so far. Natalie has requested I find someone to train her, and I'm working on that. In the meantime, I've bound her magic and warded her house, as well as the library, to protect what's in there." I watched him closely as I said it.

Finchley's look of bewilderment looked genuine. "The books? Betty's spell books, certainly, but I don't think anything else in there is particularly valuable. We want to keep outsiders away, of course." He paused. "You said something has gone missing from the library. What's missing?"

"Something Betty had in a hidden compartment in the bottom of one of the bookcases. We're not sure what it was. Any ideas?"

"None at all," Finchley said, and I believed him. "My sister and I didn't talk about magic; no one in our family does. I suppose it's always been something of a taboo subject. The need for secrecy, you see. It's not always easy to tell who might be listening."

"I understand. Other than Betty, Natalie, and yourself, who else in the family has magic?"

Finchley looked at me, saying nothing.

As a good-faith gesture, I decided to put another card on the table. "Whoever took the item from Betty's library has strong magic. I first suspected one of her children, but I've been able to eliminate them."

Finchley smiled. "As you've eliminated me, I suspect, with that long handshake."

"Yes." I smiled back.

"Well, if you've contacted my nieces and nephew, you know they have little or no magic. Natalie's mother, God rest her soul, had air magic, but not much. Is Natalie's magic strong?"

"No."

"Thank God for that," Finchley said. "It's better that way."

I didn't comment on that. "What about your sister, Helen?"

Finchley looked thoughtful. "Helen has air and fire magic, like Betty. It's not strong, but she does have it. Are you going to visit her as well?"

"I think so." My ears perked up. It looked like we were headed to Hope after all. "Can you think of anything else I might need to know about Betty that could help us figure out what she had hidden in her library?"

Finchley thought about that, then shook his head. "I really can't. As I said, we never spoke about magic. Whatever it was, I suppose she took that secret to her grave." He regarded me. "What magic do you have, Miss Worth?"

"Air and earth."

"Earth magic," he said wistfully. "I was always so envious of Betty's fire. My own magic seemed so dull by comparison." My skin prickled as a warm breeze swirled through the room, then vanished. Sean started and Finchley winked at me.

I glanced around and spotted a shelf full of small antique apothecary bottles. Finchley appeared to collect them. "May I?" I asked, pointing at the shelf.

He raised his bushy eyebrows. "Help yourself."

I fetched one of the bottles and brought it over to our host, pulling out the stopper. Finchley and Sean leaned forward to watch.

I held out my right hand, and a tendril of green flame rose from my palm. It snaked into the bottle, then coiled into a spiral. I murmured an incantation, and the flame brightened for a moment before dimming to a soft green glow. I stoppered the bottle and handed it to Finchley.

"Give it a little energy once a week to keep it charged. If you need a bright light, the spell is '*Luminous.*' The flare lasts for about a minute."

"It's beautiful." Finchley lifted the bottle to peer at the spiral flame. "An amazing construction, and you did it so easily."

"Lots of practice," I said with a ghost of a smile. I'd had many lonely hours locked in my rooms in the cabal compound to master cold-fire forms. The luminary spell was one of my favorites.

Finchley set the bottle on his side table and rose from his chair. Sean stood as well.

"Thank you for visiting me," Finchley said. "It was surprisingly pleasant to talk about magic with you."

"We appreciate you taking the time to visit with us," I told Natalie's great-uncle as we followed him back to the front door. "My condolences on the loss of your sister."

"Betty was a good person," Finchley said. "I'm sorry Natalie never knew about her magic, but I suppose my sister thought it was for the best. I'm glad she knows now, and that you were there to help her." He took my hand and squeezed it.

Sean and I said our good-byes, and Finchley closed the door behind us as we headed down the walkway.

"That was incredible," Sean said.

"What was?"

"The fire in the bottle. I've never seen anything like that. I didn't even know it was possible."

"Had a lot of downtime when I was a kid." I shrugged.

I caught Sean's look of surprise out of the corner of my eye and realized I'd just casually referenced my life prior to arriving in the city. I turned away from him to watch a tennis game in progress.

We turned in our guest IDs at the office and returned to the car. "Are we bound for Hope?" Sean asked as we got in and shut the doors.

"It looks like it. Robert said Helen has both fire and air magic, same as the signature in the wards."

"He said her magic wasn't strong, though," Sean pointed out as he headed out of the Pine Ridge parking lot.

"He might be mistaken or have been misled about how strong her magic is. We'll just have to find out for ourselves."

"He's probably calling her to let her know we're coming," Sean commented.

"More than likely," I sighed. "Can't be helped. Hopefully, she'll be willing to talk to us."

* * *

She wasn't.

Sean and I stood on Helen Matson's porch, talking to her closed front door. "Mrs. Matson—" I began.

"My brother said you were nosing around, asking about Betty," came the querulous voice from inside the house. "I have nothing to say to you. Go away."

I met Sean's gaze, then glanced at the door. Somehow, he got my meaning and turned to the door, unleashing a category-five smile. I hoped Helen Matson was still peering through the peephole, though I worried the sheer force of his grin might be too much for the old lady's heart. "Mrs. Matson, my name is Sean Maclin. Ms. Worth and I certainly don't want to bother you, but your great-niece Natalie hired us to track down some items that have gone missing from Betty's library."

As Sean was speaking and hopefully drawing Helen's attention away from me, I closed my eyes, lowered my shields, and reached out with my senses.

Sensing magic without skin contact is a very different—and much more difficult—process. Sean and Helen's voices faded into a faint murmur as I focused on the older woman's energy, which was muffled but not concealed by the walls of her home. I had to pass through the physical barrier to reach her, and it took effort. I was able to sense Helen's magic, but it was indistinct. I lowered my shields more and concentrated harder.

Finally, I sensed air and fire magic, as Finchley had said, but it was low-level, and distinctly different from the signature in the library wards. Helen Matson was not the mystery mage.

I must have swayed or started to fall, because suddenly Sean's hands were around my upper arms, holding me up. I raised my shields, took a deep breath, and opened my eyes.

"Are you all right?" Sean asked me.

I blinked at him, struggling to make my eyes focus on his face. "I'm okay. It's harder when I can't touch someone." It didn't help that I wasn't completely recovered from being nulled.

From behind the door, I heard Helen's voice. "What's going on out there? Both of you, get off my property before I call the police."

"We're leaving," I said. "Sorry to have bothered you." I turned on shaky legs. Sean guided me back to the car, loading me into the passenger seat before he got into the driver's side.

"That's a negative, then?"

"It's a negative." I rubbed my eyes. "We're out of suspects. *Again.*"

Sean squeezed my hand. "You'll figure it out. Rest for a bit while I drive us back."

"Let's head to Natalie's house. With any luck, she'll have found something helpful in Betty's files."

* * *

A wreck on the highway added almost an hour to the drive back to the city. By the time we got back to Natalie's house, it was well after six o'clock.

Malcolm had tested the containment spell on the library and pronounced it ready to go. Natalie was looking through the files in Betty's desk but hadn't found anything yet that was magic-related.

When I explained our visits to Robert Finchley and Helen Matson had come up empty, Natalie became understandably frustrated.

"I don't know what to say," I told her. "I'm still certain the magic signature in the wards belongs to a close relative of your grandmother. Keep looking through those files, and I'll work on the magic angle some more."

"I'll look," Natalie promised. "If I find anything that looks like it might be interesting, I'll let you know."

I turned to my ghost. "Earring time again, Malcolm."

He sighed.

"Tomorrow's Sunday," I said. "It's going to be my day off. At the top of my to-do list is working on a masking spell for you."

"That is very good news," Malcolm said, visibly relieved.

Once Malcolm was contained in my earring, Sean and I said good-bye to Natalie and walked to his car.

Sean leaned against the driver's door. "What are your plans for the evening?"

"I have a meeting with Charles Vaughan at ten. I'm going home to relax for a couple of hours and clear my head."

Sean looked disappointed. I knew he was hoping for that date he'd been campaigning for. I'd considered it earlier in the day, but after eleven hours in his company, I needed some space and a chance to think about what I was going to say before I talked to Charles.

Speaking of which…. "I do have a favor to ask, if it's feasible."

"Name it."

"I'm going to ask Charles for help finding a teacher for Natalie." I explained my reasoning for involving the vampire in the search.

"Asking a vampire for help is risky," Sean said, his brow furrowing. "He'll want something in return, obviously—I'm pretty sure the phrase 'quid pro quo' was coined by a vamp."

"Probably," I agreed. "I'm going to make some offers, but I have to be prepared for the possibility he may demand something I'm not willing to give."

His eyes darkened. "What do you need from me?"

I'd been pondering that off and on for the better part of the day and had come up with a plan I thought would help me avoid a confrontation with Charles that might force me to reveal the power of my magic. "A kind of backup. I text you when I go into the meeting, then text when I leave."

Sean looked thoughtful. "Bringing someone along with you signifies fear and weakness, but this demonstrates confidence and forethought. It's proactive, but more defensive. If you're having to tell him you have an ally awaiting an all-clear message, the situation has already gone south. The idea is to avoid that in the first place."

"That's a good point," I acknowledged. It was odd to hear Sean speak not as a lover or colleague, but as a werewolf alpha, used to navigating complex and often dangerous political waters. "Do you have another suggestion?"

"Vampires respect power plays and alliances. I can make you an ally of the Tomb Mountain Pack. If Vaughan threatens you or attacks, he's taking on the entire pack. Even a member of the Vampire Court would avoid that unless there was no other choice. This way, you go in as an associate of my pack. It's a move he'll understand and respect. You'll be protected, but you won't lose face."

It was my turn to think. "In return, I'll be expected to aid your pack if asked to do so?"

Sean looked surprised. "So you're familiar with the concept of pack ally?"

"Yes." I didn't elaborate. My grandfather's cabal was affiliated with two werewolf packs, so shifter politics was nothing new to me. "How will we formalize my status as pack associate?"

"I'll write you a letter you can display and present as needed," Sean said. "In the meantime, since Vaughan is a vampire, my suggestion is that I mark you with my blood. He'll understand what that means from the moment you walk into his office without you having to say a word."

An alliance with the Tomb Mountain Pack, even if it was temporary, was undeniably professionally beneficial to me. I was certainly getting the better end of the deal. "Either party can rescind the alliance with notice?"

"Standard clause," Sean assured me.

"Done. How should we do this?"

Sean produced an engraved pocketknife. He opened it, then drew the blade across the pad of his thumb. Blood welled. "Hold out your hands, palms up."

I obeyed.

Using his thumb, Sean rubbed blood onto the insides of both of my wrists. Without being asked, I pulled my hair to the side and tilted my head. He drew his thumb across my neck at the shoulder, marking me as an ally of his pack.

Instead of stepping back, Sean cupped the back of my neck with his hand. "You're off tomorrow?"

"Yep. I owe Malcolm a masking spell, and if I don't do laundry soon, I might run out of clothes."

Sean's eyes glinted. "That doesn't sound like such a bad thing to me."

I rolled my eyes.

He chuckled and released me. "What's your schedule look like for the next couple of days?"

I shook my head. "I really don't know at this point. That's one of the downsides of PI work."

"I understand. Private security isn't much different. But if we can make it work, I'd like to see you next week."

"I'd like that." I glanced down at his hand. "I was going to offer you a Band-Aid, but it looks like you don't need it."

Sean held up his thumb. The cut was already healing. In twenty minutes, there would be no sign of the wound.

He leaned down to give me a kiss, pulling me close with one hand on my hip. It was a very nice kiss: undemanding, yet full of promise.

When we broke apart, he nuzzled my neck and inhaled my scent. I shivered at the feeling of his breath on my skin. "Be safe," he said quietly. "You can still text me when you're done, if you want."

"It might be late."

"I'll be up." He gave me a wolfish grin. "I tend to be fairly nocturnal."

I laughed. "No doubt."

He gave me a kiss on the cheek, then stepped back. "Have a good night, Allie."

"You too, Sean."

He got into his car and waited until I was in mine with the engine started before he waved and drove away.

CHAPTER 16

I'd hoped to sit and chat with Adri before my meeting with Charles, but she was at the door checking IDs when I arrived at Hawthorne's and it was a busy night. We exchanged quick hellos and I went inside to find a table and a much-needed drink.

I squeezed in at the bar and flagged Pete down to order a beer. He slid it over to me, took my money, and gave me a quick smile before turning to grab a bottle of vodka off a shelf. I took my drink and headed toward my usual booth, hoping to find it empty.

To my disappointment, it was occupied by a lone man, sitting back in the shadows where I usually took refuge. I sighed and started back toward the bar.

A familiar voice stopped me. "Ms. Worth."

I turned around.

The man in the shadows leaned forward into the light. It took a moment for me to recognize him in civilian clothes, but I'd know those ice-blue eyes anywhere.

"Special Agent Lake," I said, startled. "I wouldn't have thought this would be your scene." I wasn't sure what Lake's scene *would* be, but a supe bar owned by a vampire seemed an unlikely place for a SPEMA agent to be spending his off-hours.

"Hawthorne's has the finest selection of bourbon in the city." Lake raised his glass. "The owner is a connoisseur, or so I've been told."

"That he is," I murmured.

He regarded me with raised eyebrows. "Are you acquainted with the owner?"

Before I could answer, I felt someone come up next to me. Even in my high-heeled boots, Bryan towered over me. "Miss Alice," he rumbled. "Am I interrupting?"

"Not at all," I said, hoping my relief didn't show. "Am I wanted upstairs?"

"You are."

Lake studied me. I might have been imagining it, but I thought the fact I was here to see Charles Vaughan might have piqued the SPEMA agent's interest and raised his estimation of me by several degrees—neither of which pleased me. I would rather Lake forget about me altogether.

"Enjoy your bourbon," I told him.

"I'm sure I will." A small smile turned up the corners of Lake's mouth.

I turned to follow Bryan's enormous back through the crowd, depositing my beer bottle in a trash can as I passed. The enforcer and I walked down the hall and through a door marked *Private*.

As we started up the stairs, I said quietly, "You know he's a fed."

Bryan glanced at me. "We are aware. Agent Lake comes in every few weeks, has one drink of good bourbon, and then leaves."

"Anybody know why?"

"No."

"Hmm."

We climbed three flights of stairs, went through another, much heavier door, and entered another world.

The floor above the bar was soundproofed. I knew there was music blaring downstairs, but I couldn't hear a thing. The carpet was thick, the lighting dim. It was the kind of understated elegance that would appeal to a vampire.

I'd first met Charles when I worked for Mark Dunlap. Mark was a longtime associate of the Vampire Court, doing investigative work for them. Most mages steer clear of the fangy undead, since mage blood is particularly tasty for vamps. Some are able to absorb magical energy that way, enhancing their own innate powers, and drinking mage blood can become addictive. There was a lot of mutual respect between Mark and the Court, though, and since I had no particular objection, we'd ended up doing a lot of work for them. It was lucrative as well; the vamps wanted discretion, and they were willing to pay premium rates for it.

When I left Mark's firm, I was no longer on retainer for them, but Charles had hired me on a per-job basis to do some work for his businesses and the Court when Mark wasn't available. I'd proven myself to be trustworthy and capable. Charles started inviting me up to his office for a drink—liquor, not blood—from time to time when I was in Hawthorne's. He told me my bluntness was a refreshing break from the lies, evasions, and machinations of vamp politics.

Charles had also made it clear he wouldn't mind a roll in the hay, but so far I'd managed to steer clear of that particular minefield. I figured if he was that determined, he'd have pressed the issue by now, so maybe his overtures were just one more way for a two-hundred-year-old vamp to pass the time.

I checked my reflection in the mirror in the hall. I'd dressed up for my meeting in slim black slacks, an emerald-green, cowl-neck sweater, and high-heeled ankle boots, and pulled my hair up. A pair of dangly, gold earrings danced above my shoulders.

"You look very nice," Bryan said.

"Why, thank you, Bryan." I patted his arm. "We mustn't keep him waiting, I guess."

He led me down the hall to a set of double doors on the end, where two guards almost as large as him stood at attention. He knocked twice with a fist the size of a football.

From inside, I heard Charles's voice: "Come in."

Bryan opened the heavy door and stepped aside so I could enter Charles Vaughan's office.

"Hello, Alice." Charles stood and came around his enormous desk to meet me. As usual, the strikingly handsome, dark-haired vampire wore an expensive, tailored suit cut to flatter his lean physique and a watch that probably cost almost as much as my house. He would forever appear to be in his early thirties, though no one looking into those ageless eyes would mistake him for a young man. His dark suit, hair, and eyes contrasted sharply with his pallor, but his coloring looked vamp-healthy, meaning he'd probably fed already this evening.

His skin, when he took my hands, felt characteristically cool to the touch.

As he bent to kiss my cheek, he inhaled almost soundlessly, then chuckled softly. My pack alliance had been noted.

Charles sat back down, and I sank into a leather armchair across from him. Bryan closed the door and took up a position next to it.

The vampire closed a file on his desk and folded his hands on top of it. "I hoped I might have time to honor your request for a consultation on Thursday, but as I am sure Mr. Smith told you, my meeting ran very late."

"Not a problem at all," I said. "I figured it was a long shot anyway, just dropping in unannounced. Rude of me, really, but I was out and about and thought I'd risk it."

"Scotch?" Charles gestured at his extensive private bar.

"No, thank you. But if you have water, I'd love some."

He nodded at Bryan, who went to the bar and pulled out a glass bottle of imported artisanal water. He opened it, wrapped the cold bottle in a cloth napkin, and handed it to me. I sipped the fancy water. The label said its contents were filtered through natural lava rocks in a particular region of Iceland. I couldn't tell the difference between it and what you got out of a vending machine, but what did I know?

"I hope you are recovered from your recent misadventures," Charles said.

"I am, thanks. I ran into some black wards on Wednesday night, and on Thursday, I had a spell fail and got burned by uncontrolled magic."

His eyebrows raised. "Horrifying. Your job is dangerous at the most unexpected times."

"There's always an unpredictable element when magic is involved. Even the best of us can be surprised. The case I'm currently working on started out pretty straightforward but has quickly turned…interesting."

"It would seem so, if you encountered both black wards and uncontrolled magic in a single day," Charles said. "I am pleased to see you survived."

"It was a near thing, both times," I confessed. "It's been a rough couple of days."

"And yet, you drink water. Are you sure I cannot tempt you with a fifty-year single malt Scotch? I have looked forward to sharing a glass with someone who appreciates such a fine whisky."

A fifty-year-old single malt was an offer I couldn't refuse. "Well, if you insist."

"Mr. Smith, two glasses of the Glenfiddich, if you would."

We paused the conversation to watch with appropriate reverence as Bryan took out the bottle, unstoppered it, and poured us each two fingers of Scotch. We toasted each other and sipped. I closed my eyes to better appreciate the taste and smoothness of the whisky.

"Excellent." Charles clearly enjoyed both his drink and my reaction. "Simply superb."

"Definitely the best I've ever had. Thank you very much for sharing it with me."

"It is my pleasure."

We savored the Scotch a bit more, then Charles asked, "Have you had any contact with Mark Dunlap recently?"

I blinked in surprise. "No, we haven't spoken in years."

"He was puzzled by your decision to work independently, and hurt, I think."

"I know." I pondered my Scotch. "But I like being my own boss."

"Surely it has been difficult to establish yourself as a new investigator," Charles commented. "Mark has an excellent reputation and connections in both the supernatural and mundane worlds. He told me you did not attempt to steal any of his clients when you left."

"I wanted to leave Mark on good terms," I said a bit defensively. "I had no intention of poaching his clients. I'd still be friendly today if it were up to me, but Mark made it pretty clear he had no interest in talking to me."

"Perhaps it is presumptuous for me to say this, but I think you might find Mark's attitude has mellowed." He turned his glass in his hands, watching the light reflecting in the amber liquid. "Recently, he mentioned he had heard only good reports on your work. I detected a certain...regret regarding how you parted company."

"Interesting." On the one hand, part of me still smarted when I thought of the way Mark had reacted when I'd told him I was leaving, but years had passed, and perhaps it was time to let that go. I wasn't sure what kind of relationship we'd have these days. Were we colleagues? Competitors? It was hard to say exactly. Should I pick up the phone and call him? Then again, he could have called me at any point in the past three years if he was feeling regretful.

Finally, I said, "Well, the next time you speak with Mark, tell him I said hello."

"I will do that. What brings you to me this evening?"

I sipped my Scotch. "I came across an interesting situation and thought you might have some insights."

"How can I help?" Charles leaned back in his chair.

I weighed my words carefully, as was always prudent when dealing with vampires. "I met a young woman who has low-level magic, but a family member bound her, probably when she was very young, and until a few days ago, she had no idea she or anyone in her family had any such abilities."

He raised an elegant eyebrow. "How distressing for her."

"It was quite a shock." I smiled at the understatement. "She has no control over her magic. Because the family member who bound her passed away unexpectedly a few months ago, the binding spells began to fade, which is how we came to discover her hidden talent."

"Ah, I understand. The 'uncontrolled magic' accident you experienced on Thursday."

"Yes. I was able to bind her magic again, so things are good for now, but she's decided she wants to learn how to control and use her magic."

"I am glad to hear it. One should always embrace one's natural abilities. What is the problem?"

"The problem is that her family has avoided any attention from either the cabals or SPEMA and she'd like to keep it that way. Since she's an adult, her magic is at full strength. She needs a strong fire and air mage who can teach her to control her magic, someone who isn't part of a cabal, and who can be trusted not to rat her out to the Agency."

"And my role in this?"

I leaned forward. "You know a lot of people, and you're an excellent judge of character. I was hoping you could find someone who would be a good mentor, and who wouldn't sell her out for favors or money."

Charles looked pleased at my praise. "It is a tall order to find someone honorable these days," he mused. "It is fortunate her power is not strong. She is less of a prize."

"I had the same thought. She's low-level air, mid-level fire. It's nothing a cabal would pay much for; mages of her power level are a dime a dozen. She does have null abilities, but there's nothing unique about that." Okay, I was fudging a little there, since Natalie could null a mage almost instantly and break circles simply by touching them, but he didn't need to know that.

Charles steepled his fingers. "I will need to make discreet inquiries. It may take some time to find the best candidates. Let me ask this: why not become her mentor yourself?"

"A couple of reasons. First, I don't have time," I admitted. "My schedule is completely erratic because of my job. She'll need someone to spend a *lot* of time with her, especially in the beginning, and I can't afford to take time off. Second, I don't have fire magic, and she really needs to work with someone with the same abilities she has. Third, I have no experience with training a new mage, much less an adult with fully developed power. I would suck at it."

Charles chuckled. "I doubt, my dear, if you 'suck' at anything magic-related at all, but your reasoning is sound. A second question: why not ask around for a mage to train her, rather than come to me?"

Time to be careful. Charles had no idea of my background, or that I was anything more than the mid-level air and earth mage I made myself out to be, and I needed to avoid saying anything that might cause him to suspect otherwise.

"It's mainly a matter of expediency," I said, going for partial truth. "You know more people already than I could meet in a year, and you know them well enough to know if they meet the requirements. No one I know would fit the bill."

"Perfectly logical." Charles finished the last of his Glenfiddich and contemplated his glass. "One must savor such a fine Scotch slowly, and resist the urge to drink it so frequently that it becomes commonplace." He looked at me. "So, now that I know your request, what do you offer in exchange?"

Ah, yes, the proverbial deal with the devil. Money—unless it was in significant quantities—held little interest for wealthy vampires. Their preferred currency was favors. "I have a few possibilities in mind," I said.

"I cannot wait to hear these possibilities." Charles's lips twitched in a hint of a smile.

I raised one finger. "I offer my investigative services in exchange for your time and effort in locating an appropriate mentor for my client. A single employment contract, with prenegotiated duration limit."

He tapped his steepled fingers together and regarded me with half-lidded eyes. "Perhaps."

I raised a second finger. "My expertise in wards and spellwork. I have several new and highly complex wards I can discuss in more detail if you wish. One or more projects, depending on power levels and intricacy involved."

"Including black wards, if I require them?"

"Under specific conditions that I would have to preapprove."

"Understood. Any other offers?"

I blinked at him, rather surprised he didn't jump at the opportunity to have me create wards for him. "Did you have something particular in mind?"

"I do, in fact." Charles leaned forward, his hands folded on his desk. His gaze was suddenly very direct. "I require something very particular indeed."

I began to get an *oh shit* feeling. "Yes?"

"I would like to drink from you, Alice."

I stared.

Charles's eyes never left mine. "I have known you for almost five years, and never in that time have I tasted your blood. I have never asked, but this is something I have long desired. In return for finding a mentor for your client, I require one drink of your blood, at a time and place to be chosen by you, but within the next month. I am not asking for any intimacy beyond the bite, unless you wish it."

Anxiety surged inside me, but I squashed it and concentrated on keeping my breathing and heartbeat even and slow. One did not show fear in front of a vampire; they found it arousing. Charles could *not* be allowed to drink from me. He would instantly know I was no mid-level mage. Natalie's magic made her no trophy; I, on the other hand, was a great prize. I couldn't count on our history to protect me from being auctioned off to the highest-bidding cabal.

I looked at Charles and tried to keep my emotions off my face. He'd feel my alarm, but I hoped he'd chalk that up to a fear of being bitten. "I'm no one's cattle," I said quietly, using the slang term for a vamp's food supply.

Behind me, I heard Bryan shift closer to us at my tone. As far as he knew, I was little threat, but his job was to protect Charles. If it came down to it, Bryan would kill me before he'd let me harm the vampire.

"I would not ask you to be," Charles said. "Nor would I *want* you to be. It is a one-time arrangement."

"I've never allowed any vampire to drink from me." I was surprised at how calm my voice sounded. "I have no plans to do so."

"Even if it is I who does it, and you dictate the terms?" He looked mildly surprised at my reaction. For a normally poker-faced vamp, "mild surprise" was the equivalent of being flabbergasted. I supposed Charles thought I would have no objection to donating a meal, since I'd shown no previous aversion to being around vamps.

Many people craved the bite of a vampire. It could be intensely pleasurable, if the vampire wished it to be. No vampire ever had to go hungry; there were willing donors who happily lined up around the block for the chance to be breakfast, lunch, dinner, or a midnight snack. Countless men and women would climb over each other for a chance at what I was turning down.

How on earth could I extricate myself from this without arousing Charles's suspicion and anger?

"I can't," I told him. "I'm honored you'd ask this of me, Charles, but I won't be a blood meal, for anyone, for any reason."

Charles studied my face. I tried to keep my expression neutral.

Finally, he spoke. "Then I am afraid I cannot help you." His voice was calm, perfectly dispassionate.

My mouth fell open. "Because I won't let you drink my blood, you won't help me find someone to teach my client?"

"Yes."

"Why not?" The question popped out before I could stop it. It sounded far too much like a challenge. My fingers tightened on my glass.

Charles didn't move, though a muscle in his jaw twitched. I swallowed, my mouth suddenly dry.

"I do not owe you any explanation," he said finally, his voice still cold. "But perhaps I will say that I have asked so little, and your refusal has…hurt my feelings."

Oh God. I hurt the feelings of a two-hundred-year-old vampire. I didn't wet my pants, but it was a near thing. My flat refusal was a slap in the face, and I had no way to better explain myself that wouldn't expose my secrets. I'd probably lost an employer and an ally. No more late-night drinks at Hawthorne's.

Because to leave any of the very expensive Scotch would add insult to injury, I drained what little remained and gently set my glass down on the desk. Slowly, I rose, keeping my hands in plain sight. I did nothing that could be read as threatening, very aware of the vampire in front of me and the enforcer at my back.

"I'm sorry," I said softly. The vampire said nothing.

Carefully, I backed toward the door. Charles remained motionless, his eyes on me. I suddenly felt like a gazelle under the watchful stare of a lion.

Just as Bryan reached to open the door for me, Charles spoke. "A moment."

I paused. "Yes?"

Charles rose but stayed behind his desk. "I will contact you soon about a project for the Court that requires wards: a new facility, one hour from the city. If you are available, it will be a lucrative contract."

"Thank you."

"Good night."

"Good night."

Charles remained standing as Bryan opened the door of the office. I backed into the hall, and the door closed in my face.

I'd originally intended to return to the bar after the meeting for another drink or two, and maybe a chat with Adri, but I was rethinking that plan. Despite Charles's parting comments regarding a potential contract from the Court—comments that may or may not have been designed to deescalate a tense situation—the thought of dealing with the noisy, boisterous Saturday-night crowd downstairs was suddenly unappealing.

I returned to the main floor. As I weaved through the crush of people, I noticed Lake was gone and a couple had taken his place in the back corner booth.

I slipped out the front door, giving Adri a quick wave as I passed. It wasn't until I was halfway home that I started to feel the tension seeping out of my shoulders.

When I parked in my driveway, I fired off a quick text: *Home.* I stuck the phone in my pocket and got out of the car, heading for my front door.

The phone beeped as I unlocked my door. I went inside, locked the door, and went to the kitchen for a glass of water.

Wolf: Meeting went well?

I texted back, then headed for the stairs, cup in hand.

Me: No. We could not agree on terms.

The response came back in seconds. *Are you all right?*

Me: Unharmed.

Wolf: What did he ask for?

Me: Long story. Will tell you when I see you.

A few minutes went by. I went upstairs and started taking off my clothes and jewelry.

Beep.

Wolf: I have Monday and Tuesday evenings clear as of now. Dinner Monday?

Me: Maybe. Good night.

Wolf: Good night, Allie. Sweet dreams.

I plugged in my phone, stripped, and used soap and water to wash Sean's blood off my wrists and neck. As I changed into pajamas and climbed into bed, I realized I was smiling. With a growl, I turned over to put my back to the phone, curled up under the covers, and fell asleep.

CHAPTER 17

Sunday morning, I rolled out of bed at eight and headed to the bathroom to shower. I dried my hair, dressed quickly, and released Malcolm from my earring.

"What's the plan for today?" Malcolm trailed behind me down the stairs.

"Today we're going to work on your masking spell." I went into the kitchen, fired up the coffeepot, and made myself some toast with grape jelly for breakfast.

With my travel mug filled with the nectar of the gods, I led Malcolm to the door to my basement. "Come here. I need to let the basement wards know you're allowed to pass."

Once Malcolm's energy signature was integrated into the wards, I flipped on the light, opened the door, and led the way down the stairs.

Malcolm's form shimmered a bit as he passed through the barrier, and he grimaced. "Oof. That felt intense. So much power."

At the bottom of the steps, he paused to look around.

To the right was my library. It was modest, about half the size of Betty's. When I escaped my grandfather's cabal, I left with only my scars and the half-burned clothes on my back. My personal library at the cabal compound had been massive, and it was one of the hardest things to leave behind. I'd begun building a new library the moment I arrived in the city, but it was a slow process. Spelled bookcases, carved with protection runes, ran around the outside of the room, with a large wooden table in the middle.

To the left was my spell-crafting and summoning area. Another heavy table stood against the wall. Chalk, papers, crystals, little tubes of henna, and jewelry-making materials were scattered on top of it. Four large, heavily warded oak storage cabinets against the back wall contained a variety of implements and supplies, from crystals to athames. The floor had three concentric circles inlaid into the concrete.

Malcolm studied the cabinets. "What's with those two cabinets on the end there?"

"Don't touch those."

Malcolm snorted. "No shit. Those are serious black wards. What's in there?"

"It's where I keep all my blood magic materials."

"Oh, that explains the wards. Wouldn't want anybody finding that stuff."

I went to the library and started scanning through the books. "I'm looking for how to mask your magical energy so you being a mage ghost is less noticeable," I said, hunting for helpful volumes.

Malcolm drifted over next to me. "Seems like a masking spell might work, if we can make it so anyone who senses me thinks all I have is low-level earth or water magic."

"I don't know how to make a masking spell that will work on a noncorporeal being," I confessed.

"It's not that different than a spell for a living person. I think I can show you."

We worked for most of the day on Malcolm's masking spell, taking a few breaks to chat and rest while we refined the spellwork.

Storing him in the earring helped hide him, but it occurred to me it wasn't fair of me to expect him to stay in there all the time. When I'd first put him in the earring, it was supposed to be a temporary arrangement, but then I'd let this case—and other things—distract me from working on the spell that was needed to obscure his identity. I'd been stashing him in there for my convenience and letting him out when I needed help, which was inexcusably selfish. I felt guilty about it and told him so.

"No worries," Malcolm said with way more understanding than I thought I deserved. "Since the minute I showed up in your office, you've been working nonstop on this case, and you've been injured a couple of times. There really hasn't been any chance for you to work on this spell, but we're doing it now, and that's all that matters."

"Thanks for being so patient."

Malcolm shrugged. "Hey, I've got time. It's not like I'm getting any older here."

When I was sure he was joking, I laughed. I'd had a dream about the cabal the night before, and it was a grim reminder about what he'd gone through. He seemed pretty stable for somebody who had died that way. Unlike some ghosts who go completely bonkers in the Null and come back to earth as wraiths, poltergeists, or just plain deranged, he seemed to have made it back with his sanity intact. I wondered if that was due to his strong magical abilities.

"Hey, you in there?" Malcolm interrupted my musings.

I blinked at him. "Sorry. Got lost in thought for a minute. You were saying?"

"I was saying I think I might have figured it out." He showed me the spellwork he'd been working on. It was similar to the spell I'd used to mask my own magic and pass myself off as a low-level air mage while I was recovering from plastic surgery on my face. He'd modified it to work on a noncorporeal body and to make himself seem like he had a low amount of water magic only.

"Hmm." I pondered the spell. "It might work."

"Only one way to find out."

I reached out to take Malcolm's arm with my left hand and used my right to trace the spell in the air. In moments, his energy signature muted and transformed. I added the additional disguising spell, wove it through the masking spell, and invoked both. Then I released his arm.

I could immediately sense the difference in Malcolm's energy signature. While before I could sense strong earth and water magic, now I would have sworn he was only a low-level water mage.

"Did it work?" Malcolm asked.

I remembered he wouldn't be able to feel the difference, just as I couldn't feel my own masking spell that made me seem like a mid-level air and earth mage. "Yep. I think you're officially incognito now. I guess this means less earring time for you."

"No offense, but thank God. It's weird in there."

That made me laugh. "I do want you to come up with a spell that would let you jump into the earring if you needed to. We don't know yet how well the masking spell will hold up under scrutiny, and I'd like you to have a bolt-hole of some sort in case we're out and about and encounter a strong mage or a ward that disrupts the spell."

"Makes sense. Maybe I can work on that while you figure out how to set your basement wards so they don't zap me when I cross them." He looked at me sideways.

I rolled my eyes at him. "You are such a nag. I'll work on that tomorrow. I am seriously worn out after all this work we did today. How are you not tired?"

"Um, because I'm a ghost?"

"Whatever. I'm going upstairs." I led Malcolm back up the steps to the main floor, where he braved the sizzle of the wards once more. "Sorry about that."

"It's okay. It's not like it hurts. It just feels like I'm being pulled apart a little."

I winced. "I'm not sure how much less uncomfortable I can make it without compromising the wards, but I'll look into it."

It was almost nine p.m. I threw a load of clothes into the washer, then made myself a quick dinner. As I was eating, I realized the message light on my phone was blinking. I'd missed a call from Natalie while I was doing laundry and had a voice mail.

"Hey, Alice." Natalie sounded excited. "I think maybe I found something that might help us. It's a folder of letters from a couple of years ago from a man named John West. In one of the letters, he refers to something called the *Kasten*." She spelled it. "He thanks my grandmother for agreeing to keep it. I looked through the rest of the letters, but he never mentions it again. It sounds like he and my grandmother were both in something called a harnad?"

I went cold. A harnad was an alliance of blood mages who do magic in pairs or groups to increase their power. They were extremely dangerous and had the well-deserved reputation of being ruthless. Harnads had been known to even use lifeblood—the last blood drained from a dying person, which was extremely potent—for spells and the most deadly and powerful black wards and curses. To do so was a capital crime in all fifty states, but there had been at least a dozen documented cases of the ritual being performed in the past decade, and those were just the ones that had become public knowledge.

This had the potential to be very, very bad.

Natalie was still talking, oblivious to the bomb she'd just dropped. "Anyway, I'm putting these letters on the dining table for you to look at, and I'll keep digging around. Have a good night!" *Beep.*

Malcolm and I looked at each other. "Shit," he said.

I couldn't have said it better myself.

* * *

I curled up on the couch with my laptop while Malcolm alternated between reading over my shoulder and floating around the house. I did a search for *Kasten*, but nothing came up that looked remotely useful, other than it was the German word for *box* or *chest*. I tried combining it with different search terms like *object of power* and *focus*, which were my best guesses about what it might be, but still got zilch.

After I put my clothes in the dryer, I searched for *harnad* and *Kasten* together, but all I got were news articles about harnads and websites denouncing blood magic. More than one website claimed there were at least two active harnads in the city, though not much was known about them. A local reporter believed they were responsible for a string of missing prostitutes, but the police were unconvinced.

I had no problem finding information about Betty's friend, John West. He was a high-level fire mage who lived in the city. By all accounts, he was a respected businessman who still did frequent commercial work, despite being in his seventies. I found nothing about West being a blood mage, but that wasn't surprising since blood magic was illegal.

Contacting West would be a highly dangerous proposition, since I had no desire to get myself on the radar of a member of a harnad. I leaned my head back against the couch and closed my eyes.

"What are you going to do?" Malcolm wanted to know.

"Good freaking question," I told him without opening my eyes. I briefly outlined what I'd found out about John West, the rumored local harnads, and the missing prostitutes. "Things just keep getting worse. This started out being about missing books. Now we're talking about a harnad being involved."

"If this *Kasten* doohickey belonged to the harnad, maybe they figured out who the mystery mage is and got that person to go in and get it for them," Malcolm suggested.

I'd been thinking that myself. "You're pretty good at this private investigator thing. Maybe *you* should be the PI and *I* should be the wisecracking assistant."

"That would work, except your jokes suck," Malcolm quipped.

I threw a pillow at him—they call them throw pillows, after all—and it went through him and landed over by the fireplace. "Do you think it's worth asking that reporter about the local harnads?"

"At this point, I'm not sure. I still think our best bet is figuring out who the mystery mage is and following that lead to see where it takes us."

I threw my hands up in aggravation. "Except we're out of suspects! It *has* to be one of Betty's children or siblings, but we've eliminated them all. It makes no damn sense."

"Okay, well, that's the thing. It *has* to be one of them, so either someone is capable of disguising their magic, or there's another family member we don't know about."

I rubbed my forehead. "If one of them is hiding their magic and/or disguising their energy signature, we'll need a spell that can detect a masking spell like the one we just put on you."

"I can do that, no problem."

"Awesome. Then all I'll have to do is sneak up to each of them and see if the spell triggers." I wrinkled my nose.

"Actually, I can do that easier than you," Malcolm pointed out. "I'm invisible. You can just wait in the car."

I could get used to this ghost assistant thing. "That sounds like an excellent plan, if you can design a spell that won't be triggered by the masking spell that's on you."

Malcolm gave me an insulted look. "I'm pretty sure I can do that."

"Figuring out if there's another sibling that Natalie isn't aware of might take a bit more legwork. I'm wondering if she could call Betty's lawyer tomorrow and find out."

"That's a thought. I'll work on the detection spell tonight and have it for you in the morning."

I glanced at the clock and was surprised to see it was almost midnight. "Wow. I really lost track of time. I'd better hit the hay." I hesitated, realizing I'd never "let" Malcolm out of the earring overnight. "Do you…need anything?" I asked awkwardly.

"Like what, my blankie and a bedtime story?"

I made a face at him. "Jerk."

Malcolm grinned. "No, I'm good. I'll work on the spell and maybe experiment with going out and about."

"Until we have a spell that can jump you back to me or into the earring, I don't know how comfortable I am with you going out on your own."

He scowled. "I don't need a babysitter."

"That's not how I meant it. Your masking spell isn't foolproof. We can't have anyone finding out who and what you are."

Malcolm nailed me with a hard stare. "You mean the way you can't have anyone finding out who and what *you* are?"

We eyeballed one another like two gunfighters sizing each other up in the middle of a dusty street. If a tumbleweed blew through my living room, we'd be all set.

"You can't go to a hospital, you can't let anyone get ahold of your blood, you've got multiple layers of masking spells, you don't want to ask around for a mentor for Natalie because you don't want to attract the attention of the local cabals. It doesn't take a rocket scientist to figure out that you're hiding. I'm dead, not stupid."

I kept silent.

Malcolm literally buzzed with anger, his fury intensifying by the second. "You know pretty much my whole life story, but apparently you don't trust me enough to even tell me what you're hiding from."

"No, I don't, not yet, and that's going to have to be the way it is for now, because I don't trust anyone with that information. It's not just you," I added when Malcolm started to get huffy. "I haven't told anyone about my past, and that isn't likely to change anytime soon. I value you, and I want you to be safe, which is why I'd like you to have a bolt-hole spell to get you back to the earring in case of an emergency."

I got up and headed for the stairs. "So be pissy if you want. Go out if you want; I'm not going to stop you. The house wards will let you pass. Just be careful."

I was almost halfway up the stairs when Malcolm finally spoke. "I'll make the bolt-hole spell before I go out." He still sounded angry, but there wasn't anything I could do about that.

I paused. "Thanks. Have a good night."

"You too."

I went upstairs and shut my bedroom door. It took a long time for me to fall asleep.

CHAPTER 18

When my alarm went off Monday morning at seven thirty, I'd been lying awake in bed for almost an hour. What little sleep I'd managed to get had been plagued by nightmares about blood mages and faceless, dark figures chanting around an altar and an object I couldn't see. My restless brain bounced from one topic to the next: Natalie, Malcolm, the mystery mage, Betty, harnads, John West, the *Kasten*, and even Charles and Sean. The worst part was, they were all big question marks.

Since I already had my phone in my hand, I pulled up Natalie's number and called her before I realized it might be too early.

She picked up on the third ring. "Hi, Alice!"

I was relieved that she sounded perfectly awake. "Morning, Natalie. Sorry I'm calling so early."

"Nah, I was up. Did you get my message last night? Did any of that make sense?"

"Some of it," I hedged. "Not sure what the *Kasten* is—I'm still looking to that. A harnad is the name for a group of blood mages."

A very long pause.

"Natalie?"

For the first time since I'd met her, Natalie swore. "Are you saying my grandmother was a blood mage?"

"It looks that way," I admitted. "I'd really like to look at those letters."

"I've got them here. You can come look at them anytime. God." I wasn't sure if she was swearing or if it was a prayer. "I thought I couldn't be shocked by this anymore, but I was wrong. Do you think my grandmother killed people?"

"I don't know, but we're going to be very careful. Harnads are dangerous. Don't talk to anyone about this."

She whimpered.

"I was wondering if you could do something for me," I said.

"What do you need?"

I explained that Malcolm and I were going to see if any of her aunts or uncle were hiding their magical abilities. "In the meantime, you mentioned you were still in touch with your grandmother's attorney."

"Yes. He's helping me fight my aunt in court."

"Could you call him and ask if Betty had any other siblings or children besides the ones we know about?"

Another long pause. "If my mother had any other brothers or sisters—even half brothers or half sisters—I'd think she would have told me," Natalie said finally.

"Unless she didn't know. Maybe there was a black sheep in the family."

Natalie snorted. "At this point, anything is possible. Sure, I'll call him and ask. I'm sure the answer is no, but we might as well check."

"Thanks. Let me know what you find out. I'll keep you posted on our end."

We made plans to touch base in the afternoon and said good-bye. I rolled out of bed and headed for my bathroom to shower and brush my teeth.

When I came out of the bathroom, Malcolm was in my room.

I shrieked, jumped, and almost lost my towel. "Damn it, Malcolm, what the hell? What if I'd walked out of my bathroom naked?"

He whirled around to face the other way. "Sorry! Sorry! Shit."

"We need to have some ground rules about my bedroom." I went into the bathroom, put on my bathrobe, and came back out. "Okay, I'm decent."

Malcolm turned around. "Seriously, sorry about that."

"It's fine. What's up?"

"Couple of things. I've got the masking-spell detector ready to go. I made the bolt-hole spell for your earring, but I need to test it."

"Awesome! How—"

Malcolm vanished.

I jerked. "What the hell? Oh." I went over to the nightstand and picked up my earrings. One of them buzzed with energy. "*Release.*"

Malcolm popped into my room, looking quite pleased with himself.

"Way to go. Any idea what its range might be?"

"That I'm not sure of," Malcolm said. "In theory, range shouldn't matter since this is metaphysical, but I would like to do more testing in incremental distances before I rely on it to jump me across town."

I felt a hell of a lot better about the situation now Malcolm was able to jump into the earring in case of an emergency.

"What about a spell I could use to get *out* of the earring, instead of needing you to let me out?" he asked.

I frowned. "That is going to be more of a challenge. The earring is a heavy-duty containment spell designed from the ground up to keep its contents in and only respond to my commands. I'll have to mess with it. It's possible, I think, but it's going to take some time."

I went to my closet to find clothes. "I asked Natalie to call the lawyer to find out if she's got any other relatives we don't know about. She's not very happy about the thought of her grandmother being in a harnad." I grabbed a blue plaid shirt and a pair of jeans and emerged from the closet.

Malcolm snorted. "I can't say I blame her. Imagine if *your* grandmother was in a harnad."

My grandmother *founded* three harnads, but that was neither here nor there. "I did tell her not to talk to anyone about it, which I would think would go without saying, but better to be safe than sorry. Now shoo so I can get dressed."

Malcolm went through the door into the hall. I put on my clothes, then brushed out my hair and pulled it into a ponytail before doing my makeup and putting on my jewelry.

Once I had my boots on, I opened the bedroom door and Malcolm was waiting in the hall. "You ready to go solve this thing?" he asked.

"Absolutely," I said. "Just as soon as I get some coffee."

* * *

I figured we'd start with Elise and work our way backward up the suspect list. I hit a fast-food drive-thru for a breakfast sandwich and gigantic cup of dark roast.

"How's your cholesterol?" Malcolm's disembodied voice was sardonic.

I took a big bite of my sandwich. "No idea. Probably fine, though," I said through a mouthful of food.

"You are a classy woman."

"Shut up."

By the time we got to Elise's neighborhood, I'd finished off the sandwich and most of the coffee. I rolled past Elise's house and told Malcolm to meet me around the corner.

"Roger that," Malcolm said, and I felt his energy leave the car.

I cruised down the street, turned the corner, and pulled over to the curb. I took my phone out and pretended to be in the middle of an animated conversation, as if I'd just stopped to make a call. Several morning dog-walkers and joggers passed by my car, saw me on the phone, and moved on without paying me much attention.

It was nearly ten minutes later by the time I felt Malcolm's energy in the car. I'd started to get worried around the six-minute mark. "Boo," Malcolm said.

I put my phone in my lap. "Very funny. What took so long?"

He snorted, which was a weird sound to hear from an invisible ghost. "'Gosh, Malcolm, it's pretty cool you can detect masking spells and you can sneak up on people without them knowing since you're *invisible* and whatnot, but gee whiz, can't you work faster?'"

"Was that sarcasm? I couldn't tell."

"Yes, that was sarcasm."

"Yeah, so was that. So what took so long?"

There was a pause, during which I tried to imagine what expression was on Malcolm's face. "I had to do some 'tuning' before I could get it to work," he said finally, sounding aggravated. "But I'm 99.9 percent certain Elise is exactly what she seems: a nonmagical human. She's not hiding anything. Well, except maybe alcoholism. She was drinking wine."

I glanced at the clock on my dashboard. "At nine a.m.?"

"Yup. *Red* wine. In a coffee mug."

"Damn." I couldn't decide whether to be amused, disapproving, or impressed. "Well, that's one we can cross off the list, again." I pulled away from the curb.

"Who's next on the list?"

"Deborah Mackey."

"Sweet."

* * *

Three hours later, I was parked just down the street from Helen Matson's house in Hope, crushing candy on my phone, when Malcolm returned to the car. "You won't believe this, but it was negative too."

I shut the game off and hit the steering wheel with the heel of my hand. "This is nuts. You and I both think that energy signature on the library wards belongs to a child or sibling of Betty Morrison, but you're telling me your spell is not picking up masking spells on *any* of them?"

"Yep. We've eliminated Elise, Deborah, Kathy, and Peter, and even Robert and Helen."

"And you're sure it works?"

Malcolm sighed. "Yes, I'm sure. It picked mine up before I tuned it out. It's picking *yours* up."

"Then what the hell?"

"Maybe we should call Natalie and see what the lawyer told her."

"Good thinking." I called her cell. There was no answer, so I left a message to call me.

"What now?" Malcolm asked.

I sighed. "I guess let's go back home. I want to keep looking for info on this *Kasten* and try to figure out what the hell it is. If nothing else pans out, I might try to track down John West or call that journalist about the local harnads."

* * *

By the time we got back to my house, it was almost two and I was hungry. Malcolm went down to the basement to work on spells. I started to pull a small pizza out of the freezer, but I thought about my cholesterol and decided to make a salad instead. I grabbed a diet soda and carried my lunch downstairs.

I set out my lunch at the table in the library area and pulled a couple of books from the shelves. Malcolm was using my circles in the workspace. It looked like he was trying to set up additional bolt-hole spells that could jump him to different crystals. Not a bad idea; we could leave one here and another at the office in case of emergencies.

I ate my lunch and started thumbing through the books, looking for any references to anything called a *Kasten*. I checked the indexes in the back, then skimmed them, finding nothing. When my vision got blurry, I took a break to do more Internet searches, but nothing came up, no matter what I searched for. Even alternate spellings gave me nothing.

I went back to the books, this time looking through some of my books on fire magic. Over an hour later, I still had nothing except a headache. No call from Natalie yet either.

Malcolm, meanwhile, was jumping in and out of crystals in the work area. "I hope you don't get stuck in one of those while you're testing your spells," I told him as I headed for my storage cabinets. "Before we start using them to jump you from place to place, I need some way to get you in and out of them too."

"I'm working on that," Malcolm said, disappearing and reappearing. "Right now I can jump in and out, but there's no masking spell on the crystals, so any mage who wanders by them would be able to tell I was in there."

"Good point. We should work on that too." I went to the leftmost cabinet, traced four runes on the door, and opened it. Four of the shelves held books and notebooks, the contents of my carefully curated but limited blood magic library. These books were black market and extremely hard to find. They'd been procured through third parties and delivered to post office boxes.

I pulled out any books that dealt with harnads or objects of power used in ritual blood magic. I took the books to the library table and spread them out while Malcolm went back to his bolt-hole spells. I bent my head over my books.

Twenty minutes later, I dropped a book on the table with a yell.

Malcolm popped to my side. "What?"

I pointed to the page. "I found it!"

"Found what?"

I picked up the book, a rather dry tome on harnad history and myth, and read: "'In the year 1648, a small village in Germany was destroyed by fire. Witnesses reported that the fire moved with unnatural speed, devouring everything and everyone in the village in a matter of seconds. The fire was said to have been the work of a local harnad leader, a man named Adelbert, who had been driven from the village after suspicions of witchcraft years before.'"

"What does this have to do with—"

"I'm getting there. 'Only one family survived the fire. Adelbert warned a young woman named Alide, whom he had hoped to marry before his banishment, that he was returning to take his revenge on the town and she should take her family and leave. He told her that he was in possession of an object of power he referred to as *der Zauberkasten*, which he claimed would destroy the village.'"

"What else does it say?" Malcolm asked.

I read on. "'The Adelbert *Kasten*, as it came to be called, is often considered to be a mythical object, as no reliable sources have ever documented its existence. It has been described by various anecdotal sources as a wooden box or chest with a lid. One account from mid-eighteenth-century France references the *Kasten* as a reliquary containing bones supposedly belonging to Adelbert himself. Another report, this one recorded by a monk in eighteenth-century Germany, describes the *Kasten* as wielding enormous destructive power when filled with the lifeblood or severed body parts of mages representing all four cardinal elements: air, fire, earth, and water. Such an object would be of obvious interest to a harnad, whose members regularly practice ritual blood magic, but there is no record of the *Kasten* being used since 1748 in Europe, and never in the United States. The evidence seems to suggest that if Adelbert's *Kasten* ever existed at all, it has been lost to time.' That's all it says."

"Holy shit," Malcolm said after a moment.

We stared at each other.

"So this *Kasten* is some sort of magical weapon of mass destruction that runs on the blood or body parts of mages?" Malcolm asked. "Do we think it's possible Betty Morrison and her harnad had it and she was keeping it hidden in her bookcase?"

I rubbed my forehead. "I don't know. The person who wrote this book certainly seems to think it probably didn't really exist, but Natalie's got a letter from John West to Betty thanking her for keeping it safe. Whether that was what was in the bookcase, I don't know."

I picked up my phone and called Natalie again.

"Hey, Alice," she said breathlessly. I heard traffic sounds in the background. It sounded like she was downtown. "I'm sorry I haven't had a chance to call you. I'm having to run some errands and deal with an accountant, and it's taking all day."

"That's okay. Did you get in touch with the lawyer?"

"I left a message," Natalie replied. "He hasn't called me back yet. If I don't hear from him today, I'll call him again in the morning."

I debated telling her what I'd found out about the *Kasten*, then decided it was a conversation better had in person. "Okay, great. Let me know what you find out." We said our good-byes and hung up.

"What's the plan for the rest of the day?" Malcolm asked.

I glanced at the clock on my phone. "Well, it's almost four. Now that we know what the *Kasten* is—or might be—I think I need to know more about John West."

Malcolm floated back and forth nervously. "Well, we know he's a high-level fire mage, and if he's in a harnad, that means he's probably a high-level blood mage as well."

"I'd like to get a sense of his magic so I could recognize it again, and to know exactly what I might be up against if it turns out he's in the middle of all this." I started gathering up the books on the table.

"Are you going to use a ruse so you can shake hands with him?"

I shook my head. "I don't think that's a good idea. It worked with Peter and the others because they have low-level magic and they have no idea how to use it. West is a high-level mage. If I touched him with my shields even partially down, he'd sense me immediately. I don't want to attract the attention of anyone in a harnad, least of all a high-level fire mage."

"I could do it," Malcolm suggested. "Like I did today, with the spell detector."

I thought about it but shook my head again. "No, it's dangerous for you too. Even with the masking spell, you're still vulnerable. All I need to do is get near him and I should be able to sense his magic."

My phone rang. I glanced at the screen. *Wolf.* I remembered he'd invited me to dinner tonight and I hadn't had time to think about it today.

I answered the call. "Hi, Sean."

"Hi, Allie." I smiled at the sound of his familiar voice: deep and a little growly. "I'm leaving the office and thought I'd check in and see if you were interested in getting dinner tonight."

"I was just about to head out to check on a person of interest who's come up in the last day. It may take up most of my evening."

"Want a colleague along for the ride? You can catch me up on the situation with Vaughan."

I thought about that. As a pack associate, I did owe its alpha a summary of what had transpired at my meeting with Charles. Plus, having Sean along was good camouflage for surveilling West. "That would work. I need to be at his office before he leaves work at five, though."

"It's four now. I can be at your place in twenty. Is that enough time?"

"Should be. I'll be ready."

"See you in twenty." We disconnected.

I finished collecting the books on the table and took them over to the cabinet. Malcolm followed me.

As I was putting them back on the shelves, he said, "So this thing with the werewolf."

"There's no 'thing' with Sean. He's useful."

"'Useful,' huh?" Malcolm didn't bother to hide his skepticism. "Useful for what?"

"Professionally useful." I put up the last book and closed the cabinet. "It was easier to get access to Natalie's aunts and uncle with him posing as a colleague or fiancé. I can use his car to surveil West. My alliance with his pack strengthens my reputation in the supe community and improves my bargaining position with the vamps."

"What alliance?"

I told Malcolm about my new status as pack associate and briefly recapped my meeting with Charles as we went upstairs and into my storage room.

He was understandably concerned about my close call with Charles, but wasn't easily distracted from his original question. "Sean may be useful, but it's more than that," Malcolm said as I pinned my hair up and reached for a blonde wig. "I saw the way you smiled when the phone rang."

I slipped the wig on carefully, then adjusted it in the mirror and used my fingers to gently comb out the hair. When I was satisfied with how it looked, I slipped on a pair of thick-framed fake glasses and left the storage room, turning the light off and closing the door.

"I do like his company." I checked to make sure I had everything I needed in my bag. "He's a good colleague and a good resource. Anything else that happens is purely recreational."

Malcolm grinned. "Good for you. All work and no play makes Alice a dull girl."

I scowled at him. "Whether or not I 'play' is none of your business."

"Duly noted. But if you're planning on having 'playtime' tonight, warn me so I can go hide out at Nat's house, okay?"

Aggravated, I dove at him, magic sparking on my fingertips. With a laugh, he vanished.

CHAPTER 19

Forty-five minutes later, Sean and I were parked outside a small office building just east of downtown, reading online reviews of John West's investment company and news stories about his fire magic. Most of the comments on the stories were from local contractors who had used his services. A couple of fire departments had hired him to help manage some wildfires, and apparently he'd saved a lot of lives and property.

To hear the city's fire chief tell it, John West was a hero who'd fearlessly walked into a wildfire and controlled it so it could be contained. I did an Internet search for the incident and found news footage. Sean and I watched in stunned silence.

"I can see why you're keeping your distance on this one," Sean said after we'd seen the video twice. "Have you ever seen anyone control that much fire at once?"

"Yes." My grandfather could, not that he'd ever used it to help anyone. "But it's very rare. As much as I'd like to avoid him and anyone else in his harnad, if there is one, forewarned is forearmed. If I end up having to meet him, I don't want to go in blind."

"That is true, though in this case, I'm not sure how much good it might do you."

I stayed quiet and watched the video again.

On the way to West's office, I'd told Sean about my meeting with Charles and the vampire's demand for my blood. Though his hands tightened on the steering wheel until it creaked, his only comments were professional and neutral. I'd also told him who we thought West might be—a blood mage and member of a local harnad—but didn't mention the *Kasten*. If that was what was missing from Betty's library, and it was an object of power, the fewer people who were aware of its existence, the better, until Malcolm and I knew more about it.

Once the video ended, I read up more on West's bio while we waited. As five o'clock approached, lights started turning off in the various offices and people started pouring out of the building. I didn't see any sign of John West until ten after, when he suddenly came out the front door.

"That's him," I said to Sean.

Despite being in his seventies, West looked lean, like a runner, with silver hair brushed back from hard, blue eyes that reminded me of my grandfather's cold gaze. The fire mage scanned the parking lot as he walked briskly to a black BMW, laid his suit jacket carefully across the backseat, and climbed into the driver's seat.

Sean started his car and fell in behind him, keeping his distance as we battled rush-hour traffic on our way north of town. I knew West's house was on the east side, so I wondered where we were going. It was probably too much to hope that he was headed to a harnad meeting.

When he finally turned through the gates of the art museum, Sean asked, "What are we doing here?"

"No idea." I thought the museum normally closed at six, but the parking lot still had quite a few cars in it. West parked, put his suit jacket back on, and headed into the museum.

"He may be meeting somebody," Sean commented.

"Could be." I checked my wig in the mirror on the visor, unfastened my seat belt, and opened my door. Sean and I exited the car. I slung my bag over my shoulder, and we headed into the museum.

When we stepped inside, I scanned the enormous lobby and spotted West heading toward the auditorium. An easel beside the reception desk advertised a special presentation tonight by an art historian on the Italian High Renaissance.

"Are you here for the lecture?" the woman behind the desk asked us cheerfully.

West went into the auditorium, so it looked like we were. I paid for our admission, and Sean and I put museum stickers on our shirts.

When we got to the auditorium, I spotted John West holding a glass of wine and looking over a spread of hors d'oeuvres.

Sean and I went to the cash bar. He bought water for me and a beer for himself, and then we browsed the long table of bite-sized appetizers. Food and drinks in hand, we staked out a spot along the wall where I could keep an eye on West as Sean chatted about his day. West spoke to no one; unlike most of the other attendees, he stood off by himself, sipping his wine.

A few minutes before six, people started to move to the seats. We managed to snag the seats behind West. I put my bag and jacket in the seat next to mine. The auditorium was only about a third full, but I didn't want anyone sitting down next to us.

A museum employee came out, and I half listened as she welcomed everyone to the museum and said a few words about the evening's speaker, an art historian named Dr. Jacob Altman. I pictured a dusty old man with horn-rimmed glasses carrying an overflowing briefcase.

When the presenter came out, however, I was surprised that Dr. Altman was an enthusiastic young man with unruly hair and Converse sneakers. Instead of an old, battered briefcase, he carried a MacBook Pro that he connected at the lectern, and fired up a very modern PowerPoint.

As the art historian lectured us on the finer points of High Renaissance art, I watched John West. The older man seemed to be listening intently and taking notes in a small notebook. It was looking more and more like he was simply here to learn about a bunch of sixteenth-century painters I'd never heard of.

When the presentation was well underway and I was certain West's attention was focused on the lecture, I closed my eyes and concentrated on his magical energy as it buzzed against the edges of my senses. Slowly, I reached out with my mind.

White-hot fire screamed through the crack in my shields like a blowtorch through tissue paper. The sheer power of West's magic blazed through my brain in a shockwave that felt like it would take off the back of my skull. The energy level was nearly incomprehensible. My senses shut down, and my arms and legs went rigid with strain. I had to raise my shields or risk permanent damage.

It took an excruciatingly long time and every ounce of strength I had to raise my tattered shields and block him out.

When awareness returned, I realized I was half slumped in my chair and sweating profusely. I heard a strange sound I slowly recognized as applause; apparently, the presentation was over. I had no idea how much time had passed while I was semiconscious; it might have been as much as ten or fifteen minutes. The audience was filing out of the auditorium.

My entire body hurt as if all my nerve endings had been seared, but the agony was receding like a tide going out. As the fog lifted and my vision cleared, I became aware of a different kind of pain. Sean was gripping my right wrist tightly enough to bruise, and probably had been for a while, judging by the ache.

When I looked at him, his eyes shone gold. "Allie," he said roughly. "Tell me you can hear me."

I stared at him uncomprehendingly. I heard the words, but they weren't connecting with anything. I wondered if I'd shorted something out in my brain.

A blank stare wasn't the response Sean was looking for. As West finished collecting his belongings and stood, heading for the exit, Sean gripped my chin and leaned closer. His eyes glowed. "Alice," he said, and a little shiver of something ran down my spine. "Wake up and talk to me."

It felt like someone took their hand and brushed away the cobwebs. Somehow, though I wasn't a shifter, Sean had been able to use his alpha influence to help me recover. I shuddered and exhaled a long, shaky breath. As my straining muscles suddenly relaxed, I fell forward against his chest, making a pained noise when my nose hit his sternum.

Sean tipped my chin up to look me in the eyes as I rubbed my nose. "You with me now?"

"I'm with you." My voice still sounded a little thin, but at least I could think clearly.

"Give yourself a minute," Sean said. "West went into the men's room."

How he'd seen that with his focus on me, I had no idea, but I was grateful for the extra few minutes to clear my head and regain muscle control.

By the time West exited the bathroom, Sean and I were making our way toward the auditorium doors. My legs were wobbly, but I was walking on my own.

We followed West back out to the parking lot. "You doing okay?" Sean asked as we got in the car.

"I feel much better." I put my bag on the floor and buckled in.

West left the lot, heading east, and Sean followed at a distance. As he drove, I thought about what I'd felt. John West was, by far, the most powerful fire mage I had ever encountered, and that was saying something. West made my grandfather's fire magic feel like a birthday candle by comparison. Perhaps more chilling, West's blood magic would likely be as strong or stronger than his fire magic. I thought of what my grandfather could do with his fire magic, and then imagined someone stronger, and with high-level blood magic too. I felt nauseous.

I knew what I wanted to know about West's magic, but it wasn't going to help me sleep any easier.

* * *

West drove back to his house. After a brief debate, I opted not to stay and watch his house, having no real reason to right now, other than my curiosity about his harnad. We headed home.

When we arrived, Sean pulled into my driveway and parked. Before he could say anything, I said, "I know you said you wanted to go out to dinner, but how would you feel about just ordering a pizza and maybe watching a movie here? I know my TV isn't as big as yours, but we could stream something."

"I was hoping to take you out to this great steakhouse I like, and then maybe for a walk down by the…." Sean trailed off, reading my expression. "What are you thinking when you get that look in your eyes?"

I wasn't sure what look he was referring to, but what I was thinking was that I'd never been on a real, formal date—not the kind he was describing. I hadn't been picked up and taken to dinner, or for a romantic walk. It would be difficult, or impossible, to explain why something so seemingly innocuous felt so terrifying. I tried to figure out what to say.

"Hey." Sean smiled and leaned over to kiss me. "It would be very much okay to order a pizza and watch a movie," he told me when we broke apart. "I can't think of anything I'd rather do."

Sean grabbed his go-bag out of the trunk while I lowered the house wards, unlocked the door, and went inside. I put my stuff down by the door and went around turning on lights while he changed into casual clothes in the downstairs bathroom. I grew puzzled when I sensed Malcolm wasn't in the house, but remembered his comment about going to Natalie's in case Sean and I needed privacy. I smiled to myself.

Once Sean changed into jeans and a vintage Allman Brothers T-shirt, we ordered our pizza, and then I showed him around the house. He was impressed with the renovations I'd designed. We talked home remodeling for a bit, until our tour took us to the door to the basement.

I paused a few feet from the threshold. I'd never let anyone but Malcolm into my basement, but for some reason, I wanted to show it to Sean. "The basement is my library and spellwork area. Don't ever let anyone touch the door or try to go into the basement without me. The wards could kill them. At the very least, they'd be incapacitated."

"Understood."

I drew a series of four runes on the doorframe. "What was that?" Sean asked.

"Think of it like a security code. Give me your hand."

After a moment's hesitation, Sean reached out. I took his hand in mine, placed my index finger along his, and touched the doorframe. Sean twitched when the wards gave him a little zap. "It's tasting you," I murmured, and I traced two more runes on the doorway with our fingers.

A frisson of magic ran through us, and Sean sucked in a breath. "Wow."

"The wards know you as a friend now." I released his hand and reached for the doorknob. "It will be uncomfortable to cross the threshold, but you won't get knocked out. I'd say brace yourself, but it won't be as bad as when you broke through Natalie's house wards."

"That hurt," Sean said.

I laughed. "Yeah, I bet. We've both been on the wrong end of some wards lately." I flipped on the basement lights and breathed deeply as I pushed through the invisible wall of magic to start down the stairs ahead of Sean. Behind me, Sean grunted, but he didn't falter or stagger. Either werewolf strength or werewolf pride, or a combination of both, I thought.

When he was through, I led him down the steps. At the bottom, he stopped and looked around the basement, taking it all in.

I spread my arms out. "Welcome to my lair, Mr. Maclin."

He stayed on the stair landing. "What's safe down here and what's not?"

"That's a smart question to ask. When dealing with mages and their private spaces, it's always a good idea to assume there are spells all around. In this case, you have been designated an official 'friendly' presence, so most of the spells and wards in here will be uncomfortable but not harmful to you."

"Most, huh?" Sean looked like a man standing in the middle of a minefield. "So what shouldn't I touch?"

I pointed to the storage cabinets. "The last two cabinets on the left have black wards. If you touch them, they will kill you."

Sean stared at me.

"The rest of the cabinets are safe to you, but like the threshold upstairs, it will be uncomfortable."

He looked like he was still processing the fact there were spells in the room that would kill someone. I could only imagine what his reaction would be if he knew what the basement's perimeter wards were capable of doing.

He cleared his throat. "Should I even ask what's in those cabinets on the left?"

"Dangerous magic stuff."

"'Dangerous magic stuff,'" Sean repeated. "Okay. The security consultant in me wonders if the contents are explosive."

I shrugged. "Not particularly, but all magic is volatile, even earth and air magic."

"Other than the fire in the bottle you made the other day, I haven't really gotten to see much of your magic." He started to lean against the wall, but the sizzle of the wards made him move away. "I feel like a kid asking this, but is there anything you can show me?"

I grinned. "Show and tell? I can do that. Come with me." I walked to the circles on the floor. Cautiously, he followed me. "Stand in the center circle." He stepped into it and I stood outside it.

"What are you going to do?"

I winked. "It's a surprise. Don't worry; you're perfectly safe in there." I closed both his circle and mine and they blazed with energy.

He jerked. "I can feel it."

"Good. Now watch." I raised my hands in front of me. They erupted in bright green fire.

He made a startled sound. "Are you all right?"

"Of course." I turned my hands and moved closer so he could see the flames caressing my skin but not burning me. "Cold fire. Earth magic." I drew the fire slowly up my arms and let it spread over my upper body. It took focus because I hadn't done this in a while, but I knew it looked incredible. I didn't get much opportunity to show off my fancy tricks. The bright green fire danced along my arms.

"That's beautiful," Sean breathed, watching the fire move. "How much control do you have over it?"

In answer, I pulled the fire back to my right hand, then flicked my wrist. The fire became a short rope about five feet long. The rope coiled through the air, the flames dancing. I twirled it over my head, cowgirl style, and it snapped out in front of me like a whip before coiling back into my hand.

Sean applauded. I laughed and pulled the fire back down to the tip of my right index finger. I blew on my finger and the fire went out, only to flare up on my left hand as if I'd blown it there.

It was a corny trick, but Sean grinned. I broke his circle with my hand. "Come here." He walked up close to me. "Hold out your index finger."

He held up his left—not his right, I noticed, which would have been his trigger finger. I murmured an invocation and traced a spell in the air. "Don't move." I touched my finger to his.

His eyes widened as the green flame spread to the tip of his index finger. "It's cold," he said in wonder.

I drew my hand back, and a small green flame continued to burn on his finger.

He raised his eyebrows. "Are you going to put this out?"

"Nope, but *you* can. Blow on it."

He looked at me.

"Blow on it," I repeated.

He blew, and the flame went out.

"Now, focus on your finger, envision the flame, snap your thumb and index finger together, and say, '*Frio*.'"

Sean awkwardly snapped his fingers. "*Frio*." The tip of his index finger burst into green flame. "Whoa." He stared at his hand.

I watched him admire the tiny flame. "It's a simple spell. I can take it off, or it will fade by itself in about a week."

He blew on his finger and the flame went out, then he brought it back. "Holy shit, this is awesome." He blew out the flame.

I laughed. "I guess I'll just leave it, then. But remember: always use your powers for good. Now for the big finale." I closed his circle, isolating him inside, and my hands flamed up again.

This time, as I held on to my earth magic for the fire, I brought up my air magic. An impossible breeze came up, blowing my hair back from my face. I continued to draw on the air magic until it whipped around the inner circle where I stood, contained on the inside by Sean's circle and on the outside by mine.

He watched the wind blowing my hair as the green flames on my hands danced. "Incredible."

"You ain't seen nothin' yet. Stay in your circle." *Showtime*.

I took a deep breath, exhaled, and my entire body went up in green flame.

"Allie!" he shouted, fear in his voice.

"I'm all right." I held my arms out to feel the wind on my body. Then, as the wind whipped around me furiously, I opened the valve and poured green fire from every square inch of my body.

In an instant, the circle where I stood became an inferno of cold fire. Blown by the wind, the firestorm raged in my circle while Sean stood safe in the eye of a hurricane. His mouth hung open.

I tilted my head back and closed my eyes and let the fire and air pour out of me. Like I'd told Natalie, using magic felt wonderful, like that first stretch when you wake up in the morning. There was a great pleasure to using magic, if you stayed the hell away from the cabals and were able to use it to help instead of harm.

Letting the magic flow out of me felt so good, I could have stood like that for a long time, but I remembered Sean was watching and waiting. I opened my eyes.

He was up next to the barrier of the inner circle, as close as he could get to me and my firestorm. His expression was a combination of awe, admiration, and something else I couldn't quite interpret, but that might have been hunger, and not for food.

"Do you trust me?" I asked him.

He didn't hesitate. "Yes."

I murmured an invocation, reached out, and grabbed his hand. The inner circle fell, and the inferno raged around us as I held his hand in mine, his body protected by a spell. He stood frozen as his brain struggled to process that he was standing, unhurt, in the middle of a firestorm that felt cold instead of hot.

I drew him to me and kissed him. The hunger I'd seen in his eyes was in his kiss. It took my breath away.

While my lips were pressed to his, I pulled both my air and earth magic back into myself. The wind began to fade, and the fire dwindled. By the time the kiss ended, the flames were gone, and the air was still.

Sean touched his forehead to mine. He was breathing heavily, but I was calmer than I'd been in days. I felt purified.

"Good enough for show and tell?" I teased.

"Holy shit, yes." He wrapped me in his arms.

I rested my head against his chest. "Next time, I'll do something *really* cool."

His laugh filled the basement.

* * *

The pizza arrived not long after we went back upstairs. I let Sean flip through my vinyl collection while I got napkins and beers and set up our dinner on the coffee table in the living room.

As I sat on the couch to take off my boots, he fired up the turntable and I heard a familiar sound like a heartbeat. I grinned. "Excellent choice."

"Just when I thought the evening couldn't get any better, I find out you've got *Dark Side of the Moon* on vinyl," Sean said, dropping onto the sofa and grabbing a piece of pizza. "If you've got *The Wizard of Oz,* we're in business."

"I thought that was an urban legend."

"It's not. They really do sync."

We ate pizza and drank our beers and listened to Pink Floyd. I ate two slices and lay down on the couch with my head in Sean's lap while he "wolfed" down the rest of the pizza. When the first side of the record ran out, we were both too comfortable and full of pizza to get up and flip it over. Sean ran his fingers through my hair, gently working out the tangles from the windstorm downstairs. I closed my eyes and relaxed.

After a while, he asked, "Where do things stand with your case?"

"I've eliminated all the known suspects *again.*" I told him about Malcolm's masking spell detector and our visits to Natalie's family earlier in the day. "What West's involvement is, I'm not sure, but finding out more about him and this harnad he was supposedly in with Betty is probably the next step."

I didn't have to see his face to know the idea wasn't making him happy, but he didn't object. Instead, he said, "Thanks for including me in today's adventures."

"I'm not sure anything we did today could be categorized as 'adventures.'" I shifted on the couch and looked up at him. "But there's still time to make things interesting."

His eyes glinted. "What did you have in mind?"

"For starters, how about this?" I rolled to my feet, then straddled his lap. His hands gripped my hips as I kissed him, then bit his lower lip. He growled.

I moved my lips across his jaw to his ear, tracing its contours with the tip of my tongue before plunging it inside. He jerked like I'd shocked him and growled again. I bit his earlobe and he groaned. "Allie."

I went back to kissing him, feeling the hard length of him between us as I moved against him. Sean ran his hands up under my shirt and over my ribs to cup my breasts. I gasped when his thumbs stroked my nipples through my bra.

I pulled my shirt off over my head and took his face in my hands.

His eyes glowed like golden lanterns. "Are you sure?"

"Absolutely," I told him.

He made a snarly noise, and suddenly my bra tore in half and his mouth was on me. "Hey," I said weakly.

"I'll buy you another one," he growled, then bit down. I cried out and dug my nails into his shoulders, my head falling back.

I heard him whisper something as he snapped his fingers, and when I looked back, he was tracing a line down my breastbone with the tiny, cold flame on his finger. I whimpered as the cold, tingly sensation shot through me like an arrow.

Sean held up his spelled finger. "This has possibilities," he mused.

I blew out the flame and reached for his belt. "You're overdressed."

Sean stood, his hands under my butt. "Put your legs around my waist," he instructed me. "We're going upstairs."

I locked my ankles behind his back and kissed him as he carried me upstairs. When we got to my room, he tossed me carefully onto the bed. I raised myself up on my elbows to watch as he took off his T-shirt and shoes. He reached for his belt.

"Come here," I ordered.

To my surprise, he obeyed. I undid his belt, then unfastened and unzipped his pants. His breathing sped up as I pushed his jeans and boxers down to free him.

Sean sucked in a breath when I wrapped my hand around him and stroked gently. I leaned forward and took him into my mouth. He groaned as I moved in a steady rhythm that made him fight for control.

Soon, Sean was breathing heavy, and his fingers dug into my shoulders. "Stop, stop," he said roughly, and I released him from my mouth. "Clothes off."

I stood and took off my socks, then slid my jeans and underwear off as one. I reached into my nightstand drawer for a condom, tossed it on the bed, and looked at him with an arched eyebrow. "Why aren't you naked?"

In a second, Sean was out of his jeans and boxers. With a throaty growl, he leaped and took me down onto the bed, his mouth on mine. I hooked my leg around his hip and arched up against his body in a blatant demand that made him chuckle.

Instead of unwrapping the condom, he pushed my leg to the side and reached down between us. I writhed underneath him and bit his shoulder. He kissed me again, muffling my cries with his mouth. I started to shudder.

"That's it," he murmured against my lips. "Come for me, Allie."

I was vaguely aware of my own voice calling his name as everything fractured around me in a wave of intense pleasure. A moment later, I heard the condom packet tear. In a single movement, he grabbed my hip, sank his teeth into the flesh of my shoulder, and thrust into me.

I threw my head back and screamed. He buried his face in my neck as he moved. I dug my nails into his back as he adjusted his angle and speed, driving me back toward the edge.

He rose above me, his eyes bright gold, predatory and hungry, beautiful and dangerous. "Allie," he growled. "Release your magic."

I intended to, but first, I wanted more than merely physical intimacy. I closed my eyes and dropped my shields, focusing on Sean.

Suddenly, my mind filled with images, smells, and sounds. I saw flashes of moonlight, of teeth and fur, trees and a grassy field, and smelled forest and earth. I heard a howl so beautiful that it brought tears to my eyes.

Then I saw myself, my head thrown back and eyes closed, gasping for air, the sheen of sweat on my skin, and I knew I was seeing through Sean's eyes, and feeling what he felt. Our combined pleasure was so intense, I thought I would black out.

Everything came apart in a rush. Sean's movements caught the crest of my bliss and stoked it higher. My magic tore free in a burst that felt far stronger than when we'd been together before. Once again, I heard things crashing in my room. I opened my eyes and saw the green-and-white hurricane was infused with golden, primal shifter magic, Sean's power mixed with my own.

Our magic rolled through us in a wave. Above me, Sean groaned and began to shudder. I cried out as he made a sound that was part shout, part howl, and collapsed on top of me. My inner muscles twitched around him, and he jerked and snarled.

"Did you just *growl* at me?" I asked, reaching up to push sweaty hair back from his forehead.

"Maybe." He rolled on to his side and pulled me tightly against him. "Are you all right?"

I felt so much better than *all right*. "Yes," I replied breathlessly.

My shoulder stung. I reached up to touch it, and my fingers came away smeared with red.

Sean froze. "I hurt you."

I kissed him, tugging gently on his lip with my teeth. "It's all right. I like a little pain with my pleasure."

He looked stunned. "I've never done that before. I'm sorry."

"I bit you first," I pointed out, kissing the mark my teeth had left on his shoulder. "You were just returning the favor."

"I shouldn't have—"

"Sean, shut up."

He shut up.

A few minutes later, I said, "Was this how you were hoping the evening would go?"

He nuzzled my hair. "I'd be lying if I said no, but for the record, I really did want to take you to dinner, and for a walk along the riverfront, and maybe for some ice cream, first."

This man thought I was worth taking to dinner and out for ice cream. I felt a stab of disbelief mixed with wonder. "Maybe next time."

He jerked, pulling back from me.

"What?"

He looked confused. "I thought...." He shook his head as if to clear it and pulled me close again.

"So there will be a next time?" he asked finally.

"I'd like there to be a next time."

"So would I." He ran his fingers over my hip, tracing the line of tattooed stars that ran from my upper left thigh to my rib cage. "Speaking of which...."

My eyes widened.

* * *

Some wonderful time later, Sean held me close as I lay on top of him and we gasped for air.

"I need you so much, I can't even think," he said, his lips against my ear. "I can't get enough of you, and it's making me crazy."

"We can be crazy together," I told him. "It's more fun that way."

CHAPTER 20

At a little after midnight, we lay on the bed in a tangle of arms and legs. Most of the bedding was on the floor, along with pretty much everything else in my room.

As it turned out, the rumors of werewolf stamina were *not* exaggerated. I was well past the point of exhaustion, but judging by the now-familiar glint in Sean's eyes, he was, almost unbelievably, thinking about another round, and I was thinking seriously about whether I would survive it.

Before either of us could do anything about that, however, my phone beeped. Sean had brought our phones upstairs in case he got a call from work, then abandoned them on top of the dresser. They were now somewhere on the floor.

When I groaned and started to move, he wrapped his arm around me and pulled me close, removing all doubt as to whether he was recovering. "Leave it," he growled into my ear. "You're mine until the morning."

"It might be an emergency," I pointed out. "Nobody texts this late at night with good news."

He grumbled but let me go. I slid out of bed, wincing slightly, then started pawing through the debris on the floor. I finally found my phone under some clothes.

To my surprise, there was a text message from Adri. *Mr. V would like to meet tonight to discuss a time-sensitive project that requires your expertise.*

Can you come to Hawthorne's?

I frowned and texted back. *Busy tonight. Can it wait till tomorrow?*

Adri: Mr. V believes it cannot.

I made a face. *What time?*

The response was immediate. *As soon as possible. Mr. V awaits your arrival.*

Well, that sounded serious—and potentially very lucrative. I mentally applied a multiplier to my usual Court rate and fired back a reply. *ETA 1 hour.*

Sean sat up. "What's going on?"

"Text from Adri. Charles has an urgent project and wants to meet." I tossed my phone on the bed and headed for the bathroom.

Sean was off the bed and in front of me in a blink. "Is this a trap?"

I shook my head. "I doubt it. He mentioned the other night that there was a project coming up." I was reasonably certain Charles had no plan to demand a meal or take one by force; my alliance with Sean's pack protected me, and beyond that, my abilities made me a valuable asset both to him personally and the Vampire Court. I doubted he would risk losing that resource by biting me.

"I don't like it. Not after what happened Saturday night."

I shrugged and continued into the bathroom, turning on the shower. "Come with me." I stepped into the tub and slid the curtain closed. "You can stay downstairs in the bar while I meet with Charles."

The curtain moved, and Sean stepped into the shower with me. I raised my eyebrows.

He gave me a toothy smile that brought back a rush of pleasant memories. "I can wash your back."

"Don't make me turn this shower on cold," I warned him.

He laughed and reached for my bottle of shower gel. "I'll be on my best behavior," he promised. "The sooner we get this meeting over with, the sooner we can come back to bed." His eyes gleamed, and I very much doubted he was thinking about sleeping. Truth be told, neither was I. I hoped this new project wouldn't take long to discuss. By the time we got back, I figured I'd have my second wind, and then we'd see exactly what it took to wear out an alpha werewolf.

* * *

Almost exactly an hour later, we parked down the street from Hawthorne's and strolled up the sidewalk to the door, where Bryan was checking IDs.

"Evening, Miss Alice," he boomed. "Here to see Mr. Vaughan?"

"Yes. Is he ready for me?"

"Adri will come get you in a few minutes." Bryan glanced at my companion. "Mr. Maclin should plan to wait for you in the bar. Vampire/shifter politics are touchy these days. The appearance of favoritism might cause problems." He stepped aside to let us pass.

Despite it being two a.m. on a Monday night, the bar was busy. I sent Sean to find us a table while I went to say hello to Pete.

Pete grinned when he saw me walking up, but the smile fell off when he spotted Sean behind me. *What the hell is up with that?* I wondered.

"Hey, Alice," he said. "How are you doing tonight?"

"Doing great, Pete. Just wanted to say hi. We're going to try to find a table."

"What are you drinking? I'll send it over."

I ordered two bottles of a craft beer I liked, and Pete said he had to get them out of the cooler in the back. I went to find Sean and finally spotted him at a standing table by the window.

As we stood together at the table, Sean rested his hand on my hip. I stepped away slightly to put a little distance between us, and Sean's hand fell away. Despite our physical intimacy and how content I was to be in his company, I wasn't anyone's territory. Sean looked frustrated, but he leaned down to kiss my temple and I let him.

When AC/DC came on the jukebox, Sean and I started talking about favorite rock albums. I was mounting a passionate defense of the Eagles' *Hell Freezes Over* when a server appeared with our beers.

"I guess I don't know much about recent developments in local vamp/shifter politics," I said, drinking my beer. "Is there something going on in particular, or is just the usual intrigues?"

"Nothing specific going on that I'm aware of. There are three large werewolf packs in the area—mine and two others—and a half dozen smaller packs, plus the cats, though they're more of a loose-knit clan. Everyone's looking to make alliances, and the vamps have more power and influence than any other group. Since Vaughan is on the Vampire

Court, it would probably be prudent for him not to be seen meeting privately with any of the pack alphas. The other alphas might take offense, and who knows what the cats might do. They're weird."

I laughed at that. "Such a *wolf* thing to say, disparaging the cats," I teased.

"It's not disparaging if it's true," Sean griped. "They *are* weird."

We drank our beers and listened to the music. I caught Sean looking strangely at me a couple of times, but didn't have a chance to ask him about it before I saw Adri heading toward me, weaving through the crowd with a dancer's grace. She caught my eye.

"I'm heading up." I gave Sean a quick kiss. "I'll be back."

"I'll be here."

Adri seemed preoccupied and said little on our way upstairs. Despite my earlier certainty that Charles was not a threat, Adri's silence was making me uneasy. On the other hand, maybe her mood had nothing to do with me.

When we arrived at Charles's office, she knocked twice, then opened the door without waiting for a response.

Charles rose when we entered. For a moment, I thought I saw something—anger, maybe—in his eyes, but it was gone before I could figure it out. "Thank you for coming on such short notice," he said. "Can I offer you a drink?"

"I'm good for now." I settled into the guest chair while Adri stood off the side—not by the door as usual, which I thought was odd. "You said you had a project you needed to discuss right away."

Charles sat down behind his desk and looked at me silently. I raised my eyebrows.

Finally, he spoke. "I must confess that I have asked you to meet under false pretenses. There is no such project."

I stared at him, my stomach knotting. "Then why am I here?"

"I apologize for the subterfuge, but it was necessary, for reasons that will become apparent." He folded his hands on top of his desk. "In the past few hours, I have been made aware of information that concerns you. Despite our…disagreement…on Saturday evening, because we have known one another for some time, I felt it was imperative to pass it on to you immediately, hence the urgent summons."

My uneasiness gave way to full-blown apprehension. "Go on."

"I understand you are in the company of Sean Maclin of the Tomb Mountain Pack."

"Yes," I said.

"I believe you met him for the first time in the bar last week."

"That's true." Where was he going with this?

"Forgive me for noticing, but it would appear you have become lovers."

Incensed, I stood, forgetting in my shock that I needed to avoid making any abrupt movements. Adri was suddenly beside me. "How the *hell*—"

"I can smell him on you," Charles said matter-of-factly.

Goddamned vampire senses. I blushed and hated myself for it. "What of it?"

Charles rose from his desk and came around to stand in front of me. "Maclin leads a strong pack and has a good reputation, but he is unmated, which is unusual for an alpha at his age. Werewolf packs require an alpha pair to remain stable. His lack of a mate is causing dissension and insecurity in the pack, and the other packs sense the turmoil and are circling. Recently, Maclin's beta advised him that he must find a mate, or he risks losing his pack, either to infighting or opportunistic attacks from rivals."

I felt sick to my stomach.

"The beta suggested some possible mates for him, including a female from a smaller pack, which would bring about an alliance many believe would be advantageous. According to one of the pack members, who visited our bar this night and spoke to Pete, Maclin declined the offer to mate with this female, stating that he wishes instead to find a mage, preferably a strong one, and infect her with the werewolf virus. He believes such a woman would make an ideal alpha female for the pack, protecting it from possible attacks from other packs, and discouraging challengers from within."

Charles said something else, but I didn't hear him. I thought of Sean's face, his eyes, his smile. How he held me when I was hurting. The way he looked at me while we had sex. The heat of his touch. How he'd broken through house wards to get to me, and rearranged his entire work schedule to spend two days by my side.

"I need you so much, I can't even think," he'd said.

The bastard. He'd sought me out in the bar and slept with me because he needed a mate to keep control of his pack. He planned to bite me, turn me into a werewolf, and make me his alpha female.

I felt a surge of fury so raw, so ferocious, that for a moment I went blind with rage. Blood magic sizzled on my skin, threatening to break loose and destroy Charles's office and everything in it. I closed my eyes so the vampire couldn't see them glow. With herculean effort, I pulled the magic back and regained control.

Charles moved toward me. "Alice?"

I took two deep breaths and waited until I knew my eyes were back to normal before opening them. "Thank you for telling me." My voice was so cold, it made Charles seem warm and fuzzy by comparison. Adri watched me warily. "I need to go downstairs and tell Sean that our…date…is over. We came together in his car. Is there someone who can give me a ride home?"

"Ms. Smith will take you." Charles glanced at Adri. Whatever instructions he gave her through their telepathic bond, her eyes hardened perceptibly.

He regarded me. "We will speak again."

I nodded, and Adri opened the door to the office. When we were down the hall, she said quietly, "There is a direct exit to the parking garage."

"I'm not going down the back stairs." I pushed open the door to the main staircase and it banged against the wall.

We returned to the bar. The music and cacophony of voices were almost painful after the silence of the upper floor. Weaving my way through the crowd, I spotted Sean before he saw me. He was still at the table, leaning against it, drinking a beer. Two empty bottles sat in front of him. As I watched, a cute blonde came up to him. He shook his head and said something, and she moved on.

Sean looked up. Our eyes met through the crowd, and for a heartbeat, the bar noise faded away. He set his beer down immediately and moved to intercept me, his eyes darkening. I was aware of Adri behind me, close enough to intervene if needed, but far enough away to give us the illusion of privacy.

Sean's gaze flicked to Adri and then back to me. "What's wrong?"

"I have to go." My voice could have cut glass. "Feel free to stay. Adri's going to give me a ride home."

Something shadowy and dangerous flashed in his eyes. "Just like that?"

Anger made my skin feel like it was on too tight. I wanted to confront him, but this was not the place. Not in public, not with so many witnesses—or potential collateral damage—around us. "I have business I need to take care of."

Sean's eyes narrowed. He looked at Adri again, this time with open suspicion. "What's going on?"

"I don't have time to do this with you right now. We'll talk later." I started to walk away.

He grabbed my arm. "Allie, wait." Magic crackled on my skin, and he flinched.

Adri took a step forward.

I met Sean's gaze. "Take your hand off me."

Sean let go. I felt a strange spike of something like hurt and anger that made me take an involuntary step back. I shook my head to clear it, then looked at Adri. "Let's go," I said.

I turned on my heel and walked out.

* * *

Adri took me home in a black Audi SUV. She seemed content to drive quietly, and I had no idea what to say. My fury had gone from red-hot to icy-cold, the glacial calm allowing me to think clearly. I knew now why Pete reacted the way he did to Sean being with me tonight.

Unbidden, images of the past few days, of Sean, tumbled through my brain. I felt like the world had been yanked out from under my feet and I was dangling over a long fall into nothing.

He wanted to turn me into a werewolf. My shoulder hurt where he'd bitten me.

Adri stopped for a red light. "Are you all right?"

"Yes." I turned away to look out the window.

"Do you want to talk about it?"

"No."

"Okay." A pause, then: "I'm sorry, Alice."

I said nothing. The light turned green. Adri drove on.

A few minutes later, she pulled into my driveway and parked. "Do you need anything?"

"I'm fine. Thank you for the ride home."

"Do you want me to come in?"

I shook my head. "I'm tired. I'm going to bed."

She squeezed my hand. "Call me if you need me. You've got my number."

"Have a good night."

"You too."

I got out of the SUV and headed for the front steps. Adri waited until I was inside before she started backing down the drive. I waved at her through the front window and watched as she drove away. I let the curtain fall back in place and stood in the foyer of my house.

I pulled my shirt off over my head to see the bite mark on my shoulder. What I'd regarded earlier as a souvenir of a passionate roll in the hay now looked more like a sinister brand. The light from the kitchen revealed a pizza box and two empty beer bottles on my coffee table, right where we'd left them. I knew if I went upstairs, my bed would smell like us. I might have been imagining it, but I thought I caught a hint of Sean's scent—aftershave and forest—in the air. He'd gotten past my defenses—not by much, but enough to become a presence in my home, all on a foundation of lies.

My fury erupted out of me like a volcano, and this time, I made no attempt to hold it back. My blood magic became a violent red, black, and purple storm with my body in the center. In seconds, the walls of the foyer were stripped bare of pictures, the small table by the door reduced to kindling, the curtain ripped from its rod and shredded. The overhead light fixture burst in a hailstorm of broken glass. The magic I'd accidentally unleashed in front of Malcolm when we'd first met was nothing compared to this. That had been a trickle from a faucet. This was Niagara Falls.

I roared inside while the magic tore through and around me. I wanted to burn down the world.

I realized I was angry less at Sean than at myself. *This is what happens when you trust someone even a little bit*, I raged in my head. *You can trust no one, not ever, you brainless, fucking idiot*. Furious at my own stupidity, I went to my knees and smashed my fists as hard as I could into the tile. My knuckles split. I did it again. Blood splattered across the floor, and I felt bones crunch.

I stayed on my knees, head hanging, eyes closed.

Through the fog, I heard a crash and realized the door to my coat closet had been ripped off its hinges. With enormous difficulty, I pulled the magic back into myself before I tore down my own house. My skin hummed like I was holding on to a high-voltage wire. I shuddered and bent over, resting my forehead on the tile, my head between my arms. For several long minutes, the only sound was the pounding of my heart and my ragged breathing.

I must have seemed like easy prey that night at Hawthorne's, alone and injured from my run-in with Betty's wards. I'd probably put up more of a fight than Sean had anticipated, but in the end, he'd almost suckered me into believing, if only for a moment, I could be worth something to someone for more than my magic—that I was deserving of kindness and caring for who I was, instead of what I could do.

You'd think I'd know better by now.

Out front, a car door slammed. I jerked upright with a sound that might have been a snarl. Moments later, heavy footsteps crossed the porch and a fist banged on the door, three loud booms that made it shake and the wards sizzle. "Alice!" Sean shouted. "Alice, are you hurt?"

At the sound of his voice, magic sparked on my fingertips as a cold wind blew over me.

I struggled to get my feet. My hands throbbed in time to my pulse, but the pain was distant, muted. I wrapped my shirt around my hands and staggered to the door in my bra and blood-spattered jeans. "Go away." I barely recognized my own voice. "Leave me alone and don't come back."

"I don't understand," Sean protested. "What the hell happened?"

"Someone told me some important information about your pack and how much you need a mate." I leaned my forehead against the door and the wards crackled on my skin. "Suddenly, these last few days, everything you said and did from the moment we met, it all made sense."

"It's not like that," Sean said. "I wasn't even thinking about that when I met you."

"Even if that's true, which I don't believe, I know you thought about it later, or you wouldn't have been so persistent. Don't lie to me, Sean."

"Allie—"

"Don't call me that!" I shouted, then lowered my voice. "You don't get to call me that ever again. You lied to me. You screwed me and you lied to me so you could turn me into a werewolf to be your mate."

A long silence. "Who told you that?" It was a growl.

"It doesn't matter. What matters is, it's not going to happen. Stay the hell away from me, or I will burn you."

Sean swore. "If you won't let me in, at least open the door so we can talk face-to-face. I'll stay on the porch and you can stay behind your wards, but I deserve the chance to explain."

"You don't 'deserve' a damn thing," I told him. "I deserved the truth from the beginning, and all I got was lies. But I've learned—or relearned—some important lessons because of this, so I guess I owe you some kind of thanks for reminding me why I can't trust anyone."

"Alice, please." I heard a soft thump, like Sean was bumping his head or his fist against the door. "I would never have turned you into a werewolf against your will. If you lower your shields, you'll be able to feel I'm telling the truth."

Shock left me speechless for a several heartbeats. "What does that mean?"

Silence.

"Sean, tell me what the hell that means!" I demanded.

"We have a metaphysical link," Sean said finally, sounding resigned. "I can sense your emotions, and you can sense mine."

Suddenly, I remembered the odd looks he'd been giving me all night, and the strange feeling of hurt and anger I'd felt at the bar. I went ice-cold all over.

Sean must have created a link between us when we'd slept together tonight. It was the first step in establishing a mating bond, and he'd done it without my knowledge, or my consent. The violation made me physically sick.

Up until that moment, a part of me still wondered if Charles had been wrong about Sean's motivation for pursuing me. Now I felt those last bits of doubt vanish.

"What were you going to do, take me as your mate against my will? Hold me down and bite me if I wouldn't be turned voluntarily? Rape me?"

"Of course not. What kind of man do you think I am?"

I snorted. I couldn't believe he had the balls to sound outraged after all his lying and scheming. "I really don't know what kind of man you are. I thought I did, but clearly, I was wrong."

"I can feel that you're in pain. Who hurt you?"

I ignored him. "I fell right into your trap, but I've wised up. Now go. Don't call me, don't come looking for me. We're done. Go back to your pack and find yourself a werewolf female and leave me the hell alone."

"Goddammit, Alice, at least give me a chance to explain before you do this."

"Go. Away." I was getting tired of saying it.

Silence. Then: "What the hell are *you* doing here?" he snarled.

I frowned in confusion. Then I heard another voice outside, as cold as Sean's was hot with anger. "I am here to ensure Alice's safety."

Charles Vaughan had come to my house. A member of the Vampire Court had left the security of his office and crossed the city to protect me. A dozen emotions clashed inside me, fear strongest among them.

"Alice doesn't need any protection from me," Sean growled.

"We have good reason to think otherwise."

"Are you behind this?" Sean demanded. "What lies have you been telling her?"

Footsteps on the front steps. "I have told her no lies." It sounded like Charles had joined Sean on the porch.

"Someone has," Sean retorted. "I don't know what your game is, Vaughan, but I'm going to find out."

"Are you threatening me, wolf?" Charles's voice was low and very, very dangerous, the sound of a predator. It triggered something primal in some deep part of my brain, making me tremble. I had never heard Charles use that tone before, and hoped I never would again.

What was scaring me more, however, was the prospect of Charles and Sean coming to blows on my front porch. It could be war between the Vampire Court and Sean's pack, and I would be caught in the middle of a massive shitstorm. My anonymity would be blown in an instant. I had to get them away from each other and my home.

"Get out of here, Sean," I said through the door. "Just go."

"I'm not going anywhere," Sean said. "The vampire goes, and then you and I are going to talk."

I heard an inhuman hissing sound that I realized had come from Charles. *Oh no.*

"Sean, leave *now*," I said desperately. "I will talk to you later, but you need to go."

"I'm not leaving." Sean's voice was an octave lower than normal.

"You will vacate the premises or I will remove you," Charles told him. "I will not permit you to bite Alice."

Sean snarled. "For the last time, I *never* had any plans to turn her into a fucking werewolf!"

"You lie," Charles said.

Sean's growl made the hair stand up on my arms. A pulse of magic sizzled against my house wards, and the growl turned into a howl of fury. To my horror, I heard fighting erupt on the other side of the door.

With bloody, numb hands, I dropped my house wards and fumbled to unlock the deadbolt. Before I could open the door, the front window exploded as a vampire and a huge gray-and-black wolf smashed through it.

CHAPTER 21

I screamed and turned away as shards of glass pelted me, ripping into my arms, back, and face.

The sounds of snarling and crashing caused me to shake my head and try to focus on what was happening. My vision was blurry and red; I realized glass had cut my face and blood was running into my eyes. I wiped it away as best I could and saw the fight had moved past me into my living room. The vampire and wolf moved so quickly, I had a hard time seeing what was happening, other than a gray-and-blue blur demolishing everything in sight.

"Stop!" I shouted and stumbled toward them. They were both a hundred times faster and stronger than I was, but I couldn't just let them destroy everything I owned.

Massive arms wrapped around me and held me back. "You're hurt." Bryan must have come in when I wasn't looking. "You have to stay back, or you could get killed."

"I have to stop them," I said stupidly, struggling in his grip.

"It won't last much longer. The wolf is weakened by the speed of his shift, and Mr. Vaughan is faster."

Bryan was obviously seeing something I wasn't, because it sure as hell didn't look as if—

Like someone pushed Pause in the middle of a fight scene, it was abruptly over. The sudden silence startled me.

In the middle of my wrecked living room, Charles stood over the wolf's limp body. He was fully vamped out, eyes pure black and fangs extended. His suit had been shredded by teeth and claws. Blood seeped from about a dozen lacerations, but they were already healing. I could see that the wolf—Sean—was still breathing but unconscious. Broken furniture, electronics, pictures, and glass were everywhere.

Adri came in, talking urgently into her headset in a low voice. I caught the words "cleanup," "tranquilizer," "cage," and "van" through the buzzing in my ears.

Charles's gaze shifted from the wolf to me. "Alice, you are injured."

I could see bloody cuts all over my arms, chest, and legs, and it felt like some of the wounds still had glass imbedded in them. I was standing in front of Charles, Adri, and Bryan in my bra, but was too much in shock to care.

"I'll be all right," I told him. Bryan's massive hands were under my elbows, holding me up with surprising gentleness.

Charles took a few steps toward me. I realized I was covered in fresh blood, and my heart was pounding. I was basically ringing the dinner bell, and he suddenly looked hungry.

With effort, I fought back my sudden fear. "Charles, don't come any closer," I said firmly. "I'm not on the menu tonight."

Adri and Bryan tensed. The hands on my arms tightened. I wasn't sure if Bryan would help Charles or me if the vampire lost control and attacked, and I wasn't going to wait to find out.

Bright green cold fire burst from my hands and ran up my arms. In a blink, Bryan released me and jumped away.

"Everyone stay back," I warned them. I moved until I had the wall behind me and could see Charles and his enforcers. Broken glass crunched under my boots.

Charles gazed at my cold fire, his expression somewhere between awe and appraisal. As I watched, his eyes began to return to normal, and his fangs disappeared. It was a remarkable—and chilling—display of control.

"I apologize," he said finally. "I forgot myself. You have my word I will not harm you."

We stared at each other. I read sincerity in his eyes. Slowly, the cold fire drew back to my hands and vanished.

Charles's eyes narrowed. "Alice, your shoulder."

I picked up my shirt and used it to cover the bite mark as my face grew hot. "It's nothing."

His gaze moved to my bloody and swollen hands, and his frown became thunderous. "Who is responsible for these injuries?"

I had no intention of discussing this with Charles, especially not in front of Adri and Bryan. "It's none of your business."

He looked at the blood splattered on the tile and the extensive damage to the foyer, and then back at my hands. I saw disbelief in his eyes as realization dawned. "You have done this to yourself."

Adri inhaled sharply.

My eyes stung with angry tears. Humiliated, I went on the attack. "Why the hell are you here, Charles?"

His eyes flashed silver. "Mr. Smith and I followed the werewolf when he left Hawthorne's. We believed he posed a danger to you, and it would appear we were correct."

"He says he never intended to turn me into a werewolf," I said quietly, almost to myself.

"Of course he would deny it," Charles said. "To bite someone against their will is a capital offense in both human and shifter courts."

When I stayed silent, Adri spoke up. "I have a team on its way to take the wolf into custody, sir," she told Charles.

"The window must be replaced immediately."

"I'll take care of it." Adri started scrolling through her phone.

I glared at Charles. "I don't need you to do anything for me."

"I will arrange for someone to come immediately to fix the window. Your home must be secure."

"Make sure I get the bill," I told him. "I don't want you to buy me anything."

He regarded me. "Alice, as I am at least partially responsible for the damage, I ask that you allow me to pay for the window."

"Fine," I conceded.

Adri made a call and began speaking quietly to someone about getting a window company out to my house immediately.

I shivered hard and fought back a wave of dizziness. When I glanced down, I saw blood forming a small puddle around my feet.

When I looked up, Charles was in front of me. I hadn't even seen or heard him move. Gently, he raised my hands. The movement made fresh pain surge, and I grimaced at the sight of my bloody, swollen knuckles. I couldn't make a fist with my left hand. In my blind rage, I might have actually broken something.

"I think you have," Charles said. I realized I'd spoken aloud. "Will you let me heal your injuries?"

"How?" My eyes narrowed.

"A few ounces of my blood will suffice."

"What will you want in return?" I remembered his request to drink from me and feared he would try to revisit that demand.

"Nothing. This gift of healing is freely given."

I sighed and hung my head for a moment. "All right."

"Will you permit Ms. Smith to assist you in removing the glass? You will need help to reach the wounds on your back."

I couldn't argue with that. "Okay." I started toward the stairs, then paused. "What will you do with Sean?"

Charles looked at the unconscious wolf. "He will be sedated and taken to a holding cell at Hawthorne's," he told me. "He shifted and attacked me, causing these injuries to you, and that cannot go unpunished. I will contact his pack and apprise them of the situation. For now, you must tend to your wounds. Ms. Smith, please go with her."

I shuffled across the floor to the foot of the stairs. I paused with one foot on the bottom step, looking at the wolf in the middle of my wrecked living room. I noticed then that my record player had somehow survived the destruction. *Dark Side of the Moon* was still on the turntable where we'd left it. I closed my eyes.

"Alice, do you need help up the stairs?" Adri asked me.

I looked up toward the second floor. I felt weakened and dizzy, but I shook my head. "I can make it," I said and began to climb.

When I got to the door to my room, I looked back at the trail of blood I'd left behind me. I couldn't leave my blood lying around, not with Charles and his people here. With difficulty, I crouched to put my fingertips in the blood on the floor. "Fire in the hole!" I hollered. I assumed Adri was warning Charles telepathically about what I was about to do.

"*Burn.*" With a *whoosh*, an air magic burner spell flashed through my upstairs hallway, down the stairs, and into the foyer of my house, reducing all my blood to a fine layer of white ash.

From downstairs, I heard Bryan's familiar rumble: "What the hell was that?"

I smiled grimly and pushed myself upright using the wall as leverage. "Okay," I told Adri. "Let's do this."

* * *

It took well over an hour to pull all the pieces of glass out of my face, scalp, back, arms, and legs. I had to comb glass out of my hair. My bathroom looked like a scene from a slasher movie by the time we finished. Adri stripped off my clothes and put me in the shower to rinse off the blood. I used a burner spell to clean up the blood in the bathroom and my bedroom, and Adri swept up the broken glass and ash while I sat naked in the tub.

When the floor was clean, I asked Adri to change my bedding. She did so without comment and took the other bedding downstairs to the laundry room. When she came back, she wrapped me in my bathrobe and got me to my bed, where I curled up on top of the quilt. I was bleeding from a dozen deep cuts that throbbed painfully, and my hands hurt so badly it was hard to think clearly. I was glad Sean and I had taken the time to straighten my room before we left; the thought of Adri—and Charles—seeing it in such disarray would have been more humiliation than I could have dealt with tonight.

Charles appeared in the doorway of my bedroom, presumably responding to Adri's telepathic summons. For a moment, I saw a flash of something that might have been tenderness when he saw me lying on the bed. It faded and his face became impassive once more.

Adri stepped outside the bedroom and closed the door as Charles came to sit on the edge of my bed. Someone must have brought him a change of clothes; his tattered and bloody suit was gone, and he was elegant once again.

"You are very pale," Charles told me, removing his suit jacket.

"Look who's talking," I shot back.

Charles chuckled. As he unfastened his cufflink and rolled up his sleeve, I suddenly felt terribly awkward.

He touched my face, his cool fingertips brushing my cheek. I closed my eyes.

When I opened them again, Charles's fangs were visible. He used them to pierce his wrist and blood welled up. He raised his wrist toward my mouth. "Drink from me."

Before I lost my nerve, I reached for his arm, brought it to my lips, and covered the wound with my mouth.

The first taste was of blood, coppery and cool, but somehow not unpleasant. I sucked gently on the wound, and sensation exploded in my mouth, spreading rapidly through my body. I closed my eyes as it rolled through me in a warm wave of intense pleasure. I swallowed again, and this time it felt so good that I shuddered. Strange sensations flared in a dozen places on my body. Charles gently brushed my hair back from my face, his arm still at my mouth. I swallowed again.

A few ounces, I thought hazily. Surely that had been enough. I ran my tongue over his skin to lick up the last of his blood. I heard a moan. It might have been him or it might have been me.

Charles's arm moved away from my mouth. From beyond the bliss, I felt my hands spasm and I cried out. Cool hands were resting on top of mine, holding me still with my arms against my chest while things moved under my skin in my hands and wrists. I suddenly felt as if ants were running over my skin as my cuts began to heal. Charles held me as I whimpered and squirmed.

When my head finally cleared, I opened my eyes. Charles was leaning over me, his hands still covering mine. I looked dazedly up at him. "Did it work?" My tongue felt thick.

"Yes." Charles held up my hands so I could see them. I stared at them in wonder. The skin was unbroken, the swelling gone. I flexed them experimentally, marveling at how the fingers opened and closed without pain. Vampire blood had painful healing spells beat by a mile.

Charles settled back, rolling his shirtsleeve back down and neatly fastening the cuff. His arm was already healed, the skin unblemished.

I sat up and kept looking at my knuckles. "Amazing," I said, more to myself than to him. I pulled the collar of my robe aside to see that no sign of Sean's bite or any of the cuts remained. "What's going on downstairs?"

"The wolf has been taken to Hawthorne's," Charles said. "The window is being replaced and the glass cleaned up. My crew is cleaning your floor. Within a few minutes, the work will be complete."

I gave him a small smile. "Thank you."

Charles watched me swing my legs over the side of the bed. I felt cool air on my skin and realized the bathrobe had come untied at some point, and I was naked beneath it.

Charles reached out toward me, his eyes on mine. Given the way he'd been looking at me minutes earlier, I expected him to touch me, and, strangely, I wasn't sure how I would respond. I was surprised when he gently pulled the robe closed and held it while I tied the belt. Then he stood and drew me to my feet.

"Are you well?" Charles still held on to my hands.

"I feel good." I pulled free of his grip. "Thank you for everything."

His expression became distant for a moment, then he looked at me. "My people have finished their work downstairs. You may raise your house wards."

I laid my palm against the wall. In moments, the wards crackled with their familiar intensity.

When I opened my eyes, Charles stood next to me. "Do you wish me to leave someone here to watch the house?"

I shook my head. "No. You've got Sean in custody. My wards are up, and I'm fine."

"Very well." He hesitated, then bent down to kiss my cheek. "Sleep well, Alice."

"You too, Charles."

He went to the door of my room and opened it. Adri waited on the other side. She looked at Charles, and then at me with a thoughtful expression.

"Good night, Adri," I said. "Thank you for your help."

"Anytime, Alice."

She and Charles headed down the stairs. Moments later, I felt a tingle from the wards when they left.

I stripped off my bathrobe and changed into pajamas. Then I brushed my teeth and fell into bed, pulling the covers up to my chin. In minutes, I was sound asleep.

CHAPTER 22

I'd been screaming for hours.

My voice was nothing more than a hoarse rasp. My throat must have been raw, but I couldn't feel anything anymore. Maybe I'd shorted out whatever part of my brain processed pain. It took long enough.

I'd been kept hanging on a metal rack for most of the day so the blood mage had full access to my naked body, though she'd focused most of her attention on my back this time. During rare moments of coherent thought, I wondered if my grandfather had ordered her not to damage any part of me that might be visible. Moses had to maintain the fiction that his granddaughter obeyed his every command, that she never hesitated to unleash her terrible magic according to his wishes. There could be no hint that she resisted him. He'd had people killed for even mentioning the possibility.

They said my heart stopped twice. I'd wanted to die, but like everything else I'd ever wanted, I didn't get it. They brought me back each time. The floor was littered with expended spell crystals and empty blood bags from transfusions. I'd probably bled out three times over.

I'd experienced it often enough to know I was in shock. I felt ice-cold and I was shaking so badly it looked like I was having a seizure. I'd been taken down from the rack and dumped facedown on a cot that was bolted to the floor. My wrists and ankles were manacled to the frame with spell cuffs. The metal edges cut my skin and rattled against the cot as I shook. Someone had thrown a sheet over my bare ass and legs. It had once been white but now was mostly red. My thirst was painful, but no one had offered me water.

Though shock kept me from feeling much of anything, I strongly suspected there was no skin left on my back. Odd sensations made me think things were exposed that shouldn't have been. I wondered how many healing spells it would take to fix me this time.

I'd been alone in the soundproofed torture room for a very long time. I faded in and out, though I never really lost consciousness, thanks to the spells. Perhaps they were waiting for me to bleed out, or for shock to stop my heart. I'd have wished for it if I didn't know they'd just bring me back again. Dying hurt, but coming back always hurt worse.

The heavy door swung open. My grandfather appeared, accompanied by the blood mage and one of his favorite lieutenants, a snake of a man named Kade. I felt a weak surge of something through the numbness: hate. Kade was a sadist. He supervised most of my torture sessions, and he usually became aroused watching me bleed. At least the other lieutenants acted like it was just a job and maintained a kind of clinical distance. Kade took a lot of pleasure in his work.

Moses strode across the room, walking through the blood without even looking at it. He didn't flinch in the slightest at the sight of my body or the amount of blood on the floor and walls and ceiling. But why would he? He'd have inflicted the damage himself if he'd had anything more than mid-level blood magic. Handing my punishment over to a high-level blood mage had been merely a practical decision.

"Exceptional work, as always," my grandfather said to the blood mage as they came to stand over me. "I was able to observe some of the session between meetings."

"Thank you, Davo," the blood mage said. Her gaze swept over my body like an artist surveying her work. She was clearly pleased with her efforts.

"Your precision has improved." Moses looked me over. "There is almost no skin remaining, and yet she is conscious. Remarkable."

The mage made a murmuring sound. I stared fixedly into space, avoiding eye contact with my grandfather and trying not to notice the obvious bulge in the front of Kade's pants.

"There is, however, significant muscle damage," Moses added in that same casual tone.

The blood mage appeared unconcerned. "Healing spells will repair the damage."

She failed to see the shark fin in the water, but Kade and I both spotted the signs. He tensed. I did not. The blood mage was dead already; she just didn't know it.

"Muscle damage requires extensive and lengthy use of healing spells," my *grandfather said. "Our timeline for this project is quite inflexible. She won't be recovered before the priority deadline has passed."*

The blood mage was becoming aware that she was in trouble and took a step back. "Davo, it was unclear—"

That was as far as she got. My grandfather's hand whipped out, and a coil of fire wrapped around the blood mage's neck. Her scream was piercing, and I smelled burning flesh.

"This is an unacceptable loss of revenue, and if we fail to meet the schedule, it will damage our reputation," Moses said with that same calm voice as the blood mage writhed and shrieked on the end of his fire rope. I didn't flinch. What was she experiencing that I hadn't at her hands, and for hours at a time? "Despite your skills, you continue to lack the kind of attention to detail I require in my employees. I made the timetable clear to you when you received the assignment."

The blood mage finally lost consciousness. The coil of fire released her neck, and she hit the floor in a heap, her throat a charred mess. The smell was terrible, but I was glad for the silence.

Kade stepped away to call someone to come get the mage. My grandfather looked at me. He might as well have been looking at a piece of trash on the side of the road. There was absolutely nothing in his eyes. Looking into them was like looking into hell.

"Her stupidity and your stubbornness are going to cost me a lot of money." That was the only warning I got before he brought the heel of his boot down on my back. Agony whited out my vision and I sank toward oblivion, but I could not pass out because of the blood mage's spells. I found I was still able to scream some more after all.

CHAPTER 23

I came awake with a scream that sounded like it was ripped out of my soul. With a sob, I curled up on my side, drawing my knees up to my chest, and began to shake. I swore I could still feel my grandfather's boot heel on the middle of my back.

It had been months since I'd had a nightmare that intense. It didn't take a psychiatrist to figure out what had brought on such vivid memories; Adri had spent the better part of an hour digging glass out of my back. The pain and blood from last night was more than enough to remind me of the horrors of what my grandfather had done to me.

I stumbled to the bathroom to wash my face. I was about to put toothpaste on my toothbrush when my phone rang.

It was Adri. "You must never sleep," I told her after we'd said hello to each other.

"I'm headed home. Mr. Vaughan requested I call you in the morning to let you know where things stand, but I didn't want to wake you too early."

I was quiet. "How is Sean?" I asked finally.

"Mr. Maclin is healing well. He'll be our guest for a few days. Mr. Vaughan informed the pack of his whereabouts, and his beta saw for himself that he's unharmed and being kept in comfortable conditions."

"What do you plan to do with him?"

Adri's tone was businesslike, which I appreciated. "Since he suffered no serious injury, Mr. Vaughan has decided not to file a grievance with the Were Ruling Council. He suggested you go before the council and demand a judgment against Mr. Maclin for the seriousness of your injuries and the damages to your home."

"I don't want anything from Sean," I stated. "The less I have to think about him at this point, the better. I'd rather pay for the repairs myself than drag this out."

"It would be Mr. Vaughan's honor to represent you," Adri informed me. "You'd have no contact with Mr. Maclin at all."

"Please tell Charles I appreciate his offer, but I just want all of this behind me. The sooner Sean and I have nothing to do with each other, the sooner we can both move on."

After a beat, I asked, "Has Sean said anything about…the situation?" I didn't know why I inquired or why it mattered to me in the least.

Adri didn't seem surprised at my question. "Once Mr. Maclin shifted back to human form, he was extremely upset you were hurt, and he wouldn't be calm until we convinced him that you were healed. He's also insisting he had no intention of infecting you with the werewolf virus, or claiming you as his mate against your will, though he admits you share a metaphysical link."

I scowled.

"We've been told the link will dissolve on its own given time, as long as you have no further contact with Mr. Maclin." Adri paused. "He asked that we tell you that he would still like the chance to explain himself."

"You can tell him that you delivered the message and there's nothing he has to say that I want to hear." I was pleased at how steely my voice sounded, though I felt a sharp ache somewhere in the middle of my chest.

"I will do that." Another pause. "You doing okay with all of this?"

"I'll be all right. It's not like I was in love with him, or anything close to it." I paused, then added, "He should have known I'm not prey."

"I understand."

We fell quiet.

"Oh, I almost forgot," Adri said finally. "Mr. Vaughan began making inquiries last night to find a teacher for your client."

"Really? I thought…."

"He's apparently changed his mind about requesting your blood. I believe he'll ask you to upgrade the wards on one of his storage facilities instead."

"Please tell him thank you, and that I'll be happy to work on the wards. Just tell me when and where and what kind."

"I will. Have a good day, Alice."

"You too, Adri. Go get some sleep."

I put the phone down, lay back on the bed, and closed my eyes.

My heart felt bruised. I was glad Charles was keeping Sean in custody for a couple of days, so I wouldn't have to worry about him showing up on my doorstep. Despite everything, there was a part of me that wondered if Sean had been telling the truth when he'd claimed he had no plans to turn me into a werewolf. Maybe it was unfair of me not to hear him out.

Even if that was true, I reminded myself, there was no place for me in Sean's life. He was an alpha werewolf in need of a mate, and that wasn't going to change. Until Charles had explained the situation, I hadn't really thought of Sean's role as an alpha and how different it was from a pack werewolf.

More importantly, he'd initiated a mating bond with me without my permission, and I didn't think that was something I was going to be able to forgive or forget. It was best we made a clean break. For both our sakes, I hoped by the time his involuntary seclusion was over, Sean would come to the same conclusion.

Wanting to distract myself from thoughts about Sean, I called Natalie.

She answered immediately, her voice cheerful. "Alice! No answer from the lawyer yet, so I left him another message. How are you?"

"Doing well, Natalie. Have you had any luck finding out more about our missing item?"

"The MacGuffin?" Natalie teased. I made a face at Malcolm's goofy nickname for the *Kasten*. "Nothing yet. I just got started on the papers in her desk, though. There's a lot more to go through. I'll try to get finished this afternoon."

I remembered my earlier conversation with Adri. "By the way, I'm in the process of finding you a teacher. I hope to have some news on that soon too."

"Awesome," Natalie said. "I'm actually getting kind of excited about it."

"I'm really glad to hear that. Let me know if you find anything, and I'll keep you posted." We said our good-byes and disconnected.

I took a long shower, scrubbing myself until I could no longer imagine I smelled Sean on my skin. I dried my hair and dressed.

When I opened my bedroom door, Malcolm waited on the other side. "Where have *you* been?" I asked.

"At Natalie's, giving you some space. What the hell happened downstairs? Were we robbed?"

I leaned against the doorframe and told him about my visit to Hawthorne's, what Charles told me about Sean's pack problems and his plan to turn me into a werewolf, what happened at my house, and Sean being held in Charles's custody.

Malcolm was flitting around in a rage. "That son of a bitch. I'm so sorry, Alice."

I shrugged. "He still claims he had no intention of infecting me, but he *did* initiate a bond without telling me about it. Even if he didn't want to turn me into a werewolf, an alpha has to have a werewolf mate, so it was basically doomed from the start."

"He did save your life after Natalie burned you, and he took care of you afterward. I suppose that's worth something. Though if he wanted you for his mate, that would explain why he was so strongly motivated to get through the wards. I can't believe he was going to bite you."

I headed down the hall to the stairs, Malcolm trailing along behind me. "I guess it doesn't matter anymore. He's Charles's problem for a couple of days while he calms down. After that, if he does come around, I'll just have to make it clear he needs to stay away from me."

"You need to get some silver."

I paused in the middle of the stairs, then continued on. "I hope it doesn't come to that," I said softly. "But you're probably right. I have silver, though. I guess I need to start carrying it."

When I got to the main floor of the house, I stopped and stared.

My front window had been replaced with a lovely piece of decorative fixed glass that looked frightfully expensive even without adding in the cost of having a window company come out in the middle of the night. The bevels in the glass cast rainbows of light across the foyer. The floor was spotlessly clean, and I didn't see or sense any trace of ash or my blood anywhere.

My living room was virtually empty. The books that had been in the bookcases were stacked neatly on the floor. The broken furniture, my smashed television, and the rest of the debris were gone. Only the couch and the record player remained. How they had avoided getting destroyed, I had no idea.

I went to the basement door. When I looked at my wards, I could see the golden thread that represented Sean. I yanked it out. The wards rippled, then went still. I opened the door, and Malcolm and I went downstairs.

I went to one of the cabinets, traced runes on the door, then opened it. I pulled out two small silver throwing knives and a wrist sheath from one of the cabinets, then I took out a box of silver bullets, my gun, and an empty magazine. Malcolm watched silently as I loaded the magazine with the bullets.

I felt sick at the thought of shooting Sean, but if he did intend to bite me and turn me into a werewolf, I'd do it without hesitation, even if it brought the entire Tomb Mountain Pack down on my head. My only hope in that case would be to get to the Were Ruling Council before the pack got to me and explain that Sean had attempted to bite me against my will.

There was a slim chance my strong blood magic would be able to burn the werewolf virus from my body if I did get bitten—I'd heard of it happening before—but I was certainly not going to bank on that. My best defense was silver.

While I finished loading the magazine, I told Malcolm what I'd sensed from John West at the art museum the night before.

He was justifiably troubled. "We knew he was strong, but from what you're saying, West might not just be a member of the harnad. He might be its leader."

"I'm starting to think that too. In that case, he could draw on the power of the other members to enhance his own blood magic."

"Not someone you'd want to have to face."

I snorted. "No kidding."

* * *

I went back upstairs to make coffee and toast an english muffin, then returned to the basement to look through my blood magic books for any more references to the *Kasten*. Other than the one I'd shown Malcolm yesterday, I didn't see any more mentions of the box, though a few of the books described other objects of power with similar characteristics. I made some notes on those, hoping I'd learn something that might help me better understand what the *Kasten* was—if indeed that's what had been in Betty's library—and what it might be able to do. Malcolm worked on his masking spells in the work area.

Shortly before lunch, Natalie texted that she was looking through the last of the papers in the desk. We made plans for me to come over later in the afternoon to look at the letters she'd found from John West, once she'd had a chance to look through the rest of Betty's files.

By two o'clock, I was bleary-eyed and my back was killing me. I leaned back in my chair for a few minutes and watched Malcolm jump in and out of his bolt-hole crystals.

I was reaching for another book when it felt like something kicked me in the head and I fell over. My chin hit the table and I bit my tongue. I ended up on the floor, staring up dazedly and tasting blood.

As the ringing in my ears faded, I could hear Malcolm calling my name. "What the hell was that?" he demanded. "I felt a surge of magic, and then you fell out of your chair."

I tried to think, but my brain was fuzzy. "I don't know. It almost felt like my house wards broke, but they're fine." I frowned. "Did someone try to get past my wards?"

"That wouldn't have affected me," he pointed out. "The only wards I've been working on—"

"—Are at Natalie's house," I finished. "Did someone just break Natalie's house wards?" I struggled to my feet, reaching for my phone. My call to Natalie went straight to voice mail. I didn't bother to leave a message.

"We've got to get to Natalie's house," I said. "Right the hell now. Can you jump there?"

Malcolm shook his head. "No, but I can get there a lot faster than you. Meet you there." He vanished.

I took thirty seconds to cram my blood magic books back into the cabinet. Then I grabbed my phone, my bag, and my gun on the way out the door.

CHAPTER 24

I might not be able to move as fast as a ghost, but I could haul ass in my car. I got to Natalie's house in less than fifteen minutes.

Even from the street, I could tell her house wards were broken. It felt like something was scraping against my brain, and the feeling got worse the closer I got to the house. By the time I reached the porch, I was staggering. The wards hadn't just been broken; they'd been ripped apart with brute force.

I managed to get to the house and place my palm against the doorframe. I brought down the broken wards, and the disorientation and pain vanished. I straightened up shakily and tried the front door. It was unlocked.

Inside, it didn't look like anything was out of place. Whatever happened, it happened quickly. "Malcolm?"

Malcolm appeared next to me. He flitted back and forth so rapidly, it hurt my eyes. "She's gone. There's blood in Betty's room."

"Shit." Just outside the library door, there was a large smear of blood on the floor. I wondered if Natalie was trying to get to the safety of the library, where the wards would have protected her, but someone got her just before she crossed the threshold.

"Whatever happened here, we missed it." Malcolm flitted so fast I could barely see him. "Someone took her."

"Can you sense her?"

Malcolm stopped, closed his eyes, and concentrated. He vanished for a moment, then reappeared, then vanished again, then came back.

"I can't," he said finally. "Something is blocking me. She must be spelled or inside a ward. Whatever it is, it's got to be strong."

I cursed. The library wards ran over my skin like an electric current. Whoever had come into Natalie's home, they hadn't broken them. I wondered if that was because there was nothing in the library they needed anymore, if the wards had proven too strong for them to break, or if they figured someone would feel the house wards break and come to investigate.

I put my hands on my hips. "Natalie said she had the letters from West on the dining table, but they weren't there. I'm guessing they were taken too."

Malcolm moved next to me. "Can you track her with blood magic?"

I glanced at the blood on the floor. "Maybe. The longer the blood sits there, the harder it gets. If she's protected by a masking or protection spell or ward, it gets even harder. I'll need some of the things from my basement. I'll get what I need to do the spells and be back as soon as I can."

"I'll stay here in case whoever took her comes back."

"Be careful." I shut the front door of Natalie's house and hurried to my car.

My thoughts raced as I drove back to my house. Why take Natalie now? Malcolm and I had used his spell detector on Natalie's aunts and uncle, but I didn't see how any of them could have been aware we'd done that since Malcolm was invisible. Even if they had, none of them were the mystery mage. I was pretty sure John West hadn't noticed us tailing him last night.

I almost hit a parked car when a sudden realization struck me.

Son of a bitch. The lawyer.

I'd asked Natalie to call Betty's lawyer and find out if her grandmother had any other children besides the ones we knew about. Hours after leaving another message for him, Natalie was gone. Was there a connection? If the mystery mage wasn't one of the siblings Malcolm and I had checked out, then there *had* to be another family member. It made sense. Maybe Natalie's calls to the lawyer had spooked someone, and they'd come to shut her up.

I didn't know the lawyer's name, but I'd bet it was in the paperwork on Betty's desk. I'd find it when I got back to Natalie's house, and if my blood magic wasn't able to locate Natalie, Malcolm and I would pay him a visit. If he knew who had Natalie, he'd tell me.

When I parked in my driveway, I left everything but my keys in the car so my hands would be free to carry what I needed for the blood magic ritual.

I was so focused on getting in and out of the house as quickly as possible that it took me way too long to realize Peter Eppright was standing five feet away in the shadows under my carport, and that he was pointing a gun at me.

I stared at him for a full second before reacting. I lashed his right hand with my cold-fire whip. He yelled in pain and dropped his gun, bending over to cradle his hand. I reached into my car to grab my gun off the passenger seat just as I heard a footstep crunch in the gravel behind me.

Something smashed into the back of my head, and everything went black.

* * *

The digital clock on my nightstand read 3:35 a.m. I sat cross-legged on the floor inside a circle. In front of me were three large jars filled with my blood and a spell crystal into which I was draining almost every last drop of my magic. Anyone monitoring me—which they certainly were, as I was under surveillance almost every minute of every day—would see me working ritual blood magic for my grandfather. They would not be able to see the jars or the spell crystal. I'd spent many hours crafting the circle. It was a powerful obfuscation spell, one of the most difficult I had ever attempted.

Tonight was the culmination of almost a year of planning and preparing, waiting for the right time, for the right type of contract. When my grandfather was hired by a smaller cabal to wipe out their competitor, it was the perfect opportunity for me to put my escape plan into action. Of course, I couldn't readily accept the assignment or that would have aroused suspicion, so I'd initially refused to obey my grandfather's command. I hoped Moses wouldn't suspect I'd relented too soon. I had to balance how much torture I could take with how much I would have to recover for my plan to work.

The attack would require an enormous amount of energy, which was what I had been waiting for. I had been instructed to perform the ritual tonight, when the targets would all be at a location that was less well-protected than their compound. Everything had been carefully planned. It was a shame it was about to go completely sideways.

I'd drained as much of my blood into the jars as I dared. It had to be an enormous amount, and full of magic, for this to work. When it was dispersed by the explosion, my grandfather would have to believe I had been killed. I'd been thinking about this for almost a year. Now, in the moment, I was very calm, almost detached. It was almost certainly mainly the blood loss, but the rest was cold resolve. Either I would be free, or I would be dead. There were no other alternatives. Knowing that made it easier.

I funneled all of my magic into the spell crystal until all I had left was a tiny amount of blood magic.

I opened the jars and poured their contents into the circle. The coppery scent turned my stomach. The smell of my blood was inexorably tied to torture by my grandfather, the recently deceased blood mage, and others. Tonight it would be the key to my escape—I hoped.

The blood ran across the floor in wide rivers. I left the jars where they were. There would be nothing left of them, or the room I was in.

I used a small knife to cut four runes into my forearm with quick precision. A blood-magic protection and obfuscation spell flared over my body, powered by the last of my blood magic. It had to hold or I was going to be dead in about five seconds.

I closed my eyes. Blood magic flared around me.

I don't remember the actual blast. One second, I was standing in my room. I blinked, and I was outside.

I lay in the courtyard, surrounded by burning debris. An enormous fireball billowed from a giant hole in the side of the compound where my rooms used to be. My hearing was gone, but I saw red flashing lights and knew every alarm in the compound was going off. People in black uniforms were running everywhere, some toward the blaze, some toward my grandfather's apartment, the library, and the storage areas.

No one saw me on the ground, staring dazedly at the ruined section of the compound where I'd been kept prisoner for most of my life. The obfuscation spell was holding for now, but only fumes of my magic remained to keep it going. Once it failed, I'd be visible. I had another spell in my pocket, but it was an emergency backup and I couldn't use it until I was well outside the compound walls.

I sat up and pain took my breath away. The protection spell had saved my life, but my left arm was broken at the elbow. I staggered to my feet, holding my arm against my body, and focused as well as I could to avoid bumping into anyone as I made my way through the chaos and smoke to the main gate.

Behind me, there was a second explosion; apparently, the fire had reached something volatile. I smiled grimly. Maybe the whole damn compound would burn to the ground. It was probably too much to hope for. It wouldn't destroy the cabal, but it would certainly cripple it for a while.

The guard at the gate was shouting into his radio as the heavy double doors beside the gate opened. More uniformed men and women came pouring in—they'd been outside the gates on patrol and had been called in to help. They wouldn't open the main gate; if it was an attack, that would put the compound at risk, but the small personnel doors could be opened to let in reinforcements.

I waited for my chance. When the guards stopped coming through, I slipped out and began running. Every step jostled my broken arm, but I held it as steady as possible and moved as quickly as I could through the woods surrounding the compound. I had to put as much distance between myself and that place as I was able to before blood loss and exhaustion rendered me visible and vulnerable.

Somehow, I made it the three miles from the compound to the state highway before I could go no farther. My vision was graying, and I was reduced to crawling the last few hundred yards. I'd hoped to use one of the disguise spells in my pockets and get a ride from a passing motorist, but I couldn't even stand up, much less wave anyone down.

I spotted a culvert under the highway. On my knees and one hand, my left arm held against my body, I crawled inside the drainpipe and crept back into the darkness, half burying myself under leaves. Luckily, it hadn't rained lately, and the drainpipe was dry.

Despite the warm summer night, I was shivering from shock and pain. With fumbling fingers, I dug into my pocket and felt around for the healing spell I'd brought. It was the largest of the spell crystals in my pocket; the others were mainly disguise and masking spells, plus a suicide spell that would burn my body to ash. The latter was the only one in my pocket that was distinctly cube-shaped. I was careful not to grab it by mistake.

My fingers closed around the healing spell. I had to hope no one came near this area and sensed its use before the magic trace dissipated. I knew I was risking being caught, but I also knew there was a real chance I would die from shock and blood loss if I didn't do something. I hadn't come this far to die now. I'd already gone all-

in. What was one more gamble?

I pulled the crystal from my pocket, stuck it inside my bra so it would stay against my skin even if I passed out, and invoked the spell.

Magic hit my chest like a sledgehammer, and I spun off into darkness. My last thought was of freedom.

CHAPTER 25

Awareness returned slowly, as if I had to surface from a great depth.

I'd gone through so many torture sessions in my life that it had become second nature to play possum upon first waking. Feigning unconsciousness had worked in my favor more than once. I held perfectly still, breathed slowly and evenly, and tried to figure out what the hell was going on.

The first sensations I had were disorientation and tremendous pain. The latter seemed to be coming from the back of my head. Had I fallen? I tried to remember, but everything was fuzzy. I dimly recalled going to Natalie's house after someone broke her house wards. Blood on the floor in Betty's room. Malcolm trying to find her using their connection and failing. Driving back to my house. Then…nothing. The pain in my head indicated I'd been attacked.

That hypothesis was supported by the fact I was tied up and gagged. I felt a surge of fear when I realized I was splayed out on a hard surface. My left wrist and ankles were tied with rope, but my right wrist was fastened with a spell cuff. I reached for my magic, but it was dampened completely. It took everything I had to breathe slowly through the terror. It felt like I was back at the cabal, held in restraints for torture.

I had been basically rendered helpless, and the fear began to give way to rage.

I heard movement to my right. "You can open your eyes now."

The male voice was familiar, but I couldn't place it. I didn't react.

"Miss Worth, please. You've been awake for several minutes."

I finally recognized the voice: Peter Eppright. *What the hell?*

I opened my eyes and blinked, waiting for what I was seeing to make sense.

It looked like I was in a half-finished office building. I saw scaffolding, clear plastic sheets, boxes of drop cloths, stacks of sheet rock, huge spools of cables, and tables covered with hand tools. There were lights on stands set up around us. The rest of the building was dark. It must be night.

I lay on top of a large wooden table in my bra and underwear. All of my weapons and jewelry were gone, even my belly-button piercing. I was miserably cold.

I glared at Eppright, who stood about four feet away near a smaller table covered with a black cloth. His right hand and wrist were wrapped in gauze. I got a sudden flash of him standing under my carport with a gun. I didn't think I'd been shot, but how had I ended up here? Whatever was going on, he was clearly in on it.

I heard a sound from the darkness and turned my head to look. It was a mistake.

Nausea surged. Vomit filled my mouth and sinuses, and I couldn't get any air. I made desperate noises and tried to breathe through my nose, but that caused me to aspirate vomit into my lungs.

Eppright started cursing. He untied my gag and left wrist, lifted my upper body, and turned me awkwardly onto my right side so I could vomit off the table onto the floor. As I was desperately trying to breathe, I noticed a leather cord tied around my left wrist with several spell crystals on it. I wondered what its purpose was. I saw a second table next to mine, but it was empty.

"What's going on?"

It was a woman's furious voice. If I hadn't been trying not to choke to death on my own vomit, I would have looked to see who it was. My brain felt too big for my skull. Definitely a concussion. The fact I was having a hard time thinking clearly and had been unconscious for at least several hours were very bad signs.

"She started to choke," Eppright told the woman, who stood behind him and out of my line of sight. "You said we needed her alive."

I threw up again, then started coughing up bits of stuff that had gone into my lungs.

"You should have thought of that before you and that idiot bashed her skull in," the woman said.

I decided I didn't recognize her voice at all. Also, I'd like to know which "idiot" hit me on the head so I could return the favor. My eyeballs throbbed in time with my pulse.

"That was Ray." Eppright looked a little green, hopefully due to my vomit.

"Clean that up," she ordered. I wished she would move so I could see her. She sounded like she was in charge of whatever the hell was going on. My brain started to catch up. Was this the mystery mage? With the cuff on, I couldn't sense her magic.

He looked like he wanted to refuse her order, but thought better of it. "Are you done?" he demanded.

I coughed up some vomit out of my burning lungs and spat it in his face.

He jerked back, but not in time, and my glob of spit hit him on the forehead. Eppright's face turned bright red as he pulled back his bandaged fist to punch me. I didn't give him the satisfaction of cowering.

"Stop!" the woman snapped. Furious, Eppright obeyed, dropping his fist to his side. She stepped around him and I got my first look at her.

She looked like she was in her mid-to-late fifties, but in good shape for her age. She wore slacks and a light blue shirt, her ash-blonde hair pulled back in a neat ponytail. She looked vaguely familiar, though I'd have sworn I'd never seen her before. Then I realized she looked a lot like Betty.

"So you're Betty's other daughter." My voice was hoarse from throwing up.

Eppright used a drop cloth to clean up my vomit. I winked at him and he clenched his fists so tightly that his knuckles turned white.

The woman looked surprised. "Well, aren't you smart." She didn't sound sarcastic. "I'm Amelia Wharton. Formerly Amelia Eppright."

I glanced at Peter. "Brother?"

"Yes."

I made a face. "My condolences."

Eppright flushed again.

"Now, don't be rude," Amelia said. "I can understand why you're upset, but there's no reason we can't all be civil."

My eyebrows went up. I was beginning to think Amelia might not be all there. There was something off about her tone—a kind of detachment, like she was discussing the weather report, not standing over someone she'd had kidnapped and tied up.

Kidnapped. That triggered a memory. My brain still felt entirely too sluggish. "Where's Natalie?" I asked.

Amelia glanced at her watch. "They should be bringing her here in a few minutes."

"Is she all right?"

Amelia shrugged. "She's alive."

"That is *not* the right answer," I retorted. "She's done nothing wrong. She's your *niece.*"

She looked at me with flat, expressionless eyes that reminded me of my grandfather's empty gaze. Amelia, like my grandfather, did not care about human life. She was a psychopath, just like him. Whatever she was planning, I wasn't going to be able to appeal to any kind of a conscience to get us out of this.

"I must say, I am impressed by your spellwork," she said. "Natalie's magic is better bound now than it was when Betty was alive. Judging by the burn mark on the floor in her bedroom, it must have gotten loose at some point."

"Yes." No sense revealing any details. "Why do you call your mother by her first name? Why didn't Natalie know you existed?"

I saw a flash of emotion in Amelia's eyes: pure hate. Then it vanished, as if it had never been there. "Betty sent me away when I was six years old and Peter was two. My magic developed very early, and she found it impossible to bind completely. Rather than raise me, she sent me to a…facility in Oregon. I lived there until I was twelve, and then I was sent to live in a group home in South Dakota."

"I don't understand. Betty was a strong mage."

"I was stronger. Even at six years old, she couldn't control me. She was concerned I would use my magic in public and expose her. She was hiding our magic from her husband, so she sent me away."

It was equally possible Betty had recognized her daughter's psychopathy, I thought, looking at Amelia's flat stare. This didn't seem like the time to pry into that, though. "If you hated your mother so much, why did you come back?"

Amelia smiled, but it didn't reach her eyes. "Five years ago, my harnad in Portland heard a rumor that Betty had come into possession of Adelbert's *Kasten*. It seemed impossible, but I had to find out. No one has seen it in more than a century."

"So you showed up on her doorstep, or what?"

"Yes. The prodigal daughter, returned." Her tone was dry.

"And she trusted you?"

"Not at all, but I could see she felt some guilt over abandoning me, so I used that. I showed her that I was a strong blood mage, and that I could make her harnad stronger."

"She brought you into her harnad?" I was having a hard time believing Betty would trust her daughter enough to let her join her alliance of blood mages. I'd known her five minutes and I didn't trust her one little bit.

"After some persuasion from John West," Amelia said. "I showed John how powerful I was, and he wanted me to join. Plus, after I figured out I was his daughter and I made Betty tell him, all he wanted was to know me. The poor man never had any other children, apparently."

The pieces were falling into place. Amelia was the daughter of Betty and the powerful fire mage John West. Peter was actually her half brother, the son of Betty's first husband. No wonder their magic felt similar, but Amelia's was so strong and the other siblings' magic so weak.

"So you came back for the *Kasten*?" I scoffed. "It's a myth."

"It's not a myth," she countered. "It's very real, as a lot of people are about to find out. I've been waiting a long time for this day. I wish Betty could be here too, but the bitch died before I had everything in place."

"What exactly are you planning here? And what's Tweedle*dumb*'s role in all of this?" I glanced at her half brother.

He looked like he would love nothing more than to strangle me with his bare hands. The feeling was mutual. My head was killing me.

Amelia patted Eppright's arm. "Peter is key to everything. Without him, none of this would be possible."

Eppright preened.

I would have rolled my eyes, but they hurt too much. "Then what the hell am *I* doing here?" I asked the obvious question.

"At first, I was simply curious as to how much you'd found out by snooping around Betty's house and visiting my brother and sisters. Until Natalie asked William today if Betty had had any other children, I wasn't worried." I assumed William was the lawyer. "But when he called to warn me, I realized my complacency had nearly cost me everything. William helped me get Natalie at her home. I had Peter and Ray Browning intercept you at your house and bring you here. Unfortunately, we had to get rid of William. He became too much of a liability."

I was sickened by her casual admission of murder. "How did you manage to get Betty to give you passage through her library wards?"

Amelia looked surprised. "Well, well. I clearly underestimated you from the beginning. That explains why you were visiting my brother and sisters, and why you had Natalie ask if Betty had any other children—you were looking for whoever besides Betty could pass through the wards."

"So you somehow tricked Betty into allowing you into her library. Then after Betty was dead, you waited until Natalie was out, and came in and took the *Kasten* and Betty's spell books?"

Before Amelia could reply, I heard voices. Out of the darkness, a small group approached us. I saw Deborah, Kathy, and a large man I didn't recognize. He was carrying something over his shoulder wrapped in a blanket. I saw a flash of red hair inside the blanket and felt ice in my veins. Natalie.

Deborah avoided looking at me, but Kathy gave me a big, ugly smile. "Well, hello, *Audrey*," she said in a singsong voice. "So nice to see you again. Still looking to buy a house?"

"Oh, you know," I said casually, "it's really a buyer's market right now. I'm not rushing into anything."

Her eyes narrowed. "Where's your friend?" She turned to Amelia. "She wasn't alone when she came to see me."

"The werewolf?" Amelia said.

I stiffened. How the hell did they know who Sean was?

"He won't be able to find her. The obfuscation spell she's wearing and the blood ward will block any magical or metaphysical links."

I glanced down. Sure enough, there was a dark stain on the floor in a large circle around the table I was on. The circle was about fifteen feet wide and contained both of the large tables and the smaller, cloth-covered table. I hadn't been able to sense the ward because of the spell cuff. Between that and the spell I was wearing on my wrist, there was no way for Malcolm or Sean to find me, even if Sean hadn't been in Charles's custody.

Charles.

For a moment, I felt a flare of hope, but it quickly died. Without drinking my blood, he wouldn't be able to sense my location. There was no rescue coming. I'd have to get out this by myself. Fair enough; I was used to being on my own.

"Put her on the other table," Amelia instructed the man carrying Natalie.

He grunted and dropped the rolled-up bundle with a thud that made me wince.

"Ray," Amelia scolded.

"Sorry." He didn't sound like he meant it.

So this was Ray, Elise's husband, the asshole who'd bashed in the back of my head. "Why isn't your wife here?" I asked him.

Ray scowled at me. "She doesn't believe in using magic," he said shortly. He unrolled the blanket, revealing Natalie's unconscious body. She looked extremely pale, and there was a bloodstain on her shirt near her shoulder blade.

"What did you do to her?" I demanded.

"Shut up." Ray started tying Natalie to the table with rope. On her left wrist was a leather bracelet like mine.

I looked at Amelia for an answer.

She gestured at Natalie. "I had to use magic to knock her out, as well as an obfuscation spell to prevent you from locating her. Her magic and your binding have been reacting badly to my spells. It can't be helped. I don't have time to make new ones."

"Then let me do it," I said. "It's killing her."

Amelia gave me another one of those cold smiles. "Do you think I'm stupid? You won't be using your magic here today. Tie her arm down again," she said to Ray.

I had really, really been hoping they would forget about my untied left arm. As Ray moved toward me, I fought him off for a few seconds. Then Eppright backhanded me across the face, my head hit the table, and I blacked out.

CHAPTER 26

I wasn't out for long—a few minutes at most. When I came to, Ray was tying my arm down again. When he saw me looking at him, he gave my wrist a vicious twist and something popped. I shrieked and gagged.

"Ray." Amelia's voice was sharp. He stepped back from the table and sneered at me. I lay still and focused on not throwing up again.

When the nausea subsided, I still wanted to know what the hell was going on. "Okay, I get why I'm here and why Amelia is here." My words sounded slurred. My vision was blurry and I tried to focus. "But what are the rest of you doing?"

"We're Amelia's harnad," Deborah said primly. "We're here to allow her to draw energy from us for the box."

I blinked at Amelia in confusion. "*They're* your harnad?"

She gave me a calculating smile. "Of course. They're my family."

"But you can't be in a harnad," I told Kathy. "You aren't a blood mage."

"Of course I am," Kathy said as if I was slow. "Amelia and I are sisters."

"That's not how it works. You and Deborah have only very weak air magic. Peter is a low-level fire and air mage. Harnads only include very strong blood mages, which *none* of you are."

"Alice, Alice." Amelia shook her head. "Lies will not help you here. We are a family of blood mages. Betty never wanted us to use our magic. She wanted all the power for herself, but now we will become the most powerful cabal in the country with the *Kasten*. No one will *ever* cross us again." She gestured at her half siblings. "Please, step inside the circle so we can begin."

Kathy and Deborah joined Ray and Eppright inside the blood ward. Amelia traced a rune in the air and the ward flared.

"I'm telling you, you're not her harnad," I insisted, looking at the three half siblings and Elise's dumb thug of a husband. "I don't know what she's up to, or what she's told you, but you are not blood mages—only *she* is."

"Shut up," Eppright snarled. "Or I'll shove that gag down your throat and let you choke on it this time."

I shut up. I wasn't going to be able to convince them of anything. They didn't know enough about magic to know it wasn't possible for them to be blood mages or in a harnad. She'd duped them completely.

What the hell was Amelia up to? She'd probably promised to share power with them, but somehow I doubted that would actually happen. I didn't believe a word of this "family" crap she was spewing. That woman didn't care one iota about her half sisters and half brother. If anything, she probably despised them since Betty had abandoned her and raised them.

I narrowed my eyes at Amelia and then at the cloth-draped table where, I presumed, the *Kasten* awaited. What was it the book had said? That the *Kasten* had to be filled with the blood or body parts of mages representing all four elements?

I looked at Amelia in horror. She smiled at me. "*Religo!*"

Despite the dampening of the spell cuff, I felt a wave of magic prickle over my skin. My cuff protected me from Amelia's binding spell, but Kathy, Deborah, Ray, and Peter were not so lucky. All four were frozen in place where they stood. Awareness and fear shone in their eyes, but they were immobilized.

Amelia patted me on the hand. "Relax, dear. You're just a bystander for now."

She went to the covered table and pulled back the cloth. On it sat an old wooden chest about the size of a shoebox, a small ritual knife, two spell books that were probably Betty's, and a long black robe. Rune carvings covered the box. Amelia put the robe on and picked up the knife, cutting the pad of her thumb. She smeared her blood across the lid of the box and recited an incantation. It sounded like German.

"You're going to kill them all," I said.

"Yes." Amelia's voice was emotionless. "Greedy fools. Kathy's husband spends money faster than she can make it, and Deborah and her husband have nothing saved for their retirement. Peter owes his bookie a hundred grand. Ray and Elise are so far in debt, with their house and their cars and private school tuition, he was all too eager to join us. It might be the only time he would have been better off listening to my idiot half sister. All any of them want is power and money."

"And you don't?" I said skeptically.

"Of course I do, but what I want the most is revenge. I can't get to Betty, but I can do this." She used the knife to gesture at the four terrified people standing frozen around us. "I can wipe out her family, everyone she loved after she turned her back on me. Then I'll burn the city down. There won't be a single person or cabal who can stand against me. If I fill the *Kasten* with the lifeblood of an entire family, it will be the most unstoppable object of power the magical world has ever known."

I didn't know how much I believed that, but if the legends were true, I couldn't let her unleash the *Kasten* on the city. I doubted I had much chance of reasoning with her, but I had to try. It was either that or lie here and watch her kill five people. I might not like Natalie's extended family very much, but they were still human beings. I'd seen enough suffering and death in my lifetime.

"What makes you think the *Kasten* will be as powerful as you think? Everything I read said it's a myth."

Amelia caressed the box. "Our harnad in Portland had a letter written by a mage in 1843. He described a story told to him by his father, who had witnessed a mage wield the power of the *Kasten* filled with the blood of a father, mother, and three children. It laid waste to more than ten square miles. Imagine what one filled with the lifeblood of an entire extended family would do. Four siblings, their spouses, their children, and grandchildren. And Betty's brother and sister, and her precious granddaughter." She sneered at Natalie.

I went cold at the way she casually described killing children. "So, old legends? That's all you've got?" I challenged her. "What if it doesn't work? You'd have killed all these people for nothing."

"Not for nothing," Amelia countered, picking up the box and the knife and moving toward Peter Eppright. "Even if the *Kasten* isn't even powerful enough to start a campfire, wherever Betty is, she gets to watch her entire family die. It's enough for me." She stopped in front of Eppright. His eyes were full of panic. "*Kneel*," she commanded.

All four of them crashed to their knees on the concrete floor, compelled to obey by her spell.

I struggled against my cuff and ropes to no avail.

Amelia murmured an invocation, traced runes on the lid of the *Kasten*, and opened the box. I felt a whisper of power that I recognized immediately from Betty's library; this was what had been hidden in the bookcase, behind the blood ward. The inside was stained black.

I began pulling on the rope that bound my left wrist. It hurt, but I hoped Ray might have been careless in his haste to tie me up. I twisted and pulled, trying not to attract Amelia's attention. I couldn't feel any give at all, but I kept trying.

With one quick movement, Amelia cut Peter Eppright's throat.

Blood spurted out across the floor. His eyes were wide and horrified, but he remained immobile. Amelia stood to the side for a moment, watching the blood arc through the air without so much as a blink, and then she raised the *Kasten* to catch it.

Warm blood ran down my fingers from where the rope on my left wrist had cut through the skin. Maybe the blood would make it easier to slip out.

I didn't dare look at my hand and tip Amelia off to what I was doing, so instead I watched Peter Eppright bleed out and die. It seemed to take forever, but in reality it probably took less than a minute. I felt the moment he died; it was like a frisson of energy across my skin. The *Kasten* now contained the lifeblood of one member of Betty's family. There were four more in the circle, awaiting their turn.

Amelia stepped away from Eppright's body, which, grotesquely, was still upright on its knees despite being dead. I stared at her, hoping she wouldn't notice the blood dripping from my left hand. Her face was serene.

"Blood magic is the most peaceful feeling," she said, breathing deeply. She touched Eppright's body and it fell over, hitting the floor with a wet *thump*.

Then she turned to Elise's husband Ray, who was facing me. When she slit his throat, hot blood sprayed across my stomach and legs before Amelia moved the *Kasten* between us. I flinched and continued pulling on my ropes, watching Amelia smile and hold the wooden box while Ray's lifeblood drained into it. I kept my face impassive, but inside I was screaming curses. I'd wanted him to suffer for hurting me, but this...this was a nightmare.

It took longer for Ray to die, but in the end, the life faded from his eyes and my skin tingled. More lifeblood for the triple-damned *Kasten*. At Amelia's touch, his body joined Eppright's on the blood-splattered floor.

I looked at Kathy and Deborah, and then at Natalie, still lying unconscious on the other table. "What's my part in all of this? I'm not a part of the family."

"You're actually very important," Amelia informed me. "Imagine how glad I was to sense that you have water magic. No one in our family is a water mage."

I blinked. "I'm not a water mage."

She shook her head at me. "No point in lying, dear. Not now." She walked to Kathy and casually cut her throat.

I clenched my teeth as the blood fountained from Kathy's slim neck and Amelia lifted the box to catch it. "I'm not a water mage," I repeated. "I have air and earth magic and that's all."

Amelia ignored me and watched Kathy's lifeblood drain into the *Kasten*.

I desperately tried to think, despite the pounding in my head and the nausea. I didn't understand why she was insisting I had water magic. I'd never....

Wait.

I remembered something Malcolm had said several days ago, after he'd had to use a dozen healing spells to save my life. He'd said I'd carry some of his magic as a result. Shit, I *did* have water magic—only a trace, but it might be enough. Thanks to me, Amelia would be able to give the *Kasten* everything it needed to unleash destruction on a massive scale.

I seethed and continued pulling on the rope on my left wrist as another tingle ran over my skin. Kathy was dead. A moment later, she fell to the floor.

Something started to slide over my left hand. The leather cord holding the masking and obfuscation spells had gotten slippery enough with blood that I might be able to slide it off. I scraped my wrist against the edge of the table, trying to push it over the big part of my hand, but it was stuck. I pulled harder.

If I could get the cord off, Malcolm might be able to sense me, at least enough to get close, since the blood ward wasn't specifically designed to obscure my aura like the obfuscation spells were. It was likely Charles knew I was missing by now. If I could somehow break Amelia's blood ward, someone would be able to find me quickly. I didn't know if I could break the ward without getting my spell cuff off, but one problem at a time.

I kept my attention on Amelia so she wouldn't suspect I was trying to get my hand free.

"Isn't the box full yet?" I asked her. Deborah's eyes were so full of fear, horror, and grief that I could hardly stand to look at her.

"It can't be filled." Amelia's voice sounded dreamy, her eyes unfocused. "Its capacity is endless, like its power."

The cord slid off. I caught it so it didn't fall to the floor, then tossed it up and onto the table where it was hidden by my body. The obfuscation spell was gone. Hopefully Malcolm would be on his way. Now I had to get out of this spell cuff and break the blood ward.

Sure. No problem.

My left wrist was streaming blood now from cuts made by the rope. If Amelia was paying attention to me instead of slitting throats, she'd have noticed the small puddle forming on the floor near my table. Instead, she stood with her eyes closed, swaying back and forth, presumably entranced by the power of the *Kasten*.

I twisted my left wrist just so, and the rope went slack and started to slide over my hand. My wrist was shredded, and I could barely feel my fingers.

I had a few seconds to plan at the most. If I got my left hand free, I might be able to undo the spell cuff if it wasn't the kind that required a key. Once I had my magic, Amelia was fucking toast.

Even if I couldn't get the cuff off, I might still be able to break her blood ward. It might only be down for a short time, but it might be long enough for Malcolm and whoever else was looking to find me. That was a lot of "mights," but I didn't think I had much of a choice. Amelia was heading over to Deborah, and once she was dead, then she'd be ready to cut Natalie's throat and mine. It was now or never. I was done watching people die.

I slipped my left hand out of the rope, twisted my upper body, and looked at the spell cuff on my right wrist. Hallelujah, no key required; it was the kind with two latches.

"No!" Amelia shouted. I ignored her and focused on making my numb fingers unfasten the latches. I had to get the damn cuff off or I was dead.

Just as I flicked open the second catch on the cuff, Amelia attacked, slashing me with her knife. The blade cut across my chest and blood spilled out. I shrieked and swung wildly with my left arm as I shook the cuff off my right wrist.

The second the cuff fell off, my magic roared through me like a dam had broken, and I made no attempt to hold back the surge of power. I threw my head back and screamed. The sheer force of my unleashed magic caused Amelia to stumble backward and fall, splashing blood from the *Kasten* onto her.

I fought to pull my magic back into myself and get it under control, but it was harder than it should have been; my head was pounding because of the damn concussion. I tried to move before I remembered my feet were still tied. I used my earth magic to burn the ropes off.

I staggered to my feet just as Amelia cut loose with a flash of air and fire magic. I barely had time to throw up a quick protective circle. She attacked again with a stronger blast, breaking my circle, and fire scoured my body. I screamed and lashed out with my cold-fire whip. It seared Amelia across the chest and knocked her down again. Her shriek of pain was music to my ears.

I realized Natalie was unprotected, lying unconscious on her table. As Amelia struggled to get to her feet, I threw up another circle, this one much stronger, and staggered over to Natalie. With a heave, I pushed her table over so it was between us and Amelia and made my circle larger to cover us both. The other mage blasted my circle with fire, but this time, it held.

I yanked the spell bracelet off Natalie's wrist. She was deathly pale, her breathing shallow. Amelia's spells were killing her. I didn't have time to unweave them, but if I unbound Natalie's null magic, it might disrupt the spells and keep her alive. I pulled at the threads of the binding spell and removed the one that kept her null magic contained. Yellow magic flared briefly, and Amelia's spells fractured.

Amelia sent another wave of fire, stronger than the last. My circle wavered but held. It wouldn't protect us for long, though. I needed to drop the damn blood ward and call in the cavalry. I'd hand Amelia over to the vamps.

With my right hand, I wiped across my chest, gathering up as much of my blood as I could. I steeled myself, broke my protective circle, and lunged for the blood ward. Behind me, Amelia screeched in fury.

I shoved my bloody hand into Amelia's ward and pushed energy into it, chanting "*Obliterate, obliterate, obliterate*," until it broke with a surge that made me stagger. I wiped my foot through the ward on the floor and smeared my blood across it so she couldn't close it again. Now maybe Malcolm and Charles could find me.

I turned around and realized Amelia was right behind me. The light glinted off the edge of her knife as it arced toward my heart.

I stumbled backward, but I was dazed and disoriented from breaking the blood ward and moved too slowly. Screaming incoherently in rage, Amelia buried the blade in my chest, just above my right breast.

I stared dumbly at the knife for several confused seconds before Amelia yanked it out. My feet slid out from under me and I collapsed.

As I slumped against a large crate, Amelia picked up the *Kasten*. With the knife in one hand and the box in the other, she walked toward me. I tried to use my earth or air magic to push her back, but I was too dizzy and weakened to do more than raise a gentle breeze and a few paltry green flames.

With my lifeblood, she would have all four kinds of natural magic. If the legends were true, she would wield the *Kasten* and destroy the city, killing everyone in her path. With it, she might become the most powerful blood mage in modern history.

No.

There was no Malcolm. No Charles. There was only me here to stop her.

I forced myself to think. What could I do? I was having trouble breathing; my lung was probably punctured. Blood pumped out of the stab wound in my chest at an alarming rate. I wasn't going to be able to put up much of a physical fight. I didn't know if she would try to slit my throat or just catch the blood coming out of my chest. All I knew was that I was not going to give up yet.

I looked up at the half-finished building we were in. If I could spool enough earth magic, I could bring the building down on her. On us. Let's see the bitch get out of that one. I smiled and coughed up some blood.

Natalie and I might survive, if we were lucky. If not, at least we'd take her with us.

Amelia knelt in front of me, knife poised, and rested the *Kasten* in my lap. It looked like she was going to slit my throat after all.

I started spooling my earth magic. She either didn't notice or didn't care.

Amelia leaned close to me. "I enjoyed this. It's rare I find someone so near my own skill level. I'm almost sorry to have to kill you."

"Fuck off," I mumbled, which would have been more impressive if it hadn't come out in a bloody gurgle.

She opened the *Kasten*. Despite having its contents splashed around several times, the box was still full of blood. The power it gave off was enormous.

"Leave it be," Amelia said. "There's nothing for you to do now." I realized she was referring to my spooling earth magic.

She was wrong about that; I could bring down the building. Either she didn't think I could or she didn't think I would. I certainly didn't want to, but I didn't think I had much choice.

I looked down. My bloody hands tingled with the power of my earth magic, but I wasn't sure it was going to be strong enough or fast enough. I put my palms on the floor and prepared to shove every last ounce of magic I had kindled into the concrete.

I caught movement out of the corner of my eye and glanced up. To my shock, Natalie, pale and shaken, was standing behind Amelia. She gestured at me as if to say, *What should I do?*

Amelia raised the knife.

"Just touch her," I whispered.

Amelia paused, her blade an inch from my jugular, and stared at me. "What?"

I'd been on the receiving end of Natalie's nulling once, but I'd never seen anyone hit with it before. When Natalie's hands came down on Amelia's shoulders, the flare of bright yellow magic seared my eyes. Amelia screamed in anger and panic, and I felt a strange pulling sensation on the edge of my senses, like I was too close to the big drain at the bottom of a pool. Natalie's powerful nulling magic sucked Amelia dry in an instant.

With a cry of rage, Amelia staggered to her feet, knife in hand. She might be nulled, but she was far from defenseless.

"Look out," I rasped.

Natalie dodged the knife as Amelia lunged. As the older woman stumbled, off-balance, Natalie reached for a stack of short metal pipes, grabbed one, and swung it two-handed at Amelia's head.

The pipe connected with Amelia's skull with a sickening, wet *crunch*. She went down, and I seriously doubted she'd be getting up again.

Natalie dropped the pipe and stared at Amelia's body. "Oh God."

Before I could speak, a wave of gray-and-black magic swept over me, and a surge of pure power whited out my vision. The *Kasten* had lost its host and moved on to the strongest mage in the vicinity.

As if in a dream, I stuck my hand into the box. The blood felt thick and warm. In the bottom, I felt small, knobby objects that I realized were finger bones. *Adelbert.*

Hallo, meine Liebe. The voice in my head sounded like it originated in the depths of hell.

Power coursed up my right arm and through my body. It was the most incredible feeling I'd ever experienced, and with it came the desire and the power to annihilate. I could destroy the building, the city, the world, and I wanted to.

I closed my eyes. The *Kasten* showed me a vision of my mother, beautiful and gentle. My mother, who promised me that soon she and my father would take me away from my grandfather to a place where he'd never find us. My mother, whose own father had burned her alive, along with my father, when the guard she'd bribed to help her get me out of the compound betrayed her. I saw my mother and father, two piles of ash, on the floor of their house. My grandfather had taken me to see them when it was over so I could see what happened to people who crossed him.

Then the *Kasten* showed me my grandfather. Moses Murphy sat in his office, reading an offer from a prospective client. People were to die. Moses had only to agree to a price. He would never stop killing, unless someone stopped him.

Grief and rage rose within me like a tidal wave. I could level the compound, kill everyone in it. Moses would be dead. I could burn him to ash, and I could stand in front of him when I did it. I would be free forever. The *Kasten* offered it to me as a gift, and I wept in joy at the thought.

Then I would destroy everything and everyone else who stood against me. I would bring the world to its knees.

No. I wanted no one on their knees, not ever.

Ja, the *Kasten* said. Somehow, though I'd never spoken a word of German, I could understand it. *We will have vengeance. All will suffer for what was done to you. Take us and destroy.*

No, I am not a destroyer. I struggled but sank further into the darkness that was spreading through my brain.

Alice. I heard a different voice in my mind. It was gentle, like a caress. *Alice, come back.*

I opened my eyes. My brain processed a series of images, like a slideshow.

My right hand was wrist-deep in the blood in the *Kasten*. My left arm was wrapped around the box, holding it against my stomach.

Charles crouched in front of me, his hands on my bloody, burned legs, fangs extended, eyes solid black. Somehow, he had found me within minutes of the blood ward falling. He must have been nearby when I broke it. I wasn't sure I liked the covetous way he was looking at the box on my lap.

Amelia lay dead on the floor next to him in a puddle of her own blood. I felt nothing at the sight, not even satisfaction.

Natalie stood next to Bryan, her eyes as wide as saucers. Malcolm floated on the other side of her, looking at me and the box in horror.

I was burned again. Blood pumped sluggishly out of the stab

wound in my chest. I should be dead, but I wasn't. I knew the box was keeping me alive so we could become the Destroyer.

I never needed to fear again. The *Kasten* would free me.

I would become a monster. I'd run away from the cabal so I didn't become one.

His eyes shining silver, Charles reached for the box. The *Kasten* struck with a bolt of black-and-gray magic that knocked him back several feet and left a scorched and bloody gash on his chest.

Natalie shrieked. Bryan was instantly at the vampire's side, but Charles held up his hand and stared at the *Kasten*.

"*Fass mich nicht an*," I heard myself say, my voice flat. "*Ich bin für dich nicht da du Toter.*" Do not touch me. I am not for you, dead man.

Unlike me, Charles apparently spoke German. "*Was willst du?*" the vampire asked me, his voice hard. *What do you want?*

"*Rache*," I rasped.

Revenge.

The *Kasten* showed me a vision of endless devastation, of blackened earth and mountains of corpses. I understood then that Adelbert's thirst was unquenchable. I could not just use the *Kasten* to kill my grandfather; once released, Adelbert would control me. Through me, he would destroy everything in his path.

If I gave in to what the box wanted—what this terrible part of me wanted—I might as well be dead. As badly as I wanted Moses to die for everything he had done, I couldn't surrender my soul to this darkness. I couldn't unleash the *Kasten* on the world.

And yet, I couldn't just let go of the box either. No one else should have this kind of power. Charles wanted it. Others would kill to possess it. There was no choice here; the *Kasten* must be destroyed.

I met Charles's gaze and coughed up more blood. "Thank you for finding me," I whispered.

The vampire's eyes widened almost imperceptibly. He recognized a good-bye when he heard one. He reached out cautiously to touch my foot, and I heard his voice in my head: *Alice, no!*

I closed my eyes and shoved every ounce of magical energy I had down my right arm into the black void that was the soul of the *Kasten*. *Die,* I ordered it.

From deep within the emptiness came a roar of fury: NO. YOU

WILL DIE.

I'm already dying, I said simply. *And I'm taking you with me.*

The only response was a wordless scream out of the darkness.

The *Kasten* lived on the life energy of those whose blood made it whole. I felt familiar magical traces: Amelia Wharton, Peter Eppright, Ray Browning, Kathy Adams. My own. Beyond that, deep in the core of the box, I sensed a dark malevolence, a spirit so filled with hate and malice that it made me shudder.

Adelbert's enduring evil was the soul of the *Kasten*.

I had not used my blood magic to kill in a very long time, not since I left the cabal, but I still remembered how. I reached into the vile nothingness at the center of the *Kasten* and ripped out its heart with a single power word.

The darkness receded. With a howl of rage, the box died.

I let out a long, gurgling sigh. Without the *Kasten*'s poison in my veins, I felt completely at peace. Amelia was dead. Natalie and Deborah were alive. Despite the power it had offered me, I'd resisted long enough to destroy the *Kasten*. This was going to be a giant mess, but it was going to be someone else's job to clean it up.

I realized I was no longer sitting up. At some point, I'd fallen over and was now lying on my back on the cold concrete floor. A face appeared above mine, but I couldn't see who it was.

My heart stuttered in my chest. I didn't think I was breathing anymore, but that was all right. Maybe it was time to rest. Some part of me was breaking free.

Strong arms gathered me up and cradled me like a child. Something cool and delicious filled my mouth and ran down my chin. Vampire blood.

You must live, Alice. Drink from me. Charles's voice in my mind was urgent.

I couldn't obey. *Tired.*

I know. Drink.

...

I was too far gone to frame a thought.

Alice, you are not permitted to die.

Arrogant vampire. As if it was up to him.

I used my last bit of strength to comfort Charles with my mind. It was all I could do. Then I slipped away.

CHAPTER 27

I woke in an unfamiliar bed to the sound of an argument.

"Your anger is unwarranted." Charles's voice was quiet and calm.

"It's been almost a week, Vaughan," Sean growled, also in undertone. It sounded like they were on the other side of the room. "A *week* you've kept me waiting to see her."

I could not open my eyes, or move, or speak. That should have frightened me, but strangely I felt entirely contented. I lay still and listened to the steady beeping of a heart monitor, the soft whirring sounds of machines, and the voices of Sean and Charles.

"Your presence would have done nothing to improve her condition," the vampire replied. "As you can see, she is comfortable and well cared for."

"Damn it, that's not the point and you know it," Sean snarled. "I had the right to see her as soon as you knew the accusations against me weren't true. The Were Ruling Council cleared me three days ago, and still you turned me away."

"I am aware of the council's findings, but Alice is under my protection here, and I had no intention of permitting you access to her until *I* was personally satisfied the allegations were false."

"And it took you three extra days to come to that conclusion?"

"If it had taken a year, I would not have risked her safety by allowing your presence one day too soon," Charles countered. "If you care for her as much as you claim, you would understand my diligence.”

“I didn’t come here to argue with you; I came to see Alice. If you’ll leave, I’d like a few minutes with her.”

A long silence. “Speak of nothing that will trouble her,” Charles said at last. “If she can hear you, I would not have her be distressed.”

“I will keep that in mind,” Sean said icily.

A door closed. Footsteps approached my bed, and Sean took my hand. His skin felt almost painfully hot.

“You’re so cold.” Sean’s voice was rough. He brushed hair back from my face, his fingers lingering on my cheek. “Damned vampires. I’ll tell them to turn the heat up in here. You shouldn’t be so cold.”

Minutes passed. Sean rubbed my arms, warming me.

“I spoke to the nurse, and she said hearing familiar voices might help you find your way back,” Sean said finally. “I don’t know if you can hear me, but I’m here. I want you to know I found the source of the allegations that I planned to turn you into a werewolf. One of my wolves, Mike Holleman, wanted to take over my pack, but he knew there was no way he could win a challenge. He started spreading rumors that I planned to bite a woman to make her my mate, thinking I would be arrested or shot dead. It was one of Mike’s buddies who told the bartender, Pete. After reviewing the evidence, the Were Ruling Council cleared me immediately of all charges, though apparently it took far longer to convince Vaughan that the whole thing was false.”

Sean began rubbing my hands. “He wouldn’t let me in to see you until now. I’ve been here every day for the last week, but this is the first time I’ve gotten to see you except through a video monitor. You’re at Hawthorne’s, but you probably guessed that.”

Another pause.

“I have a lot more I need to say to you, but I’m going to wait until you’re awake.” Sean held my hand in both of his. “Allie, wake up. I know you’re there. Just open your eyes, damn it.” His voice was tight with frustration and grief. “Open your eyes and *look at me*.”

My fingers moved. Sean froze.

It was nothing more than the slightest twitch, but I *moved*. I was elated.

“Allie, I can feel you,” he breathed. “Do it again, baby. Squeeze my hand.”

For a long moment, nothing happened. Sean's hope washed over me through the link that stretched between us.

My fingers tightened again.

The warmth of his happiness was a welcome feeling after my long, lonely wandering in the darkness. "Now I know you can hear me," Sean said softly. "It's time to wake up, baby. You've been asleep long enough."

I sent a blast of annoyance down our link and felt his surprise. "Don't call me baby," I murmured. My lips barely moved, and the sound was softer than a whisper, but his werewolf ears heard me.

Sean raised my hand to his lips and pressed a kiss to my knuckles. I managed a ghost of a smile before sleep took me away again.

* * *

The next time I woke up, it was the middle of the night, and there was a vampire in my bed.

"Alice?"

With effort, I rolled my head on the pillow to look at him in the moonlight spilling through my windows. Charles lay on his side, facing me. I noticed he wore a button-up shirt and khakis, and his feet were bare. I'd never seen him dressed so casually.

"Ch...Charles." My voice was hoarse from disuse.

"I am here, Alice. I feared you would wake during the day when I could not be with you, but Ms. Smith was here so that you were not alone. You were cared for at Hawthorne's until early this evening. Once your condition improved, I believed you would be more comfortable in your own home."

I frowned. "But...the wards?"

"Your ghost was able to adjust the wards to permit us to enter." Charles took my hand. "I am glad you are back with us."

"Glad...to be alive. How did you...find me?"

"The werewolf sensed the attack on you through your link. Since he was still in my custody at the time, he and Ms. Smith went to your house immediately and attempted to find out what had happened to you. They found your blood in your driveway, but you were gone. Maclin recognized Peter Eppright's scent from your previous meeting, but they had no idea where you had been taken. Once your ghost arrived, he was able to communicate with the werewolf and tell him of Ms. Newton's kidnapping. When I woke at sunset, I tasted the trace of your blood found at your home and attempted to locate you, but it was so degraded by then that beyond a general sense that you were on the east side of the city and alive, I was unsuccessful. The wards hiding you were too strong."

Charles tucked my hair behind my ear. "Maclin was driving around the area, trying to reach you through your link or catch your scent, and I was attempting to locate you when I felt you break one of the spells. I still could not sense your exact location, but we were close when you broke the blood ward. We arrived soon after, but it was almost too late."

His gaze was troubled. "You went into cardiac arrest. Maclin arrived and performed CPR. Once we resuscitated you, we brought you back to Hawthorne's for medical care."

"Thank you for taking care of me." It was getting easier to speak, thank goodness. "What have I missed?"

"The building where you were held was a site belonging to Browning Construction," Charles told me. "We removed everything belonging to you, Ms. Newton, and Ms. Newton's grandmother, and your ghost dispersed your magic trace. I arranged a fire that consumed the building and destroyed much of the evidence."

I stared at him in shock.

"At this time, the police and coroner's office believe Amelia Wharton sacrificed Browning, Eppright, and Kathy Adams as part of a blood magic ritual, then lost control of the power she had gathered and burned the building down, killing herself. The case has not been closed, but unless additional evidence surfaces, I believe your involvement will remain unknown."

"What about Deborah Mackey?"

"While I feel certain Ms. Newton can be relied upon not to divulge your secret, especially as she would then be implicating herself in Wharton's death, I doubted Mrs. Mackey could be trusted. I glamoured her, and she remembers nothing of knowing Wharton or going to the construction site that night. It was, I believe, the best course of action, besides leaving her to perish in the fire. Your ghost was most insistent you would not have permitted her to die."

"Malcolm was right about that," I said. "Enough people died there."

"Then I made the correct choice." Charles's brow furrowed. "A man by the name of John West has been making discreet inquiries about the fire. There is some concern, as West seems to suspect there were at least one or two other mages present at the ritual who are not accounted for among the dead. As your ghost dispersed all magic traces other than Wharton's, how he came to this conclusion is not clear, nor is his involvement in these events."

Slowly, with frequent pauses to catch my breath, I explained how I'd been taken from my house by Peter Eppright and Ray Browning, who Amelia Wharton was, what she was doing with the *Kasten*, and why John West was involved. When I described how Adelbert and the *Kasten* had attempted to take control of me, Charles's face grew even more grim.

By the time I finished the story, I was breathless and covered in a cold sweat. Who knew talking could be so exhausting?

Charles touched my face. "You must rest. Your strength will return."

"I'm a little surprised to be so weak. You saved me with your blood, didn't you?" When I woke the morning after being cut by window glass, I felt fully recovered; this time, I felt as wrung out as a dishrag.

"It took a significant amount of my blood just to save your life. You had a deep stab wound, significant blood loss, a punctured and collapsed lung, first- and second-degree burns, a skull fracture, a severe concussion, a fractured wrist, broken ribs—"

"Broken ribs?" I didn't remember that.

"From chest compressions."

"Oh."

"I was concerned too much of my blood might have long-term effects. We used primarily human blood transfusions once the major injuries were healed, which is why you are weak."

I tilted my head to look at him. "What long-term effects were you worried about?"

"At first, I feared you might become a dhampir, since you had already consumed my blood just the night before. Once that danger was past, it was possible more blood could create a permanent telepathic bond between us. You might be able to broadcast thoughts and emotions as well, and there would surely be a dramatic increase in your libido."

I blinked at that. "Well, I definitely want to skip the first three, but that last thing might not be a complete disaster."

With a cool fingertip, Charles traced a line down my forehead and nose to my lips and chin. "A *dramatic* increase," he repeated.

I spent a few moments thinking about what would constitute a *dramatic* increase. "Well, it's just as well, I suppose. I wouldn't want to go around wanting to f—"

I was abruptly silenced by his mouth on mine.

Charles's lips were as cool as the rest of him, but the kiss was anything but chilly. His hunger was its own warmth. I'd never kissed a vampire before, but he didn't taste any different from any other man.

Heat blazed through me as my body responded to his touch, and I moaned. If there was anything in the world I wanted more than Charles at that moment, I didn't know what it was.

Through the haze of desire, I felt a strange sensation, as if something was nagging at me. Even as my body was responding to the feeling of Charles's hands on me, I was starting to realize something was terribly wrong. Charles was dangerous. I didn't want him touching me, or kissing me. My body was betraying me because of the blood he'd shared with me. My brain screamed to get away, even as I pulled at his clothes and dug my nails into his flesh. *No,* I thought desperately, as his cool hand slid under my pajama top. *No, I don't want this.* If he heard my thoughts, he ignored them.

Charles's blood might be powerful, but there was one emotion in me that was stronger. Fear of being victimized was at the core of my being. It rose in me like a tidal wave and broke his influence.

I took a ragged breath and looked up at the vampire. His eyes were silver. "Charles, stop."

"You are afraid, Alice." Charles's voice was low, almost a purr. "It is arousing."

"Well, it's *not* arousing to me," I snapped. Anger was clearing the fog of desire away. "Take your hands off me. I'm not thinking clearly. You know that what you're doing isn't fair."

"I never claimed to be fair, my dear," he said, lowering his head.

"But you've always been honorable," I said quickly, before his lips could touch mine. "There's nothing honorable in taking advantage of a woman whose judgment is impaired, or ignoring her when she says no. And have you forgotten my alliance with Sean's pack? An assault on me is an assault on the pack."

Charles chuckled, flashing his fangs. "Oh, yes, your alliance. 'Well played,' as they say." He rose smoothly from the bed and tucked in his shirt, stepping into a pair of Italian loafers. I wrapped my arms around myself.

Charles crouched at the side of the bed, his face level with mine. "Soon you will come to me," he said, and his voice made me shiver. "You may say what you feel is because of the blood I shared with you, but we both know it is not true. You fear me, but you desire me as well." He stood and looked down at me. "Sweet Alice," he murmured.

He moved to the bedroom door and opened it, then vanished into the darkness.

* * *

I slept for a few more hours and woke just before dawn, feeling surprisingly clearheaded and alert. Instead of getting up, however, I lay in bed and tried not to think too much about Amelia Wharton and the horrors I'd witnessed at the construction site.

Though I tried to distract myself, I kept coming back to John West. The thought of West digging around made me nervous. I wasn't sure how he had been able to tell there had been any other mages at the construction site once it had burned down, unless he was able to sense the magic Malcolm used to remove my blood and trace. If it was Malcolm's magic he was tracking, that was still very dangerous since Malcolm was bound to me and I carried some of his magic within me.

Not long after sunrise, I thought I heard a car pull into my driveway. When the engine shut off and a car door slammed, I rolled out of bed and went to the window. I recognized the silver Mercedes even before I saw who was walking up the sidewalk.

Sean.

I froze, my hand on the curtain. After he'd spoken to me while I was in a coma, I knew we needed to talk about where things stood between us. I'd felt his truthfulness when he said he'd never intended to turn me into a werewolf. There was still the matter of him being an alpha in need of a mate, though, and the metaphysical link he'd created without my permission.

I'd planned on talking to Sean about all that when I was ready, but it looked like he was done waiting for me to call. Never mind I'd only been out of a coma for all of—I glanced at the clock—five hours.

Sean looked up and saw me at the window. A surprisingly overt parade of emotions moved across his face: relief, anger, determination.

I could claim I was exhausted and ask him to come back another day, but I didn't want to be a coward about this. It wasn't like the conversation would get any easier if I put it off.

I heaved a sigh and held up a finger, indicating I would be down in a minute. Sean nodded and pointed at the porch.

As I was debating whether to put on a robe or get dressed, my phone rang. Someone had plugged it in and left it on the nightstand. The screen said *Bryan Smith*. "Hello?"

"Do you require assistance?" Bryan's voice was a deep rumble.

I frowned.

"Alice? Do you need us to come to your house?"

"What? No, why would I?"

"Sean Maclin is at your house," Bryan said.

I glared at the phone as if the enforcer could see me. "How the hell do you know that? Are you people *watching* me?"

A pause. "Mr. Vaughan is concerned about your safety. We are monitoring your visitors."

My face grew hot. "Well, you can tell *Mr. Vaughan* when he wakes up that this surveillance had better be gone by tomorrow. And no, I do *not* require assistance. I can take care of my own damn self."

I threw the phone on my bed in disgust and stomped over to my dresser for clothes, then stuck my feet into flip-flops and braided my hair. Good enough. Anyone who showed up unexpectedly at my house at the crack of dawn got what they got.

I yanked my bedroom door open and walked straight into Malcolm; like, literally *into* Malcolm.

We both yelped and jumped back. I shuddered and rubbed my arms. "Son of a bitch!"

"Sorry!" Malcolm flitted around the upstairs hallway. "Damn it, sorry. I was about to tell you Sean is here."

"Yeah, I know. I'm going down to talk to him." I walked around him and headed for the stairs.

"Are you sure?" Malcolm trailed after me.

"Yes, I'm sure!"

"Jeez. You're really grouchy when you wake up from a coma."

I sighed. "Sorry." I explained about Bryan's phone call.

Malcolm did not look happy. "The vampire's spying on you, huh? What are you going to do about that?"

"First off, get someone in here to check for hidden cameras and microphones, that's for damn sure." I stomped down the stairs. "And you are going to fix those wards so Charles and his people can't get back in here."

The ghost followed me. "I'll do that right now. You want backup with the werewolf?"

I squared my shoulders. "No, I want privacy. We have to get this over with."

"Okay, Alice. I'll be downstairs. Summon me if you need me." Malcolm disappeared through the basement door.

Before I chickened out, I marched to the door, opened it, and came face-to-face with Sean.

He wore a faded Rolling Stones T-shirt that stretched across his broad chest, jeans that fit very well, and sneakers. "Hello, Allie."

I hadn't seen him—not in human form—since I left him standing in Hawthorne's more than a week ago. It felt like eons since that night, and yet, when I looked at him, I felt a surge of something so powerful that it hit me like a physical blow.

To cover my reaction, I moved over to the porch swing and sat down. That made me think of the night I'd been burned by Natalie's magic, and how he'd held me on the swing while I was unconscious. I scrubbed my face with my hands.

"Allie?"

I peeked through my fingers. Sean was crouched in front of me. "What's going on?" he asked me.

I blew out a breath. "I don't know, Sean. I really don't. I thought you wanted to turn me into a werewolf. I watched three people get their throats cut, and I was helpless to do anything about it. I damn near died trying to save the city from a crazy woman with a box full of mage blood. I was in a coma for a week. Charles has people watching my house. It's a lot to process."

Sean stared at me. "Well, when you put it that way, it *does* sound like you've got a lot on your mind," he said finally.

Despite everything, that made me smile.

He put his hands on my knees, his eyes turning serious. "We need to talk."

"I know. But first, thank you for saving my life at the construction site."

Sean looked grim. "When the blood ward fell, I was several miles away. When I got there, Bryan was holding you and Vaughan was trying to get you to drink his blood, but you were already...." He paused. "I hoped you would use our link to reach out to me and tell me where you were, but you never tried."

I was startled. "It never occurred to me," I confessed. "I doubt it would have worked through the blood ward, anyway, but you got there in time to save my life." I hesitated, then covered his hands with mine and squeezed. "I heard you speaking to me while I was asleep. Thank you for not giving up on me. It just took me a while to find my way back."

"So you heard what I told you about Mike?"

"I heard you. Are you going to have any more problems with this guy?"

"No. He's dead."

I blinked.

Sean's face was hard. "I confronted him the day after the construction site murders. He challenged me and lost. Two of his buddies stepped up after him. They're dead too." He looked at me. "Does that bother you?"

"No." I'd seen my share of challenges when I was part of my grandfather's cabal. I remembered how Sean had looked in wolf form, and my mind conjured up an image of him fighting another wolf to the death. It would have been bloody and vicious. His werewolf physiology meant he healed quickly, but three fights was a lot, even for an alpha. "I'm glad you're all right."

Sean took my hands. "You must have spent some time around a pack at some point," he said, his eyes searching my face. "Most people aren't this calm when they find out they're alone with someone who recently killed three people."

I didn't comment on the first part of his statement. "You killed them in a fair challenge," I said, raising my shoulder in a half shrug. "They were trying to kill you. I know what it means to be an alpha." I'd assumed Sean had fought and killed numerous times as a wolf; alphas didn't get—or keep—that position by popular vote. "Mike gave you no choice. He sealed his own fate when he tried to get you killed."

"I tried to tell you it was a lie."

I shifted uncomfortably. "I know."

Sean pinned me with his stare. "I walked through Natalie's house wards when you called me. I helped Malcolm save your life. I held you and kept you from hurting yourself when you were delirious and hallucinating."

I'd hallucinated after being burned? I didn't remember that at all. Neither he nor Malcolm had ever said anything to me about it.

While I was still trying to wrap my brain around that news, Sean continued. "I did all those things because you are worth it, and I wouldn't hesitate to do them again. I let you set all the limits and call all the shots while we were working. You say you know what it means to be an alpha, but I'm not sure you know how difficult it was to let someone else have that much control. Believe me when I say that I have never done anything like that before." His gaze was fierce. "Before I met you, I never *wanted* to do anything like that for anyone who wasn't part of my pack. And despite everything we went through and everything I've done, you never gave me a chance."

I said nothing. What could I say? He was right.

Sean wasn't going to let me get away with silence. "Didn't I deserve the benefit of the doubt, Allie?"

"Yes, you did. I'm sorry I didn't give you the chance to explain. I was so angry that I couldn't think."

"I can understand that." Sean squeezed my hands. "My guess is that up to now, you've probably known a lot more betrayal and lies than people you could trust."

He wasn't wrong about that either, but that wasn't a topic I was interested in discussing.

Sean rose, then sat on the porch swing next to me. "What happened between you and Vaughan last night, after you woke up?"

I looked at him.

"Did he hurt you?" When I didn't immediately respond, Sean's eyes turned bright gold. "He did," he snarled. "Tell me."

"He didn't hurt me. He kissed me and…wanted more. I said no, and he left."

"It was more than that," Sean said flatly. "I felt you through our link earlier. That's one of the reasons I came over."

I scowled. "Were you eavesdropping on me?"

Sean shook his head. "Not on purpose. I had the link wide open while you were in the coma, trying to sense you. I closed it when Adri Smith texted me that you were awake, but my shields must have gone down while I was asleep. I thought at first it was a dream, but then I realized what I was sensing. I felt your desire, and then I felt your terror. I knew you were with Vaughan. I was throwing clothes on to come over here when the fear subsided."

"He healed me with his blood. I wasn't thinking clearly, and I asked him to leave."

"But not before he scared you so badly that I felt it all the way across town. He didn't want to take no for an answer, did he?"

"I took care of it. It's over. I don't want a repeat of what happened over here a week ago."

Sean's anger prickled on my skin. "The vampire and I have unfinished business," he informed me.

My stomach lurched. "He was wrong about you and your supposed plan to infect me. Please don't—"

"That's not all of it," Sean said. "I'd have confronted him earlier, but he had you until last night and I'm not going to jeopardize you again. I underestimated Vaughan's ruthlessness last time. I won't repeat that mistake."

"What do you mean?" I asked with a frown.

"Vaughan deliberately pushed me through your window."

I stared at him.

"I had no intention of letting our…disagreement endanger you. I was trying to take the fight into the yard. Vaughan maneuvered us in front of the window, then pushed me through it." Sean's eyes became amber fire. "Even if he was just trying to use your wards to injure me, he *knew* you were standing right there. I don't know if he wanted you injured or if he simply had no regard for your safety, but I can tell you that he did it on purpose."

I tried to remember the scene the night Charles confronted Sean at my house. Sean *had* come through the window first, but when I replayed it in my head, the wolf's body had its back to the window. Charles would have been in position to take the fight through the window and into my house.

My thoughts raced. Why would Charles have wanted to injure me? He'd implied Sean was responsible for my wounds, thus further driving the wedge between us, and he'd held Sean in custody, effectively preventing Sean from warning me. Charles had offered to heal me that night, knowing his blood would influence me. I'd certainly lowered my guard around him after that. He'd played me like a violin, and I hadn't even realized it.

Cold fingers closed around my heart. Charles had several opportunities to taste my blood: before the burner spell turned it to ash, from my driveway after Ray Browning hit me on the head, when I'd been bleeding at the construction site, and then while I lay defenseless in a coma. If Charles had bitten me while I slept, I wouldn't know; vampires didn't leave fang marks unless they intended to brand their cattle.

In any case, if he'd tasted my blood, he knew I was no mid-level mage. There was a good chance my identity as Alice Worth had been irrevocably compromised, at least as far as Charles was concerned.

There was little I could do about it at this point except stay the hell away from him and make sure his prediction about us being lovers never came true.

"Allie, I'm sorry. It's my fault. I should have protected you better."

"It's not your job to protect me." My voice sounded mechanical, flat. "I knew he was a threat. If it's anyone's fault, it's mine."

"If he ever touches you again, I'll kill him," Sean stated.

"If he ever touches me again without my permission, you won't have to." I spent more than twenty years belonging to a cabal, with no control over my own body, and nearly died to regain my autonomy. I'd be damned if I'd let Charles, or anyone, take that away from me again.

We looked at each other.

"You mean that," Sean said.

"I do."

Sean didn't ask how it was possible I could kill Charles; he simply accepted it as fact. Maybe I shouldn't have been surprised by his confidence in me, but I was.

I took a deep breath. "I have a couple of things I have to say."

"Say them."

"You're an alpha werewolf. You have to have a werewolf mate, and soon, or you could lose your pack. I'm not a werewolf, and I never will be. There's no future for us together."

"My mate doesn't have to be a werewolf."

I felt like my world had just tilted ninety degrees.

"Traditionally, yes, the alpha pair are both shifters, but there's no written law that says that has to be the case. In fact, there are a number of alphas with nonshifter mates. Several are mages. It's not unprecedented."

I looked him in the eye and lowered my shields to feel the link that stretched between us. It was thin and fragile but still strong enough to sense him. "Did you seek me out because I'm a mage and you want a mage for a mate?"

Sean met my gaze and didn't blink. "No."

Truth. I relaxed minutely.

Sean continued. "I saw you at the bar, and I thought you were the most beautiful woman there. I wanted to be with you for the night. By the next morning, I knew I wanted more than just one night."

Truth. Now I had to ask the hard questions.

"You created a link between us without my permission. Just when I thought I could trust you this much"—I held up my thumb and index finger a centimeter apart —"you tried to make me your mate without me knowing. That's not something I'm going to be able to get past, not very easily. Why did you do it?"

Sean rubbed his face. When he looked back at me, his eyes were troubled. "I didn't intend to form a link with you. When we were together here that last night, it felt like you were in my head. I don't know why it happened; I must have lowered my shields and reached out to you without realizing I'd done it. My wolf recognized a strong female he thought would be a good mate and created the link. I sensed something new in my head, like a door opening up, but I didn't understand what it meant, not until later that night. Suddenly, I could feel your emotions, and then I realized what had happened."

Truth.

I leaned back in the swing and stared at him. Acting on instinct, I had lowered my shields to feel closer to Sean during the most intimate moments of making love. I should have known that with magic and metaphysics, there could always be unexpected outcomes. His wolf had simply responded to my presence in Sean's mind.

I felt like someone had kicked me in the stomach.

"I screwed up not telling you about the link the minute I figured it out," Sean said. "I don't know if you'll believe me, but I was going to tell you as soon as we got back here from the bar."

I barely heard him over the rush of guilt I sensed through the link. I'd decided not to tell him at the time about lowering my shields, worried he would be upset I had seen some of his memories. My instinct was always not to volunteer information that could be used against me. I'd learned that the hard way. I wasn't in the cabal anymore, though, and Sean was not my grandfather. I swallowed hard.

"Allie? What are you thinking?"

"It's my fault, Sean," I blurted out. "The link is my fault."

"What? How is it your fault?"

"When I…." I cleared my throat. "When we were having sex, I lowered my shields. I wanted to feel what you were feeling. I saw little flashes of memories, of you as a wolf running through the woods at night. Nothing specific—just glimpses, really—and I saw myself through your eyes for a few seconds."

Sean looked stunned. "Why didn't you tell me?"

"I thought you'd be angry that I accidentally read your mind." I looked away. "I should have said something. It's just…."

To my surprise, Sean took my hands in his. "Thank you, Allie."

Confused, I frowned at him. "For what?"

"For being honest and telling me about what you saw. I wish you'd told me then, but I can understand why you didn't. Now at least I know why it happened."

I was silent.

"Alice?" he prodded.

"I don't get it," I said.

"You don't get what?"

"What you could possibly see in me."

Sean stared at me.

"I had sex with you, then I kicked you to the curb with no intention of ever calling you. After you nearly killed yourself getting through Natalie's house wards to save me, I made you work for the dubious privilege of a date with me. Then I dumped you like last week's garbage the second someone told me something about you that I immediately believed, instead of giving you the benefit of the doubt, or letting you explain yourself. I blamed you for a link I caused, and I almost let myself get seduced by a vampire whose ulterior motives have ulterior motives. I'm an asshole *and* an idiot."

Sean said nothing.

I kept going. "I'm rude, secretive, and stubborn, and I have massive trust issues."

Sean waited. "Are you done?" he asked me finally.

I thought about it. "Honestly, I'm a mess, but you know that by now, which is why I have *no idea*—"

For the second time today, I was interrupted by a kiss.

This time, however, my desire wasn't tempered by fear—only by my uncertainty over why Sean Maclin, alpha werewolf, wanted to put up with me and my shit. It was not enough, however, to make me want to stop, not even close. And if Charles's people were watching, well, so much the better. I hoped they reported it all back to him, every last detail.

Sean pulled back, his eyes flashing.

"What?" I asked, breathless.

"I can feel your confusion. You really don't know how incredible you are, do you?"

I scoffed.

Sean leaned forward until his forehead touched mine, his eyes glowing softly. "You are brave, strong, beautiful, and *literally* magical."

I snorted inelegantly. "One out of four."

"*Four* out of four," he corrected me. "I'm an alpha. We're always right."

I laughed.

"What now?" he asked.

I thought about it. "Why don't you come inside. I still have my turntable and my couch. We can listen to side two of *Dark Side of the Moon* and figure out where we go from here."

Sean kissed the tip of my nose. "Sounds like a plan."

CHAPTER 28

The next morning, I was sitting in Natalie's living room with a cat in my lap and another on the arm of the chair. My client was curled up on the couch across from me. We both had mugs of tea.

Natalie told me how Betty's lawyer, William Benson, showed up on her doorstep with Amelia, who tore apart the house wards and took her out with a spell just before she could get to the safety of the library.

"That's what we figured," I said. "Malcolm and I both felt when your wards went down, but by the time we got to your house, you were already gone."

Natalie rubbed her arms. "I don't remember anything until I woke up tied to the table. I could see Amelia standing over you, and Peter, Ray, and Kathy were dead. Deborah was frozen, like a statue, and there was blood everywhere. I was in such a daze, I barely remember getting myself untied."

"You were incredible," I told her sincerely. "If it weren't for you, we'd both probably be dead. Nice work with the pipe, by the way. You've got a hell of a swing."

"I paid for my art history degree with a softball scholarship," she said, wrapping her arms around her knees. "Never thought it would save my life."

Benson had vanished without a trace; what Amelia had done with him, I had no idea. His disappearance had been in the local news, but so far, no one had connected him with the construction site murders.

"How are you doing with all of this?" I asked.

Natalie blew out a breath. "I'm doing okay today," she said. "Sometimes it's hard to believe that I actually…killed someone." She swallowed hard. "But she murdered three people, and she was about to kill you and me too. I know I didn't have any choice. I've been talking about it with Malcolm, and that helps."

Malcolm had been spending a lot of time at her house lately. Considering what Natalie had been through in the past couple of weeks, having a ghost as her new best friend seemed strangely appropriate.

Natalie shifted on the couch. "The hardest part was lying to the detective who came by. I hated to lie, but the vampire, Mr. Vaughan, explained it was best if I said I didn't know anything about Amelia or what happened."

The more I heard about how Natalie was dealing with everything, the more impressed I was with her newfound moxie. The Natalie who sat in front of me today was very different from the one I'd met two weeks ago at Janie's Downtown Café. Since learning about her grandmother's magic and her own abilities, and especially after what she'd done to save our lives at the construction site, Natalie had toughened up considerably.

"I have some good news for you," I told her. "I'm going to be interviewing a couple of potential mentors for you in the next few days. With any luck, I'll find someone to help you with your magic soon."

"I'm glad," Natalie said. "Are you sure you can't do it? I'd be so much more comfortable with you."

"I would if I could, but I don't have fire magic, and you really need someone who has the same kind of magic you do. I'll stay in touch, though, and keep track of how your training is going." I smiled at her. "I'm excited for you. I look forward to seeing you show off your skills."

It occurred to me then that Natalie had never gotten to see real magic up close; she'd seen it almost kill me twice, and Amelia killed three of her relatives to get more of it. For her, it was still a scary unknown. I hesitated, then asked, "Do you want to come over to my house sometime this week and see some cool magic?"

"Sure!" She lit up and looked at me hopefully. "Can you show me something now?"

I held out my right hand, palm up, and a tendril of bright green flame spiraled up. Natalie gasped in wonder. I spun the single flame into a small fireball, then blew gently, sending it floating across toward her.

She watched it move, her eyes wide with awe. "Will I be able to do this?"

"That's earth magic. You have fire magic. You'll be able to do that, but your fire will be hot instead of cold." I crooked my fingers and the fireball zipped back to me. I let it grow until it consumed my entire hand. We sat and watched the bright green flames dance.

"That's incredible," Natalie said. "It's so beautiful."

I looked into the flames. "Yes, it is."

Finally, I drew the magic back into my hand, and the fire went out.

"How long before I can do things like that?" Natalie asked.

"It will take a while," I told her honestly. "Learning control takes time and hard work, but children learn to control their magic. You will too. I'll find you the best teacher I can."

"Thank you, Alice. For everything."

"You're welcome." I got up and went to the kitchen.

As I was standing at the sink rinsing out my mug, I glanced out the window.

And froze.

A familiar black BMW was parked across the street. Inside, behind the dark-tinted glass, I saw a single figure, sitting motionless, as if watching the house.

"Shit," I breathed.

The car glided smoothly away from the curb and drove past Natalie's house, only to make a three-point turn and come back. I moved away from the window as the BMW rolled slowly past my car, as if John West wanted a good look at it. Then the car took off down the street, paused at the stop sign, and disappeared around the corner.

* * *

A few days later, I was sitting on my couch in the middle of the afternoon, holding a mug of coffee that had long since gone cold and staring blankly at my empty living room.

For days, I'd barely slept. Nightmares left me restless and prowling the house at night. I'd gotten so crabby from lack of sleep that Malcolm had taken refuge at Natalie's house. I was letting my voice mail take my calls. I had two messages from Adri, three from Sean, two from Natalie, and a couple from my office line that were probably potential clients. They sat untouched in my inbox.

At a little after two, I heard heavy footsteps on my porch and someone knocked on my front door.

I frowned and made no move to get up. I wasn't expecting visitors and had no desire to talk to anyone. Besides, I hadn't showered or even brushed my hair and I was wearing pajamas and a robe.

More knocking, much louder this time. It sounded like someone's fist. My frown deepened. "Go away," I muttered. Apparently, whoever it was couldn't take a hint.

My phone rang. Listlessly, I picked it up and glanced at the screen: *Adri Smith*. Damn it, were they still watching my house? I thought I'd made it clear I didn't appreciate being spied on.

With a snarl that would have made a werewolf proud, I swiped at the phone's screen, rejecting the call. I stomped to the front door and peered through the peephole.

When I saw who was on my porch, I froze.

"Ms. Worth, please open the door." The voice was calm, with an authoritative tone that set my teeth on edge.

Reluctantly, I turned the deadbolt and opened the door.

If Special Agent Lake was taken aback by my dishevelment, or the fact I was wearing pajamas at two o'clock in the afternoon, he didn't let on. His eyes swept over me analytically before meeting my gaze. "Good afternoon, Ms. Worth," he said, reaching into his inside jacket pocket for his identification. "I'm sure you remember me."

"I do, but I'd like to see your credentials anyway." The last time he'd shown them to me, I'd had a flashlight in my face and hadn't been able to read them.

Lake flipped open the leather wallet and held it up. The top section contained the SPEMA seal and next to it, his photo and name: Special Agent Trent Lake. Below was his shield. I looked at the picture for a moment, then studied the man as he returned his ID to the inside pocket his suit jacket.

No coat today; it was warm and sunny, and he wore a dark gray suit with a blue tie that matched his eyes. Up close and in the light of day, I could see a faint scar on his chin and another that had split his left eyebrow. In my bare feet, I felt dwarfed by his size.

I stood in my doorway and regarded him with a distinctly unwelcoming stare. "What brings you to my door, Agent Lake?"

Lake gave me a smile that was surprisingly charming. "Can we go inside?"

"Nope, not unless you have a warrant."

The smile faded. "I'm not an enemy, Ms. Worth."

That was debatable. "You're not a friend, either." I stepped out onto the porch and pulled the door closed behind me. "Where is Agent Parker today?"

"At a crime scene." He was watching me closely. "The local police have called us in to help with the investigation into the murders at the Browning Construction site."

I probably deserved an Oscar for the mildly interested expression I gave him. "I heard about that. Really awful. Mages like this Amelia Walker give all of us a bad name."

"Wharton," Lake corrected me.

His gaze was intense, but I didn't blink. "Oh. Wharton. Right." I shrugged. "I'd never heard of her before she was in the news. I thought I read somewhere that she was from Portland."

"That's what it looks like. You're sure you didn't know her?"

I frowned, feigning puzzlement. "I'm sure," I assured him. "I don't know anybody in Portland. Plus, I stay away from blood mages. They're dangerous."

Lake stared at me, saying nothing.

I raised my eyebrows and leaned back against the doorframe. "Any particular reason why you'd think I'd know a blood mage from Portland?"

"I wondered, since the victims were all related to your client, Natalie Newton." I saw a flash in Lake's eyes that said, *Gotcha.*

I blinked at him innocently. *You've got nothing, Lake.* "That is true. Both Natalie and I were very surprised—and horrified—by what happened to her uncles and aunt. I'm sure Natalie told you she never met or heard of Amelia Wharton. Neither had I, until I saw it on the news." I tilted my head. "How did you know Natalie was one of my clients?"

"We've been speaking to members of the extended family, gathering background information on the victims. When I met with Ms. Newton yesterday, I remembered seeing you together at Janie's Café downtown, and she told me she'd hired you to put wards around her home."

"Ah," I said, mentally applauding Natalie for successfully bluffing Lake. "You've got a good memory for faces, Agent Lake."

"It comes in handy in investigative work. As a private detective, I'm sure you agree." The smile was back. If I didn't know it was nothing more than an interrogation technique, I might have been fooled by it.

"Oh, definitely." I regarded him. "I'm sorry I can't help you with your current investigation. I didn't know Amelia Wharton."

"But you *did* know Natalie's aunts and uncles," Lake said.

I strongly suspected he was fishing, trying to catch me off guard. I declined to bite the hook. "I spoke to a couple of them, very briefly, while I was looking for the person who had attempted to enter Natalie's home without her knowledge. I wouldn't say I 'know' any of them."

"So you spoke to the victims?" Lake pounced on that. "Why didn't you mention that?"

"I only spoke to Peter Eppright and Kathy Adams for a few minutes. Once I determined they hadn't gotten into her home, I had no further contact with them."

"How did you know they hadn't been in her house?"

"Interested in my investigative techniques, Agent Lake?"

"Simply curious."

I shrugged. "It was rather straightforward, actually. Whoever crossed the wards left magic trace behind. No one in Natalie's family has magic, so it was easy enough to rule them out. We've suspended the investigation pending any new information." I met his gaze without flinching. He might suspect my involvement, but there was zero evidence tying me to the construction site. As long as I kept my cool, he had nothing.

Lake reached into his pocket. I tensed, but he only pulled out a card and handed it to me. "If you think of anything that might help us, please give me a call. My cell number is on there."

I tucked the card into the pocket of my robe. "I'll certainly do that," I lied.

We looked at each other. His gaze was sharp. Mine was guileless.

Finally, Lake squared his shoulders. "All right. Have a good afternoon." He turned to leave.

Just as I reached for the doorknob, Lake turned back, one foot on the porch steps. "Oh, one more question."

His casual tone immediately put me on alert. "Yes?"

"When I ran into you at the café, I noticed your earrings. Where did you get them? I remember thinking my sister would love a pair like that."

I shrugged. "I made them."

"I see." Lake dug in his pocket and pulled something out. "Did they look something like this?" He held out his hand, stepping back up onto the porch so I could see what he was holding.

My earring.

It was sooty, the wire bent, the crystal cracked and dark, but I recognized it just the same. Apparently, so had Lake.

I remembered how when I came to at the construction site, all my jewelry was gone, removed by either Amelia or Peter Eppright. Charles had told me they'd taken everything of mine and Natalie's from the crime scene before the fire, but it appeared they'd missed at least one piece of my jewelry, and Lake had found it.

I frowned and looked at the earring. "Sort of, but mine had little beads at the top. Not all crystal jewelry is the same, you know."

Lake's gaze was razor-sharp. "I'm pretty sure this is yours, Ms. Worth. Guess where I found it."

"It's not my earring," I told him flatly. "I have mine."

"Then let's see them."

I narrowed my eyes. "Agent Lake, I don't have to show you anything." I did have another pair, actually—not exactly the same, but very similar—but I would be damned if this man was going to bully me into getting them.

He shifted his feet, planting himself more firmly in place on my porch. "Show me your earrings and I'll go."

Despite our height difference, I refused to be intimidated. "You'll go anyway, since you don't have a warrant."

We stared at each other.

"Ms. Worth, I'm starting to think you know something about what happened to those people."

"Agent Lake, I'm starting to think you're grasping at straws," I countered. "That is *not* my earring, I have *never* been to that construction site, and I *do not know* anything more than what I have told you."

It occurred to me then that Lake having my earring in his pocket wasn't exactly procedure. If he was treating it as evidence, it should be in an evidence bag, its chain of custody clearly preserved. It looked more like he'd found the earring while poking around in the debris and decided to do a little independent investigation.

The corners of my mouth twitched when realization dawned. If he told anyone how he knew me, it might jeopardize the official story of how Scott Grierson, the half-demon "Full Moon Stalker," ended up dead in the park with a knife through his eye. Lake and Parker had already taken credit for bringing an end to Grierson's killing spree; there was no room in their tidy narrative for my involvement. So Agent Lake was in a bit of a pickle: he suspected it was my earring but couldn't tell anyone why he thought that. No one would believe he remembered it from a chance encounter between strangers in a café weeks ago.

I met Lake's gaze. "I'm sorry I don't have any information that might help you. I'm sure Amelia Wharton was nothing more than a sick, delusional woman who murdered three people in some bizarre blood magic ritual and then died when she lost control of it and brought the building down on herself."

Lake seemed to be weighing my words. "It would help our investigation a great deal to have corroboration from someone who was there," he said finally. "If someone was merely a witness—or an intended victim—there would be no reason for that person to fear prosecution, or even have their name released." His piercing blue gaze took in the shadows under my eyes, my tangled hair, and the robe I'd thrown on over my pajamas because actually getting dressed seemed like too much effort.

I didn't like the way he was looking at me, as if he could see the nightmares in my head. My expression grew cold. "I'm sure it would, but just looking at the scene on the news, it seems unlikely anyone got out of there alive."

"Or at least, nobody got out unscathed." Lake glanced meaningfully at the burned remains of my earring.

"Well, it's been lovely chatting with you." I turned toward my front door. "Best of luck in your investigation."

"I know you were there, Ms. Worth."

I spun back around.

Lake held up his hand to stop my angry retort. "I may not be able to prove it yet, and maybe there's nothing more to what happened than, as you say, a woman who sacrificed three victims and lost control of the ritual. But that's twice now you've been in the middle of something big here in the city. I think it would be in my best interest to keep an eye on you from now on."

"I'm just a private investigator. I'm nobody." My heart pounded so loudly, I feared he could hear it. "I'm not worth your time."

"I disagree. I think you are. See you around, Alice Worth."

With that threat hanging in the air, Lake turned and headed down the steps toward the unmarked black SUV parked at the curb, tucking my earring back into his pocket as he walked.

I went inside, slammed the door, and locked it. Then I thumped my forehead against the doorframe and took a deep, shaky breath.

See you around, Alice Worth.

Fantastic.

THE END

Turn the page for a sneak peek at the next book of the Alice Worth novels,

FIRE IN THE BLOOD

LISA EDMONDS

Coming Soon from City Owl Press

PROLOGUE

When the half-drunk graveyard shift cook with singed eyebrows and Johnnie Walker breath says you're looking rough, you know you've got problems.

"Thanks," I said wearily, dropping my change into the tip jar by the register and heading for the door.

"Your food!" the cook hollered, gesturing with his spatula at the counter, where I'd left behind an empty coffee pot and untouched club sandwich.

"Guess I wasn't hungry after all." I pushed the door open and headed out to the parking lot.

When I'd arrived, despite it being after midnight, the only available spot in the tiny lot next to Nancy's Diner was at the back near the dumpster. I unlocked my car, tossed my bag onto the passenger seat, and started to get in.

Someone screamed.

My head whipped around. The sound cut off abruptly, but not before I was already running toward the alley on the other side of the dumpster.

When I rounded the corner, I saw what looked like three or four people fighting about twenty feet away. As I got closer and my eyes adjusted to the dim light, I realized with horror that three young men had cornered a blonde girl by a large trash bin. She kicked wildly as one of them tried to pin her against the wall and another covered her mouth while the third yanked her bag away and dumped it on the ground.

"Hey!" I yelled.

The men looked up. One of them, the skinny kid who took her bag, dropped it and headed toward me, while the other two continued to struggle with the girl. She looked at me, her eyes huge and panicked.

"Bitch, you better get out of here," he told me. A blade glinted in his hand. It was shaking.

"I don't think so," I said, advancing. "Put your little knife away before you hurt yourself."

Twitchy raised his knife and spun it between his fingers with surprising dexterity. I was close enough now to see he wasn't trembling because he was afraid. His pupils were dilated, and despite the cool night, he was sweating. *Shit*. He wasn't scared; he was high.

The girl suddenly screamed again, and one of the other thugs swore. "She bit me!" He punched her in the jaw and she fell, unconscious. *Double shit*.

I took a deep breath and said little prayer to whoever might be listening. I was about to do something really stupid.

"Look at you losers," I taunted them. "Three of you against one hundred-pound girl. Is this the only way you can get any action?"

That did it. With twin snarls, the other two joined their friend, leaving the girl on the dirty pavement behind them.

"Maybe we start with you instead," the tallest of the three said. "You got a big mouth. It'll feel real good right here." He grabbed his crotch, and the other two laughed.

Two of them—Twitchy and Dip-stick, the tall one—had blades. The third cracked his knuckles while he leered at my chest. His hands looked bloody, either from hitting the girl or someone else earlier in the evening. All three of them twitched like they were holding onto a high-voltage wire.

Well, I'd gotten them away from the girl for the moment, but she was out cold and unable to run away, and now I had become their target. Three against one wasn't great, but I wasn't nearly as defenseless as they probably thought I was.

Dip-stick came at me first. I waited until he was about four feet away before I flicked my right wrist to manifest my cold fire whip. His eyes widened, but he had no time to react before I whipped the stream of cold fire through the air and lashed his knife hand. He screamed and dropped the knife, doubling over and clutching his hand. I struck again, knocking him flat, then stepped forward and kicked him in the jaw. He went still. One down.

Knuckles took a step back, but Twitchy advanced, his lip curled and knife raised. He turned back to his companion. "Come on!"

They rushed me.

I went for Twitchy, striking out with my whip and connecting with his chest. He staggered back but managed to hang onto his blade. Knuckles came at me from my left side, which was smart…or might have been, if my whip was my only weapon.

Knuckles took a swing at me and I ducked. My cold fire vanished, and I struck out with my hands and hit him in the chest with both palms. A strong blast of air magic sent him flying backward ten feet to smash into the wall of the building. The impact knocked him out, and he hit the pavement in a heap. Two down, one to go.

In the meantime, Twitchy was on the attack. A streak of fire seared across my right forearm and I cried out. Before he could strike again, I lashed out and my whip caught him across the neck. He shrieked and stumbled, dropping his knife to grab his throat. I took two steps to pick up momentum and kicked him in the groin. He doubled over with a breathless scream and I brought my knee up into his face. Cartilage crunched and he went down, blood streaming from his nose. One kick to the head, and then there were none.

Breathing hard, I looked at my arm. Blood dripped from my fingers. I couldn't see how bad the cut was in the dim light, but the tear in my sleeve was about six inches long, and the wound stung.

Before I could deal with my injury, I had to make sure they stayed down until the girl and I were gone. I touched Dip-stick's arm, using a "nap" spell that put him out cold for about an hour. I went to the other two and repeated the spell.

With them taken care of, I went to check on the girl. She was still unconscious, her jaw swelling where Knuckles had hit her.

At a glance, I guessed she was a working girl: short black skirt, high heels, mesh top over a bright pink bra. The contents of her bag were scattered around her.

While I waited for her to wake up, I unfastened one of the charms on my bracelet—a small, blue crystal—and moved until I was leaning against the wall, out of sight of the street and the diner parking lot. I pushed up my sleeve, held the crystal to my bloody right forearm, and invoked the spell. "*Helios*."

It was a mid-range air magic healing spell, the strongest I dared carry with me. I breathed deeply through the pain as the spell worked to heal the knife wound. The pins-and-needles sensation lasted for about a minute.

When at last the magic faded, I tucked the spent crystal into my pocket and looked at my arm. The cut was mostly healed, reduced to an angry red line. Another healing spell would heal the injury altogether.

I rolled up my sleeves to hide the blood and moved over where I had been standing when my arm got cut. I crouched and put my fingertips in my blood on the pavement. "*Burn*." With a *whoosh*, white fire—my air magic—consumed my blood, leaving behind a fine grey ash that would blow away.

Once my blood was gone, I went through Dip-stick's pockets. His wallet contained a few bucks in cash, no cards, and an expired driver's license identifying him as John Andrews. I put the cash in my pocket, left the wallet on the pavement next to him, and turned his jeans pockets inside out. Nothing but some loose change and a lighter.

Nothing interesting in Knuckles's pockets either, though I confiscated about forty dollars in small bills.

I hit pay dirt with Twitchy. No ID, but in his front pocket, he had a respectable roll of cash and two small plastic bags containing marble-sized amounts of black crystals. The bags were marked with black flames. I frowned. *What the hell is this?* I wondered. Some new kind of meth? What were these guys on?

I tucked the money in my pocket and the drugs in my boot and stood. Behind me, I heard a moan. When I turned, the girl was blinking dazedly and looking around, plainly confused.

I approached slowly so I didn't startle her. "Hey, are you okay?"

Her eyes widened. "Where are they?"

"They're napping." I crouched down. "You're safe."

The girl groaned and pushed herself up to lean against the brick wall. She touched her jaw gingerly. "Where did you come from?"

"I was in the parking lot at Nancy's when I heard you scream."

She looked at the three unconscious thugs in disbelief. "What are you, some kind of superhero?"

I snorted. "Hardly. I didn't know if they were trying to rob you or rape you or both, but I wasn't going to stand by and let it happen. How do you feel?"

The girl started cramming stuff back into her bag and flexed her jaw. "It doesn't feel too good, but I'll be okay. I've had worse."

"What's your name?"

She stared at me, her eyes narrowing. "Why?"

"No particular reason. I'm Alice."

"Where's your rabbit, Alice?" The girl grimaced as she started trying to stand up.

I rose. "Can't find him. Little furry bastard runs too fast."

She laughed and used the wall to push herself to her feet. "Ow, my ass," she breathed, rubbing her tailbone.

"Is anything broken?"

She shook her head. "I don't think so. Just bruises, probably. I'm Carrie."

"Hey, Carrie. Why don't you take the rest of the night off?" I dug in my pocket and handed her the cash I'd collected. "It's all they had."

Carrie grinned. "Sweet. I like you, Alice." She took the money and stuck it in her bag. "Wish I could have seen what you did. First time anyone ever came to my rescue, and I missed it."

"It wasn't all that exciting. Really, they went down pretty quickly." I reached into my boot and pulled out one of the little plastic bags. "What do you know about this stuff?"

Carrie glanced at the bag and grimaced. "Haze," she said with disgust.

"Haze?" I'd never heard of it. "Is that a new nickname for meth?"

She held out her hand. I handed her the bag and she looked at it closely. "It's not meth. This shit starting showing up a couple of months back. Now it's like everybody's on it. They always mark the bags with the flames. They call it Haze or Black Fire. It's bad stuff, makes you real mean and paranoid. My old roommate took too much and jumped off a bridge."

"Wow." I stared at the little bag in surprise.

Carrie was quiet for a moment. "I'm not gonna lie: I take pills. You gotta have something to take the edge off, you know? But I don't want any part of that garbage." She handed the bag back to me.

I stuck the bag back in my boot. "Thanks for the info."

Carrie gingerly put her bag over her shoulder. "Thanks for kicking their asses. Hope you catch that rabbit," she added with a smirk, and headed off down the alley and out of sight.

I took one last look at the thugs, then cradled my sore arm and headed back toward the parking lot, tossing the bags of Haze into the dumpster as I passed.

I'd accidentally left my car unlocked, but by some miracle, no one had stolen it. I got in and locked the doors, wincing as I used my sore right arm to turn the key in the ignition and shift out of park.

I turned out of the lot and headed down the street, driving with my left hand while my right arm rested in my lap. I had healing spells at home that would take care of the knife wound, and then I'd have to try to get some sleep.

I sighed. I probably wouldn't have any more luck sleeping tonight than any other night in the days since I'd woken from the coma, but I always hoped.

The nightmares had to stop at some point, right?

Thank you for reading! Catch book two of the Alice Worth novels, FIRE IN THE BLOOD, coming soon from City Owl Press!

But first, want an exclusive look at the playlist for HEART OF MALICE? Check out her website: www.lisaedmonds.com

And be sure to find Lisa Edmonds across social media.

Facebook: www.facebook.com/Edmonds411

Instagram: Edmonds411

Twitter: @Edmonds411

Please sign up for the City Owl Press newsletter for chances to win special subscriber-only contests and giveaways as well as receiving information on upcoming releases and special excerpts.

All reviews are welcome and appreciated. Please consider leaving one on your favorite social media and book buying sites.

For books in the world of romance and speculative fiction that embody Innovation, Creativity, and Affordability, check out City Owl Press at www.cityowlpress.com.

ACKNOWLEDGMENTS

Many wonderful people helped this novel grow from an idea to a published work. First, I want to thank Heather, Tina, and Yelena at City Owl Press for their guidance and assistance in bringing Alice to life.

I am deeply and forever indebted to my cadre of wonderful and patient "beta" readers, whose sage advice and constructive criticism helped HEART OF MALICE evolve from its first highly imperfect draft to the version you hold in your hands. Many thanks to Dr. Adrienne Foreman, Dr. Kimberly Dodson, Dr. Amy Montz, Amy Hopper, Dr. Robert James, Dr. Marie Guthrie, Holley McLane, Shannon Butler, and Laura Shelton Hicks.

I am grateful for the unwavering love and support of my family and friends, many of whom provided helpful information or advice in response to texts or Facebook messages that began with the words "So, random question…" A special thank you to author Danielle Fifer for sharing her insights on the publishing industry, and to Deborah Rebisz for introducing us; Dr. Robert Shandley for the German translations; Dr. Rick Moberly, my official source for medical knowledge; Dr. Galen Wilson, Scotch expert; and Dr. Nicholas Lawrence, who knows which songs and albums are not overrated.

I am especially thankful to Stacey Kelley for more than thirty years of friendship, and for hanging onto the only existing copy of a short mystery novel I wrote while a senior in high school, and surprising me with it this past year.

When I was five or six years old, I wrote a (very) short story on a piece of Big Chief tablet paper about a rainbow and a flower who were friends. I gave it to my mother, who still has it in a box somewhere, and told her I wanted to be a writer. I did a lot of other things while I was pursuing that dream, including earning a Ph.D. and becoming a professor of English, but writing was always the goal that mattered most. Thanks, Mom, for always believing in me. I am also thankful for the love and encouragement of my father, the late Loren Edmonds, who passed away in 1997.

Much love to my sister Susan Michelle Edmonds, my brother-in-law Josh Herrin, my sweet nephew Madden, and my cousin Antoinette Eve, for always being there for me when I need them.

Finally, and most importantly, I would like to thank my (patient, long-suffering, wonderful, thoughtful, and helpful) husband, Bill D'Amico, for so many things that I would need a whole other book to list them all, but most of all for being ready with a Starbucks gift card, an idea, or an (in)appropriate Family Guy quote when I need one. It's hard being married to a writer; we're weird and obsessive and we stay up all hours writing when you'd rather be snuggling and watching a movie. We also constantly interrupt what you're doing to ask questions such as: "If you were a werewolf, how would you respond in this situation?" or "Which AC/DC song best goes with this scene?" Through it all, every single day, Bill has been my strongest supporter. I love you so much.

ABOUT THE AUTHOR

© Madison Hurley Photography

LISA EDMONDS was born and raised in Kansas, and studied English and forensic criminology at Wichita State University. After acquiring her Bachelor's and Master's degrees, she considered a career in law enforcement as a behavioral analyst before earning a Ph.D. in English from Texas A&M University. She is currently an associate professor of English at a college in Texas and teaches both writing and literature courses. When not in the classroom, she shares a quiet country home with her husband Bill D'Amico and their cats, and enjoys writing, reading, traveling, spoiling her nephew, and singing karaoke.

Want an exclusive look at the playlist for HEART OF MALICE?
Check out her website: www.lisaedmonds.com

And be sure to find Lisa Edmonds across social media.

Facebook: www.facebook.com/Edmonds411

Instagram: www.instagram.com/edmonds411/

Twitter: www.twitter.com/Edmonds411

ABOUT THE PUBLISHER

CITY OWL PRESS is a cutting edge indie publishing company, bringing the world of romance and speculative fiction to discerning readers.

www.cityowlpress.com

66693801R00191

Made in the USA
Middletown, DE
14 March 2018